W9-BRC-292

earth
BOUND

earth
BOUND

APRILYNNE PIKE

razOr
bill

An Imprint of Penguin Group (USA) Inc.

razOr bill

Published by the Penguin Group
Penguin Group (USA) Inc., 375 Hudson Street, New York, New York 10014, USA
Penguin Group (Canada), 90 Eglinton Avenue East, Suite 700, Toronto, Ontario M4P 2Y3,
Canada (a division of Pearson Penguin Canada Inc.)
Penguin Books Ltd, 80 Strand, London WC2R 0RL, England
Penguin Ireland, 25 St Stephen's Green, Dublin 2, Ireland (a division of Penguin Books Ltd)
Penguin Group (Australia), 707 Collins Street, Melbourne, Victoria 3008, Australia
(a division of Pearson Australia Group Pty Ltd)
Penguin Books India Pvt Ltd, 11 Community Centre, Panchsheel Park, New Delhi–110 017, India
Penguin Group (NZ), 67 Apollo Drive, Rosedale, Auckland 0632, New Zealand
(a division of Pearson New Zealand Ltd)
Penguin Books (South Africa), Rosebank Office Park, 181 Jan Smuts Avenue, Parktown North 2193,
South Africa
Penguin China, B7 Jiaming Center, 27 East Third Ring Road North, Chaoyang District,
Beijing 100020, China

Penguin Books Ltd, Registered Offices: 80 Strand, London WC2R 0RL, England

Library of Congress Cataloging-in-Publication Data is available

Printed in the United States of America
1 3 5 7 9 10 8 6 4 2

ISBN: 978-1-59514-650-2

This is a work of fiction. Names, characters, places, and incidents either are the product of the
author's imagination or are used fictitiously, and any resemblance to actual persons, living or dead,
businesses, companies, events, or locales is entirely coincidental.

To Scott, whose high level of dedication to my research was NOT appreciated. Still cheering for you every day.

CHAPTER ONE

I remember the plane going down.

Not the crash exactly, but the moments before—and while it *must* have been only moments, when I look back, it takes much longer.

I was sitting with my forehead pressed against the tiny window, looking through the cloudless air at farms and settlements passing below me, when the engine exploded, rocking the plane into a crazy tilt that tossed me back and forth in my seat. The actual blast was surprisingly quiet—muffled by the insulated fuselage, I imagine—but the billowing clouds of coal-black smoke pouring off the wing were impossible to miss.

Every nerve in my body clanged, but my eyes stayed riveted to the roiling smoke that streamed back from the engine just feet from my window. My aching fingers clung to the armrests to hold myself steady as the plane dipped forward, then plunged, the momentum forcing me against my seat.

The pop and hiss of hundreds of oxygen masks, springing from the ceiling like venomous snakes, startled my attention away from the smoking wing. Reflexes honed by dozens of droning safety speeches sent hands darting out to grab the oxygen masks, the adults *securing their own masks before assisting others.*

But I didn't bother with mine.

Not even when my mother pushed it at me, her eyes dancing with terror as she gripped my father's arm so tightly I knew her fingernails must be drawing blood.

It was the flight attendant who made me understand. Two of them were standing in the aisle, trying to get everyone's attention, demonstrating the crash position—like that was going to help. But I focused on the third one. He wasn't attempting to buckle up or help the passengers; he just stood, his body strangely still amid the chaos, looking out the window, two tears rolling down his cheeks.

That's when I knew we were all about to die.

And in that moment, my fear melted away and I felt completely at peace. No life flashing before my eyes or sudden aching regrets. Just an overwhelming peace.

I relaxed, stopped struggling, and watched out the window as the ground rushed up to swallow me.

▲

I stare at the photos in horror. It has to be true; there's no other explanation.

The timing couldn't be better.

Or worse.

"She's gone?" I ask in my iciest voice. I'm not mad at him; I'm mad at myself for not seeing it sooner. I should have. Everything balances on a knife's edge and this could destroy it all.

Or save it.

"We're doing everything we can." He's nattering on about their efforts, but I don't have the patience to listen. I walk over to the window, arms crossed over my chest, staring down at the lush garden below, seeing nothing.

Not nothing. Seeing her face. That face I've known since almost before I can remember my own. That face I thought I was finally free of.

Except now I can never be free. I need her. We need her. It's difficult not to choke on the bitter irony that after everything she's done, I need her. Without her, everything will fall to pieces.

Worse than it has already.

And I almost killed her.

▲

CHAPTER TWO

Therapy is the epitome of the best and worst of everything in my life. I sit ramrod straight on the couch, tears threatening to spill. I blink, forcing them back. Not because I'm embarrassed—I've cried gallons in front of Elizabeth. I'm just sick to death of crying.

I don't like to talk about my parents, but it's Elizabeth's job to make me once in a while. Like today. She tried to focus on happy memories, but this time all that did was remind me that they're never going to happen again. That chapter of my life is over.

Gone.

Forever.

A huge, gaping forever.

"Hey," Elizabeth says, startling me back to her office with an audible gasp. "It could be worse. You could be a brain-injured orphan with a weak leg *and* be having a bad hair day."

For just a second I stare at her, wide-eyed, trying to decide if the joke is funny or not. But her expression—melodramatic concern with just a hint of true sympathy behind it—cracks through my shell and I start to laugh and swipe at my eyes at the same time.

I have, I admit, kind of a weird relationship with my therapist. I theorize it's because neither of us thinks I'm crazy.

She doesn't even let me call her Dr. Stanley—which is what the diplomas hanging on her wall say—just Elizabeth. At first I thought it was one of those cheap shortcuts adults try to take with teenagers to get them to relax and spill their guts, but Elizabeth seriously squirmed every time I called her *Dr. Stanley* and after a while I finally switched. Now it comes naturally.

"Seriously, Tavia," Elizabeth says, her voice soft and sober. "It's not supposed to be easy. I think you're very brave and that you're handling things extremely well."

"It doesn't feel like it," I admit, shrugging into a black hoodie. I've always liked sweatshirts in general, but these days, anything that covers my head—and with it the scar beneath my still-too-short hair—is a distinct preference.

"Then trust my professional analysis," Elizabeth says with a smile as she escorts me through the darkened and empty waiting room. "You're not walking home, are you?" she asks once we reach the exit. We had to reschedule our regular appointment, so it's after hours and her secretary—Secretary Barbie, I call her, because her face looks like plastic and she basically never talks to me—has already gone home.

"No, Reese is coming." I usually do walk—on the orders of my physical therapist—but since it'll be getting dark soon, Reese insisted on picking me up today.

I guess that's fine.

True to her organized, punctual personality, my aunt is already waiting for me, her BMW parked right in front of the door. She leans across the car, pushing the passenger door open and giving Elizabeth a little finger wave.

"Hey, Tave. How was it?" she asks as she pulls away from the curb, her eyes scanning the road.

"It was therapy," I say, clicking my seat belt. "It was *therapeutic*." I lean my head against the passenger-side window, not wanting to talk about it. Therapy is . . . well, it's personal. And even though I'm immensely grateful to Reese and my uncle, Jay, for taking in a step-niece they hardly knew, they don't really feel like *family*.

Luckily, Reese takes the hint and flips the radio on as we turn out of the parking lot. She has a never-ending well of patience. For me, at least. Clients on the phone? Not so much.

As we drive, I take in the streets around me—Portsmouth, New Hampshire, is one of the United States' oldest cities and they do a really good job of preserving colonial sites. I'm a closet history nerd, and the first couple of months I was here, I would walk for as long as my injured leg would let me, exploring the monuments and markers and museums. It feels fitting, somehow—a city mired in its past, me trapped in my own.

And the whole city is so beautiful. I love old buildings—they just don't build them the same way anymore. There's a grace and beauty to them that society has lost. No matter how elegant the whole deco thing is supposed to be, there's something in the hand-carved intricacies of colonial architecture that sets off a mourning within me for what once was.

My favorites are the occasional perfectly preserved eighteenth-century houses nestled amid modern homes in a normal neighborhood. Like a treasure, hidden in the sand, just waiting to be discovered. It's hard to find them while driving around at the breakneck speed Reese favors, because they're usually set back from the road and often sheltered by the leafy canopy of an ancient tree. But when I walk alone, I look for them. I'd love to know the stories behind them, but I'm too nervous to go knock on some stranger's door.

I take pictures instead and make up stories in my mind. I swear I have about a thousand photos on my phone. I wish . . . I wish I could sketch them, paint them.

But I haven't been able to draw since the accident.

Still, something about these old homes soothes me; calls to me, almost. I pull out my phone and scroll through to one of the pictures of my favorite house and zoom in, trying to imagine painting the wooden slats in watercolors, the hint of sheer curtains I can see through the windows.

"I got stuck on the phone until just before I had to pick you up." My brain slowly realizes that Reese is talking to me. "I didn't think you'd mind." She looks at me expectantly.

"I'm sorry, I . . . what?" I shove my phone in my old red backpack. I'm afraid spacing out is my specialty these days.

I didn't used to be like this.

"Do you mind if I stop by the store for milk? We're out," Reese repeats, turning the radio down a little lower.

I dolefully consider the snooty, locally grown, organic food store Reese frequents. Great. "Can I wait in the car? My—my leg is sore," I lie.

Sort-of lie. It's been three months since I got out of the cast, but *shattered* is the word my doctors used to describe the breaks both above and below my right knee. Something like that takes time to bounce back from, even without taking into account my decreased gracefulness since brain surgery last year.

At least that's what the physical therapists keep telling me when I get discouraged.

A wrinkle appears between Reese's brows for just a second before she accepts my excuse. "Sure thing—I'll only be a few minutes."

She leaves the car running. As soon as she's out of sight, I turn the heater up and lean my head against the window.

The edges of the parking lot still have a few mounds of slate-gray snow that haven't quite melted, but it won't be long. Green blades are poking through last year's crinkly brown grass and tulips are popping up all over town.

At least it's not hailing, like yesterday.

It's that almost-spring time of year—jacket weather, not overcoat weather. But the weather has been weird all year. In February *all* the snow melted and the newscasters were predicting drought and heat waves. But two weeks later three feet of snow dumped on us in a single night. Once the snowplows finally dug themselves out and cleared the roads, everything more or less went back to being winter. But still, it's been a strange few months.

I pull my jacket a little tighter around me, remembering the couple days we had below zero—not to mention the killer ice storm right before— and hold my hands out in front of the vents. Other than the hoodie, I'm not really dressed for winter. I should probably wear something other than my old tank tops and screen tees, at least until summer, but that would require going shopping and I don't like spending money that isn't mine. Even if Reese *says* her money is my money. I'm going to have to break down and buy a new pair of jeans soon, though—these ones are pretty threadbare at the knees. Because I'm tall and fairly thin, but with very long legs, I always have trouble finding jeans that aren't too short. So when I do, I wear them to shreds, which is about where this pair is sitting now.

As my fingertips warm, I scan the slowly darkening street, letting my gaze linger on a house across the road. It's painted a cheery red and has a whole bed of maroon and gold tulips in front of the veranda. A little girl is sitting on the porch, playing with a doll. I smile when I see she's dressed in a cute old-fashioned dress and pinafore—not unusual, here. In towns as old as Portsmouth, there's always some kind of reenactment going on, usually of the American Revolution. This little girl looks great. Authentic.

Well, her clothes are probably a little too brightly colored and those curls are undoubtedly from a curling iron, not overnight curling rags, but hey—that's what modern conveniences are for. A smile steals across my face as I realize the doll is even that old-fashioned rag type.

Her cute little chin jerks up and I see a man walk out of the house to join her on the porch.

Not a man, I guess. Too young to be her dad. I only see a wisp of his face, but he looks about eighteen, same as me. Maybe a tad older. Reenactments must be a family affair in the red house because he's dressed in a navy-blue jacket and has a tall hat atop golden blond hair that's pulled back at the nape of his neck.

He's nice to look at; I won't complain about that.

Sadly, his luxurious hair is probably a wig. Most people aren't hard core enough to actually grow it out. And the ones who are; well, they're a little scary in their own right.

As the guy crouches by the little girl, I wonder why breeches went out of style. Let's just say they look amazing from the back. I arch an eyebrow in appreciation and squint to get a better look, glad the Beemer has dark-tinted windows and I can enjoy my little eye-candy feast in private. It seems like my moments of casual contentment are so few and far between these days.

The guy stands with the little girl's hand in his. Showtime, I suspect.

As if sensing my laser-focused gaze, he pauses, then turns. My mouth goes dry when he stares pointedly in my direction.

He can't see me, can he? The tinting on Reese's car windows is almost a mirror from the outside. But his eyes stay focused and widen in an expression of surprise I can make out even from here.

He takes a few steps in my direction and I clench my fists as his eyes burn into mine. I'm certain he can't know I'm here. How . . . ?

On the second step he stops and looks back at the little girl, who's gripping his hand and pulling him back. He pauses, hesitates. He looks at the girl for a moment, then back at the car, his expression conflicted.

I can't look away, even though I feel warmth rushing to my cheeks. From this distance I can't tell what color his eyes are, but they pin me in place and it takes a few seconds to realize I'm holding my breath.

A sudden chime from my phone shatters the silence and breaks the spell. I look down to see a text pop up labeled *Benson Ryder*.

All done?

"Perfect timing," I mutter. But I can't suppress a smile as I jet off a quick response.

I had friends back in Michigan—in my former life, as I tend to think of it—but they were casual. My art was my life, and friends tended to pull me away from that. At-school friends, I guess. When Reese and Jay told me I'd have to cut contact with everyone in Michigan to keep my location a secret from the media, I admit I wasn't sad to give them up. They felt . . . frivolous.

Benson, is . . . well, it's just different. I see him almost every day. We text a lot. Have long phone calls sometimes.

And he knows. *Everything.*

No one else does.

Being the sole survivor of a major disaster leads to attention. Questions. And that means having to remember—the pain, the surgeries, the shaky memories.

My parents.

It's easier to lie, to just tell everyone I broke my leg in a car wreck. No one questions it. Sometimes they tell me I'm *lucky to be alive*.

The people who say that have never lost anyone close to them.

My doctors know what happened, my physical therapist, Elizabeth, and of course Reese and Jay, but no one else. Fewer people to leak my location to the media, who would love to swoop in and grab an exclusive story, even months after the fact.

Well, I told Benson too. Or perhaps it would be more accurate to say Benson worked it out of me. Not exactly unwillingly. The closer I got to Benson, the more I *wanted* to tell him. To stop lying. When it finally came out, it was a huge relief. It was nice to tell the truth. Especially to someone *I* chose.

I haven't mentioned to Reese that I spilled it all to him. I don't know if she'd be mad or not—it's my life, after all—but the fact that I'm not sure is reason enough for me not to tell her.

Besides, Benson will keep my secret.

Sometimes I think I need him—need our easy camaraderie—and that scares me.

Everyone I've ever needed in my life is dead.

As soon as I hit send, my eyes dart back to the tall boy on the porch with the little girl, but they've gone in. I try to shake off the bizarre melancholy that has enveloped me. I stare at the house—wishing, I guess, for the strangers to reappear—and just as I blink, something flashes over the door. I open my eyes wide, but the flash is gone.

No, not *completely* gone—

Almost like a shadow in my peripheral vision, so faint I have to blink a few times to make sure I see it, a shape glitters just above the door. A triangle.

And for reasons I can't comprehend or explain, my heart begins to race.

CHAPTER THREE

Usually my nightmares are about the crash, about those moments I don't remember. Sometimes I'm forced to watch as my parents' bodies rip apart in slow motion, blood splattering across my eyes and painting my vision that unmistakable red. Sometimes it's me—my hands—being crushed in the debris. They curl into unnatural angles, the bones snapping until they're nothing but a mangled mass.

Which is what should have happened.

Maybe I'm morbid, but while I was in the hospital I spent a lot of time on the Internet looking at photos of the crash site. And even though the media didn't get my name, they knew which seat I was in.

"According to analysts, the frame should have crumpled here, and here," one reporter said as she pointed to two places on the frame of the cabin. "But instead you can see that the interior of the plane looks completely untouched. The passenger in 24F, who the airline will only confirm was a female minor, sustained life-threatening injuries but survived in this unlikely cocoon, which experts are at a loss to explain. It's as though this section of the plane wasn't in the crash at all."

I stay away from the reports where they show the casualties. Rows and rows of bodies, sometimes with broken arms and legs flopping out from beneath the drapes. Those I simply can't look at.

Part of me fears I'll recognize my parents among the bodies: my mother's left hand with her wedding ring, my father's ankle with an army tattoo twisting up his calf.

Another part is just overwhelmed by guilt that out of 256 passengers, I was the only one who somehow survived.

But tonight there are no bodies, no blood.

There's no plane at all.

I'm floating.

Floating in water. The ocean? A river? A lake? I can't be sure.

But it's cold. The kind of cold that feels more like a blade against your skin, flaying away your flesh and exposing your bones. Even though I somehow know it's a dream, I shiver.

My hair is long and loose, billowing around me, and when I realize I'm being dragged under, I reach for items that are just suddenly *there*—a life jacket, a floating log, a small boat. But as soon as my fingers make contact, they pop out of existence, less real even than the dream. Exhausted, I simply flail in the water, but my hair gets wound around my arms, trapping me like ropes.

Something is pulling me down. I can't tell if it's a current or my heavy clothes. Why am I wearing heavy clothes?

I can't stay afloat.

I fling my arms out, looking for something else to hold on to, but the water is rising. Or I'm sinking.

I raise my chin, desperate for one more breath, and see a big, bright moon shining down on me. Tears sting my eyes as I realize it's the last thing I'm going to see before I die—but I don't feel fear. I feel something else.

An aching loss.

This water is taking something from me.

I open my mouth to scream, but icy liquid rushes in, filling my throat and making my teeth ache all the way into my jaw. The surface closes over my face, but my eyes remain open, looking at the bright, silvery moon.

Desperate, I manage to rip my consciousness away from the dream and force my real eyes open, where a similar moon greets them. Thankfully, this one is shining through my window, not the wavering surface of icy water. My lungs burn and I suck in air as though I had actually been on the verge of drowning. As my heartbeat slows, I touch my forehead and find beads of sweat. It's been weeks since I had a nightmare this bad.

Weeks. I remember when nightmares like this happened every few *years*.

And when they did, I had a mother's bed to jump into.

I toss back the duvet, and even though a chill ripples up my legs when the night air hits them, the shock assures me that I'm awake—the nightmare is over. My feet are resting on solid wood, not flailing in the impenetrable blackness of a bottomless lake.

Lake—it was a lake.

But I push the thought away. I don't want to dwell on the dream. Its effect on me is lingering too long anyway.

Everything's been a little off since therapy. Talking about my parents does that.

No, I have to be honest with myself. It's more than that. It's that guy. That house. The triangle.

It's been nagging at me all evening—like I've seen it before. But where? I rise on shaky limbs and cross through the shadowed room to the door.

Warm milk—the age-old remedy for nightmares.

In the kitchen I try to keep quiet, but when I hear a squeak on the stairs, I'm unsurprised to see Jay's face poke around the doorway. "You okay?" my uncle asks softly.

"Nightmare," I reply, waving my spoon at the microwave. It's all I need to say. They're used to it.

Jay steps fully into the kitchen, leaning one shoulder against the wall. There are light but definite shadows under his eyes.

"I'm sorry I woke you," I add, but he dismisses my apology and runs his fingers through his sleep-tousled hair.

"I was up anyway. Been feeling a little off—insomnia, you know. Maybe Reese is right and I've been working too hard," he says with a self-deprecating grimace. "But the boss has everyone putting in extra hours on this new virus." He wrinkles his forehead. "It's . . . not like *anything* I've seen before."

Jay's got to be about thirty-five, but he looks like a twenty-something running around in big person clothes. If I saw him on the street, I'd never believe he was a scientist, but he's actually some kind of specialized biochemist.

He's nice, though. Easy to talk to.

I didn't know him before my parents died. Reese's mom and my grandpa got married after she and my dad were mostly grown up. I was like eight. Reese had just started college and lived on campus, and I didn't even meet her for the first several years. So finally getting to know Reese and Jay has been great.

I just wish there'd been another reason.

"Plane crash again?" Jay asks softly, noticing the expression on my face.

I pull the door of the microwave open, stopping it two seconds before it finishes so it doesn't beep and wake Reese up too. "Actually, no." I reach for the porcelain canister of sugar and spoon a generous helping into my mug. "Drowning, of all things." I avoid his eyes, stirring intently.

"Think maybe your mind is moving on?" Jay asks, ever the optimist.

"Maybe." I glance up at the clock on the oven.

2:36 A.M.

"I'm fine, Jay," I insist. Now that reality is fully with me again, I wish he wasn't here—wasn't witness to my freak-out. "You can go back to bed. I'm just going to finish this and then that's where I'm headed too."

"Are you sure?" Jay asks, his pale blue eyes glinting even in the murky shadows of the half-lit kitchen. "Because if you don't want to be alone, I'll wait till you're done."

"I'm good. Like I said, it wasn't about the plane, just a regular nightmare." Even as I say the words, I remember the iciness of the water and that strange, hollow sense of loss. *Regular* isn't the right word either.

I force a small smile onto my face and take a sip of the foamy milk. *Ahhh!* Almost worth the nightmare.

Almost.

Jay gives me a long look, but there's nothing more he can do and he seems to know it. With a nod, he turns before I can catch him yawn—I do anyway—and heads back upstairs.

As the steps squeak lightly, I drop into a chair at the kitchen table and sip my milk. My eyes skim the moonlit backyard, so silvery it looks staged. The warmth from the mug spreads through my body, and by the time it's empty, I'm feeling much better. The bitter cold has left me, and I think maybe I can sleep again.

Maybe.

I rub at my temples for a moment, then my fingers freeze as the realization settles almost with a *click*.

I know where I've seen that triangle.

I try to be quiet as I hurry upstairs and grab my phone off my bedside table. My feet wander over to the window as I scroll through some pictures I took on one of my history walks. Down off Fifth Street—between Piper and Sand. In the Old Money part of town.

There! A white house bedecked with six gorgeous gables and curlicued eaves. I scroll forward a few until I reach a good shot of the front entrance—a cheerful green door, stark amid crisp white walls.

And there it is. In the picture it doesn't flicker and glimmer the way the triangle at that guy's house did. And while it's not exactly clear, it's definitely there—a faintly glowing triangle, just like the other one.

I didn't even notice it when I took the photo. What does it mean? Part of me thinks it's probably just some kind of weird builder's mark, but for some reason that doesn't seem quite right. I sit on my window seat and lean back against the wall, tugging nervously at a short lock of my hair as I peer down into the backyard.

A movement catches my eye. A large, dark shape is emerging just at the edge of the trees. *Probably just some hungry deer*, I think. Squinting, I peer into the deep darkness and startle when a *person* walks out onto the grass. He's wearing a long coat and hat and—

It's the guy from the porch. The one I saw this afternoon.

Shock rattles through me, jarring bones that are suddenly chilled again. It doesn't make any sense, but I see the blond ponytail and I . . . I just know. It's him.

He's at my house in the middle of the night.

Did he follow me? What the hell is he doing? Every sliver of logic within me is screaming to go get Jay. He's just down the hall.

But instead I sit there, staring.

The blond guy walks across the backyard, very slowly, kicking grass with the toes of his knee-high boots. His hands are wedged deep in the pockets of the breeches I was admiring earlier, pushing his long coat back at the waist and showing off an embroidered vest. He seems completely unconcerned by the fact that he's standing on someone else's property at a totally inappropriate time. He's not hiding or even keeping to the shadows. He's just ... walking.

The tip of my nose brushes the chilly glass and I realize I've practically pushed my entire body up against the window. He turns and looks right up at me. Our eyes meet.

I freeze.

There seems to be something wrong with my body the last twelve hours; my fight-or-flight mechanism isn't working quite right; it's stuck on simply *stop*. I don't so much as twitch as his gaze takes me in—my wide eyes, my open mouth, my fingertips making ten little smudges on the frosted glass.

Then he *smiles*—half interested, half amused, as though this were some kind of game.

But I don't know the rules.

Strength seems to drain from my arms and my hands drop slowly, my fingers making lines down the clouded windowpane. We both stand there, frozen in time, just staring.

He raises one hand and crooks a gloved finger at me, inviting me out. I squeak and pull away, flattening myself against the wall, out of sight.

Hiding *him* from my sight.

My heart pounds in my temples and my fingertips as I stand there counting my breaths, trying to calm down. Who *is* this guy? How did he find me? After ten long breaths I scoot over and turn, peeking out from behind the curtain. *I don't have to hide,* I rationalize, *I'm not the one doing something wrong.*

But though I stand at the window staring down for several minutes, nothing stirs, nothing moves.

He's gone.

I'm so confused. I don't know this guy—I've never seen him in my life before today.

So why do I *miss* him?

CHAPTER FOUR

I don't see Benson when I enter the library—not entirely unheard of; he does *occasionally* have to do actual work. But despite my homework, the real reason I came here was to see him, to talk to him, and my nerves are so frazzled that when I don't immediately catch sight of him, my still-recovering brain finds it impossible to formulate a plan B.

"Oh, Tavia dear." Marie's soft voice scares me so badly I spin with an audible gasp. I have *got* to simmer down. "Benson's back in the file room. Would you like me to get him for you?"

Marie is the head librarian and technically Benson's boss. She's about as strict as a bowl of whipped cream, and Benson adores her. Which means that she adores him back—and who wouldn't?—but also that she often hovers when we're working and pays me extra attention because I'm *Benson's special friend*.

And she *always* pronounces my name wrong. We've had the conversation—Tave, it rhymes with *cave*, not *mauve*—but it never sticks.

"Y-yes please," I answer, hoping she didn't notice the stutter. She just smiles and heads toward the back of the library at a maddeningly slow pace, her silver, wavy hair bouncing as she walks.

I suppose it's not a particularly complimentary testament to my social life that my only friend is a library intern, but considering I'm attending high school online and don't have a classmate within a hundred miles, I can hardly be choosy. After missing four months of school for physical and neurological recovery, online was pretty much my only option if I didn't want to be a "super senior."

Besides, Reese and Jay thought it would be better for me to get a whole new start out here, a thousand miles away from my old life. At first I assumed they just didn't want to move, and I didn't blame them. But in the end I think they were right. I like being someplace new—where I'm not immediately labeled the poor girl who lost both her parents. Broken and orphaned. Something tells me there's no going back to normal after either of those, much less both.

Plus, classwork gives me an excuse to get out of the house almost every day to come here and see Benson. Not that I *need* an excuse, but I don't want Reese and Jay to think I'm trying to get away from them.

And I'm not . . . exactly. It's just weird to be in the house with Reese all day long every single day. I'm eighteen; I should be out doing high school stuff. Football games, school plays, hanging out at McDonald's eating my weight in french fries. The kind of stuff I used to occasionally let my friends drag me out for, back in Michigan. The kind of stuff I'd decided to do more of my senior year at my new art school. Maybe even with a guy—a nice, artsy guy.

And then my plans crashed along with the plane.

Things like that don't interest me anymore. I'd accepted that I would have a secluded senior year when an English assignment sent me to the library for the first time a couple months ago and Benson Ryder was the one who introduced himself to me.

Then taught me how to use microfiche. Friendship at first sight.

Literally.

I slip into a chair at our usual table and knead the muscles on my right leg—they're always a little tender after the half-mile walk here—before glancing around the sparsely populated library. It generally isn't too busy between nine and four, unless one of the local elementary schools is having a field trip. It gets busier in the afternoon, when school's out, but one of the advantages of online school is that I can go to the library anytime I want.

Plus Benson is more likely to be free to "study" with me when fewer people are there to ask for his help—or overhear the conversation we're about to have.

As I reach into my backpack to pull out my textbooks, I'm dismayed to see my hands are shaking. Am I nervous to tell Benson? That doesn't seem quite right. Maybe I'm just still so messed up from everything that's happened.

And I'm not sure exactly *how* to tell Benson about the blond guy from yesterday.

And last night.

This morning, technically.

I don't even know his name, but he feels special somehow. My secret. Not the kind of secret that makes you feel guilty and empty inside; he's a cappuccino secret—something sweet and frothy that warms me from the middle out.

Still, I need to tell Benson. I should tell *someone* in case . . . in case this guy really is dangerous. Though even the thought makes me prickle in defense.

As though I *know* him.

Benson will understand, won't he? Benson knows everything about me. *Everything*. It's been a slow process—you don't just walk up to someone and say, "Hi! I'm the orphaned sole survivor of one of the biggest plane crashes in history and I've been hiding from the media for six months and oh, by the way, did I mention I'm recovering from a traumatic brain injury?"

But slowly—and without me consciously intending it to—it all sort of spilled out. About a month ago, when I finally confided that the "car crash" was actually a plane crash, I expected Benson to be mad. *That* fact I'd outright lied about. More than once.

He just laughed and stretched his arms out to the side and asked, "Seriously, is there anything else I should know about you? Long-lost twin? Secret baby? Toenail fetish?"

I love how he makes me laugh at myself.

But his smile was a little strained until I assured him that, no, there was nothing more and he now knew all my deep, dark secrets. And it was an incredible relief to tell him. To stop lying.

To one person, anyway.

I think that's the day I realized I was falling for him.

Not that it'll ever happen. Probably. He's so focused on school and I . . . I'm kinda broken. Not just my injuries. I've *changed*. In ways I can hardly put my finger on, but I can't deny it. Concentration is harder than it used to be. Everything is harder, really. My brain injury was considered moderate and my recovery pronounced by the doctors to be "miraculous," but simply *living* is a tiny bit less natural, a shade less instinctive. A little less . . . everything. I've mostly come to terms with it. But I don't know that I'm ready for a real relationship with anyone yet. Or even soon. My life is a tangle of uncertainty.

Besides, he has this girl. Dana. I haven't met her—I don't *want* to meet her—but apparently she's gorgeous and funny and smart and amazing and . . . well, an angel come to earth, according to Benson. They aren't dating. *Yet*, as Benson says. But he talks about her all the time.

When I can't get him to change the subject.

He won't even see me; not compared to that. And I'm not willing to lose his friendship just because I can't have it both ways.

Pushing away my self-pity, I look down and realize I've been sub-consciously doodling. Just scribbles. Rubbing my pencil back and forth, essentially. But . . .

But . . .

I turn the paper sideways and swallow hard as a jolt of adrenaline tingles down my arms. The dark smudges definitely look like someone's shadow.

A guy's shadow. A guy who's tall and slim and has a hint of a ponytail.

I let the pencil slip from my fingers and clench my fists, trying to get control of my breathing, my panic coming from a completely different source now.

I haven't drawn a thing since the day my plane went down. Not that I haven't tried. But art is the symbol of my ruined dreams.

And the reason my parents are dead.

I know technically it's irrational, but if I hadn't insisted on going to tour the fancy art school that offered me a scholarship, we never would have boarded that plane. Elizabeth tells me I'm mis-assigning blame. But knowing that and *feeling* it are two very different things. Every day I fight the guilt.

Sometimes I win.

Most days I lose.

Someone at the school—Huntington Academy of the Arts—saw my work when it was displayed at the Michigan state capitol. They contacted me and requested a portfolio of every piece of art I'd ever done, tempting me with full-color brochures of a beautiful campus where students could apparently take out their easels and paint sunsets at their leisure.

Mom and Dad were skeptical at first, but when the school sent me a full-ride scholarship for my senior year to the tune of about $50K, they had to at least agree to let me go see it.

After the crash I was surprised to realize that I still wanted to go. It felt wrong, yet something inside me still wanted to reclaim what I'd lost.

But the first time I tried to pick up a pencil, it fell out of my fingers. I couldn't even hold the stupid thing. The doctors told me it was because my brain was still healing; that they expected me to regain all my motor function with physical therapy.

And time.

I insisted Reese call Huntington. After she explained everything, I was surprised how willing they were to defer my scholarship—to let me start up in January when my injuries were healed.

But the fall months passed and I could still barely write my name. Every time I tried, I'd turn into a crying mess all over again. Reese encouraged me through November, December. She told me art was an inherent part of me, part of who I am. To this day I'm not sure why she cared so much. But New Year's came and even though my hands were better, my *artist's block* was all too firmly in place. I called the school myself, on my last day in the neuro-rehabilitation center, and withdrew.

Reese and Jay didn't try to talk me out of it.

I sigh, loudly. With Benson still AWOL and the weight of anxiety pressing down on me, I cast about for something to keep me busy—to distract me—while I wait. I grab a newspaper from the table next to me and start mechanically reading the words, hardly taking them in. I'm on the second page before I feel an arm drape around the back of my chair.

"Sorry I took so long," Benson says. I have only a moment to take in a blur of khakis and a pastel green and blue plaid shirt before he's there on the chair beside me. His breath feels warm on my neck as he glances at the paper, and I feel my fingers tingle. I grip the page tighter and force myself not to lean in—not to press my forehead against his cheek and see if it's as soft as it looks or gritty with stubble. "Marie had a crapload of filing saved up for me."

"I hardly noticed you were gone," I say with mock-loftiness, though my body has practically gone limp with relief. "I was too busy reading about the plague that's going to destroy the world," I say, but my humor falls flat.

"That virus again?" Benson says grimly, pushing up his glasses as he leans in to read the story over my shoulder.

"Yeah. They found a new case in Georgia. Dead in twenty-four hours, just like those six people in Kentucky." I flip back to the front page and point to the first part of the story, then hand over the section.

Since almost dying, I feel like I'm surrounded by death. People are constantly killed in accidents, from diseases, flukes. I know it's always been that way, but now I'm hyper-aware.

"Sixteen victims so far," I say quietly. But Benson doesn't respond—his eyes dart back and forth as he reads. "Jay's lab just started him working on this," I add as Benson flips to the second half of the story.

"Really?" Benson's sudden attention startles me.

"Really, what?"

"Jay's lab?"

"Yeah. New assignment. You want me to ask him about it?" Benson's been following the story pretty closely since the first mini-epidemic in Maryland last week. Then Oregon, then Kentucky just a few days ago.

Benson meets my eyes for a second and sits back and pushes the paper away. "Nah. I imagine everybody's working on it. Hoping to be the one who makes a big breakthrough. It only makes sense."

"I guess."

Benson glances down at my backpack. "So what do you need my incredible expertise with?" he asks. Technically Benson doesn't actually do all that much helping anymore—mostly I just needed the microfiche thing—but we sit and discuss my assignments and readings and he often returns the favor with his own suggestions. It's why I started reading Keats.

"Nothing but calculus today, actually."

"Please, a waste of my creative skills. Also, way too hard," he says with a grin. "I'll let you do that one on your own."

"Thaaaaaanks," I drawl, whapping him on the nose with a pencil.

He pulls my backpack open with one finger and peeks inside. "Don't you have anything fun in there? Like history?"

"I'm completely finished with my history class for the rest of the semester, as of that paper we researched last Friday. We ate our dessert too quickly." Since Benson and I are both history buffs, it was just too big of a temptation to work ahead.

"More's the pity," Benson says in a faux British accent.

I shake my head at his dramatics. The first time I saw Benson, I thought he was just a run-of-the-mill library nerd. But his comfortable grip when he shook my hand and the way his light green button-up shirt and gray sweater vest had an all-too-purposeful touch of wrinkling told me this was a carefully crafted look—not a persona he stumbled into after a geeky childhood.

In some ways, he keeps me sane better than my shrink. Reminds me of the normalcy life used to have.

He's an intern from UNH, but even though he's in college, we're practically the same age. His birthday's in August and mine's in December, so we're both eighteen, just on opposite sides of the school year cutoff. Not that he doesn't take every opportunity to bring up the fact that he's *older and wiser*.

I'll give him the *older* part. But only just.

"I just had to get out of the house." It's only a half lie. A few more seconds of procrastination as I try to decide how to start the real conversation.

"Admit it, you missed me."

"Pined," I say with an eyebrow raised. But it's the truth. More than I like to admit.

I rummage through my backpack—not actually trying to find my math book, just avoiding looking him in the face. "Hey, Benson?" I begin. "Is . . . is stalking ever acceptable? Like, justified and not weird and creepy?"

"Oh, absolutely," Benson says in a very serious voice.

"Really?" I say, and I feel my heart speed up as hope leaps into my chest.

"Yes. When Dana McCraven is stalking me. That is completely acceptable, rational, and even expected as far as I'm concerned." He strikes an exaggerated thinking pose, resting his cheek on his fist. "No, other than that it's pretty much always weird and creepy. Why?"

"No reason," I grumble, going back to my pointless poking around.

"Oh please," Benson blurts after nearly a minute of silence.

"What?"

He runs his fingers through his light brown hair, styled in a casual messy look today. "'What did you have for lunch?'" he says in a high, mocking tone. "*That's* a question that people sometimes ask for no reason. 'What did you do last night?' is also a random question. I would even accept 'Did you shower this morning?' as a question without *true* motivation since you are aware of the fact that my hygiene habits are beyond reproach. Whether or not *stalking* is socially acceptable is definitely not a random, casual question."

I refuse to meet his eyes.

He angles himself toward me and lets his arm rest on the back of my chair again, as if that didn't make this whole conversation even more awkward. "Tave, seriously. This isn't funny. Are you the stalker or the stalk-ee?"

"That's a stupid word."

"Is someone seriously stalking you?" Though he remains calm, all traces of humor are gone from his voice.

"No! Yes. Sort of." I groan as I cover my face with my hands. "It's complicated."

"Reporters?"

I shake my head.

"Cupcake, spill." He always refers to me as some kind of confection when he's trying to worm information out of me. Which, considering my somewhat sordid past, happens on a semi-frequent basis. I caved once to *muffin* but put my foot down at *croissant*.

Cupcake is acceptable, though, so I give up and tell him. Once the words start, it gets easier. Then it's a relief. Then I'm talking so quickly I'm having a hard time enunciating. The guy, the triangles on the houses, everything. By the time I reach the part where the guy tried to get me to come outside, Benson is done joking.

"Tavia, you need to call the police. This is some seriously scary shit."

"I think that's a little extreme, don't you? I've only seen him twice."

"No!" Benson says, leaning closer, his arm tightening around my back. "He tried to *lure you out of your house at two in the morning.*"

I know it's true, and I know I should be as freaked out as Benson. But somehow I'm just . . . not. "He's not some creepy old man. He's, like, our age. Or close to it."

"Oh, good point," Benson says, but his tone is flat and dry. "Because the rule book says that all dangerous stalkers are ugly and old."

"That's not how I meant it. I didn't *feel* afraid. Maybe 'stalker' isn't the right word." I rub my temples and gather my thoughts, trying to figure out what the right word *is*. "I don't think he wanted to hurt me. It's more like he . . . he wanted to *tell* me something."

"Like, 'Get into my car before I blow your brains out'?"

"Benson!"

Benson senses that he's pushed me one step too far and stays quiet for a while. Finally he offers an apology. "I'm sorry. I know you're not stupid, and I don't mean to treat you that way. I just . . . I'd hate to see you get really hurt because your instincts might be . . . off."

He doesn't have to tap one finger against the side of his head for me to take his meaning. A lot of my reactions are still a little off-kilter. Maybe that's all this is. This overwhelming draw to be near a strange guy—to talk to him, to sit in silence, to just *be* the two of us—it's a ridiculous feeling, a terrible instinct, and I *know* it. But telling myself that and turning the feeling *off* are two vastly different things.

The moment gets a little heavy, and to cover my anxiousness, I lean away from Benson and start digging around in the bottom of my backpack again.

"What are you looking for?"

"My ChapStick," I grumble. The cold air here is surprisingly hard on my lips. The winters were plenty harsh in Michigan, but Reese says that the salt from the ocean is what's making my skin dry out. So now I carry ChapStick everywhere.

Except when I misplace it.

Which is frequently.

"Look in your pocket," Benson says with apologetic warmth in his voice. "It's always in your pocket when you can't find it."

Making a silent wish, I dig into my pocket and breathe a sigh of relief when my hand closes around the familiar tube. "You're a genius."

"You're an addict," he counters.

"I'm telling you," I say, pausing to rub my lips together, "in five minutes I'll just have to do it again. I think I've become immune."

"I think you have a serious problem, Tave. You need to go to therapy."

"You're so weird," I say, turning back to my homework.

"No, seriously," Benson says. "It's almost three o'clock. You need to get to physical therapy."

I hesitate. In the face of everything that has happened, going to physical therapy seems so small. So unimportant.

As though reading my thoughts, Benson squeezes my hand as he says quietly, "Let me think on this for a bit. It's hard to take in all at once. Go ahead and go to your appointment and text me later, deal?"

I muster up a smile and say, "Deal," feeling a little better. I pull on my jacket and, in a playful impulse, grab Benson's face, planting a Chap-Stick kiss on his cheek.

As soon as my lips make contact with his skin, he stills, his hands tightening on my arms, and I wonder if I've made a mistake.

But then he's wiping his cheek and his eyes aren't on me and I'm not completely sure it happened at all. 'Tavia," he protests. "Gross!"

"See you tomorrow," I say with a little finger wave.

"Addict," Benson hisses one more time just before I reach the front doors.

CHAPTER FIVE

The route from the library to the physical therapy center takes me up Park Street, through an old section of town. This area is an eclectic mix of old and new: a gas station, an ancient brewery, a famous house that's now a historic monument—beautifully restored—all amid a formless mix of office buildings, many in the shells of their original two-hundred-year-old structures. It's a clashing of times that feels dissonant, yet reeks of awesome. I love it.

But enjoying the scenery is kind of low on my list at the moment. I'm trying to keep my pace up while walking to a steady four-count in my head. One, two, three, four. One, two, three, four. It's a trick my physical therapist taught me a couple weeks ago.

"Tavia Michaels, you should *not* have a limp anymore," she insists. But after months of shying away from the pain, it's become a habit—my natural cadence even though the pain is gone.

Most days.

Pure physical therapy only gets you so far; now it's a question of resetting my mind. So I count. A lot.

But my even pace is a little hard to maintain when my eyes are darting to the space above every building, every front door, looking for symbols.

I blink. *Was that a flash?* I peer harder, blink again. Nope. This time I really am just seeing things. Great.

I try not to look at the next house, but I can't help it. My eyes wander to the door all on their own.

What the . . . ? I come to an abrupt halt, and a man in a jogging suit mutters as he sidesteps to keep from running into me.

It's not a triangle this time, and it's not glowing, either. This one looks solid and . . . real. I take a few steps toward it, peering at the symbol carved into the beam above the door. It's so worn—not to mention painted over—that I can't quite tell what it is; something round but elongated over some curvy lines. It could be anything, but it's definitely *something*, and it sets my heart racing the same way the glowing triangles did.

I attempt to look casual—like I'm not some creepy voyeur—as I pull out my phone and take a quick picture. As soon as the phone clicks, I shove it in my pocket, hoping no one noticed.

I lower my chin and start counting my strides again, trying to take my mind off the symbols. *One, two, three, four. One, two, three, four.*

When I look up to gauge how far it is to the end of the block, a hint of gold flashes through gaps in the pedestrians in front of me. *It's him!* Over the shoulder of the man in the jogging suit, not far past a lady with a stroller, I make out that now-familiar blond ponytail at the nape of his bronzed neck.

Apparently his long hair *is* real.

And it looks silky and soft.

My jaw tightens against the thought and I begin walking again, faster now, marshaling my courage. I should at least talk to him—find out what he thought he was doing last night.

I shoulder my way around a couple holding hands. Only two more people between us. My leg twinges, but I ignore it. I've stopped counting, too. Never mind my gait, I'm totally focused on *him*. I can't yell—he'd probably run—but I'm almost close enough to grab his arm.

Almost there.

Almost.

But as I reach out to tap his shoulder, he steps around the corner into a narrow alley and is gone.

"No you don't," I mutter, and pivot without slowing, determined to catch him.

Pain hits me as I slam into a wall and the collision radiates down my spine, collapsing my knees and dropping me to the sidewalk. I blink and try to focus as faces enter my field of vision.

"Are you okay?"

"Someone call an ambulance."

"She's having a seizure!"

"Miss? Miss?"

"I'm fine," I mutter, blood rushing to my cheeks. And despite being at a higher risk for them since the accident, I most certainly am *not* having a seizure. I rub a searing spot on my head and squint up at what I thought was an alley.

There is *no* alley there.

It's a gray stone real estate office—a newer building, with flashy posters of available properties hung all over the windows.

But . . .

I want to die of humiliation as about six people help me to my feet. Their hands worry over me, touching me, violating my bubble of personal space—which has always been large, but has expanded with the isolation of the last several months. I put my arms out, nudging people away, chanting, "Thank you, I'm fine, thank you, I'm fine, thank you, I'm fine," until they finally leave me alone, only one or two glancing after me.

"You have a scrape on your forehead," a woman says. She looks at me so intently I wonder if she knows me. If I know her. Worse, if she knows Reese and Jay—it's not a particularly large city—and is about to open up her cell phone and call them. What a disaster *that* would be. I open my mouth to speak, but before I can, she presses a Band-Aid into my hand, turns to cough politely into the crook of her arm, then walks up the street.

I watch her go, and just as I start to look away, she flickers.

What the hell?

I study her back—a spot of blue pastel among the pedestrians—willing her to flicker again, to have someone else notice, to prove to myself that I'm not crazy. But after about ten seconds of nothing weird happening, she takes a left and walks out of sight.

I brace my shoulder against the gray stone of the realty office and try to convince myself that I must have just blinked or that it was my imagination or something.

The blond guy is nowhere to be seen, which is probably a good thing since I'm not sure I could keep myself from screaming at him. He wants me to come to him; he runs away from me.

Down nonexistent alleys, no less.

Boys.

The again-milling foot traffic flows around me, but there's something . . . something else making me uncomfortable. A niggling sense of—*there!* I catch sight of a man across the street, watching me. He's wearing khaki cargo pants and sunglasses; pretty nondescript.

But he's watching me. Great.

I meet his eyes—I think, stupid sunglasses—and glare, daring him to keep staring at the klutzy girl. He immediately turns his head and begins walking in the opposite direction. I *hate* embarrassing myself in public.

Distantly I hear the crinkle of the Band-Aid wrapper as I crumple it in my palm and my chin drops to my chest. I stride up the still-crowded boardwalk, forgetting to count as I work my way along, hoping no one looks at my bright red face too closely.

At the end of the block I turn and head to a much newer part of town, where my physical therapy center is. My mind races faster than my feet.

Who the hell is this blond guy? He could be a reporter. Seems awfully young for that, though. I got a good look last night and he can't be much older than me. And based solely on statistics, he's *probably* not a serial killer. He could be some kind of bizarre stalker, but why?

Maybe he's just a weirdo. I mean, he grew his hair out for a reenactment costume he wears every day; he could simply be way hard core into that kind of thing. Like the old men who spend all their spare time building model trains or painting Civil War miniatures. Or this guy in my old school who was really into theater and would dress and talk like his character all day, every day whenever he was cast in a new part. It would be about three steps beyond "quirky," but not unheard of. In fact, that might be the best explanation—for my safety, at least.

But Mr. Ponytail did try to get me to come out last night. Why would he do that? If he were so into his reenactment life, it seems like he would approach me during the day and introduce himself with some kind of overdone wave of his hat or something similarly dramatic.

And that flicker when the woman walked away. . . . Just one more bullet point on my list of topics I really don't want to think about.

When I arrive at the PT center, a glance in the passenger-side mirror of a random car in the parking lot shows me my injured forehead. There's a scrape with a little line of dirt on one side. I lick my finger and try to clear the smudge away. The raw skin stings each time I touch it, but I ignore that and scrub until the grayish streak is gone. I adjust my short bangs over the shallow cut and try to convince myself no one will notice.

I'm about to head in when my phone rings. "Elizabeth?" I whisper to myself. It's not like she never calls—she used to check up on me somewhat regularly. But it's been a while. "Hey, Elizabeth," I say.

"Got a second?" she asks cheerily, but I'm totally nervous anyway.

"A few," I say, glancing at the PT center.

I hear her draw in a breath, then hesitate. "I spoke with your uncle this morning. He said you were up very early. Two o'clock early."

My mouth drops in surprise. "Jay?" *Traitor,* I think, and kick the tire of the car I'm standing by.

"Don't blame him," Elizabeth says. "He just thought it might be important."

Like *that* makes everything okay. "Well, it isn't. I had a nightmare. That's all."

"About the crash?"

"Didn't *Jay* tell you?" I sound petulant but can't bring myself to care. I already feel like I'm living my life in a fishbowl; I don't need further confirmation.

Elizabeth says nothing, but the truth is, she doesn't have to speak; I know the words intrinsically. *Tavia, you're avoiding the issue.*

"No," I finally answer, one hand fisted on my hip. "It didn't have *anything* to do with the crash—that's why it's not important."

"You know, just because the dream didn't have a plane in it doesn't mean it isn't related to your mind trying to deal with the crash. Many dreams—most, really—aren't literal."

She lets the conversation hang, waiting for me to direct it. I know her tricks.

But that doesn't mean they don't work.

"I was drowning," I say, turning my back to the physical therapy center, as though someone inside could hear me. "A stereotypical dream. The kind *normal* people have," I add, emphasizing the word *normal* and clearly leaving myself out of that category.

"Would you mind sharing?" Elizabeth asks.

I don't want to talk about the water. Even thinking about it makes me shiver all over. So I give her as fast a version as I can, skimming over the way it made me feel.

"Were you able to get back to sleep or did this dream continue to bother you?" She uses the word *dream* instead of *nightmare*. I suspect it's to make it sound more neutral, but I wish she'd call it what it was. Dreams don't terrify you until you stop breathing. "I went downstairs and had a snack, and that calmed me down."

Then silence. Elizabeth knows there's more and she waits. Just waits. She does this in her office, too—it's maddening.

But it works.

Almost against my will, I start to speak. "There's . . ." I know that once I tell her, there's no going back. I can hardly believe I'm doing this. My shrink. I'm taking my guy troubles to my shrink. But who else can I take them to? Not Reese or Jay. Just . . . no.

And Benson already told me what *he* thinks I should do. I think I need to talk to another woman. Maybe the romantic chromosome we all seem to have will help her understand this weird feeling.

"There's a—a guy. I just saw him for the first time. Actually, like the third time and—" I force myself to stop and calm my nerves. I have to start from the beginning. "Yesterday, after our session, I was in the car while Reese was getting milk."

She listens without comment—though she breathes a soft, "Oh, Tave," when I get to the part about him being in the backyard at two A.M.—until I wrap up with the *incident* at the realty office. Though I fudge the details a teeny bit to make it sound like I'm not seeing fake alleys or flickering women.

"And he was just *gone?*" Elizabeth asks when I finish.

"Gone," I say, and that weird sad feeling swirls in my chest again. "Benson says I should call the police," I add when the silence makes me nervous. "But I don't think this guy's dangerous. And if . . . if I call the police, he'll—" I cut off my own words. I don't even want to say it.

"He'll leave?" Elizabeth asks, and anguish drowns me, filling me so completely I can't speak. I only make a vague noise of agreement. Part of me hates the way this guy makes me feel—it's overwhelming and awakens emotions I don't recognize. It's different than the way I feel about Benson—he's a soft, steady light, while this guy is like a firecracker—blindingly bright, but here and then gone in an instant.

But those brief moments are like liquid joy pouring over my head. That part, I like.

"You seem to be feeling some very strong emotions here."

"I guess." I brace myself for her to tell me that this is a side effect of my grief, or that I'm projecting unrequited love on an inappropriate target, or that it's the brain damage talking.

I'm irrationally relieved when she doesn't. I *want* to see him again, even though every shred of logic within me is shouting that it's a bad idea.

I can't help but wonder if this is a sign that I'm getting better or that I'm truly broken.

"Tave, I really want to make sure we talk about this more tomorrow when we can discuss it face-to-face. Is that okay with you?"

"Sure, I guess," I say, almost hating that I told her at all now that the panic has passed. But she's my psychiatrist—this is the kind of crazy stuff I'm *supposed* to tell her. Still, I feel like I just spilled someone *else's* secret rather than sharing my own thoughts.

The silence stretches again, but I'm in no mood to deal with it anymore. "I gotta go," I mumble, looking for an excuse to hang up. "I have a physical therapy appointment." I force a sharp bark of laughter. "You know, my *other* therapist."

Elizabeth chuckles and then says, "Okay. Go in and . . . stretch. We'll talk more tomorrow."

"Thanks," I say dryly, and hang up. I walk toward the center, trying to sort through my conflicted feelings.

She didn't tell me *not* to see him again. But I feel like it was too easy. Mentally, I know Benson's reaction made more sense. Perhaps part of me wanted Elizabeth to confirm that I really *should* stay away from him.

But she didn't. And I can't help but wonder why.

CHAPTER SIX

"Hey, Tave," Jay says as I slide into the passenger seat, my leg throbbing from ankle to hip. Usually Reese picks me up from PT because Jay's at work.

"No lab Nazi today?" I ask, buckling my seat belt. The combination of aches from therapy and knowing that he tattled on me to Elizabeth makes me much less than happy to see him.

"Worse," Jay says, pulling into traffic. His voice is scratchy and he stifles a yawn. "I have research to do at home."

"The virus?"

He pauses, so briefly I almost don't catch it. "Yeah." But he doesn't elaborate. "What happened to your head?"

My fingers fly to the scrape, preemptively sabotaging any lie I might have tried to tell. Clearly, my bangs aren't doing their job. "Um." I fumble for an explanation. "I ran into a wall."

"Let's see," he says when we hit a red light. He stretches his arm out toward my face. I try not to flinch, but when his hand stills midair, I know I've failed. I don't like people reaching for me—not anymore. Too many months of doctors and nurses checking my eyes, my stitches, my ears, my temperature, my scar, and—of course—about a million needles, all pointed toward me.

He doesn't push it. Jay's always pretty good with stuff like that.

"Please, Jay," I say, rubbing my eyes with the heels of my hands as I feel a headache building. "I'm totally feeling like a dork already—I was just a stupid klutz. I promise."

He hesitates longer than I think is really necessary. It's just a scrape.

"I know you talked to Elizabeth," I blurt after a short pause, my anger making me brave. When in doubt, go with a diversion. Or better yet, an accusation.

He smiles guiltily, tilts his head like a puppy that got caught chewing on a shoe. "I didn't really tell her anything," he protests. "Not even what the dream was about."

"Did you tell Reese? What it was about?" I clarify.

"You know I tell Reese everything."

I can't be mad at that. They're married. And family or not, I'm an intruder in their life. "Light's green," I mutter.

"It was really casual," Jay says, trying to placate me. "Dr. Stanley calls once in a while to make sure everything's going well at home, and she happened to call this morning." He pauses, glances over at me. "I didn't think it was confidential; I mean, was it?"

"Not really," I admit, feeling my frustration ebb. It wasn't *that* big of a deal. "I just feel like I don't have any privacy. Like, ever."

"I'll warn you next time," he says earnestly. "In fact—peace offering—when we get home, you go upstairs and put a dab of makeup on that scrape before dinner and I'll make a teeny exception to my tell-Reese-everything rule. Our little secret," he whispers with a grin. "Truce?"

I go ahead and give him a weak smile. It isn't that I *don't* want Reese to know, exactly. But she worries. A lot. Not that I blame her—her step-brother died in a plane wreck and she inherited his crazy, damaged kid. Death makes people paranoid.

I should know.

Just before we pull into the garage, I catch sight of the billowy curtains in Reese's office fluttering through her open window. Wind chimes that Reese let me mount across the front porch a few weeks ago sway in the slight breeze. As I take in the ringing of the chimes and the classic beauty of the house, I feel my whole body relax. For some reason, I've always found their home comforting.

"You'll have to excuse me," Jay says as we walk in the back door, "but I do need to get some work done before dinner." He yanks off his already-loose tie and tosses it over the arm of a chair as he heads into his "office." It's more like a lab, complete with three computers, charts of molecules plastered on the wall, and one side of the room entirely taken up with bookshelves full of colorful reference books in very non-alphabetical order.

His actual chemistry stuff is at the lab—he says it's too dangerous to bring home—but every simulation and research tool you could possibly want is in there.

Assuming you can find it.

Jay drops into his office chair and gets right back to work, and I tiptoe upstairs to fix my forehead.

Reese's office is down the hall from my room and I hear her inside, humming off-key. I creep by the barely cracked door and into my room before she can catch me. My makeup bag is sitting on my vanity, and I pull out my best cover-up and examine the scrape in a decent mirror for the first time.

It really isn't that bad; it just stings like crazy.

I dab pancake-y makeup on it and it stings even more, but at least it's hard to see now. I finish the job off with a little powder and check out my handiwork.

Pretty good.

I still look stressed, though. They don't have makeup to cover *that*. It's something in the eyes. But I think I have reason to be. I'm tired of listing the psycho things that have happened to me in the last twenty-four hours. Tired of trying to figure out how I'm going to talk to Elizabeth about them all without sounding like I've taken some pretty massive steps backward in my recovery.

Avoiding eye contact with myself, I run my hands through my short, dark hair, but all that does is make it look wild and unkempt. With a sigh I smooth it back down and click my compact closed.

It didn't used to be short. I wish it would grow faster.

They shaved the right side of my head for surgery, and when the bandages finally came off, it was covered in matted fuzz while the other side was still halfway down my back.

That was the first time I cried. Until then, everything was numb and I felt disconnected—like all this medical stuff was happening to someone else. Someone with no parents and very little chance of a normal life.

Not *me*.

But the hair. The hair was mine.

And if the hair was mine, the rest of it was too. The broken brain, the dead parents, all of it. Mine.

At least I could do *something* about the hair. I decided then and there to shave the other side too, so at least I would match. I don't know that it was the *wrong* decision, but having a shaved head isn't exactly my idea of pretty.

I thought it made me look insane.

Two hundred years ago, they would shear the hair off all the "patients" in asylums to keep them from getting lice and nits. So for weeks after surgery, whenever I caught a glimpse of myself in a mirror with my stubbly hair and hospital gown, I felt like a prisoner in an old-fashioned madhouse.

And thought it rather apropos.

Tentatively, I poke at the scar that runs along my head, fingering the raised edge. The doctors told me that it will gradually get flatter and less noticeable, but it'll always be there. It's about eight inches long and stretches back diagonally from just above my hairline on the right side of my head. Luckily, once my hair got to be about an inch long, it covered the scar almost completely. The four inches I have now is dark enough that no one can see my scar at all unless I run my fingers through my hair.

I don't do that in public; I'm very careful.

Still, maybe a visit to the salon would help.

"How was PT?" Reese asks, making me jump. At least she waited to swing by my room until after I hid all evidence of my latest injury.

"As good as torture ever is," I mutter, shoving my makeup bag aside. My leg is *still* aching.

"And how about your session with Dr. Stanley yesterday?" she continues. Reese and Jay apparently didn't get the memo about the Elizabeth thing; they always call her *Dr. Stanley*.

"Fine," I say, peeling off my sweater; all this adrenaline is making me hot. The air from the open window cools my prickly skin.

"So things are going well?" she asks. "Progress?"

I look up at her, suspicious; this is more than she usually delves.

Or maybe I just haven't noticed, but today everything makes me feel paranoid.

"I'm only asking," Reese says quickly, "because I need to visit a client out of town in the next week or so. I wondered how you would feel about me being gone for a couple days."

"Oh, that would be totally fine," I say, too fast. "Is Jay going with you?"

"Don't I wish. He's got a new project. There's no way they'd let him take a week off now." She's leaning against my door frame, her voice distant—wistful. If she weren't answering a direct question, I would wonder if she was talking to me or herself.

Then, abruptly, she straightens, and looks at me and smiles. Big.

I like Reese; I really do. But she tries so hard. Too hard, I guess. Jay takes everything more naturally, and it's easy to sit and joke when it's just him and me. Or even all three of us. When I'm alone with Reese, it takes effort.

"Dinner'll be ready in about ten minutes," she says cheerily. "I made lasagna."

I grin and she interprets it as excitement for the lasagna—which is understandable. It's great lasagna! But really I'm laughing at her use of the word *made*. Because in my opinion, the guy at the deli *made* the lasagna. All Reese can take credit for is slipping it into the oven and setting the timer.

That might be baking, but it's definitely not *making*. When Mom made lasagna, she'd spend hours rolling fresh noodles and crushing tomatoes and chopping oregano. Nothing came from a pouch or a can or a deli; for Mom, food was art. Reese's lasagna is different—just like everything else in my new life. So different that it doesn't seem entirely real sometimes.

There are days when my life here feels like I'm at an exotic summer camp and after a few more candlelit meals and nights under my silky down comforter, I'll go home and my parents will be waiting back in middle-class Michigan.

Other days it feels so different that the fact that my old life is gone seems all the more real.

And depressing.

Luckily, most days are somewhere in the middle.

"My favorite," I blurt at last.

Reese plays with the edge of her untucked blouse as her mind churns almost visibly. She's trying to think of something else to say.

I avoid the tension by looking out the window at the frothy Piscataqua River and almost choke in surprise, my heartbeat immediately back up to full speed. "You know what, Reese? I'm kinda hot. I'm going to go outside for a little bit."

I hope I sounded sufficiently casual as I squeeze past her and make it halfway down the stairs before she can respond, my leg throbbing as I nearly run.

"Dinner in ten," she yells after me. "You need to eat!"

But I barely hear her.

I burst out the back door, my eyes scanning, searching. *Please don't let me be too late*, I mentally beg.

But I'm not.

He's still there. Crouched on the riverbank.

CHAPTER SEVEN

He doesn't seem to take any notice of me as I walk up, blinking furiously and trying to make sure I actually see him. That he's real.

But as usual, there's no flickering, no glowing. Not like the woman by the realty office or the triangle at the house. Just . . . him. Real and solid. I'm both relieved by and afraid of that.

The jacket and hat are gone, but he hasn't exactly replaced them with jeans and a polo. He's wearing a linen shirt tucked loosely into brown canvas breeches and his feet are bare, toes half buried in the rocky sand. I glance around at the ground next to him and don't see any shoes. But then, if he was crazy enough to come to my house uninvited and unannounced two days in a row, maybe he walks around barefoot, too.

In March.

As I watch, the air frozen in my lungs—is my heart even beating?— he lifts a hand and tucks a strand of that silken hair behind his ear. Then he bends forward, the linen straining across his shoulders, and picks up a small rock. With a leisurely motion he swings his arm around and releases the stone to go skipping over the face of the river.

The stillness is gone.

A hot fountain of anger and need and want and fury bubbles up in my stomach and as I cover the distance between us, I'm not sure which are stronger—the feelings holding me back or the ones propelling me forward.

Then I'm there. Beside him.

He doesn't look up. Doesn't give any indication that he knows I'm standing here at all.

It just makes me angrier.

"I saw you," I say, just loud enough for him to hear—I don't want to draw anyone's attention, especially Reese's. "Yesterday. Today, I mean. Two in the morning."

I wait for him to explain, to defend himself. To lie even. But he says nothing.

"And then on Park Street too. I don't like that you're following me and I want you to stop." My teeth nearly clamp down on the lie I didn't know was a lie until it came out of my mouth.

But at least I got it out. Benson would be proud.

Still the guy says nothing. Just reaches for another stone and lets it fly, like the first one.

"I'm serious," I say.

I'm not.

"I want you to leave me alone."

I want you to talk to me.

He's still. Still and silent.

"Hey!" I snap, folding my arms across my chest. "Are you even listening to me?"

He reaches for another rock and I move in front of him to block his throw.

"You can't just—" I look down at his face and my words cut off.

It's the most beautiful face I've ever seen.

Leaf-green eyes look up at me with a calm as deep as the waters of Lake Michigan. His jaw is angular, but the curve of his mouth softens the lines and his sooty lashes do the rest. As I drink him in, a strand of golden hair slips loose from behind his ear and casts a dark shadow across his cheek. Air hisses through my lips in a gasp, and though I'm trying to form words, my mouth doesn't obey.

As if sensing that he's the source of my distress, he looks away, back over the water, and I can move again.

"I beg your forgiveness," he says, and his voice is deep, but soft. Dark chocolate. "I approached you badly. Botched it all up." His words sound a little off—accented maybe, but not with any lilt I can place.

I don't know what I was expecting, but an instant apology wasn't it. Excuses, denials, that's what I was ready for. I'm stunned by his admission and, for a moment, stand with my mouth slightly open.

"I ought to have introduced myself in the traditional way." His eyes meet mine again and I can't look away.

"Yeah, that would have been better than standing outside my kitchen at two in the morning," I force myself to say.

"I frightened you."

Again the bluntness. I want to deny it—to insist I wasn't afraid at all. But I was. Terrified and exhilarated in equal measure.

"But I am not the one whom you should fear."

I study him. There's . . . something. Something *familiar*, now that I see him up close. "Do I . . . do I know you?"

He grins and I have to take a step back as he pushes to his feet, the deep V of his loose shirt falling forward, and I glimpse well-defined abs.

I'm not the kind of girl who goes for muscles and tans and all that—brains over brawn for me—but I find it impossible to avert my gaze. It's as though this body was made explicitly for my adoration. As he straightens, his shirt falls flat against his chest once more. My eyes travel upward.

And upward.

I'm not short. I'm five eight. But this guy is a good six inches taller than me, and he stretches his lanky arms above his head in a leisurely gesture. "No," he says, and his eyes sparkle with some kind of mischief. "But you will."

And then we stand.

And stare.

At each other.

This isn't *me*, tongue-twisted over some guy, drooling over a granite physique. It makes me feel right and wrong at once and by turns until I want to walk out of my skin to get away from the contradiction.

"I'm Tavia," I say, thrusting my hand out. I have to do *something*. The tension is killing me and I can't figure out what I want. What I don't want.

They seem to be the same thing.

He looks at my hand but ignores it. "I know who you are."

Of course he does. I wait.

And wait.

Is he going to make me ask?

"We should talk," he says as he stoops to grab a coat from the sand, then slips his lean arms into it. "I have things to show you and our time is short."

"I don't know your name," I blurt.

He smiles all the way now, showing broad teeth and tiny crinkles on each side of his eyes. "You're beautiful, you know that?" My legs shake as he lifts his hand to my face, his fingers just a hair's breadth from my cheek. "I like you this way," he whispers. I close my eyes, waiting for the touch to land.

It doesn't.

After a few seconds I open my eyes, embarrassed. But he's not looking at me. He's turned half away and his eyebrows are folded low.

"Why are you doing this?" I choke. "I don't understand any of it."

"I wish I could explain everything right now, but it will take time. You must trust me. I know I've done nothing to deserve it," he adds before I can argue. "But please, please trust me."

My head is nodding even as I bite my lip, letting go when my teeth touch the sore, cracked skin. Stupid ocean air. It gives me a moment of clarity and I fight the woozy, agreeable feeling that fills my head. "No offense, but why should I trust you?" I snap. "You won't tell me anything and you keep running off. I need you to talk to me."

"Next time," he says, a touch of promise in his voice. "You know I cannot linger tonight. A promise," he adds. "I shall bring something to help you understand next we meet. Agreed?"

"You can't come *here* again," I warn. "Not like this. You'll get us both in trouble."

He nods soberly, almost as if he expected that. "Don't look for me. I'll find you."

It appears that's the best I'm going to get. He's right—he can't stay. Not now. "Okay," I concede. My whole body trembles as I say it. I'm afraid of what I've just agreed to.

He turns and his long coat billows out for just a second, falling back around his legs with a whisper. "Be safe," he says. I *think* he says it. But it's so quiet I might have imagined it.

"Wait!" I say, jumping after him.

"Soon," he calls without turning. "Soon."

"But—" I don't even know what to say; I'm completely out of control here. Of the situation. Of him. Of myself.

A light laugh escapes him and I start to feel angry, but he spins to walk backward and his eyes meet mine with an innocent playfulness. "Since names matter so much to you, it's Quinn," he says with a smile. "Quinn Avery."

Quinn Avery.

Two simple words, but they mean everything.

CHAPTER EIGHT

Where are you? My fingers shake as I text Benson.

Library. About to leave, he replies about a minute later.

We need to talk. I feel weird texting Benson, the guy I liked last week, about Quinn, the guy I apparently like *this* week.

The *other* guy I like this week. It's so weird, when Quinn is around, it's like I can't focus on anything else. He overwhelms my senses and I float in a cloud as blissful as it is terrifying. But when he's gone, reality creeps back in and I don't know what to think.

I know I should give Benson up as a lost cause, but he's like a forest fire—everything started off with a spark too small to even notice until it blazed into something more. I couldn't simply douse those feelings even if I wanted to.

And now I'm going to tell him about Quinn? What am I doing?

But I'm bursting with this new revelation—he has a name and he wants to see me again! And who else can I tell? I'm not about to call my therapist—again—at almost eight o'clock at night.

I try not to think about his other words. *I am not the one whom you should fear.* I've spent the entire day being afraid. Right now I want a few minutes, an hour maybe, to just be happy.

After pleading a forgotten homework assignment to Reese, I get her to let me borrow her car to run to the library. I've got less than half an hour before it closes. When I get there, I park and walk through the front doors as fast as my sore leg will let me, looking for Benson. I don't care if he doesn't understand. I've listened to him practically compose sonnets about Dana McCraven for the last two months and dealt with it; he can listen to *me* now.

It's better this way, I tell myself. *Now we'll both have someone.* But the thought makes me feel strangely hollow.

He's leaning over the counter, talking softly with Marie. My heart gives a funny leap as my eyes skim him from head to toe—taking advantage of the moment before he realizes I'm there. He's still wearing the soft gray sweater-vest over a light green button-up shirt from earlier, but now the sleeves are rolled up, emphasizing the definition of his forearms. As I watch, he pushes his glasses up his nose a little and makes a face at Marie.

He looks totally at home among the stacks of books.

And totally charming.

I swallow, remembering the reason I'm here.

As soon as Benson sees me, his mouth closes and I catch a strange, melancholy look in his eyes before his lopsided smile erases it. I need to remember that he's worried about me. That I'm giving him even *more* reasons to worry about me. Benson is so constant, so mellow, it's hard to remember that he's one of those guys whose emotional river runs deep.

I walk over, trying to avoid eye contact with Marie before she can give me a chirrupy greeting and start asking about my day. I don't have time for her tonight.

"Hi, Marie," I toss off quickly without looking directly at her, then turn to Benson. "I *really* need to find that book before the library closes. It's in the back, right?" I add meaningfully.

"Yeah, I'll show you," Benson says, eyeing me quizzically. He puts one hand on my shoulder and steers me toward the far end of the library, where no one hangs out—not that there's more than a handful of people here now anyway. And most of them are preteens crowded around the computers.

I head to the middle of a shadowy aisle—after checking that no one is browsing—and run my fingers along a variety of spines—newish paperbacks, crumbly ancient hardcovers. I don't think this library ever gets rid of their books. Any of them. There's a single-bulb light fixture above us and it illuminates dust motes swirling in a tiny breeze from the heater.

I feel fluttery now that the nerves are starting to wear off, and I attempt to cover up my awkwardness by pulling a tube of ChapStick from my pocket and reapplying it.

"Oh, hey, that reminds me," Benson says, digging into his own pocket. "I remembered to bring your other one."

I look up into Benson's face. "What?"

"Your ChapStick. I found it in my car after I took you home the other day. I brought it for you. Now you'll have two." He holds out a tube of cherry-flavored ChapStick, identical to the one in my hand, and grins. "Double your pleasure, double your fun."

"Not mine. I need to get a new one, but I haven't yet." I look up at him with one eyebrow raised. "Must belong to one of your girlfriends," I add, trying to sound cheerful while wondering if Dana finally succumbed to Benson's many charms.

Not that it matters.

I don't care.

I *don't* care.

"No, it was on the seat after you left," he insists, still holding it out. "It must have fallen out of your pocket."

I don't know why he's pushing this. "Benson, I'm not going to take some other girl's ChapStick; that's gross. *This* one's mine."

He's looking at me funny. "But—"

"It really doesn't matter, Benson. Just throw it away; I have to talk to you *now*."

"Your loss," he says, and tosses it in the air. It spins several times before he catches it. "You should switch to a new brand anyway. You've been complaining this stuff doesn't work anymore."

"It's just the salt in the air," I say, putting the cap back on my Chap-Stick. The one from my pocket. The one I *know* hasn't touched anyone's lips but mine.

Technically, if he made out with her before she put some on, Benson's germs could be on there too. It makes my stomach feel funny, and I don't like the simmering feeling. I twist the ChapStick in my fingers just to have something to do.

And maybe so I don't have to look at Benson.

My fingers clench around the plastic tube for an instant, then the space where it had been is empty and my fingers touch together. "Holy crap!" I jerk my hand back.

"What?" Benson asks without looking at me, tossing the ChapStick again.

"It's gone!"

"What's gone?"

"The ChapStick!"

There's a slight hesitation before he shrugs. "Look on the floor."

"Benson!"

"What?"

I wait for him to look at me. "I was holding the ChapStick, and then it was gone."

His face is a mask of confusion and he opens his mouth to speak, then closes it and just stares at me. Looking for something in my eyes.

"It *disappeared*, Benson," I say, struggling to keep my breaths from turning into ragged gasps. "I was holding it and it literally disappeared."

Another few seconds of silence pass before Benson swallows and holds the other tube out to me with a half grin. "Well, now you have another one."

"Benson—"

"Jeez, Tave," he snaps. "It's just ChapStick. Take it or don't, but it's not mine."

His sudden flare of temper shocks my thoughts and a second later I realize my cheeks are wet. It's not crying exactly, but the tears are pouring from my eyes as though my emotions are leaking out. Good, bad, terrifying, exhilarating. I've just had too much today and now I'm overflowing.

And embarrassed. I'm completely out of whack.

I snatch the stupid ChapStick from Benson—I'll throw it away later—then open my purse, looking for one of the many packs of tissues I keep in there. Since my parents died, I cry randomly in public on a pitifully frequent basis.

When I sniff, Benson looks up and his whole face crumples in regret. He reaches out, hands finding my shoulders. "Aw, Tave, I'm so sorry. I'm a total jerk. I—"

But I cut his words off with a sharp wave of my hand. I reach into my purse and pull out a tube of ChapStick. Then, just to make sure, I lift my hand and uncurl my fingers to reveal the one Benson just gave me.

Two. Three, if you count the one that disappeared.

I feel myself losing control and have to force a few breaths into my lungs as an awful thought occurs to me. With my hands almost numb in fear, I reach into my pocket again.

At first I feel nothing. But I dig deeper, into the bottom corner where the pocket lint tends to accumulate.

And pull out another tube.

Benson was right; it's *always* in my pocket when I can't find it.

I hold the three tubes out to Benson and he instinctively lifts his hands to take them.

I drop them into his palm. Benson has to see.

If Benson sees them, I'm not crazy.

Or at least I'm not hallucinating.

I reach into my pocket again and meet Benson's eyes as I pull out another tube of ChapStick and place it with the other three already cradled in his hands.

Four. I reach again.

Five.

Six.

I don't want them to cut open my brain again.

"You're weirding me out," Benson says, his eyes boring into mine.

"Ssh!" I hold my finger up to my lips. "Watch."

"Tave—"

"Just. Watch," I insist.

The seriousness in my voice finally gets through to him and he keeps his eyes on my half-dozen lip balms with a skeptical look like he's waiting for me to pounce on him and yell *"Gotcha!"*

I wish.

I wish it were that simple.

A few minutes have passed, and my eyes are already weary from glaring at the tubes. Benson takes a breath and I can practically feel him getting ready to say something when the middle tube pops out of sight.

Benson gasps as he drops the rest of the ChapSticks. He scrambles out of the way—almost knocking me over—and they scatter across the carpet. "Holy mother of Max!"

"Ssssshhh!" I whisper-command, putting my hand over his mouth and stepping right up close to him.

Right against him.

I look up, our faces only a few inches apart, and my chest freezes. My hand lowers slowly, his lips soft against my fingertips, until only one finger rests on his bottom lip. A distant part of me hears Benson's breath, unsteady as it speeds up, his eyes burning into mine.

I'm not sure who reaches out first or how it happens amid everything going on, but in an instant my fingers are grasping at his hair, pulling his face down to me, his hand behind my neck, pulling me up, tilting my mouth to his. His lips are desperate on mine, seeking, demanding, taking.

But how can they take what I'm savagely giving?

His whole body trembles as he steps forward, pressing against me, trapping me between the bookshelf and the warmth of him. The corners of books dig into my back as our bodies meet, push, wrap. I grasp at the soft fabric of Benson's sweater-vest, and my fingers dig into his ribs just beneath. His hands are still behind my neck, my head—fingers weaving through my hair as he brings my mouth harder against his—but the length of his body rocked snugly against mine feels like its own kind of embrace.

I rip my mouth away to gulp for air but return immediately to his lips, needing more of him. Tiny groans vibrate in his throat and they make me want to hold him tighter, kiss him deeper. I don't know how long it lasts—forever and yet not nearly long enough—before Benson throws his head back and lets out a long sigh. His hands frame my face and he lets his forehead rest against mine as we both struggle for air. His breath is hot on my lips and when I breathe, it smells like him.

And something in me knows that everything is different now.

Better? I hope so.

"Is this the part where I'm supposed to apologize?" Benson asks, and his voice is so low, so weak, it makes me want to cry all over again.

"*Are* you sorry?" I whisper. And I don't know what I want to hear.

"Never," he says, his whisper barely audible.

A strange joy fills me and this time it's not overwhelming. It's calm. Peaceful almost. "Then don't apologize."

But he stands up, his hands sliding away from me to take a new stance on his hips, and he looks at the bookshelf just to my left. "The timing, it was bad, you were crying, and I . . . I should have, no, I *shouldn't* have—"

"Benson," I interrupt. "It's okay."

"It's not okay, I didn't mean—"

"Benson," I say, more firmly. I step forward and slide my hands down his arms, forcing his fists off his hips and sliding my fingers between his. "It's *okay.*" I don't want to ask, but I know I have to. "Is this why you dislike Quinn so much?"

Benson swallows hard before he speaks. "He has a name now?"

"Yes."

"It's one of the reasons," he finally admits. "But the others are just as valid."

My mind is having a seriously hard time thinking rationally. "What about Dana McCraven?"

Benson's face flushes so red it's almost maroon. "I made her up," he admits. "I didn't want you to see how puppy sick I was."

"Really?" I ask, genuinely shocked.

And pleased.

"You asked one day and I just . . . came up with a name. It wasn't supposed to become such a big lie. It was supposed to help me keep my distance," he mumbles. Then his eyes dart up to mine for just an instant and the emotion I see makes my heart pound. "Didn't work, I guess."

"Well, *I* was convinced," I say with a giggle.

"Dana McCraven can't hold a candle to you," Benson murmurs, grinning.

"Why didn't you tell me before?" *We could have been kissing like this for months!* I want to shout.

"I didn't want to lose what we had," he mumbles. "I really liked you coming in every day."

I start to grin like a sappy idiot.

Benson likes me.

Me!

He always did.

It's a tiny spark of goodness in a world that has become so confusing lately that I feel like I've forgotten what to do with good news.

But, of course, my eyes choose that moment to catch sight of the ChapStick on the floor. "Benson!" I gasp, my hands tightening and probably hurting his fingers. "They're gone!"

There's only one lonely tube of ChapStick lying innocently on the carpet.

My face turns back to Benson and I resist the urge to grab the front of his shirt and shake him. "You saw them, right? I'm not imagining this. There were *six*, right?" My voice is getting high and loud and Benson rubs his hands up and down my arms as he shushes me.

"Yes, I saw them. They were there." His eyes are wide again, his jaw set as he and I both stare at the carpet where the tubes all landed, as if they'll suddenly appear again.

Our heads jerk up as Marie's voice fills the library via the PA system. "The library will be closing in five minutes. Please bring your books to the front for checkout. The library will be closing in five minutes."

"I have to go. I told Reese I'd be right back."

Benson's jaw is clenched so tightly I want to run my finger along it, make him relax. But after a second he says, "We need to talk about this. Tomorrow."

"You work tomorrow afternoon. Should we just meet—"

"Not here," Benson says firmly. "Maybe my place?"

My place—a pleasant ripple travels down my spine at the thought. But when Benson leans down to pick up the remaining ChapStick, I'm completely sober again.

"I'll call in sick if I have to," Benson says, running his hands through his hair and looking off into the distance. "I can figure this out," he says softly. Then he turns and carefully takes my hand. "*We* can figure this out."

I nod, feeding off his confidence. Mine is gone.

"Here," he says, handing me a random book. "Go check this out. That way Marie won't ask questions."

"Okay." I hold the book to my chest and start to walk away, then turn and look at him, desperate to kiss him again.

He leans ever so slightly forward.

But somehow, it's just not right. Without the passion of the frantic moment, it's like there's a barrier we can't cross. I settle for squeezing his hand before slipping wordlessly around the corner. I force myself not to look back, as if the entire world didn't just turn upside down behind that row of dusty old books.

It's only when I'm easing the car out of the library parking lot that I realize I never told Benson about Quinn. That I've hardly thought about Quinn since the moment Benson's lips touched mine.

CHAPTER NINE

"So have you seen him again? Your mysterious, um, *guy*?"

No pretense, no greeting, no small talk. Elizabeth just jumps right in.

"Briefly," I reply, and the words are out of my mouth before I remember it was in my aunt and uncle's yard again. Will she tell Reese and Jay? Will she force me to call the police? She should. At least I *think* she should. My mind is still a frazzle of delight and confusion about Benson. About Quinn. Little details like when and where don't seem to register.

"In public?"

I nod instantly, hoping she doesn't sense the lie, the betrayal.

"So, then," Elizabeth begins, and she's speaking slowly, like she's trying to decide what to say next—giving herself those extra few seconds to make up her mind, "what is it exactly that's attracting you to him? I mean, I'm assuming I can conclude that you're attracted," she says with a shade of a laugh, tapping her pen absently against her notepad.

I force myself to leave Benson behind—to focus on Quinn. Just for a few minutes. "I—I don't know exactly. He . . ." I pause, but then the feelings tumble from my lips before I even know what I'm saying. "He makes me feel like a whole new person. I know that doesn't really make sense, but that's how it is. He makes me happy that I . . . exist. At all." I sound so lame. But even though I recognize that, the emotions pile up further—the ache inside me that I don't realize is even there until he makes it go away, the way he seems to detach me from the ground, freeing me so I can fly.

I gulp. Where is this all coming from? I've only exchanged a handful of words with him and literally *just* made out with Benson yesterday.

It's almost like I'm two people—one who can't stop thinking of Benson . . . one who can't stop thinking of Quinn. I'm quiet for a long time—minutes, I think—as Elizabeth looks at me intently, twirling her pen. Am I in love with them both? Or am I just exhibiting symptoms of that "socially inappropriate behavior" my neurologists are always going on about?

"Tavia," Elizabeth says after a while, setting her legal pad and ballpoint pen on the brown coffee table in front of me, "I get the feeling there's something you're not telling me. From the facts you've shared, I feel like I should be concerned for your safety. But you don't seem to share that concern. Is there something you'd like to tell me about this guy?"

"He's kind of different," I say, stalling for time.

"Is he good-looking?" Elizabeth asks with one eyebrow raised and a girlish lilt to her voice. I can't help but smile, and maybe blush a little, as I think of his silky blond hair, his pale green eyes.

That perfect physique.

Now I'm getting warm.

I describe him to Elizabeth in general terms: tall, blond, kinda tan. But those parts don't add up to *him*. He's more. Infinitely *more*. My fingers trace the edges of the table, pulling the pen and legal pad closer. "He has this look to his eyes," I say, and I barely watch my own fingers as they shape the planes of his face—those dramatic angles that are so unique to Quinn.

I'm halfway done with the rough sketch before I realize I'm drawing. I'm *drawing*.

My hands begin to tremble so hard I can't put the pen back on the paper without making wavy lines. I came here thinking about Benson and now I'm *drawing* Quinn. Drawing, for the first time since the accident, and—

I slam the pen down on the table.

"Tavia." Elizabeth's voice is so quiet my ears barely hear her, but my mind latches onto her words like a lifeline, holding tight to stave off the panic that's threatening to crush me. "It's okay. It's just a sketch. A tool to let me know what you saw."

I look up at her, awareness dawning in my eyes. *She* put down her legal pad. Close enough that I could instinctively reach for it. To *make* me draw without thinking. "You did that on purpose."

Her lips hold a ghost of a smile. Her tone is casual—as if we were discussing the decor. "Maybe. Tavia, it's just a tool. Would you like to finish?"

Her quiet question calms me. I look back at the rough sketch and do as she asks, though my lines aren't as true as before. I don't draw much more, but enough that Elizabeth could probably pick him out of a crowd—or a lineup.

Enough that I know I can do it.

"This is amazing, really," Elizabeth says when I put the pen down. "You have a real gift."

I shrug.

"He must be someone very special to break through your artist's block like that," she adds in a soft voice. "What's his name?"

"Quinn. Quinn Avery." It's the first time I've said his full name aloud and it echoes in my head, setting off a mass of tingles in my brain, like static electricity trying to escape.

Elizabeth nods. "So you've spoken to him. That's reassuring."

"There's . . . there's actually something else," I say, suddenly desperate to not talk about Quinn anymore. Part of me wants to change the subject to Benson—to get Elizabeth's advice about him. But how would *that* look? Not going there.

"I think . . . I think I'm seeing things," I force myself to say before the terror can seal my throat.

Elizabeth leans forward. "What kind of things?"

I meet her eyes. "Triangles."

Her head tilts ever so slightly to the side, but she doesn't break eye contact. "Triangles?"

"On his house," I add, trying not to sound *completely* insane. I don't want her to tell me that triangles are everywhere. These triangles are *different*. "There was a triangle over the door of the house where I first saw Quinn."

"Have you seen that triangle again?"

"On another house. Down on Fifth Street—in the old section of town. I like to take walks there. I didn't notice it at the time, but I found it later in a picture I took."

"Can you show me?"

I nod and pull out my phone. When I reach the right photo, I zoom in on the white wood above the door and point. "There," I whisper.

Elizabeth looks, squints, looks again. She doesn't say anything, but I can tell she doesn't see it. My hearts slides into my stomach and I want to crumple into the couch.

After zooming in and out a couple times, Elizabeth hands the phone back. "Why didn't you want to tell me before?"

"I was afraid," I admit in a whisper.

"Afraid of what?"

"That you would say I was crazy. Or worse, that I needed to go back to the neurologist." There's a long hush, then I rush on. "After everything that's happened, you would think that would be the least of my worries. But when it feels like nothing else in my body works, at least I'm still sane and if—if you take that away . . ." I can't finish. There are no words for the darkness that losing my mind represents.

The darkness that feels like it's looming, waiting to devour me.

"I don't think you're crazy," Elizabeth says gently, but with a firmness that tells me she's telling the truth. Or, at the very least, that she *thinks* she's telling the truth. "You've made so much progress lately that I've actually been expecting you to start experiencing some . . . some changes."

"What do you mean, changes?" Like my pockets of infinite Chap-Stick? Should I tell her about that too?

But even as I think it, I know I can't. Seeing things? Well, that can be explained. Hallucinations are an ordinary side effect of traumatic brain injury. Magic pockets are not.

"I want to continue to explore some of these things. Quinn, the triangles," she says, not really answering my question. "And Tavia, you might have more strange things happen. Unexplainable things. And that's okay. Just know that you can trust me and that I'll do my best to get your life back on track. That's what I'm here for."

I nod, but I don't mean it. It's not that I *don't* trust her; it's just that this is too big, too impossible. Maybe after I figure it out—when I can explain myself before she has me committed.

Or arrested.

What do you do with people who can magically pull lip balm from their pockets?

"Do you think maybe you'll draw anything else before our next appointment?" Elizabeth asks, sounding light and casual; but we both know we're walking on thin ice with my artist's block and if she pushes too hard, it'll break. *I'll* break.

"Maybe," I mumble, not willing to commit to more than that.

"Well, do you mind if I keep this picture until our next session?" Elizabeth asks, pulling me out of my thoughts.

She holds up the drawing and a zing of jealous possession rushes through me. I suppress the urge to snatch the drawing back, take a breath, and remind myself that if I managed to draw one, I can draw another. Or ten. Or a hundred.

Besides, it's only a couple of days.

So then why does my heart ache like it's gone forever? Like *he's* gone forever?

CHAPTER TEN

It's *pouring* by the time our session is done. Elizabeth offers me a ride, but I turn it down. I have a lot to mull over—a walk in the rain is just what I need. And I managed to have the foresight to wear an actual raincoat today instead of my usual hoodie; I'll stay dry enough. Elizabeth tries to insist—says I'll get too cold. But she finally lets me go when I tell her I'm just heading to the library.

When I reach the curb of the parking lot, I look up and barely catch sight of a man half hidden by a bush. He's leaning casually against one of the buildings across the street from Elizabeth's office plaza and doesn't seem to have seen me yet. But he looks familiar.

It's only when he lifts one hand to adjust his sunglasses—sunglasses in the rain?—that I realize it's the man who was staring at me when I ran into the wall. Have I got another stalker? Or should I add paranoia to the list of mental disorders brought on by my injuries? Most likely he just lives nearby, and now that I've noticed him, I'll see him all the time—like how when you buy a new car, you suddenly start seeing the same model everywhere you go. Still, I'm creeped out, so I duck my head and grip my backpack straps as I pivot and head in the opposite direction.

I'm only two blocks from Elizabeth's office when my stomach rumbles. I was so nervous about my appointment—not to mention keyed up about Benson—that I forgot to eat breakfast. Now I'm famished.

I've been hungry a lot lately. Like, *starving* hungry. When I came in from seeing Quinn yesterday, I think I ate twice as much lasagna as usual. I was going to ask Elizabeth about that, actually, but after everything that's happened this week, I kinda forgot. I assume it's a sign that I'm healing—that my body needs more fuel for repairs. Whatever it is, my stomach is screaming for food.

Part of me wants to head to the library anyway—maybe Benson and I can go grab lunch. He *did* say we should get together, away from work. But sanity worms its way into my brain and I realize that showing up soaking wet and bedraggled at someone's work is not really a great way to fish for a date. Home first. And maybe I should borrow Reese's car to go to the library; it is really coming down.

Looking nice for Benson didn't matter before. But now . . .

When I reach the house, the front door opens on silent hinges and I'm several steps up the stairway before I hear Reese's voice.

"It's really not a good time, Liz. Tavia took off this morning and didn't tell me where she was going. Did she even make your appointment?" Pause. "Oh! Well, in that case."

Startled, I turn my head toward the kitchen, my ears perking up when I catch my own name. Reese's steps are coming toward me and I instinctively duck out of sight as she carries the phone into the front room to peek out the window.

Watching for me.

"The blond guy again?"

Liz. *Elizabeth?* My stomach clenches within me as betrayal fills my chest. She's telling them! Therapists aren't supposed to do that. I clench my jaw, but I creep quietly down the stairs as Reese says, "She drew him? That's excellent!"

I curl my knees up to my chest, shrouded by the shadow of the winding staircase, and try not to make a sound, to not even breathe.

"You're sure? He looks just like our descriptions from Sonya? But—wait, he *talked* to her? That doesn't make any sense, does it? Is there a possibility of a mistake?" She fumbles for a second. "Let me write that down. Quinn? Okay. A-ver-y," she says slowly, writing. "I'll look him up. It's not a name I recognize, but you know how extensive our files are. Plus I can call in a favor. I have a friend in records who'll keep it quiet."

I hear her sipping something and she swallows quickly, then says, "The Earthbound triangle? At his house? So you think he knows what he is?"

I'm sick as I hear all my secrets dropping from Reese's lips.

"No, I agree, it must be. I'm happy to check out the one on Fifth as well. Were you able to get a house number from the picture? Maybe whoever lived there was a Curatoriate. There might be something left that we can use. But get me the sketch for sure—this could be the break we need."

The sketch… why did I have to leave my drawing with Elizabeth!?

"How long do you think we have before we have to do the pull?" A long pause follows and I can hear from her footsteps that Reese has started pacing again. "I *am* still worried about it burning her out. I always have been. We both know she's no good to us if her brain is destroyed. But if she's basically doing a slow pull on herself?"

She pauses, listening, for a long time while I assume Elizabeth is talking. As the seconds tick by, I start to sweat, wondering what in the world Elizabeth is telling her now. Finally Reese makes an affirmative noise, then says, "If it really is him, then she must be—" Her feet stop. "Liz, do you think she's too damaged to resurge?"

I swallow, hating the word *damaged* coming from Reese's lips, no matter how frequently I apply it to myself.

Reese sighs. "I wish I shared your confidence. But then, you've observed her much more closely than she ever lets me. Thank the gods for you or we wouldn't know anything." She changes position now, one hand resting on a jutted hip. A power position. "The triangle changes everything. He knows something. What are the chances he's a Reduciate? Oh forget it; anything higher than zero is bad news. No, no, I think trying tonight is hurrying too much. Especially when we're so close. *Might* be so close."

Not tonight. Not for whatever it is that they want to do to me. Is relief the right thing to feel in the face of all this?

"I'll move my trip up; I don't think I can get out today without the higher-ups finding out, but I can swing tomorrow, assuming the sketch matches our descriptions." Reese murmurs several affirmative noises before taking a shaky breath. "We have to watch her carefully. If she figures it out on her own, best-case scenario we lose her. Worse case, it damages her beyond use."

Damages me?

"I hope so," Reese says after another long pause. Her voice carries a melancholy I can't reconcile with the content of the conversation. "We can't hide her forever. I'm already worried. My sources are giving me mixed messages. That usually means they've found something and are trying to hide it. We all know what happens when they start circling," she adds, and though I can't say why, a tremor of fear shoots down my spine. "We can probably keep her alive for at least another week, but after that . . . all bets are off."

Keep me alive? I can't breathe. It's like taking one hard punch after another. Darkness scrabbles at the edges of my vision and I want to throw up and black out all at once.

Reese turns, heading back to the kitchen, and I try to curl up smaller—draw even deeper into the shadows.

"Just pray this Phoenix connection is legit. I have zero leads if it's not, and we'll have to proceed on our own. And that probably means running." She sighs. "I hate running. Yeah, I know; one step at a time. I'll be there soon."

I hear the beep of the phone disconnecting, then the familiar sounds of Reese pulling on a coat, grabbing her jingly keys, the hum of the garage door opening.

I throw myself away from the wall and crouch by the window, parting the blinds just enough to watch Reese's car slip down the street.

Once she's out of sight, I count to ten, slowly, then flee from the house, half running down the sidewalk, momentum fueling my gait until I have to slow down, clutching an ache in my side. My breath comes in ragged gasps and all thoughts of hunger have flown from my mind.

I look around, unsure for a few moments of where I am. My mind tries to sort through the conversation I just heard, but nothing makes sense; everything is wrong. So very wrong. I don't know what to think and all I really want to do is sink to the ground and cry.

The words I heard ring through my head over and over, but the more I consider them, the less sense they make. Why would Quinn have anything to do with my past? I would remember if I'd met him before.

Wouldn't I?

My memories were pretty patchy right after surgery, but they've been mostly whole for months now. Surely I wouldn't forget *him*. Not with the way he affects me.

Unless that's *why* he affects me.

But why would the triangles change anything? They're just weird glowing things. I want to groan out loud. Why did I have to tell Elizabeth about them? Stupid!

I'm walking without any sense of direction and hardly see the other people on the sidewalk as I pass. I don't know what to do. Betrayal is an icy spike through my chest; I'm more alone than ever with no idea who I can trust.

It was always Elizabeth.

Now there's no one.

Only myself.

And Benson.

My phone is in my hand before I can reconsider, a toneless ringing trilling in my ear. "Please answer, please answer," I whisper as three rings sound, then four.

"Tave?"

"Benson." I look in both directions before whispering, "Can you come get me? I'm in trouble."

CHAPTER ELEVEN

Benson parks against the curb in front of his off-campus house and by the time he gets around to my door, I'm already out and shifting from foot to foot, anxious to get inside. "You okay?" he asks, his hands softly rubbing up and down my arms. It's the first thing he's said since picking me up.

It was a little awkward—should I have greeted him with a kiss? Are we pretending last night never happened? I don't even know.

So I said nothing.

Did nothing.

"Yeah. No," I mumble. *What was the question?* "Can we go inside?"

Benson opens the door and beckons me in. There are a half a dozen guys lounging in the great room; three are playing some sort of video game in front of a humongous television and one in a chair near the front window looks at me with a flirtatious grin.

"New girlfriend?" he asks, addressing the question to Benson, though his eyes never leave my face.

"Not my girlfriend," Benson responds blandly, without looking at him, his hand on my shoulder, ushering me toward the stairs. I stiffen, trying to shove away the dart of hurt that goes through my heart at his words.

"Good news for me," the guy says, his smile growing even bigger.

"Underage," Benson calls back.

"I am not," I whisper.

"Trust me, it's better if Dustin thinks you are," Benson whispers back. "World's only virginal self-proclaimed *seducer*, and he's *so* desperate to lose it he'll hit on anything even remotely feminine."

I snicker.

"Don't laugh," Benson says wearily as we reach the top of the stairs. "He's my roommate." He pushes open the door and my eyes widen at the two walls so completely covered in topless women it might as well be the wallpaper.

"Nice," I say dryly.

"I did warn you." He shakes his head, then motions to the other half of the room. "This is my side."

Benson's bedroom is exactly what I would have expected. Sparse, but neat, with an eclectic collection of posters and knickknacks. He picks up a polo shirt draped across an armchair and gestures for me to sit.

"So?" he asks, taking a seat at the foot of his bed and tossing the shirt up onto his pillow.

Silence settles between us.

"I saw Quinn yesterday," I blurt, realizing I'm going to have to start my confession there before I can explain the rest.

Benson just grimaces.

"It's why I came to the library in the first place." I clamp my mouth shut; that wasn't the right thing to say either. *Hey, guy I made out with last night, I only came to see you because of another guy. And then we kissed. And then*

I pulled magical ChapStick out of my pockets. Now I'm running from a conspiracy that might be trying to kill me. I groan and put my face in my hands. "I know this is so incredibly awkward, but I have to tell you about him or none of the rest makes any sense."

"I'm listening," Benson says, and though his voice is tight, it doesn't sound angry.

Tentatively I say, "His name is Quinn."

"You mentioned that. So . . . you guys talked?" Benson asks, still not looking at me.

"I told him that the stunt he pulled at my house was unacceptable."

A tiny tick of a smile. "And he said he won't do it again?"

Kind of. "Basically." But it tastes like a lie and I don't like to lie to Benson. "He talks kinda strange."

"It sounds to me like everything about this guy is strange."

I can't argue with that. Instead I relay the whole conversation.

"*Things to show you?* What does that mean?" Benson asks.

"I don't know, but . . . hopefully I'll find out next time I see him."

"Next time? You're already planning it, aren't you? Even though he's talking about time running out and people you should fear."

I just glare.

Benson fiddles with the zipper on his backpack sitting next to his bed. "I don't understand, Tave," he finally says, not meeting my eyes. "You're so logical, so smart. It's like all that disappeared when this guy showed up."

My knee-jerk reaction is to be hurt, but a sting of conscience makes me admit that he's right. I hardly recognize myself, my decisions, since this guy walked into my life. "It isn't that I'm not being smart," I insist automatically. "It's something else, something I can't really explain. I *know* he won't hurt me. You have to trust me on this one."

"What does he look like?" Benson asks after a minute.

"Why does everyone want to know what he looks like?" I ask, rolling my eyes.

"Who else did you tell?"

"Elizabeth totally dragged it out of me."

"You told your *therapist*?"

"It is her job," I mutter, even though I still kinda hate that I told her. "So?"

"So what?"

"What does he look like?"

I tilt my head at him, not sure why he cares, but I rattle off the basics. "No horns, no fangs, no wings," I tack on when I'm done.

"What did Elizabeth say about him?"

"She kind of encouraged me, actually," I mutter, feeling instantly guilty.

He raises one eyebrow sardonically. "What the hell are you supposed to do when your shrink is crazier than you are?"

"You try not to let her kill you, I guess," I say, my voice hollow. We've finally reached the reason I called him.

Benson bolts to his feet, staring down at me. "What do you mean, Tave?"

"After my session with Elizabeth, I went home. And I guess Reese didn't hear me come in because she was on the phone with Elizabeth— she called her Liz, by the way, not Dr. Stanley—and they were talking about all kinds of crazy stuff." As I speak, Benson drops to the floor in front of me, rubbing warmth into my icy-cold hands as I relay the conversation as best I can remember. I close my eyes and focus on the feeling of his hands on mine, trying to remember every secret, every threat, the fact that they expect me to be *dead* in a week. The words become heavier as I repeat them, as though my uttering them aloud suddenly makes them real.

"Tave?" Benson asks when I've finished.

He hesitates and I'm amused that he's worried that he might be able to say *anything* to ruffle me. I feel like we're miles past that point.

"Do you think this Quinn guy is the one looking for you?"

I was wrong.

My fingers clench around his and I clamp my teeth so quickly I catch the skin of my cheek. I wince at the pain and touch the tip of my tongue to the stinging spot in my mouth. "No," I say without further explanation.

"Tave, you have to at least consider it."

My head is already jerking back and forth. "No. He would never want to hurt me."

"You don't *know* that," Benson says, leaning forward. "All kinds of people can want to hurt you. People you would never—you can't *know*."

"It could be anyone else, Benson. Like this lady when I scraped my head or—" My voice rises as soon as I think of it. "There's this man with sunglasses. I've seen him twice now and—"

"And you've seen Quinn *three* times. Twice *at your house*," Benson interrupts.

"He wouldn't—" My voice cuts off as my head falls into my hands. "How can I explain it to you? I can't even explain it to myself." I slump against the arm of the chair. "I'm just so tired."

"Stay here," Benson says. "I'll be right back."

What?

I recline into the surprisingly soft armchair as Benson slips out the door, leaving it a few inches ajar. My head is starting to ache and I remember that the whole reason I went home at all was because I skipped lunch . . . and breakfast—I've *got* to start taking better care of myself. Woman cannot live on caffeine alone.

In a moment of clarity I wonder just how bad this can be. So my shrink is sharing information I gave her in confidence . . .

With my guardian who took me in with basically no warning and has provided for my every need for the last eight months. And who's trying to hide me from someone. And getting ready to run. With me? Without me? After getting *rid* of me? I don't even know.

No matter how I justify it, everything comes back to that.

Could Elizabeth be trying to hide me from Quinn? That doesn't make any sense—why would she tell me it was okay to see him if she knew he was dangerous? And I refuse to consider that Benson might be right—that Quinn is the danger. It doesn't fit.

I look over at Benson's desk, trying to distract myself. There's a small, framed picture and I lean over and grab it to get a better look. Benson, probably two or three years ago, with an older guy and a woman. His mom and brother, I assume. He mentions them fairly often.

I study their faces. Benson and his brother don't look alike at all except for their matching brown hair, but I can see his mother's features in his face. The angular jawline, high cheekbones, and wide eyes. They're all smiling. Part of me feels like I should be jealous, resentful even. Benson has a family—minus a dad, apparently, but still—and mine are dead.

Of course I could never wish such a thing on Benson. I'm completely happy for him, I realize as I put the picture back. I'm glad I can be. Elizabeth says empathy is the most important part of being human.

Elizabeth.

I lean my head back and focus on Benson with his family instead. Dare to imagine myself in the scene with him. It feels like the most far-fetched of fantasies at the moment. My eyelids grow heavy and I let them slip closed. Just resting my eyes a bit.

I don't hear Benson's footsteps until the soft snick of the door closing makes my eyes snap open. "Here," Benson says, handing me a large Tupperware. "I've been saving these since Halloween. The guys had this stupid idea that we should be ready to hand out candy even though I told them no kids live around here. But they bought a ton anyway and there are *still* leftovers."

I lift the lid to find an assortment of mini candy bars, and my mouth instantly starts to water. I scarf about five of them before everything starts to feel significantly less stressful. "Thanks," I say, unwrapping another mini Snickers.

Benson leans forward, his hands sitting on each side of my knees. His thumbs rub little circles on my jeans, soothing some of my tension as I eat a rather embarrassing amount of chocolate while I talk.

"What am I going to do, Benson?" I finally ask. My energy and resolve seem to have left along with the tension, and my bones feel like noodles. At this moment I'm not entirely certain I could stand up if my life depended on it. "They expect me to be dead in a *week*."

He scoots forward a few more inches and his hands slide up my thighs. I don't resist—it feels good. The warmth from his palms seeps through my jeans and into my skin and makes my fingers tingle, reminding me that I'm not numb. Not completely.

Not yet.

"I'm not going to tell you empty words," Benson murmurs. "I won't patronize you like that. But whatever's going to happen, I'll help you. I'll be there with you." He leans forward and I feel my heart pounding in my ears as his face draws closer.

Closer.

"It'll be dangerous," I protest, the words barely audible as they escape through my teeth. It's my last opportunity to lean back, to pull away. But I don't want to. All I can focus on is his face, his mouth. My nerves crackle and my tongue darts out to touch my bottom lip.

"I don't care."

My eyes drift closed and—

"Aw yeeeeaaaah!"

My head jerks up as the voice intrudes and we both look up to see Dustin's face framed in the doorway.

"Not your girlfriend, my ass," he says with a suggestive laugh that fills my stomach with mortification.

"Get the *hell* out of here," Benson snaps.

"Next time put a sock on the door, bro—you know the rules," Dustin taunts, still firmly wedged in the open door as my face burns crimson.

I clench the arms of the chair as my embarrassment boils over.

"Get the sock if you want to—ahhh!" A cascade of water hits Dustin in the face, forcing him to stagger back. His gurgling scream startles me, and the water stops.

I clutch my hands to my chest as Benson kicks the door closed and scrambles to his feet to turn the dead bolt.

"Jeez, Ryder. What the hell was that?" Dustin yells through the door. "My nose is bleeding; you could have killed me." He continues to yell, but he could be a faintly buzzing fly for all I hear him.

"Benson?" I say quietly.

"I'm so sorry," Benson says. "I should have bolted it when I came up, but I was focused on getting you food and—"

"Benson?" I ask, my voice a little higher.

"I just didn't think. I mean, he never comes up here except to sleep and—"

"Benson, I did that!" I shriek.

He finally turns and looks at me, his eyes confused.

"The water," I say, struggling to keep my voice down. "I did that!"

"It's okay; he'll get over it. And truth is, he deserved it. Needed to cool off."

"No, I *made* the water."

That stops him. "Made?"

"Like the ChapStick," I say slowly. "Where else did you think it came from?"

"Oh," he says, and runs his hands through his hair before crossing his arms over his chest. "Yeah. We should probably talk about that."

CHAPTER TWELVE

But instead of talking, he pulls out his cell phone. "Hey, Marie, it's Benson," he says a few seconds later. "I know I said I'd be late, but this cold has only gotten worse and I don't think I should come in this afternoon at all. Yeah, I know, I'm sorry. Yes, of course. I will." He pushes a button to end the call and stares at his phone for several long moments. Then he slides it into his pants pocket and looks at me.

I squirm. He's tall enough that from down here I feel very small.

As though sensing it, he reaches out a hand. "Come here."

I grab on and he pulls me to my feet and turns me around. Soon his hands are gently rubbing my shoulders and neck. I give a sigh and let my head hang forward as he massages some of the tension out of muscles I didn't even realize were sore.

Though I guess I should have assumed.

"Better?" he whispers after a few minutes. His face is just over my right shoulder and close to my ear. My knees feel wobbly as I try to respond, and I have to clear my throat.

"Much," I finally manage to say. His hands are still on my back and his fingers tighten for the tiniest instant before starting to move down, running along my ribs, stopping at my waist.

After a pause, they sink a few inches lower, resting at my hips.

His breath warms my neck as he lowers his lips to brush the skin just above my collarbone. A shiver ripples up my spine.

Benson freezes.

"Good shiver," I whisper.

His arms move again, twining around me—one arm around my waist, the other diagonally over my chest, his fingers curling around my shoulder, pulling me close against him.

I grip his arms like lifelines.

He doesn't kiss me again. We just stand there, holding each other as if the entire world would tear us apart if we let it.

I wonder how true that might be.

"Tell me what to do." Benson's voice is low and gravelly right next to my ear, the vibrations on the side of my face sending a dart of warmth all the way down to my toes.

I close my eyes and lean my forehead against his cheek—just a touch stubbly, like I always suspected. I feel tears build up and blink them away—not now. "I wish I knew. I've spent months trying to piece my life back together, but I don't know what that even means anymore! I'm so confused, Benson. I don't know what to think, or do, or who to trust. I can't trust *myself.* I don't even know what I am!"

"You're beautiful," Benson murmurs, then begins to unwind our arms, turning me to face him. "And smart, and brave, and strong." I'm all the way around now and Benson's hands are framing my face, warming my cheeks. "And completely irresistible." He finishes. "The rest is just details."

I smile a little—it's all I can manage—and Benson leans in to kiss my forehead, each cheek. His nose touches mine and I can hardly breathe,

I want him so badly. His face is so close that I can feel his breath on my mouth, and the moment that his lips touch mine is sublime. Soft and warm, his hands move to my waist, pulling me forward as his lips delve. I push against him, pressing, wanting more. Closer. Deeper.

Then his face is gone, but his hands are pulling me downward, onto his lap on the chair I vacated a few minutes ago. A breath shudders into my chest as I slide, limp, into his arms, my knees hugging his thighs as he reaches for my neck and brings me back to him. I grasp at his shirt, needing something to hold on to, and a hint of a growl escapes Benson's mouth before his kiss deepens, sweeping me away with exquisite gentleness and the roar of passion I can feel held back behind it.

Everything I've craved since we met, wrapped into one moment of bliss.

And all I want is more.

My fingers spread against his chest and for a moment, I remember Quinn's chest—the glimpse of skin last night as he got to his feet.

But I push him away.

This moment is Benson's.

And mine.

Ours.

Ages pass before I'm curled comfortably against Benson's chest, my head resting on his shoulder, his fingers stroking idly up and down my hip. The sugar has finally taken effect and my body seems to hum like a well-oiled engine as I sit and draw warmth from Benson's skin.

"Why can't we just stay here forever and never think about anything else?" I ask, almost sleepily, my eyes still closed.

"I wish we could."

I tilt my head back and touch his nose. "You make me feel braver."

He grins. "Good." Pause. "I think?"

I laugh and the sound is unfamiliar. When *was* the last time I laughed? "It *is* good."

"Well, though I could kiss you all day," he says, dropping a quick kiss on my forehead. "And all night." On my nose now. "And all the next day." Now my chin, but I'm shaking with suppressed giggles. "We do need to talk about this."

I slide regretfully off Benson's lap and take the seat he had before, on the end of his bed. "I can make things, Benson. Out of thin air." I'm not sure if I feel better or worse for having said it out loud. It sounds stupid. Crazy. The sort of thing you might say if you had a traumatic brain injury that resulted in paranoid delusions. "I thought maybe it was something about my . . . pockets, I guess. But that water didn't come from my pockets."

"Can I assume this is a new thing?" Benson asks.

"Unless my memory is seriously whacked, yes."

Benson nods. I'm grateful that he doesn't point out the very real possibility that my memory is in fact seriously whacked.

"But the ChapSticks were gone when we . . . when we were done," I say, feeling my cheeks heat up. "So . . . I guess they appear and then disappear?"

"The floor's dry," Benson says, nodding toward the door where I soaked his roommate. "I don't think carpet dries that fast. Can you do something else?"

"What do you mean something else?"

"Something *else*," he repeats. "I don't know. A pencil. A dollar. A hundred dollars. Whatever."

Something like water that could drown someone inside a house? This all feels too close to my nightmare, and whatever it is that I can do, I don't like it.

But I can't ignore it.

I take a deep breath and push back my fear. I need to find out.

Except that I have no idea what to *do*.

Ultimately, I decide that my best bet is to go for a repeat of last night. I reach my hand down, planning to look in my pocket, but before I get there, my fingers close around something slim and round.

"Oh, shit!" I exclaim in surprise, dropping it. The pencil bounces to the floor between our feet. I didn't expect it to be that easy. I kind of hate that it was that easy.

"I got it," Benson whispers, bending deftly.

He holds the pencil between two fingers, studying it. He glances at me, then grabs a note card from his backpack and writes his name before setting the pencil back on the floor, the note card beside it.

An entirely new kind of tension fills the air.

One minute.

Two.

Three.

Four minutes pass and my fingertips are white from pressing so hard against my thighs. Then, with no warning, the pencil is gone.

And Benson's name on the note card with it.

"Well," Benson says in a voice that would sound casual if it weren't for the brittle, glass-sharp edge, "now we know why your ChapStick was working so poorly."

Hadn't I commented that it seemed like I had to reapply every five minutes? But how could I have even considered guessing that it was *literally* disappearing?

"Do it again," Benson says in a whisper, his jaw flexed so hard my own teeth ache.

"No," I whisper back. I can't. I just *can't*. This whole thing is terrifying and I just want it to go away.

He looks like he's about to say something, then he turns abruptly and grabs the candy bowl, unwraps a Milky Way, and shoves it into his mouth, starting on another wrapper before he's even begun chewing. Some people are emotional eaters; apparently Benson is a thinking eater.

As if abruptly remembering that I'm there, he holds the bowl out to me and I grab three. For a few minutes we both munch in silence and I suspect the sweet candy is helping to center him as much as it is me. The silence is deceptively companionable with nothing but the crackle of wrappers to mar it.

Benson leans forward on his elbows, fingers laced, staring at me with hard eyes until I have to suppress the urge to squirm. I wish he would hold my hands. Maybe run his fingers up my legs again. Something to remind me that he's here.

But he just sits, silent and separate.

"Surely it all fits together somehow," Benson says after a while, and I nod. But it's like trying to put a puzzle together without half the pieces.

And without the picture on the box.

Not to mention a death threat hanging over you if you don't solve it fast enough.

"I just don't see how it could," I admit.

"Well, you can make stuff. Surely if anyone found out, they'd want to use you, right?" He swallows and then pushes a half-eaten candy bar away from him like he's lost his appetite.

I, on the other hand, have found mine again. I start unwrapping another Kit Kat.

"Maybe they're hiding you from people like that."

"What, so I can make a big stack of diamonds that will disappear in five minutes?" I say through a chocolaty mouthful.

Benson shrugs. "Maybe with some kind of—I don't know, training?—it wouldn't disappear."

"That might make sense," I say, sifting through the bowl for another Snickers. "But if so, why wouldn't they tell me?"

"Stress, recovery," Benson says, spreading his long arms out to the side. "It sounds like at least Reese *wants* to tell you."

"Maybe." I don't want him to turn them into good guys. If he does, who will I have to be mad at—to pour my frustration into?

"What about Quinn?" Benson asks softly, and the awkwardness is back.

"What about him?" I say, feigning disinterest as I try to keep from squishing my candy bar. It's not fair; Benson deserves a straight answer. But if I *had* a straight answer, I'd be giving it to myself.

Benson hesitates, then looks up and meets my eyes. "He's got to know something. Reese said the triangle changed everything, and the first time you saw it was at Quinn's house, right?"

"Above the door, yeah."

"And didn't he tell you he couldn't explain, but that he would bring something to *show you*? Isn't that what he said?" Benson pauses. "Maybe he's going to show you what you can do."

I pull the cuffs of my jacket over my suddenly chilled hands when a thought occurs to me. "Maybe he can do it too."

Benson gives one jerky nod. "Maybe."

Whoever Quinn is, he's wrapped up in all of this. Benson's right—he has to be. I'm not sure I want to talk about Quinn with Benson, not after . . . but what choice do I have? "Do you think I should tell him I already know?"

"I guess you have to decide how much you really trust him," Benson says quietly.

With my life.

The thought comes unbidden—feels more like an invisible someone whispering in my ear. Reflexively, I pull away, but of course no one is there. I try to shake off the eerie feeling and rub the goose bumps from my arms.

"Tave." Benson hesitates and I know what he's going to ask. "What . . . what *is* he to you?"

I swallow and look at up Benson—the person who has single-handedly gotten me through the last few months, to say nothing of the last forty-eight hours. Yes, there's been Reese and Jay and Elizabeth—not that I'm certain anymore that they had my best interests in mind—but really, the person who pulled me through was Benson. Benson, who I've now been kissing for twenty-four hours.

I wish I could talk to him about anything but this.

"I don't know," I finally whisper, looking down into my lap.

"Even now? After . . . after everything. You *don't know?*"

I lift my shoulder into a shrug, hating that it's the truth.

"It's just that—" He cuts off, his fingers gripped tightly together. "I'm not sure I can keep doing this if it's only . . . if it's only kissing for you. If that's all I wanted, honestly, it would be great. It'd be fun. But . . . but it's more than that to me," he finishes, looking up and meeting my eyes for just a moment before turning away. "*You're* more than that to me."

To me too! The words are on the edge of my tongue, but I can't say them, not until there's only one guy in the arena. Until then, I can't take anything to the next step. It wouldn't be fair to Benson, but it's not fair to me either.

The thing is that it should be easy. I have no reason to even *like* Quinn, much less be obsessed with him the way I am. I know what I *want*; I want Benson. So why does my heart ache at the thought of never seeing Quinn again?

A door slams downstairs and startles me from my haze enough to glance at Benson's clock. "Crap! I gotta go. Reese and Jay are going to start wondering where I am and I can't let that happen," I rattle distractedly as I grab my backpack. "Would you mind taking me home? Maybe dropping me off a block from the house so Reese doesn't suspect anything?"

"You're going back? Tave, don't. It's not safe. Stay here with me," Benson says a little too seriously, then breaks the tension by tacking on, "I promise I won't let Dustin grope you in your sleep if that's what you're worried about. I'll make him stay on the couch. He passes out there half the time anyway."

"I can't," I say, and my voice sounds utterly defeated even to myself. "I have nothing with me and I don't know what I'm up against yet. I need some time."

Benson reaches out for both of my hands in a gesture that speaks more of desperation than affection. "It doesn't sound like you have much time, Tave."

"I have some," I say, squeezing back. "It's just one night."

"And tomorrow night?" he asks.

"I guess I'll make that decision tomorrow."

CHAPTER THIRTEEN

Despite vehement protests about the rain—which, of course, started up again about two minutes after I got into Benson's car, stupid weather—I make Benson drop me off down the street from the house. I want everything to appear normal.

After he tells me to be careful, I start to lean in for a kiss.

But stop.

I can't go there—*we* can't go there—until I figure this out.

I plod home slowly, rain trickling down my neck from where the wind blows it into my face. The chill wakes me up. Its bite is so sharp it seems to scrape the skin on my cheeks, but it grounds me, reminds me that I'm *here*. That I'm alive.

It used to only take simple things to do that—the feel of fresh air on my skin, the smell of bread baking, the sound of children laughing.

Now my reminders have to be harsh, and I admit, it frightens me.

My head is spinning. Being betrayed by Reese and Elizabeth was bad enough. The rest is hard to even contemplate.

I can make stuff.

Stuff that disappears in about five minutes.

It's not so bad, I try to convince myself as I turn up the front walk. *I'm breathing. I'm healthy.* And that doesn't seem to be changing. At least not in the very immediate future.

As in, *tonight*.

But the sight of the house—the place I have, until this afternoon, thought of as my home—brings everything back. Truth is, I'm seeing things that aren't there, people are both hunting for and hiding me, and, oh yes, the laws of physics apparently no longer apply. Did the brain surgeons do this to me? Is it something I could do before? Am I dying as a result, or is someone trying to kill me?

I don't even know for certain which side my aunt and uncle are on.

I reach for the doorknob but can't make myself turn it. Instead I sit on the top step of the porch, barely protected from the downpour, and curl my arms around my knees, pulling them close to my chest. For hours now my mind has been racing. Running around and around the same problems, worries, and suspicions until my brain feels physically tired.

Everything with Quinn and now Benson is tipping me over the edge. I'm not sure I can handle things changing with Benson—even a good change. He's my rock, the one solid thing in the hurricane of my life.

But the feel of his lips on mine . . .

I jerk my hand down from where my fingers are gingerly touching my mouth, reliving those minutes. Perfect minutes.

Not now.

I have to figure things out with Quinn first.

Quinn, who I might be in love with.

It sounds crazy, but I've never in my life felt an emotion this over-powering. It's like quicksand, threatening to drag me under the more I try to fight it. He makes me feel like someone I know I'm not—someone who'll take risks, throw logic out the window, gamble it all for the thrill.

I've been a stranger in my own body before, and I don't like the similarities.

If only it was merely a matter of the heart. But Quinn has answers; I'm sure of it. He *knows* me. The way he looks at me—as though he hears my inner thoughts, my darkest secrets. Things I don't know about myself.

A week ago I had a normal crush on Benson. Steady, comfortable Benson. Now I've moved on to an intense physical relationship with *him* even while I'm obsessed with another guy who I can't find, can't contact—and yet he makes me feel more alive than I have since my parents died.

It's too much. Too fast. With both of them.

And where does that leave me?

I stare out at the storm lashing the bushes and trees now as it ramps up its violence; it's a fitting mirror of my own emotions.

The screen door behind me opens and my spine snaps straight. "Tavia? Is that you?" Reese peers at me down on the steps. "Are you okay?" Her brow is crumpled into the slightest furrow; enough to look concerned, but not fake. You'd think she wasn't nosing behind my back with my therapist just a few hours ago.

My mouth is dry and sticky and I can't say anything. Reese drops onto the step beside me. "I'm fine." I choke out the words, a little surprised when my ears hear my voice and it sounds okay.

But Reese isn't quite convinced; I guess I'm not as good a liar as her.

"Long day," I tack on, and smile weakly.

Reese pulls in a breath, as though through a straw, then hesitates. "Where have you been?" she asks, the words coming out in a rush, like it was difficult to say. "You were gone all day."

She rarely asks. Elizabeth told her not to. No questions when I go out, no bugging me for my whereabouts. I am eighteen, after all. I used to think Elizabeth was protecting me, but now I see it for what it is—a false sense of security to keep me off guard. Not freedom, merely the illusion of it.

Now Reese is breaking the rules. She's asking.

I try to decide what that means and it only makes my head ache. "With Benson," I mumble, too tired to think of a lie.

"Did . . . did you guys have some kind of a fight? You look a little sick. Pale," she amends.

"I skipped lunch." Sadly, also true. Maybe I could cope better if my stomach wasn't getting angry with me. But it's still roiling and churning despite the pile of mini candy bars I ate with Benson.

Or perhaps *because* of them.

"Tave," Reese scolds, rising to her feet. "You can't skip meals—your body needs the nutrients. You're still—" Her voice cuts off.

But I practically hear the word as if she shouted it.

Healing.

More than any of the others, Reese has always avoided talking about my injuries. Before this evening I liked that. It made me feel less self-conscious, like she saw *me*, not a walking mass of stitches and scars.

Now? I don't know what it means.

"Growing," she finishes lamely.

Growing, right. I was done growing three years ago. But I numbly accept her fussing and rise to follow her into the kitchen. She chatters about work as she warms me a bowl of gourmet butternut squash and free-range-chicken bisque. I suppose it's her version of comfort food. I spoon the rich, golden soup into my mouth, but it's bland gruel on my tongue. I can't bring myself to touch the buttered sourdough bread on a little glass plate beside my bowl, even though it looks great. My stomach feels hollow, and I'm not sure how I'm managing to feel such an empty hunger and complete lack of appetite at the same time.

I glance up and Reese is scrutinizing me. I hear some kind of sports game playing on the plasma in the adjoining room and wish Jay would come in. Disrupt this strange playacting with Reese. We're both dancing our routine of deception, and neither of us wants the other to find out. So we dance. We laugh. We smile.

Not that it would be any more real with Jay, I remember, and the soup I've just eaten turns sour in my stomach.

Does he know?

His words from yesterday echo in my mind: *I tell Reese everything.* But does Reese return the favor?

I'll have to hide from both of them. I hate the thought.

"Tavia," Reese says quietly, "do you remember the business trip I told you about?"

"Yeah, sure," I say, developing a sudden interest in my bowl.

"I was hoping to leave tomorrow," she says hesitantly, and I'm gripping the spoon so hard my fingertips are white. "But if you need me to stay—"

"No," I blurt, too loudly, panic jolting through me.

"I can," she rushes to assure me, but I hear a desperation in her voice and know it's the last thing she wants to do.

"No," I repeat, calmer. "I won't forget to eat, I promise. I just ... I was reading at the library and lost track of time, that's all." And it's kind of true; I absolutely lost track of time.

And space.

And sanity.

She opens her mouth to speak, as if to correct herself and let me know what her actual concern is. But she changes her mind and only nods. "It's an important trip," she says. "It'll take a couple of days max."

"Where are you going?" I ask, and my throat freezes up as I wait for the answer.

She hesitates, then says, "Phoenix. Client there who I need to see personally."

I confess to being rather shocked that she told me the truth. Kind of the truth.

What's really in Phoenix? Something that affects *me* or she wouldn't have brought it up when she was on the phone with Elizabeth.

I don't know anyone in Phoenix. But . . .

"I'll be fine," I say, forcing a smile. "And Jay will be here."

Reese's eyes turn to the half circle of a head she and I can just see over the top of the couch and her eyes soften. I don't know exactly what roles they're playing, but I can read in her eyes that she actually loves Jay. Somehow, that makes me feel better. Two people who love each other couldn't mean me harm. Not really.

I convince myself it's a good argument even though I know it's completely crazy.

Not crazy.

Just irrational.

"Please go," I say, startling Reese's attention back to me. She doesn't look quite convinced and I pull out my final ammunition. "I don't want to be an inconvenience." I lower my eyelids as I speak. It used to be the truth—and it embarrassed me as fully as I'm feigning now. I've always thought myself an inconvenience to them.

I'm not. I'm some kind of project, which is worse. But tonight I'll make it work in my favor.

Reese nods and her warm fingers cover mine the way they often have in the last eight months.

All those times in the hospital.

It makes me want to throw up.

"Okay, I'll go." She pauses and I know there's more.

I wad up my linen napkin and toss it onto the table beside me. "What?"

"Dr. Stanley wants to see you tomorrow."

My mouth dries up and I blurt, "Why?" before I can stop myself.

"She called this afternoon and told me she wants to follow up with what you talked about today." I can tell Reese is trying to pick her words carefully. Not to let me know that she knows *everything* I talked to Elizabeth about today.

I look down at my bowl, trying to get a grip on my anger. I know the truth; they don't trust me to behave—or maybe *survive*—while Reese is gone. They want to babysit me.

Maybe I need it.

"Whenever you want. She'll make time for you."

"But—"

"It can be fast—she just wants to touch base."

I say nothing.

And nothing.

Until finally Reese has to ask. "Will you go, Tave?"

I still. There's something in her question. A wisp of emotion; I've heard it before. It screams to me that she cares. *Really* cares.

But I don't dare believe it.

"Whatever," I mutter. "I don't have anything else to do." We may as well both lie.

I plead a headache and dutifully swallow the two white pills Reese places in my palm. She says they're Tylenol and I see the little words stamped into the tablets, but part of my mind wonders what else they could be.

Paranoia.

I fight it. I will *not* go down that road.

But when I drag myself upstairs and into my room, my legs tremble and I can only hold back the urge to run for a few steps before the flight impulse kicks in and I launch myself onto my bed, cursing under my breath when the bed frame bellows an earsplitting creak in protest.

I've been sitting in my dark room staring at my ceiling for a good half hour when I hear Reese shush Jay as they tiptoe by my room. I'm never going to get a better chance than this. I peek out the crack in my door, and as soon as they're out of sight, I follow them, my feet silent on the runner carpet.

Their door is open just an inch or two and loud voices sound from inside as hangers audibly slide along the metal closet rod.

"I'll take a cab—if Daniel calls . . . tell him I'm ill."

"We should tell Tave first," Jay says, sounding weirdly serious.

"I can't. I can't—" Her voice breaks off, and even after everything that's happened the last few days, I'm shocked to realize she's crying! Strong, nearly emotionless Reese. "You do *not* understand what it was like last time. I won't put her or myself through that again. I have to be sure before we do this. I have to *know* it's him."

"Sammi—"

"Don't, *Jay*," she hisses.

"Samantha." The word is a whisper, but Reese doesn't retort. "Come here."

When he speaks again, his words are muffled, and in my mind's eye he's holding her, his face buried against her neck.

"Whatever you need," he says. "Just tell me what to do."

My hands are shaking as I back away and flee to my bedroom. *Tell me what to do.* The same words Benson said to me a few hours ago. I don't like the comparison.

I rub my eyes with the heels of my hands, trying not to cry. I'm so sick of being helpless in my own life. No one will tell me anything; I'm trying to figure everything out on my own with only half the information I need. I hate this!

I blink into the darkness as a thought occurs to me.

Forget this waiting-for-Quinn crap. I know where he lives—tomorrow I'll go to *him*.

CHAPTER FOURTEEN

My lungs ache—I can't breathe.

Wake up!

Wake up!

Finally the dusky gray of sunrise pierces through my eyelids and I sit straight up, gasping for air. My head spins and an ache lingers in my chest as I suck in breaths as fast as I can.

The drowning dream again. Again I was flailing about in desperation, reaching out for things.

But it makes a little more sense now; I'm reaching for things I *made*. Just like the ChapStick and pencil and water. I'm trying to save myself—to survive. My brain figured it out before I did.

I blink away the murky blackness of the water and my room swims into focus, illuminated by the just-rising sun. My nightgown is damp with sweat, but I'm so cold I can't feel my toes or fingers. I stagger to the bathroom and scalding water pours over my trembling limbs for several minutes before I can feel all my digits.

Then I remember. Reese is leaving today.

Samantha. I raise my face to the steaming shower and try to let the water wash Jay's voice away.

Downstairs, Reese and Jay are having coffee: Reese getting ready for the cab to take her to the airport, Jay to go to a normal day of work.

Despite the storm last night, the day is bright and clear, the sun shining. Perfect—I'm going on a *long* walk today.

I hide upstairs, waiting for both of them to clear out. It's cowardly, I know, but I'm going to need all my courage to deal with everything else in my life. Finally I hear the clack of the front door and that unmistakable thud of the dead bolt turning.

They're gone.

I tiptoe to the end of the hallway and pull the edge of the curtain back with a tentative finger, watching them share a goodbye kiss—*that* makes me feel conflicted all over again—before Jay heads up the street on foot and the yellow cab rolls in the other direction.

My chest loosens and I breathe easily for the first time since . . . I don't even know.

When I'm dressed and ready, I go downstairs and see a pot of coffee with two or three cups still warm in the bottom. I grit my teeth against the thought that it was a considerate gesture. I switch off the burner plate and wish that switching off my brain—or better yet, my problems—was so easy.

But a note on the refrigerator incinerates that wish.

Dr. Stanley, 10:00. Don't forget!

As if I could.

When I reach for my house key, my hand pauses at the sight of Reese's key chain hanging innocently beside it.

I reach out a finger to touch the enormous key ring—Reese has more keys than my old high school janitor, I swear—and my fingers begin to tremble as all sorts of possibilities race through my mind.

Terrifying possibilities.

I don't take the keys.

Not yet.

As I stand on the porch, a cold wind cuts through my hoodie and I almost unlock the door again to grab a windbreaker. Despite the clear, sunny sky, the wind is unusually frigid. But it's not that far, and as I make my way down the sidewalk, I realize the bitter wind is eating away at the fog that has enveloped my thoughts all morning.

Better than coffee.

I almost pull up short when I see Sunglasses Guy again. Once is nothing, twice could be a coincidence. Three times? I don't think so. And I am nowhere *near* Park Street or Elizabeth's office. He's just standing there, leaning against the sign for the rarely used bus stop about two houses down, but I'm not fooled. He's watching me.

I act like I haven't noticed him even as my heart races, the beats pounding in my head, blocking out the rush of the wind. But I can't bring myself to actually walk past him, an arm's length away, so after a quick glance I cross the street and watch him out of the corner of my eye, each of us pretending not to see the other.

As I round a corner, someone falls into step with me, but I'm so distracted wondering how long it's going to be before Sunglasses Guy is on my trail again that it takes a good thirty seconds before I realize it's Quinn, rather dashing in all dark gray and black.

"Quinn!" I gasp, stopping completely as I feel my pulse pounding in my fingertips. "I was coming to find you."

"Walk with me," Quinn says out of the side of his mouth, as though he doesn't want anyone to notice he's talking to me.

Resentment flares—like I'm the embarrassing girlfriend or something—but I shove it away and hurry to catch up. "Quinn, I have to talk to you about—"

"'Tis trouble," he interrupts.

"Excuse me?" I ask. *'Tis? What the hell?*

"They've discovered us." He pauses and looks over at me for the first time. "You know it."

I swallow hard and nod, his words confirming my suspicions. I don't actually know for sure who *they* are—Reese and Jay? The people they're hiding me from? Sunglasses Guy? But *someone* has definitely found me.

"We must go to Camden. We've no cause to wait any longer."

I clench my teeth, not wanting to be mad at him but hating the way he jerks me around. Jerks my emotions. But I'm helpless to resist. And I resent that.

Not that I'm giving up. "You said you'd bring something. Something to help me understand." I want to stop, to put my hands on my hips and refuse to walk anywhere else with him until he gives me answers, but a quick glance over my shoulder shows me a distant smudge of black that I'm pretty sure is Sunglasses Guy and I don't want to take the chance that he'll catch up.

In fact, I'd rather *quicken* my pace.

"Camden. Everything waits in Camden."

"*What* is in Camden? Where *is* Camden?" I snap, the tension of Quinn's mystery act and the fact that I'm *being followed* not a very happy-making combination.

"I'll meet you there," he says, as though I hadn't said anything.

"Why can't you just *talk* to me?" I ask, exasperated.

He says nothing, only lengthens his stride. "Tell no one," he hisses.

"Quinn!" I reach for his arm as he turns from the quiet neighborhood street onto a busy boardwalk in the touristy zone, but at the last second he skirts out of reach. I try to follow, but there are people in my way now, though he weaves through them nimbly. My bad leg twinges, as if in warning. I'm not sure I could have caught him even with two good legs.

I curse under my breath. Curse myself, Quinn, my heart and its wild beating. Why can't he just stay in one place? Or, at the very least, give me a straight answer? In *regular* English. I guess he's left me in a better place than the empty street we were on, as it's hard to lose a tail in a nonexistent crowd, but it wasn't what I wanted! He knows something and I have to find out what it is. I have a suspicion—a *rational* one, under the circumstances—that my safety hangs in the balance, and he runs away. Jerk.

Still, based on the direction he took off in, I'm pretty sure he's going to the same place *I* was headed before I ran into him. And I am not letting him get away this time. Today *someone* is going to tell me *something*.

I take a circuitous route and after about six turns, I'm pretty sure I've lost Sunglasses Guy. I go straight for a few blocks, glancing behind me every hundred feet or so, but no tail in sight. I let myself breathe just a little easier and get back on track. It takes another ten minutes to reach my ultimate destination, but finally I see the specialty food store that started the whole fiasco my life has become.

But Quinn's house isn't there.

The white porch, the red door, the triangle, even the cheery maroon and gold tulips—all gone. The whole space is covered with grass and a couple of trees, and I think it's actually part of the yard of the house to the right . . . and has been for a long time.

The minutes fly by as I stand in the middle of the parking lot thinking about everything bizarre I've seen this week: the house, Quinn, the triangles, the alley that disappeared, the flickering woman, the vanishing ChapStick and pencil.

Benson saw them too, I remind myself. *Some of them.* My chin trembles as I fight back tears of despair. I clench my fists and suddenly there's an icy, cold weight in one of them. I open my palm and drop its contents to the ground as though it would burn me.

It's the locket my mother used to wear—one she got from her mother. She was wearing it on the plane. I never saw it again. Couldn't bring myself to ask about it.

Now it's here. On the ground. I *made* it. Without even thinking.

Like the water. The water that could have killed Benson's roommate.

Terror makes my whole body shake. How do you run away from *yourself?*

"I'm not crazy," I whisper into the wind, then stand and stare at the curlicued silver on the ground until the locket pops out of existence.

CHAPTER FIFTEEN

I'm exhausted already. Not only from my long walk to avoid my tail, but because of everything that has happened. That keeps happening. My pace is slow and dragging, but eventually it gets me to Elizabeth's office, where she invites me in as though it were just another day.

It's not.

She doesn't even mention that this appointment is at *her* request, not mine.

Or that Reese is gone.

The only reason I'm even there is to keep up the appearance that everything is normal—that I'm still the ignorant child they think I am. My emotions are completely muddled; I'm angry and frustrated and confused, and desperation is slowly devouring me from the inside. I know I need to do *something*, I just don't know what.

However, the first thing I have to do is sit through at least fifteen more minutes of BS with Elizabeth. Then I can make my escape. Until then, I'm stuck here with my lying shrink, trying to convince her I'm okay.

I'm not good at lying. But I'm pretty good at not saying anything at all. So, here we are at a total impasse as I sit silently on her couch and try not to glare at her.

Or maybe just glare on the inside.

Part of me wishes I could spill everything, but after yesterday I know it's impossible. I scoff inwardly at how close I came to telling her about making stuff out of thin air.

What would she have told Reese then? I vividly remember Reese's all-too-serious question: *Is she too damaged?* If I had confessed it all, would Elizabeth have said yes?

"Why don't you want to talk, Tavia?" Elizabeth asks, after I let too much time pass in silence. She's calm and quiet, but I swear I can hear the frustration bubbling beneath the surface like a river of lava.

Or maybe it's my imagination.

If it was, how would I know the difference?

"I have nothing to talk about," I burst out, the thought of Quinn's refusal to tell me anything unraveling my patience. "I don't even know why I'm here; I'm *fine!*"

I rub my neck; it's sore from carrying my lies, and the tight control I used to have on my temper is gone.

Now Elizabeth sighs and it sounds real, but I know better. "Tavia, I have no idea what's changed, but I've lost your trust."

Liar.

She straightens and then leans forward, her elbows on her knees. "I don't know how to convince you that all I want is for you to be okay. You used to believe that."

I *did* used to believe it. I wish I still did. She has no idea how much I wish it.

"You didn't bring a new sketch." Her voice is calm, casual. Her shrink voice.

That's because you'd just show it to Reese and Jay. "I had homework," I mumble, staring down at my fingers twisting around each other until they ache. *Homework, creating things from thin air, the problem of two boys who've each laid claim to half my heart, whatever you want to call it.*

"Have you seen Quinn again?" Elizabeth continues without pausing to give me a chance to deny it. "It would be natural to want to keep a new romance like this secret—special, I guess. But you know you can tell me anything."

Right.

I sift through the last few days, wondering if there's anything I *can* tell her—something true to keep her swallowing my lies.

But I hesitate too long. Her shrink instincts latch on and she pounces like a cat.

"Come on, Tavia. Talk to me," Elizabeth pleads. "I know strange things are happening to you. That's what I'm here for. To help you understand." She reaches out and grabs my wrist before I can draw away, her fingers tight against my skin. "I want you to understand, Tave. Everything. But you've got to give me something to work with."

"Th-there isn't anything," I insist, pulling my hand back hard. But even if the stutter hadn't given me away, my words are obviously a lie. "I haven't seen him."

Elizabeth studies me for a long time until I squirm. I don't like the look in her eye.

Not because it looks dangerous, but because it looks *safe*.

She's as good an actress as Reese—maybe better. I meet her eyes and all I can see is genuine fondness, a real concern and desire to help.

Maybe I want it so badly I'm *making* myself see it.

Or maybe I'm just easy to trick. The last eight months certainly support that theory.

But those eyes . . .

"Are we done?" I barely whisper the words, but it's enough of a distraction to let me rip my gaze away from hers—to break the hypnotic influence she seems to have on me. Our session is less than half over, but we've always had the rule that I can leave if I feel the need.

And I am feeling the need.

"Are we?" she asks.

I don't look at her; I can't. I just nod and pick up my backpack from beside the couch and tromp to the door.

"I . . . I've been speaking with your aunt lately," Elizabeth says, stopping me.

I manage to not snort in derision.

But only just.

"And I know she's gone on an important business trip for a couple days." Elizabeth hesitates and my nerves are suddenly tingly. I glance back, my fingertips resting on the doorknob, itching to escape.

Something's crackling in the air—a change—and it frightens me.

"When she returns, we're going to try a different method of . . . of therapy. I think you'll like it," she adds.

I nod and my fingers pull on the knob, granting me my escape. I slip through the doorway without opening it fully, hoping she doesn't see the quaver in my now-weak knees.

They're really going to try it, the *pull* or whatever it's called—the thing that she's afraid will fry my brain.

Thoughts of electricity and hot acid float through my head and I try not to dwell on them—surely she wouldn't.

But then, what the hell do I know about what Elizabeth would and wouldn't do?

I fight the urge to run out of the office as her words echo through my head. *I don't know how to convince you that all I want is for you to be okay. You used to believe that.*

Am I so gullible that I believe *everything* I hear?

Maybe.

As I step out from under the awning in front of the office building—it's raining *again*, of course—I pull my hood up against the wind and the drizzling mist, blocking out my peripheral vision. I almost miss the guy standing on the northern corner of the parking lot.

I'd have ignored him entirely if I didn't—even in my panic-driven haze—recognize him.

Recognize his sunglasses.

CHAPTER SIXTEEN

Fear courses through me and I avoid looking at him and start walking toward the library.

When I catch sight of him again, he's walking casually, a good block back, but it's the second turn he's followed me around. His black pull-over—almost identical to my own—blends in with the sparse foot traffic, but it's not hard to pick him out.

Still. I don't want to be paranoid. There is the slightest of possibilities that we just happen to be going the same place.

Twice.

In the same morning.

I hesitate and then turn left instead of right—it'll only extend my walk by a couple of blocks, but I don't want to lead him straight to the library.

My steps slow as I approach the first corner on my new route and I sneak a peek behind me. I don't see him yet.

Slower.

Slower.

Angling to the right, I glance up the sidewalk from beneath my lashes.

Just as I'm about to step out of sight he comes around the corner, his eyes darting about. I snap my face away and begin power-walking again.

Terror ratchets through my legs, tingling in my toes, and I wonder briefly if it was a really bad idea to slow down enough to see him, if I should have gone with my gut and made my escape while I had a chance.

Problem is, I don't trust my gut anymore. It was wrong about Reese, it was wrong about Elizabeth.

And while I wasn't exactly wrong about Benson, I apparently was misreading him.

And I don't even *know* where my gut stands with Quinn.

But now that I'm sure this guy *is* following me, I want to hide. Flee. Or maybe . . . to *do* something. It's an instinct I don't recognize as my own—or maybe just one I'd forgotten, after months of helplessness in a hospital bed and further months of painstakingly gradual recovery. Regardless, it's unmistakable now. *Do something.*

But what?

Make something, I finally realize, identifying the unfamiliar urge. But I reject the possibility. No. Not a chance.

I duck into the doorway of a colorful candy shop, hoping to maybe lose Sunglasses Guy that way. After a minute or so a very tall man walks past the door going the opposite direction I had been walking and I decide to fall into step just behind him, use him as a human shield. I'll follow him to the end of the block, then double back on another street.

I stall, pretending to mess with the zipper on my backpack, then edge into the crowd so close behind him that I almost step on the heels of his shoes. Even with his head hunched down and the way he pulls his coat around him like he's tired—or sick, maybe—the man is huge and makes me feel safe and hidden.

Until he flickers.

Just like that lady the day I ran into the wall.

I draw in a loud breath but manage to keep walking. I glance around me, but no one else seems to have noticed. I look at the tall man again, his back broad and solid. He's still hiding me.

I squint, focusing on him, waiting for it to happen again.

But I don't expect him to disappear entirely.

I stop walking and someone plows right into me, making me stagger forward.

"Watch it," the woman says, hardly glancing back as she and her boyfriend step aside and keep walking.

I whip around. No one else even pauses.

They didn't see him disappear? But he was really tall—and now it's like he was never even here. Like he blinked out of existence.

I tighten my fists over my backpack straps and face forward, trying to walk evenly—*I have to get to Benson*, I think. *He'll help.* Good sense manages to pierce through my panic and I begin counting so my limp doesn't make me conspicuous.

One, two, three, four. One, two, three, four.

I've completely lost sight of my tail, and I don't dare look around to check.

I'm about two blocks from the library when the sky bursts open and starts really pouring on me. "Wonderful," I mutter under my breath. "Just fan-freaking-tabulous."

I'm soaked in seconds—as if the world seriously wants to spite me—but I can see the library now and it looks like a sanctuary. I know it's not, not really—Sunglasses Guy can go in there too.

But Benson is inside and *he* makes me feel safe.

Nervous sweat trickles down my back as I reach the stairs and adrenaline fuels my steps. I pull the entrance door too hard and it clatters against the wall behind it, earning me the attention of every library patron within earshot.

Great.

I'm soaked to the bone as I step into the warm lobby, wishing I didn't look quite so bedraggled. Benson is by my side before I can take more than about three steps and I want to throw my arms around him, hold myself against his chest until the trembling stops.

The impulse shocks me into stillness. I shouldn't want Benson so strongly—especially after having *just* seen Quinn this morning—Quinn, who makes my chest ache with longing and my mind spin in bliss.

So why do I?

I don't know. But I keep coming back to the burn of Benson's lips on mine, the possessive way his arms wound around me, how warm it felt to have his body pressed against me. I look up at him and know the sheen of wanting is shining in my eyes. But I don't have the energy to hide it.

"You okay?" he asks, his face lined with concern. "Rough morning?"

Tell no one. "You could say that," I grumble.

The main doors open, and just past Benson's shoulder I catch a glimpse of dark hair. I take half a step to my right to put Benson's admittedly slim profile between us and peek out.

Black pullover and sunglasses.

He found me.

"Can we go to your office?" I ask, desperation in my voice. "Right now? Please?"

"Yeah, sure," Benson says, looking confused. He doesn't ask any more questions, though, and leads me zigzagging across the floor, through the study tables, to the doorway of a barely closet-size alcove.

With a fast but searching glance behind me, I sit in the chair across from Benson and shove my backpack underneath the table. Then I scoot to the side of the chair, attempting to hunch out of view.

"If it's about yesterday, we can find another way to get some privacy," Benson whispers—his *office* doesn't have a door, or even a proper doorway, so it would be ridiculously easy for someone to overhear us. "We could even go somewhere else if you wanted—"

"It's not about that," I murmur. But just bringing up yesterday makes my head pound. It was too strong a mix of amazing and devastating. I sit up and within seconds am squishing a stress ball first in one fist and then the other. I've passed it back and forth a few times before I realize I *created* it without even thinking. Horrified, I thrust it onto Benson's desk, where it rolls innocently across the uneven surface until it collides with a pile of paper clips.

Benson leans forward, reaching for my hand, doing his best to ignore the yellow ball. "Are you okay?"

My nod is more than a little spasmodic and I pull my hand out of reach. My thoughts are caught in a whirlpool of confusion and I can't let the touch of his skin make things worse. I begin to wonder if this is what having a mental breakdown feels like.

"Are you sure? Because, um, you're sweating." He looks meaningfully at my forehead and I realize I didn't even feel the drop of sweat that's now tickling my cheek. I lift my sleeve to wipe it away, feeling gross.

"Benson?" My throat freezes and I can't continue.

"Yes?" he says after a long pause.

"Remember the man I told you about?" I say it before my jaw can clamp shut against the words.

"You mean . . . Quinn?"

"No." *Please don't mention Quinn. I can't talk about Quinn. Not just yet.* "No, the man with the sunglasses; the one who I've seen a couple times."

"Yeah . . ."

"He's been following me since I left home this morning. Down into the historic district, then to Elizabeth's office. And now he's here and he—" I shut my mouth. I'm rambling.

"Did he see you . . ." He hesitates and leans forward before finishing in a whisper, "Did he see you *do* anything?"

"Make anything? No!" But I remember the locket and add, very quietly, "I don't think."

"Okay. That's good, right?" he asks, peering out at the library floor over my shoulder.

"I think maybe Reese and Jay sent him."

He looks confused. "Why would they start having you followed?"

"Why would they decide to fry my brain?" I ask, feeling both questions are equally valid. "Point is, this guy's been following me, and now he's here, and you have to help me get away."

"Can you point him out?" Benson asks.

If only it were that simple. "Just in case he doesn't know I've spotted him, I have to keep pretending I don't see him."

"Good point," Benson says. "Tell me what he looks like."

"He's got dark brown hair, he's probably about six feet. He was wearing sunglasses and a black pullover."

Either of which he may have taken off on entering the library.

I sift through my recollection. It's amazingly hard to describe someone when all you have to go on are furtive glances. "Brown shoes. He's got brown shoes. Lace-ups, like Docs or hiking boots."

"Okay," Benson says, writing something I can't see on a Post-it note.

"I'll find that for you." His voice is just a little louder as he rises from his chair.

I open my mouth to protest and realize he's pretending to find a book. Perfect. I turn and watch him go—that would be natural, right?—and my eyes instantly find the man, sitting at a corner table, pretending to read.

My gaze jerks away as if he'll sense everything if I look too long.

Benson won't be able to miss him. Surely.

I sit at the desk, breathing in and out and forcing myself to calm down. I'm here with Benson; he's going to help me.

I'm almost calm when the stress ball I'd nearly forgotten about suddenly disappears. I squeak and shrink away.

Ten seconds later Benson touches my shoulder and I almost jump out of my skin. "Sorry," he says, but there's a question in his voice when he sees my reaction.

"I'm okay," I say, trying to whisper. "I promise, I'm good now."

After studying me for a moment Benson sits down again and places a large reference book on top of his desk. "I saw him," he says quietly as he riffles through the pages, pretending to show me something. "I think you should head home."

"Home? Why?"

"It's close enough to walk and probably safer than here." He glances back out at the library over the rim of his glasses. "Reese is gone, right? I'll find a way to distract this guy, then I'll meet you there. It'll be just the two of us and we'll talk about everything we know and figure something out."

"What if he's dangerous? He could hurt you."

Benson laughs wryly. "He's in a government building—trust me, he doesn't want to cause trouble here. Besides, he already *knows* how to find you. This is just a temporary fix so we can buy some time."

I nod hesitantly. "Okay. But you'll come after me, right?"

The only thing more intense than Benson's whisper is his steady blue-eyed gaze. "I'll always come for you."

CHAPTER SEVENTEEN

I check the gap in the curtains for about the hundredth time—Benson still isn't here. I collapse against the sofa, pulling the throw blanket off and wrapping it around me as if it might somehow protect me. I've stripped off my wet hoodie and toweled my hair, but violent shivers rack my body and I don't think they have anything to do with the temperature. I close my eyes, wishing things were as simple as when I was a little girl.

And my parents were alive.

And I was a promising young artist.

And there was no one following me.

And I didn't have weird powers that I don't know how to control and strange visions that can't be unexplained.

Mostly that.

A light tapping on the door makes my eyes snap open, and I get tangled in the blanket and slam my knee against the coffee table. Benson slips in the second there's enough room and pushes the door shut behind him.

"I'm pretty sure I lost him. You were right, by the way. You left and five seconds later he was up and out of his chair, ready to follow."

Then he sees my face, the blanket all crumpled up on the floor, and the crooked table.

"Oh, Tave, it'll be okay," he says, pulling me into his arms. And even though I know he must be able to feel me shaking, I'm too tired to be embarrassed. His face is nuzzled against my neck and it's the only source of warmth I can detect in my entire body. "I'm sorry for everything that's happened to you," he whispers, his lips brushing my sensitive skin. "It's more than any one person deserves. Especially you."

I let myself stand there for a moment, leaning on him, borrowing his strength until I can find my own again. Just for a second. Two. Three. "How'd you get rid of him?" I finally choke out.

"Spilled coffee on him, actually," Benson says. "Marie agreed to help. Fussed over him while I took off." He looks up and meets my eyes. "I don't know how much time it will really buy us, but it got me here without him on my trail."

"Is your car out front?"

"I walked—okay, I kinda jogged. It's not that far."

I laugh. Not heartily; it's a weary laugh. But at least I still can.

"Okay," Benson says. "So tell me what happened this morning with Elizabeth."

"Nothing," I say, suppressing the urge to squirm as I completely avoid talking about my run-in with Quinn. *Tell no one* echoes loudly in my head. "I lied, she lied; it was pretty much what I expected."

"But when you came out, this guy with the sunglasses was waiting for you?"

I nod and remember that today also brought with it the tall man who disappeared, but my head starts to ache at the thought and I can't bring myself to mention him. Not yet. "He's got to know what I can do—it doesn't make any sense otherwise." Out of nowhere, my stomach rumbles. "Are you hungry?" I ask, sliding from Benson's grasp and heading into the kitchen.

"No," Benson says, but he follows me anyway.

"Well, I'm starving," I mutter, grabbing at snack food I usually never touch: a carton of Reese's yogurt, a container of sliced pineapple, a package of Genoa salami. I don't even know what Genoa salami is, but I'm going to eat it.

"Do you think this guy is who Reese and Jay are hiding me from?" I ask as I open the various packaging.

"It's possible." He doesn't meet my eyes, and I think it's because he doesn't want me to see the fear in his face.

"Well, it's been nice knowing you, Benson." I say the words mockingly, but there's an icy edge to them—an unfamiliar bitterness that I don't like in myself.

"Hey." Benson's soft blue eyes are looking at me again. "Just because you have a tail doesn't mean you're about to die. I mean, he hasn't actually tried to do anything to you yet, right?"

I shrug noncommittally.

Benson purses his lips, then leans forward on his elbows. "So let's assume this guy does know that you can make stuff—and I think you're right that he does," he adds, before I can defend my theory. "Do you think Reese and Jay know? Elizabeth? Your doctors? Just how far into *The Truman Show* do you think this all goes?"

I stop with a slice of pineapple halfway to my mouth. *How far does it go?* "Hell if I know. Reese, Jay, and Elizabeth seemed to be focused on Quinn and the triangles. I don't even know what's special about them, except that I can see them and Elizabeth can't."

"And all these things started happening at the same time as you making things, right?"

I don't want to even talk about *that*, but I guess I don't really have a choice anymore. I have to face it. "It seems like too big a coincidence for them not to be all wrapped up together. I just don't see the connection."

"Reese is out of town and Jay's working a ton, right?" he says, clearly hinting at something.

I nod and start on the salami, rolling up one of the slices and taking a tentative bite. Pretty good. "Where are you going with this?" I ask once I swallow.

"Maybe she wanted some extra security while she's not around. You know, eyes and ears." Benson grabs a piece of salami too and puts it in his mouth, but the movement is so instinctual, I'm not sure he's tasting anything.

"Like a bodyguard?" I like the sense that makes, even though—if it's true—it would mean that Reese and Jay are lying to me again.

Still.

"Yeah," he replies, taking another bite.

"I dunno," I muse. "My *magical power* is pretty damn lame. Why would they bother to go through all this trouble for someone who can make stuff that poofs into thin air? There must be more."

Benson just stares at me. "Could you do anything . . . I don't know, supernatural when you were little?"

"Yeah, I made the glass on a snake's cage disappear right before my acceptance letter from Hogwarts arrived."

Benson just raises an eyebrow at me.

"Seriously, I had a totally normal childhood. There's really nothing stand out about me."

His hand intercepts mine as I reach for another slice, tightening around my fingers so quickly it almost hurts. "That's not true," he whispers. Then, as though it hadn't happened at all, he lets go and continues. "Is there any possibility your parents were in some kind of organized crime?"

A bark of laughter flies out of my mouth before I can clap my hand over it. "Hardly," I say. "Trust me, not the type. And, uh, we certainly didn't have enough money for either of my parents to be secretly involved in something that extreme."

"What about Reese and Jay?"

I'm sober again. "It wouldn't surprise me at all, actually. Reese especially. She's really closemouthed about her business." I hesitate, then voice the suspicion that's been eating me since Jay called Reese *Samantha* yesterday. "What if . . . what if they aren't really my aunt and uncle?"

Benson's eyebrows scrunch. "Is that even possible?"

"Sadly, yes. I didn't know them before. They could be anyone. And it just seems too big a coincidence for them to be so into whatever is happening to me when they weren't a part of my life until eight months ago."

"How can you not know for sure?" Benson asks. "Didn't you meet them before the crash?"

"It's a little . . . complicated." *Like everything in my life.* "They're practically shirttail relatives who weren't even around until the last, I guess ten years, and some of my memories from before the crash are shaky. I *do* remember Reese, I think, but it's been long enough that it could be memories of someone who looks a lot like her."

"Can't your, I don't know, grandparents tell you?"

"My step-grandma died a couple years ago. Her funeral was actually the last time I saw Reese, but she was all blotchy and had one of those fancy veil things on her hat that covered part of her face. When I think back, the veil is all I remember. It was sheer, I'm sure. But in my memories, it blocks out everything."

"Other siblings?" Benson asks, though I suspect he's expecting my answer.

"Well, you know I'm an only child. My dad was too, till Grandpa married Reese's mom. And she mostly lived with *her* dad."

"And you never reached out to anyone, like, back home?"

My memories of Michigan are the shadiest of them all; names and phone numbers flit away from my consciousness like sand through my fingers. But it's more than that—and hard to explain to someone who still has a family. "When you lose . . . everyone . . . no one looks at you the same. Even the doctors and nurses who didn't know me gave me these awful looks."

"Pity?" Benson whispers.

"It's more than pity." I feel the tears build up in earnest now and shake my head. "My mom and dad—" My voice cracks and I take a breath and try again. If they were alive, none of this would be happening—well, I guess I don't know that. But even if it was, I'd have them to turn to. "I was still trying to deal with everything, so when Reese and Jay basically offered me total seclusion at their house, I took it." I realize, as I say it, that I really am a recluse.

If I disappeared, like that man outside the candy store . . . no one would know.

The possibility horrifies me.

"I just didn't want to go back," I finally say, "and be so much less of a person than I was before."

Benson's thumbs rub against the backs of my hands. "You're not less. Different? Maybe. I didn't know you before. But you couldn't be less."

I nod glumly. He's brought me back from the edge of tears, but only just. Because I do feel less. *Everything* is just . . . less.

"So," Benson says, distracting me again. "Let's say Reese and Jay aren't who they say they are—and they might be. How would they have even gotten you? You were still seventeen. Child Services isn't going to just hand you over to someone claiming to be your next of kin."

"They got custody through my parents' will, I think. Would it be all that hard to make a fake ID?"

"I think you'd need more than that," Benson presses.

"I don't know. You can pull off just about anything with enough cash. And if they're involved in some kind of organized crime, I guarantee they have resources."

"Okay, let's say that's the case." He spreads his hands to the side. "Where are the real Reese and Jay?"

I suck in a breath. I hadn't thought about that. *No.* I force myself to be honest. *I didn't* want *to think about that.* "Is it all that far-fetched to believe they killed them?"

"I guess not. Or," Benson continues before I can go too far down that morbid path, "they might be living on a farm in Kansas with a fake death certificate and no idea you're alive at all."

"How pathetic is it that I find that idea remarkably plausible?"

"Well, one way or another, we're going to figure this out. Together," he adds, his eyes boring deeper into mine. "I'm not backing out now. Whatever you want to do next, I'm right there."

"Well," I say, leaning forward, trying to amp up my bravery. "Maybe we should take advantage of Reese being gone."

"How so?"

I swallow hard, and it's that moment when I realize how serious this next step is.

And how committed I am to it.

"I have an idea."

Benson just rolls his eyes. "Why do I have the feeling I'm not going to *like* this idea?"

"Well, that depends," I say in a faux casual tone. "How do you feel about breaking and entering?"

CHAPTER EIGHTEEN

I've tried every key twice, and the door to Reese's office remains stubbornly locked. Filled with frustration, I lean my head against the door, a total failure. Benson stands behind me, his arms crossed over his chest, saying nothing.

"I'm sorry," I say, feeling utterly dismal. "I thought for sure one of these keys would do it."

"It's understandable," Benson says with just a hint of humor. "I don't think I've ever seen so many keys in one place."

"I know, right?" I say wryly, holding up the weighty ring.

"Maybe you should just make a big hammer? Or, like, a chain saw or something."

"And destroy the door?" I sigh. "Talk about massive evidence."

"Touché." Benson glares at the doorknob, his jaw muscles standing out. Then, making some kind of decision, he drops into a crouch and pulls his wallet out of his back pocket. "May I?"

"May you what?"

He removes what look like two slim sticks from his wallet and, after a little fiddling, unfolds them and snaps them into place.

"Are those *lock picks?*" I ask, completely shocked.

"Maybe," he says, inserting one carefully into the doorknob.

"*Wallet-size* lock picks?" I press.

"First rule of Fight Club," he mutters, focused on his task.

"Fight Club my ass," I whisper, watching as he expertly works at the dead bolt.

After some fiddling, Benson cranks one of his sticks around—and the knob turns with it. The door glides open on well-oiled hinges. "There you go," he announces, folding his little lock picks back down and dropping them into the bottom of his wallet.

"Where did you learn that?" I stare at him in shock. And possibly awe.

But he just shrugs, and I suspect that's all the answer I'm going to get.

Reese's office looks . . . normal.

It's not as though I haven't been in here before. Reese often leaves her door open while she's working. I even asked her one day when I first moved in why she kept it locked, and she smiled and patted my shoulder. "I have a lot of trade secrets in there." Then she sighed, looked away, and said, "But truth be told, it's mostly just habit."

Habit. Right.

Drawing a deep breath, I cross the threshold into the office. Everything is super-organized, with perfect stacks of papers on the desk, a file cabinet with a potted flower on top in one corner, and a corkboard mounted on the wall, covered with pins and Post-its.

I reach for the filing cabinet first.

Locked.

Of course.

Benson is bent over, looking under the neat stacks on Reese's desk.

"Maybe a drawer," he mutters, opening the shallow pencil drawer at the front of the mahogany desk. "Bingo," he says with a grin as he holds up a small key chain with one key dangling from it.

"What's that?"

In answer, he walks over to the gray filing cabinet and inserts the key into the spring-loaded lock. His body is so near I catch a hint of his deodorant. I breathe deeply.

He turns the key.

The lock pops with a *click*.

"Excellent," Benson says, drumming his fingertips together.

"Library nerd," I mutter, mostly to cover the disappointment I feel when he steps back and gives me some space.

The drawer is full of files labeled at the top, mostly in Reese's neat print, but some are in another handwriting. It looks male, but not Jay's, and I wonder who she's been working with. I've never seen anyone else around the house. Or, at least, not anywhere near the office. The labels are all names. I look at the front of the drawers and they show what letters are in each one.

"Let's start at the beginning," I say dryly, and begin sifting through the *A*s. "Reese told Elizabeth she'd check her files for Quinn. I guess these are the files." *A-r, A-t, A-u, A-v, A-w.* "Nope. No Avery at all," I say, checking through several files on either side of where it should have been, just in case it wasn't alphabetized *exactly* right. I pause, my fingertips keeping my place among the files. "So I guess the possibility exists that he doesn't have anything to do with this." It's a wish more than a logical conclusion, but I'm not above wishing.

"Or that he gave you a fake name," Benson says, looking weirdly broody leaning against Reese's desk.

I ignore him—not to mention the butterflies in my stomach—and take a shuddering breath as I close the *A–F* drawer and move on to my real task. *My* file.

M–T.

Michaels.

The third one down.

The drawer seems to glow like a neon light, and I'm simultaneously desperate and terrified to open it.

Benson draws near and raps a knuckle softly against the label when I continue to stall. "It's what you came in here for," he murmurs. A soft hand touches my shoulder, and I try to draw strength from him like an emotional osmosis.

After a long moment I nod and reach for the handle, carefully pressing the latch that lets it slide free, revealing dozens upon dozens of cream-colored files. I feel my world melting around me when I see it.

Tavia Michaels.

I knew it would be there—it's the reason we broke into Reese's office in the first place. For answers! But confirmation is a bitch.

I pull it out and stare at it in horror and fascination.

It's pretty nondescript. A cream-colored folder with a small graphic on the upper right-hand corner of a feather floating above a flame. I peek back into the files; the others have the image too. But I don't know what it means and don't have the time to theorize.

I need to look at *my* file.

It's pretty thick—I don't know whether to be encouraged or discouraged by that. I flip the top and look down at a picture of myself as a sophomore.

And, um, it's *not* a great picture. Sophomore year was kinda awkward.

"Awww, look at you," Benson says with a grin, his arm resting around my back. "You're so cuuuuute."

"Shut up, jerk," I say, but he's managed to break the tension. I lean very slightly into his arm and flip to the next page.

A birth certificate. My Social Security card. High school transcripts. A copy of my parents' will. Exactly the kind of stuff you'd expect to find in a filing cabinet in the office of someone who had received surprise custody of an injured teenager.

But past all that—pictures of my art. And not just any pictures. I recognize these photos—*I* took them.

"How did she get these?" I ask aloud, holding up several.

"Hey, did *you* paint that?" Benson asks, pointing to an oil on canvas of my mother sitting by a window, slicing strawberries.

"Yeah," I manage to choke out. It's one of my best pieces. Somehow I managed to capture the . . . *essence* of who my mother really is. Was.

I can't think about my mother right now. I swallow down the grief— push it away—then flip the photo, blocking her face from my eyes.

But there's still another photo of a painting. And another, and another.

"You're really good," Benson says, taking one from me to get a closer look.

It's strange to realize that he's never seen my work. Art was my life for so many years. And now Benson is such a big part of my life. And art isn't.

It feels wrong.

"I took these pictures and sent them to the art school that wanted me," I explain, as much to distract myself as anything. "How did Reese get them?"

"Um, Huntington?" Benson asks in a wary voice.

"Yeah, how . . ." But my words fade away as I look down at the first piece of paper beneath the stack of photos.

It's the letter I first got from Huntington.

No. A *draft* of the letter.

With notes in the margins in Reese's handwriting.

"What the hell?" I grasp at the corner of the letter and lift it up only to find a finished copy beneath it. And the pamphlet they sent with it.

And copies of the photos *in* the pamphlet.

"But . . . but I didn't send my stuff to New Hampshire—it went to upstate New York."

"How hard is it to have mail forwarded?"

"But there was a website. And a phone number. I *called* them!" I'm almost shrieking. Huntington was the *reason* we got on the plane in the first place. If it's fake . . .

"Here," Benson says, pulling his cell out of his pocket. "What was the website?" He brings up the Internet on his phone and I recite the web address in a near monotone.

"Here we go," Benson says once it loads. "Huntington Academy of the Arts. The website is still up and there's a phone number."

We both look at the screen for a long, silent spell.

"I can call it," Benson offers.

I'm afraid to say yes. Despite everything we've discovered, this feels like a major turning point.

Benson looks down at his screen, and his thinking wrinkle appears between his eyebrows.

Every nerve is on edge as I nod. "Let's do it."

He waits a few seconds—giving me a chance to change my mind maybe—then touches his screen and raises the phone to his ear.

Nothing.

Nothing.

Nothing.

Then the phone on Reese's desk lets out a shrill ring.

My knees collapse and I sink to the floor, drained of the will to support my own weight. "But I talked to them!" I shout, and my voice is so shrill—I hardly recognize it. "There was a woman, and it wasn't Reese," I add before Benson can say anything. "She wasn't like Reese at all. I talked to her like *six times*. There's no way it was Reese. Or Elizabeth. She was kind of cutesy and peppy, like a cheerleader. Like . . . like . . ." *Like Barbie. Like Secretary Barbie. Who does her best never to talk to me, who's hardly ever there even when I have an appointment.*

My heart is pounding in my ears.

One, two, three, four. One, two, three, four.

"It was all fake," I say, my voice shallow and strained. "Why . . . why would they do that?"

I hear Benson breathe in and out slowly a few times. "I've been thinking about this."

"You knew?" I almost shout.

"No, no," Benson says, his hands coming to my arms, rubbing up and down to calm me. "I didn't know about the school thing. I mean I've been thinking about the whole plane thing, in light of everything else that's happened."

"And?" I say after the silence grows heavy.

"I hate to bring this up, I mean, I'm sure it's still kind of fresh and all, but maybe . . . maybe you being in a plane wreck isn't a coincidence."

"What do you mean? Like someone—" But the words are hardly out of my mouth when I realize what he's implying. "No," I whisper. "No way."

"Tavia, with everything that's happened, you have to at least consider it."

Despair rips through me. "No. No! I am *not* important enough for someone to bring down an entire *plane!* Do you know how many people were on that flight?" I'm managing to not yell, but only just.

"Two hundred and fifty-six," Benson whispers. Of course he looked it up.

"It was an accident." The words are shaky as they wisp from my mouth.

Benson is quiet, but his eyes don't leave mine. Just as I'm sure I can't look at him anymore, he says, "I don't think it was, Tave."

I sink to the floor, defeated. It's one thing to lose my parents in a tragic accident—I've learned to deal with that—but murder?

Murder that was intended for *me?*

"Benson?" His name is a croak from my dry throat. "I'm no one."

"You're not no one." He reaches an arm around me, pulling me to his chest, where I bury my face. He strokes my short hair. "Think about it. Someone must have found you when you were living in Michigan. They sabotaged your plane, tried to kill *you* because of what you can do. It all fits."

Like a glove.

The most horrendous glove in the world.

I think I'm going to throw up.

"Then why am I still alive?"

"Maybe . . . maybe something changed."

"Did *I* change?" My voice is so hollow even I can hear it, and I can't bring myself to meet his eyes.

"What do you mean?"

"Everything went crazy after the plane wreck. Did the crash change me? Have I always been this way, or did the crash turn me into something... something strange?" I look up at him now. "Did I survive a plane wreck because of my powers, or do I have powers because I survived a plane wreck?"

"Does it matter?" Benson whispers.

I look down at my file. "Maybe." As I stare at that name—*Tavia Michaels*, is that even really me anymore?—a conviction solidifies in my chest. "I have to leave, Benson. I have to get out of here. Away from them, from everyone."

"You can't leave, Tave."

Our heads jerk up to Elizabeth standing in the doorway.

With a gun.

Pointed right at us.

CHAPTER NINETEEN

I don't think.

I don't have time.

There's a picture in my head—a flicker of a picture—and metal bands appear from nowhere, wrapping around Elizabeth's body, around her hands, forcing the gun from her fingers. More bands. And more. *Iron. Cast iron*, I realize, and it feels vaguely familiar, as if I've done this very thing before.

But now I can't stop. More metal wraps around Elizabeth—her arms, her shoulders. Soon the weight drags her to the ground.

"Tavia, you . . . holy crap, what did you do?" Benson stares in horror at the uneven contraption holding Elizabeth to the floor.

"I don't know. It just . . . it just happened." *Again.* What is wrong with me that I can hurt people without even consciously thinking about it!

Shaking the thought away, I scoop the files from the floor. "Come on! We only have five minutes."

"Tavia! Stop! Talk to me!" Elizabeth calls, but I ignore her as I scoot through the doorway and sprint to my room, Benson close behind. "You don't understand what this all means," she yells. "There's more than you could possibly know."

"Tavia, stop, you need to slow down and think about this." Benson's face is white and his words tumble like white water. "What exactly are you doing?"

I scarcely hear him as I stuff socks, underwear, and my favorite jeans in my backpack. "I have to get out of here. I need answers," I mutter, more to myself than to him. A pair of red bikinis drops to the carpet and I don't feel even the barest twinge of embarrassment when Benson looks down and sees them a second before I snatch them up and stuff them in with the rest of the clothes.

We are *way* beyond that.

"Tavia, seriously. Where are you going to go?"

"I don't care. Away. That's all that matters. I have to go now!"

"Go *where*?" Benson demands, grabbing my shoulders to make me look at him.

I don't want to—I let my eyes dart to the ceiling, his shoulders, the window, anywhere but his soft blue eyes. He gives me a gentle shake and I can't avoid it anymore. I let my gaze rise to meet his.

"Where?" he repeats. "And what are we going to do with her?" He inclines his head to where I can still hear Elizabeth calling me, begging me to come back.

"They killed my parents, Benson. Reese, Jay, and Elizabeth—they're *all* involved. They murdered them. They *got* me on that plane! I *know* that Reese and Elizabeth are working together; they're just trying to get something out of me and then they will Fry. My. Brain." A sob builds up in my throat as hopelessness washes over me. "If I don't leave, I'm as good as dead."

He says nothing, but his hands loosen on my shoulders, and when I pull away to stuff things in my backpack again, he doesn't try to hold on.

"Can I stay with you for a few days?" I ask on impulse.

"I guess," he says. "But . . ."

I'm not sure I can stand to hear what he wants to say. I'm already so overwhelmed my fingers are trembling as I dig into a sock and pull out the money that represents the extent of my personal fortune.

It's less than forty dollars.

I'm so screwed.

Maybe Benson will lend me some.

No. I can't. I can't ask him for anything else.

Maybe I shouldn't even stay with him. What if they decide to just murder him too?

"I'm going to see if Reese and Jay have any money sitting around in their room." I should just say what I mean: *I'm going to see if I can steal some money from Reese and Jay.*

What else can I do?

I guess if I had to, I could magic myself some money when I went to buy something, but when it disappeared five minutes later, wouldn't I still be a thief? I can hurt people and steal stuff. Why the hell is this happening to me?

If I have to take something from someone, at least I know Reese and Jay are the bad guys.

So why do I still feel guilty?

Maybe because I know my mother wouldn't be proud of me at this moment, and that thought makes me want to die inside.

After a quick glance down the hallway, where I can still hear Elizabeth yelling, I go and stand in front of Reese and Jay's bedroom door. When I reach for the knob and turn it, it gives easily.

They didn't lock it.

They trust me.

It's a thought so jarringly dissonant from my actions that I stop, hand still poised on the knob as I try to think clearly. Why *should* they trust me? Do they think I'm that ignorant? Or do they think I'm so under their control that I couldn't possibly be dangerous?

Do they control me? Even after everything that's happened, the fact is that I don't know what I am.

And they do.

The door skims across the carpet as I push it open, a whisper in the silent bedroom. They have a chic, deco-style room with a sleek black king-size bed and square silver bedside tables. Wondering if I'll leave foot prints on the carpet—and then deciding it doesn't matter—I stride first to Reese's side of the bed, then Jay's.

The top of Reese's table is empty except for the lamp. I'm not surprised. Bedside tables tend to reflect a person's personality more accurately than any clinical test, in my opinion. Sparse, elegant, and organized. That's Reese.

Still, a peek into the table's shallow drawer nets me seventeen dollars, crisply folded.

Jay's side is more profitable—forty-six dollars—but also a thicker, more crumpled wad. It's probably been weeks, maybe months, since he cleaned up the pile of junk he's clearly been emptying from his pockets each night.

I have about a hundred dollars.

That won't last long. But it's a start.

I turn and Benson is waiting for me in the doorway. His eyes are concerned.

Of course they are. I just used my supernatural powers to incapacitate a grown woman and now am stealing things and running away like a crazy person.

I slide past him without looking and stuff the cash in the small pocket of my backpack. I look around my room, wondering what else to bring. Is it stealing to take the laptop they gave me? That seems worse than the money I just filched. But the computer technically is *mine*.

I pause. What if it's bugged?

Not bugged exactly, but what if they can find me through it? You see that kind of stuff in crime shows all the time, and I honestly don't know if that's one of those "facts" they've grossly exaggerated or if it's actually true.

Still.

Making a split decision, I grab it and shove it into my backpack, then yank the zippers closed before I can change my mind.

I can't look at my art supplies. They feel important again. Necessary—like I can't find Quinn without them.

And I *have* to find Quinn if I want answers.

But I can't take them. There's just no room.

And now I have to decide: Phoenix or Camden?

Quinn told me to meet him in Camden, but Reese seemed to think there was something important in Phoenix. Something to do with *me*. But . . . Phoenix is a big city. I wouldn't know where to start. I've never been there before.

I sigh. Somehow I always wind up forced to trust Quinn. Quinn who never stays, who never answers questions.

Who makes my heart leap and my blood warm.

Camden it is.

"I'm ready to go," I say to Benson, and I hate that my voice wavers.

I feel weak, confused. I can create things out of nothing—I should feel strong and in charge.

But I don't.

"Tavia, we . . ." Benson pauses and licks his lips nervously. "We should get out of the house," he finishes, though I know that's not what he was going to say.

We walk out into the hallway and Elizabeth yells, "I think they've found you, Tave. You're not safe out there. The Reduciata will get you— they want you more than any of our other Earthbounds. They—"

"Earthbound," I whisper, not hearing the rest of Elizabeth's sentence. I've heard the word before—in Elizabeth's phone conversation with Reese. But it's something more. A word that echoes in whispers in my head. *Earthbound . . . Earthbound . . .*

Benson is tugging lightly on my hand. "We have to go."

"Please," Elizabeth adds in a softer voice—but one I'm obviously meant to hear, "you don't know how to use your powers well enough to truly protect yourself."

I gasp and whirl around to face her. She *knows.*

A phrase rises into my mouth and spills off my tongue before I can stop it. *"Sum Terrobligatus; declarare fidem."*

Elizabeth's eyes grow so wide I can see the whites all around them.

But she says nothing.

Anger boils inside me and I stoop to pick up the gun she dropped and turn it around on her. *"Declarare fidem!"* My hand shakes—a hand that doesn't feel like mine. *What are these words? What am I doing?* I choke back a sob as everything I thought I knew about myself blows away.

I'm a monster.

"Curatoria," she gasps.

147

"What did you just say?" Benson whispers.

"I have no clue," I whisper back.

And I don't. But I should! I'm sure I should! The same way I *ought* to know the meaning of all the words Elizabeth just said. Pushing those thoughts away, I cock the pistol, letting the eerie click fill the office. "You want me to trust you; why were you pointing a gun at me?"

"Because I didn't know how much you knew about your powers," Elizabeth answers instantly, her neck craned awkwardly to look up at me. "How much control you had."

I don't like it, but what can I do? I *might* have been dangerous. I probably could have killed her. I wonder if she kept that gun in her office too—if she got nervous every time I walked into her waiting room.

Her empty waiting room.

It's *always* empty.

I am such an idiot.

Why is it that I always see everything *after* it's too late?

The waiting room has been empty every single time I have *ever* come in to see her—except, occasionally, for Secretary Barbie. Every. Time. Even when I drop by unannounced. I guess I figured no one ever stuck around because, seriously, who wants to be caught in a shrink's office?

But I should have seen it sooner.

"I want answers!" I say fervently. "And if you lie, you will *never* see me again."

To my surprise, Elizabeth smiles. Not a mocking, cruel smile, but a gentle, *relieved* one. I don't get it and for a moment it knocks me off-kilter.

But I dig my toes into the ground for better balance—an old yoga trick. "I won't," Elizabeth says, holding statue still—probably not an easy task.

I swallow a lump in my throat. I can't start feeling guilty now.

"Do you have any patients other than me?" Begin with one I've already figured out.

"Not at the moment."

I rock back a little on my heels, utterly shocked at her honesty. "Are you really a doctor?"

"A psychiatrist? Yes." She laughs lightly, then grimaces as her body shifts. "Trust me, med school was no walk in the park."

"Then why are you working for Reese? And don't even try to deny it," I warn. "I heard you two talking on the phone yesterday."

"Perfect. Just perfect," she grumbles, then turns her attention to me. "I'm not denying that I work *with* Reese," she says carefully, "but in the spirit of complete truth here, I don't work *for* her. We work for the Curatoria."

The unfamiliar word again. I ignore it—pretend I know exactly what it means. "Why the charade?"

"To give you a chance to heal before—"

The front door bursts open, cutting off her words. "Don't shoot!" Jay yells. "Tavia, please, you don't want to do this!"

My borrowed gun swings to Jay, then back to Elizabeth. I can feel Benson behind me, silently willing me to be cautious, but there are two of them now and I don't know who's the bigger threat.

Jay, I decide; Elizabeth's contained—at least for now, though the metal has got to start disappearing soon. I turn to face Jay as he reaches the top of the stairs.

"Don't shoot," he gasps, raising one hand, the other clutching his side. "It's just me."

As if that makes any difference.

"Mark, she knows," Elizabeth says.

Mark?

"Liz," he scolds, his eyes wary. And tired. He looks like he hasn't slept in days. I probably look the same. He glances between Elizabeth and me and I can tell he's trying desperately to catch up.

I don't intend to give him the opportunity.

"Why are you here?" I ask in a deadly whisper, taking half a step toward him, gun extended.

"Because you broke into Reese's office," Jay says, his hands raised in front of him.

"How do you know *that?*"

"There's an alarm on everything in this house, Tave. That's why both of us are here."

I grit my teeth, hating that I didn't think of that. "Why the *hell* is everything so safeguarded?"

"Well, consider—"

"Tavia?" Benson's voice interrupts me, filled with panic. My eyes dart away from Jay for a second and I see the bands holding Elizabeth beginning to dissolve.

I close my eyes and new bands form, prompting a quiet squeal of pain from Elizabeth.

"Tave, Jay!"

My gun swings back around to Jay, who apparently attempted to take advantage of my back being turned. His arm is raised, but as soon as the barrel of the gun points his way again, he mutters a curse and lets his hands fall.

Shackles form around his ankles, wrapping around the banister and pinning his feet into place.

"Come on, Tavia, this is ridiculous," Jay says, looking more annoyed than threatened by his bonds.

I set my jaw and point the gun again, hating myself for it even as I know there's nothing else to do. "Don't follow us or I'll use this . . . or worse," I add, feeling really stupid, but they seemed truly afraid of my abilities. "Come on, Benson," I say, shouldering my backpack. "We have to go *now*."

"Don't go with *him*," Elizabeth shouts. "You know who you need to find and it is not Benson!"

"I'm not listening to you anymore," I hiss at her.

"Please, Tavia, don't let him confuse you. You're meant for another. I know you can feel it."

I clap my hands over my ears and start down the stairs.

"Tavia, wait, don't leave," Jay says, and I almost turn at the panic in his voice. "My work, we've found connections between the Reduciata and the virus, and if you walk away, I'm not sure I—"

"I can't—I can't listen to either you anymore," I yell, cutting him off. "I can't believe anything you say." *And if I don't leave now, who else will arrive? How many people can I really hold off with my ephemeral magic tricks?*

I glance around the living room and kitchen as Benson and I pass through to the garage door. So many memories. Good ones. The awkward but strangely motherly moments with Reese, hilarious times with Jay when, for the first time in my life, I felt like I had a brother.

All lies.

Before anger can suffocate me, I turn my back on everything and head out to the garage, slamming the door on my old life.

As soon as I'm out of the house, I let Elizabeth's gun clatter to the cement.

Benson opens his mouth—he probably thinks we should take it with us—but I silence him with a look. I can't. I just can't. I hate being dangerous just by being me; I won't carry a weapon on top of that.

Acknowledging my refusal, he instead pulls the huge bundle of keys out of his pocket. "We've already broken and entered; how do you feel about grand theft auto?"

"You think we should take Reese's Beemer?" I ask, recognizing how ridiculous my words sound, as though *this* were the most awful thing that's happened today.

Benson swallows. "Not really. But my car's at the library, and I don't want to expose you to whatever's out there. I guess you could try to make one, but . . ."

"It'll disappear in five minutes," I say, cutting off his answer before I have to consider actually doing it.

"Right," he agrees. "Besides, it's black; it's not flashy. It'll work."

I stare at the sleek, shiny vehicle. "She's going to call the cops."

"She won't."

"It's an eighty-thousand-dollar car, Benson. Trust me—she's going to call the cops."

He turns to face me. "No. She'll chase you down on her own. And now she'll have to find a car to do it. No cops; she won't risk exposure."

"That's one hell of a gamble," I say softly.

"Let's chance the odds."

I hesitate, not wanting to hurt Reese and Jay more than I already have.

"Tavia," Benson urges, "they may have been complicit in the murder of your parents."

"Fine," I say, swallowing the pain that comes with his reminder. "But I drive." Because if someone's got to steal a car, it's going to be me.

CHAPTER TWENTY

My thoughts and I are silent for the first few minutes as we drive along. I stick to quiet neighborhood streets, avoiding anywhere people might be looking for us. For *me*.

Benson is texting someone. "My mom," he explains.

I'm already too full of guilt to feel any more.

I don't know where we're going—I decided against my earlier plan of staying at Benson's pretty quickly. All that matters now is that I'm putting some distance between us and Reese and Jay's house. *Mark and Samantha's* house, I guess. Enough distance to think, to plan. To figure out some way to keep from getting killed.

Or killing someone.

We're passing through an older neighborhood with no sign of Jay, Elizabeth, or Sunglasses Guy on our tail. I'm glad I'm busy driving; otherwise I'd be obsessively scrutinizing every house for a glowing triangle. Just as I have this thought, the street sign catches my eyes and I realize I'm about to pass Fifth. Impulsively, I stomp on the brake and swerve to the right, nearly dumping Benson into my lap.

"Jeez, a little warning next time," Benson grumbles, rubbing his side where it hit the gearshift.

"Sorry," I say, and though I really am, I'm so focused I know I don't sound genuine. I suspect the time for subtlety is long past, so I just pull up right in front of the old house and point. "Do you see that?" I ask, suppressing my nervous tension as I swing my pointer finger to the house's door.

If I didn't look like a creeper before, I do now.

"See what?" Benson asks warily.

"The triangle." It's light, but it's definitely there. "Do you see it?"

"Where?" Benson asks, squinting.

"Above the door. It's kinda gray."

He peers across my lap, then leans a little closer, pressing against me. I hold my breath.

"I . . ." He pauses, and in that second I allow myself to dream that maybe he too can make out the mysterious shape. "I don't see anything, Tave."

I swallow a lump of disappointment and silently start to pull away from the curb, but I only make it one block before I pull over again.

"You okay?" Benson asks, his fingers brushing my hand.

Tears start to sting, but I refuse to let them fall. "No . . . I'm—I'm not."

"What's the matter?" he asks gently.

My chin quivers and I clench my teeth down to make it stop. "You— you need to get out. You can walk home from here."

Benson sits back against the seat, his arms crossed over his chest, and raises one eyebrow. "Oh, really?"

"Benson, seriously, I—I have to go and you're not coming with me."

"What are you talking about?" he asks, almost icily.

"I'm running away from some kind of supernatural *mob*. You saw what I did to Elizabeth and Jay—hell, what I almost did to your room-mate. I'm crazy dangerous and you shouldn't be around *me*, much less the people who want to *kill me*."

He's quiet for a long time, then he turns his face toward me and reaches out tentatively with his hands, wrapping his long fingers around my thigh. "Look at me."

I don't want to. Don't want to feel that slow, easy comfort that's spreading from his hand on my leg. Don't want to face what it means.

Or what it might not mean.

But he's silent, waiting.

I lift my chin, trying to look tough and strong. Like I'll kick his ass if he tries to follow me. But I suspect my trembling lip ruins the effect.

"I'm not leaving you," Benson whispers. "I—I've only just come to understand what you really mean to me. I know this is dangerous." He pauses, pressing his lips together. "Probably even more dangerous than you think. But I'm coming with you."

His other hand is on my face now, cradling my cheek and forcing me to look up. I resist; keep my eyes closed. But soon I can't bear it. His blue eyes stare down at me, so steady and sure it makes the butterflies take flight in my stomach again.

"If you kick me out of this car and drive away, I will walk to the library—which is several miles away at this point, I might add—get *my* car, and drive around all day looking for you." He cracks a half smile. "Save us both the trouble, will you?"

"You don't know what you're getting into," I protest.

"I know *exactly* what I'm getting into."

He kisses me so softly, so briefly, it would be easy to deny that it hap-pened at all except that my mouth feels like it's on fire.

I pull away before I can lose my wits completely. It's not fair. "But . . . doesn't it bother you that I spend half my time thinking about Quinn? You know," I add in a mumble, "whenever I'm not thinking about you."

His face is close to mine and I know I should turn away—let him go—but after the stress of the day I crave contact. I crave *him*. His mouth closes over mine and a tiny sound escapes my throat as I curl my fingers behind his neck, pulling him closer.

"Think I'm afraid of a little competition?" he taunts playfully, pulling back ever so slightly.

"I . . ." My thoughts are a jumble of Benson and Quinn, but I close my eyes and kiss him, hold him, surrendering to the taste of him on my tongue.

A deafening noise throws us apart as something shatters through the back window, striking just behind my shoulder with a thud that reverberates through my seat.

"Go!" Benson yells, and as I peel away from the sidewalk I hear more shots ping into the body of the car, making the frame shudder as I try to keep control and stay on the correct side of the road.

Benson is on his knees, his face shielded behind the headrest, poking out to get a better look as I crazily whirl around the corner. "It's the guy from the library!" Benson yells.

"How did he find us?" I ask as I squeal the tires around another corner. "We're *miles* away!"

"I don't know. He must have . . . I don't know, tracked me to your house?" He sits back in his seat, buckling in. I don't blame him.

I take the first two turns I see—one right, one left—and hope for no dead ends.

"He may be on foot, but he's cutting through all the yards. We gotta get out of this neighborhood."

I nod and look for a good outlet.

"This guy needs to run a marathon or something. He is *fast*."

"I'm faster," I say, finally pulling onto a busy street and flooring the gas.

A minute later, Benson casts one more look over his shoulder. "He's totally out of sight now," he says, buckling his seatbelt again. "I'm pretty sure he got a damn good look at the car, though."

"So spilling coffee on him wasn't as effective as we'd hoped?" I joke, tossing one more mock-condescending look at him. Something—maybe the adrenaline—has given me both my nerve and my sense of humor back. Or maybe it's just what happens when you're behind the wheel of such a nice car.

"Guess not." Benson gives me a hint of a smirk, but he's the one who looks nervous now.

I've figured out where I am and take one more right, heading toward the interstate. "Last chance," I say as I pull to a stop at a red light less than half a mile from the freeway entrance. "This is real, Benson. And if you come with me, there's no turning back."

"There's already no turning back," he says, staring studiously out the front windshield.

"Benson?" I ask as we approach the 95. "Do you know where Camden is?" *Tiny detail.*

"Camden, Maine?"

"Is there another Camden?"

"Not that I know of. Not around here anyway."

"Then yes, that one."

"Yeah, it's this cool old town . . . probably five or six hours from here. East. Well, northeast. Along the coastline."

Perfect. "Let's start there," I say, clicking on the right-turn signal.

"How come?"

Tell no one. The words sound in my head as if Quinn was sitting in the backseat screaming them. "Just a hunch."

"They headed east," he says, standing in front of my desk. The one I despise.

I look up into my own reflection, fish-eyed in the dark glass. "Take those off; I hate when I can't see your eyes," I say sharply. As sharply as I can in a whisper.

He removes his sunglasses sheepishly. A sheep, I think acerbically. That's exactly what he is. *It's what most of these humans are. Not that it's really their fault. It's what we always wanted them to be.*

"Did you get a couple shots in?" I ask once his eyes are visible.

"Any more and I might have actually hit her."

I smile, just a little. "Perfect," I say. "Scared and on the run. Just the way I like her."

"Should I move my guys in?"

"Not yet," I say, picturing her in my mind. Panicking. Doing everything wrong. Acting like the human she still thinks she is. "Stay close—watch her." I lift one eyebrow. "Don't you want to see what happens next?"

CHAPTER TWENTY-ONE

I'm not sure why I'm not telling Benson the truth about where we're going. *Why* we're going there—aversion to drama, maybe. I hardly need
the guy I'm kissing to spend *hours* in my stolen car driving to the guy my
heart can't leave alone. Awkward silence much?

Instead, we talk about anything and everything except the last week
and Benson does a good job of distracting me when I lapse into silence
for too long. When I'm quiet, my mind races, and I can't help wondering
who—or what—I really am.

Part of me is actually relieved—relieved that Elizabeth showed up
with a gun, relieved that Sunglasses Guy tried to kill me—because it
means I'm not crazy. On the other hand, today I put my therapist and
guardian in chains and stole a car to get away from them. There's something inside me that knows how to do that. Something I don't understand—a person I don't know. It makes me question everything—my
life, myself, my memories. How much of my life has been a lie? Am *I* a
lie?

But a light touch of Benson's fingers against my hand, a lame joke,
pointing out a funny billboard—those pull me back into the now. Once

I get out of this car, I'll have to think about the disaster of my life. But until then, Benson and I laugh, and talk, and tease, wrapped up in a small, four-door-sedan world of our own.

Due to construction and traffic, five or six hours turn into eight. Every time we have to slow down, I find myself drumming my fingers impatiently on the steering wheel. Benson's been keeping a watch out the back windshield and, as far as we can tell, no one's tailing us. With that worry at least temporarily assuaged, all I can think of is getting there.

Camden means Quinn.

And Quinn means answers.

I'm not sure which one I'm more anxious for. I can't give up the idea of being with Quinn despite the last two days with Benson. Quinn makes me feel alive in a way I haven't experienced since the plane crash, like a part of me has lain dormant and only he can bring it back into existence.

And there's that familiarity. I can't shake it.

Hopefully once we find him in Camden, I can sort it out. Maybe I do know him. Maybe I've *always* known him.

Regardless, he'll have the answers. I *have* to believe that.

Jay has tried to call four times. Well, four times before I turned my phone off. I wonder if I need to get rid of it. I hate feeling like I have no good choices. And I hate that I can't trust Jay. I guess I really was clinging to that thread of hope that it was only Reese and Elizabeth who were involved—that Jay was as clueless as me.

After what feels like an eternity, Benson and I pull into Camden about the time everyone is closing their stores and heading home.

The buildings are all old and fairly short, two floors at the most, and there isn't a chain store in sight. But neither are there the bright storefronts I'm used to seeing in Portsmouth. Everything has a tidy-but-subdued brick-red hue about it. It's like the whole town got lifted out of the 1950s. Trees shade clean sidewalks, and all around me shopkeepers are sweeping their walks or pulling in sandwich boards so they can lock up. The closed shops are free of metal grilles, lending the impression that nothing bad ever happens here.

Maybe it doesn't. Maybe that's why Quinn sent me.

Quaint, I decide. *And classic.* If I was here for a different reason, I'd probably start scouring the city for interesting houses and historic markers, the way I did in Portsmouth. But if I should be seeing something special here, we haven't reached it yet. Quinn seemed to think I would know exactly what he was talking about when he told me to come here.

Have I been here before?

It doesn't feel familiar. I scan the shops around me, looking for symbols, but I don't see anything like that, either—though, with as dark as it is already, I might have to check again when the sun's up.

"We need gas again," I say, peering at the gauge.

"I'll get it this time," Benson says as we pull into a faded gas station. He gets out of the car and walks around to the pump.

"What are we going to do when we're out of gas money?" I ask as we both watch the dollar signs click up.

"I have a credit card," Benson says, nonchalant, but I can tell he's concerned too.

"Can't they track those things?" I sigh and lean against the driver's-side door.

"There's another option, Tave . . ." Benson begins hesitantly, and I know what he's going to say. I've been avoiding this conversation since I realized how little cash I had back at Reese and Jay's.

"If we do get desperate, couldn't you just . . . you know?"

"It disappears in five minutes, Benson. It's still stealing."

"I did say desperate. I'm not talking about now."

I look down at my shoes as Benson replaces the gas nozzle after the tank is full. Full of gas he paid for from his own—likely meager—student funds. For me.

"It's not really even the stealing," I blurt, and considering the ownership status of the vehicle we're both leaning against, I think the clarification is necessary. "Everything began when I started using my . . . powers—whatever you want to call it. Even before I knew what I was doing. Like with the ChapStick. Everything has gone to hell since then. Not you, obviously, but pretty much everything else. I just don't think it's a good idea to use my *talent*"—I whisper the word—"unless we have no other choice. It's unpredictable and *dangerous*."

"It's your call," Benson says, draping his arm lightly around my shoulders. "I won't push you." He glances around the gas station parking lot, then leans close. "Let's get out of here, though. I don't like being out in public when, for all we know, our names and faces could be on the evening news."

I sigh, hating that appearing on someone's Most Wanted list seems an only too likely ending to our little "adventure."

"You want me to drive a bit?" Benson asks, and the cramps in my legs insist I accept his offer. He gets into the driver's seat and looks at me for a minute before I realize he's waiting for me to give him directions.

But I don't have any. Now that we're here, his guess is as good as mine. Eventually he pulls back onto the road and continues in the direction we'd been going.

Within a few minutes, I realize that the last two houses we passed were a good two blocks apart and there's nothing in sight ahead of us. We were *in* the town, and then rather abruptly, we were *out* of it. "Uh, Benson?"

"Yeah?"

"I don't think we're in Camden anymore."

He looks around at the thick grass on either side of the road and the dense forest beyond, outside the range of our headlights. "I guess that was it," he says, sounding uncertain for the first time since he decided to come with me.

"What do we do now?"

He looks over. "You're the one who wanted to come. I thought you had a plan."

"Not really," I say, suddenly interested in the scenery outside the window.

"Well, we can't just leave, right?"

"I don't think so."

His eyebrows scrunch up for a few seconds, then he turns on the blinker and steers carefully onto a dirt road.

"What's down here?"

"A hiding place for the night," Benson says, peering into the rearview. He pulls Reese's car off the dirt road and right up alongside a copse of trees. "There was no one in sight behind us, and the trees will hide us from cars on the road."

"Do you think the guy with the gun is still following us?"

He's quiet for long seconds that tick off in my head. "I think anyone who's motivated enough to shoot a gun at someone isn't going to give up without a damn good fight," he says in a steady, even tone that makes fear ripple through my whole body. "But after everything that's happened today, I'm exhausted. And if you actually let yourself feel anything for a minute, I bet you are, too."

I don't have the energy to try to argue with the obvious.

"If we don't sleep, we'll be useless tomorrow, and that's no way to outrun someone who wants to kill you," he says, more gently this time, lifting a hand to stroke my face.

I look down at the backpack between my feet and realize what I forgot—pillows, blankets. I didn't exactly have much time to plan. "We have to turn the car off, don't we?"

"Can't waste the gas."

"It'll get cold."

"Our body heat will keep the small space warm enough."

I nod, numbly. I'll be the first one to admit that I wasn't feeling very optimistic about my life this morning, but even I didn't expect to be spending the night in a stolen car, in the middle of nowhere, wondering if I'd be warm enough to sleep at all.

Benson gives me dibs and I go for the passenger seat laid down almost flat while he stretches across the back, his body perpendicular to mine. He's right—even wrapped in a coat I'm starting to feel his body heat rise from where he lies, inches from my face.

Making me feel rather *un*-sleepy.

"Everything will look better in the morning," he mumbles, half-asleep already.

"Certainly couldn't look worse," I whisper, but quietly enough that he can't hear me.

After Benson's breathing deepens and slows, I let the tears come. *Quinn!* I shout in my mind. *I'm here—I did what you said. Where are you?*

CHAPTER TWENTY-TWO

I don't expect to fall asleep quickly; I figure I'll spend hours drowning in fruitless self-pity. Not to mention the general discomfort of sleeping in a car. A *cold* car. But when my eyelashes flutter open to show me a snow-blanketed forest lit by an unearthly glow, I know I must be dreaming. A glance down at the gorgeous gown that swirls around my legs in glistening silver folds confirms it.

I walk aimlessly through the sparse forest, snowflakes dotting my skin with a burst of chill against my otherwise warm body. The wide train of the dress skims the powdered snow behind me, leaving a shallow trail that curls through the trees as I circle and weave, not hurried, but looking for something.

His profile is the first thing I see. As always, his hair is pulled back at the nape of his neck, though a few tendrils lie in wispy streaks on his tanned cheeks. A cloak covers his shoulders, veiling his body in a blackness that almost blends in with the tree he's leaning against. He turns his head and leaf-green eyes meet mine. My chest convulses and I suck in a gasp of air at the sight of him. His eyes look through me, into me, seeing my soul. After a moment of contemplation—as if discovering something inside me that surprised him—his face relaxes into a smile. He holds out one gloved hand, and as his fingers come together, a bloodred rose appears between them.

"I knew you would come to me."

Quinn's words break an unseen barrier and I'm running, my bare feet silent in the soft snowfall. The rose drops to the ground when his arms stretch out, a mirror to my own as we reach.

Reach.

Reach.

My body slams into his warm chest and his hands are on my cheeks, pulling me near, grasping at the back of my neck. I don't have time to raise my eyelids before his mouth finds mine, his lips soft. It's as though a dam has broken inside us and every longing, every moment of wishing, is released. Fingertips graze down my sides, then curl behind my back, pulling me in harder, closer. I grasp his shirt, thin white linen beneath his cloak, and pull him down.

Or maybe I'm lifting myself up.

Whatever it takes to be nearer. As near as two souls can be without blending into one. His lips leave my mouth, and before I can make a sound of protest they find my neck, the hollow of my pulse. My fingers run through his hair and I tug the hair tie away so the strands tumble around my hand, silk against my skin, as good as I knew it would feel.

With a reluctant growl Quinn pulls back. His hands cup my face and his eyes bore into mine. "I have things to show you," he says, and my whole body stills at the seriousness laced through his words.

"Then show me," I whisper with greater effort than I think it should take. My words are a puff of mist in the air that hangs unnaturally between us for a few seconds before an errant wind blows it away.

Quinn draws me back against him and his mouth settles near my cheek. "I have things to show you," he whispers again, his lips brushing the tips of my ear, making a shiver course down my spine.

Then he pulls back and there's a strange shadow in his eyes. His arms fall from my waist and he takes a few steps backward.

Then he turns.

And walks away.

"Quinn?" The words are a whisper. It's *my* dream; he can't walk away. "Quinn?" Louder now, my voice echoes off the trees, making the icicles rattle. "Quinn!" The trees shake at my piercing cry; the icicles clatter to the ground. I lift my skirts and try to run after him, but the forest is darkening around me and soon I can't see anything.

I fling my arms out in front of me and grope through the darkness, my palms scraping painfully against blade-sharp bark each time I find a tree. Soon I can feel blood running down my arms, warm and thick.

Over and over I call his name, knowing somehow that if I can just find him, I can escape this darkness. The cold that was unable to touch me just minutes ago sears into my bones, and soon I stagger and fall.

Then the snow collapses beneath me and the cold multiplies drastically. I flail about, and as I lift my face heavenward, I realize I'm back in the drowning dream. The icy water cuts to my bones as blackness closes over my head.

Quinn . . . Quinn . . . My thoughts get quieter as pain envelops me and I let go.

I clap my hand over a scream as I try to make out my dark, unfamiliar surroundings.

Reese's BMW.

I'm safe.

I'm *alive.*

Settling back against the seat, I lie in the darkness as waves of emotion wash over me, swirling into eddies that shake my body from within. Fear, longing, and desperation in an overwhelming blend.

Not simply desperation for Quinn, but for answers, explanations. I know nothing, and it traps me as surely as an iron chain.

Outside the car, something flutters in the darkness. The windows are fogged from the heat of our bodies, and I lift my sleeve to clear a circle in the misty glass.

Something moves.

They found me! My entire body tenses up and I'm about to elbow Benson awake when I see a flash of golden hair.

"Quinn." The real Quinn. His name escapes my mouth in a barely audible whisper as he draws nearer.

He's close to the window now, his eyes boring into mine. He crooks his finger at me and then turns and walks out of sight.

I click the door locks, and the sound seems deafening in the quiet interior. Thankfully, Benson doesn't stir. I try to slip out without waking him, but as soon as the door opens, light from the dome floods the car. "What's wrong?" he asks in a scratchy voice, pushing up on his elbows.

"Gotta pee," I lie. "Go back to sleep."

Benson's eyes are already closing as I slip out, the cold air hitting me like a slap after the warmth of our bodies in the car. It's snowing hard, and the world around me has that intense hush that only heavy, powdery snowfall brings.

I clasp my arms around myself and peer into the darkness, through the huge lacy flakes, but I don't see Quinn.

I hope I'm not making a mistake. Quinn wouldn't lure me out into danger, though; I *know* it! Nonetheless, I peer into the darkness around me and my chest is tight as I see nothing but stillness.

I glance back at the car. Benson will worry if I'm gone long. Determined to get my answers as quickly as possible, I take off in the direction I think Quinn went. The snow is already an inch or two deep and I look down at my tracks. I can follow them back if I'm fast.

My head is low, studying the camouflaged ground, when I hear it. "Miss. Miss?"

Miss? My head whips around, and for a moment I see nothing. Then a flicker of movement in the trees makes my heart race. A face emerges and, if anything, my pulse speeds even faster.

He's beautiful in the moonlight, a dark, snow-spotted coat wrapping him from his neck to his ankles, his face soft and almost expressionless.

"I knew you would come to me."

The wind carries the soft words to my ears, and for a moment I think I'm back in my dream. He lifts his hands as though to reach for me—exactly like he did in the dream—and I have to stop myself from running to him, from burrowing into his arms with the same abandon I felt in that illusionary forest.

When I hesitate, he lets his hands fall and the moment is gone.

Why *didn't* I go to him? I'm not sure I know the answer.

Quinn turns his head before I can see if there's disappointment in his eyes.

"I . . . I dreamed about you." My words are a low murmur, but they sound loud in the stillness around us. "But you already know that, don't you?"

His jaw tightens. Answer enough.

"You made a rose in my dream," I say, and my chest is tight in anticipation. "You're like me. You . . . you make things."

Again he doesn't answer, but I'm sure I'm right.

"Quinn, please, what am I? What are *we*?" The word *Earthbound* flashes through my head again, but it brings more questions than answers.

"I have things to show you," he says simply. "This way." He turns and heads directly into the woods without looking back to see if I'm following.

The same words. That weird cadence. *I have things to show you.* Not *I have something to show you.* I hesitate before I step into the spidery shadows of the branchless trees. It's like every horror movie I've ever seen. The kind where the stupid girl ends up dead.

But isn't this what I wanted? Didn't I drive all the way up here to find him?

I search my feelings, straining for something—a sign, an omen, I don't know—but even though my head is spinning and my fingertips tingle, it's with anticipation, not fear.

With one more glance at the dark car where Benson still sleeps, I pull out my phone and turn it on. Four new messages: three from Jay and one from an unknown number. I close the notification and activate the flashlight feature before plunging into the blackness of the forest, following Quinn. Remembering the darkness in the dream, I rub my arms and shiver.

Quinn is like a will-o'-the-wisp, always ten feet ahead no matter how fast or slow I walk. I've given up trying to catch him; it only makes him go faster. Better to focus on not running into bushes or low-hanging branches—I already have one stinging scrape on my cheek.

The fear I pushed away when I started following Quinn is back.

Even if Quinn won't hurt me, I'm completely exposed. Not to mention that I've left Benson totally unprotected. If anyone found the car—Sunglasses Guy, Elizabeth, hell, who *knows* how many people are looking for me—they could easily off Benson and then put a bullet in my head from behind.

Worst of all, in this forest, my body might never be found.

The thought sends a new chill up my spine and I clench my fists and force myself to pick up the pace. It's too late to turn back—I'm just going to have to deal with the consequences.

CHAPTER TWENTY-THREE

We walk—Quinn heading roughly back in the direction of Camden, but still deep within the trees—for what feels like hours. With nearly numb fingers I check the time on my phone.

I left the car almost an hour ago. I'm so cold I can hardly move my toes, and it's snowing hard enough I can barely see Quinn just a few feet in front of me.

"Quinn," I call softly, jogging forward to try to catch up with him yet again. "I can't go on much longer," I say, surprised when he lets me draw close. "How far is it?"

But he's silent, still. I look around, my light flashing narrow beams over the dense forest. We've got to be almost two miles from the car, but other than that, I have *no* idea where I am. I try not to think about how cold I'm going to be by the time I get back.

Or how far up the sun will be.

"There are people—" I stagger and have to take a second to right myself. "People following me. *Shooting* at me. I can't just wander off like this. My . . . friend Benson is still back at the car. Quinn!" I whisper-yell, but my voice is muffled by the fresh powder.

A mound of earth covered in snow, with withered grass barely poking up through it, catches my attention as my light skims over it, and even as I take a step toward it, Quinn is moving with me.

"This way," he whispers. He gestures to the small hill and I walk, leaves and snow crunching beneath my feet.

Suddenly my feet break through some kind of weedy covering and I fall on my butt, with my legs sunk to my knees in foliage.

"I crafted these steps specifically to blend in." Quinn's voice is quiet above me.

"Well, thanks for the warning," I mutter, the cold taking its toll on my attitude. I can already feel the soft snow melting through my jeans, soaking my underwear. Fabulous. This midnight stroll had better lead somewhere good. My patience is past the *wearing thin* point, and hypothermia is not going to improve my mood.

Quinn says nothing, just looks off into the distance as I clear away enough debris to make my way down six stone steps that end in front of a weather-worn door that looks like it was laid right against the hill. *Shelter, finally.*

I pause as something prickles at my awareness. I study the door and the stairs, covered with old leaves and sticks. Despite knowing where this place is, Quinn hasn't actually come down these steps. At least not recently. You can't fake this kind of overgrowth. "Why didn't you come here before?" I ask, staring at an elaborate locking mechanism. "Maybe clear things away before you came to get me?"

"I was waiting for you."

I give myself a moment to stare back, to let that liquid heat in his gaze slip into me and warm my chest. Just for a moment—I'm so cold—then I turn regretfully away and try to open the round latch.

"It's locked." I wonder if this whole trip was for nothing and try to tamp down my frustration.

"You can unlock it. Anytime you desire."

"How about now?" I mutter. My toes and fingers are starting to ache and I wish I could get out of the wind, even for just a few minutes. I'm wondering briefly if I can simply *make* heat, or maybe just something that produces heat, but I shy away from the idea. I'm not desperate yet; and with my track record I'd probably burn down the whole forest, and Camden with it. Quinn's voice breaks into my dreary thoughts.

"I'll talk you through it this time, Becca."

"Tavia!" I correct through chattering teeth, wanting to lash out at him. I laid my very *life* on the line to get to him—not to mention Benson's—and he calls me the wrong name. I fight down the urge to just leave. But then this whole escapade really would be a complete waste. I *need* to know what's behind this door. But frustration simmers in the back of my head.

More than simmers. *Boils.*

Maybe *that* will keep me warm.

"See the four pegs?" he asks.

I look down and notice that there are four iron pegs in a deep niche just above the strange lock. I blow on my hands to warm them, then reach for the pegs. They're the same width, but each one is a different length. I crouch down beside the door and shine my light. There are six holes in the lock, just the right size for the pegs.

"The longest goes in the third one down," Quinn says, and I fumble for the pegs, slipping the longest into the small hole, having to jiggle it a little before it snaps into place.

Quinn talks me through the next three pegs and when they're all in, I grasp a large knob and turn it clockwise until I hear something metal click. My hands touch the surface of the door but are so numb I don't feel anything.

I push, but nothing happens. In the end I have to ram my shoulder against the door before it pops open a few inches with a squeal that cuts the silent night air. I try not to consider all the people who could have heard that who would love to kill me right now.

When I glance back, Quinn doesn't look nearly as nervous as me, but then, *he* knows what's going on. Freed from the time-shrunken door frame, the ancient door swings on its squeaky iron hinges. The sound grates in my eardrums and I open it just enough for Quinn and me to slip through.

The scent of mold and paper and damp dirt hits my nose in a pungent wave. I gag and then cough as I pull in another lungful of the musty air and remind myself how glad I am to be out of the falling snow and swirling wind. I flash my light around, but the beam is too small to make out much. Crates, mostly. What look like books bound in thick brown paper but torn through on the corners. Chewed through, maybe.

Don't even think about that.

Or the fact that my phone's battery is going to give out any minute. Maybe I could *make* a flashlight? Do I know how to make a flashlight? I grit my teeth—I'll cross that bridge when I come to it. Hopefully I won't have to.

There's a long wooden table, covered with grainy clumps of dirt—probably from the root-braided ceiling—strewn with papers and several items I'm not close enough to identify, like whoever made the place left in a hurry. I step forward, my feet silent in the warm, soft-floored burrow.

A book, several scattered bits of paper, some pieces of tarnished silver jewelry. Coins.

Coins?

I squint at them, then pick one up. The metal is heavy in my hand. Solid gold. I don't think these are actual money, but I feel like a thief even touching one. The ice-cold surface seems to burn into my palm.

I set it back down and turn to the open book instead.

It's covered with the same layer of dirt as the rest of the table, and I lean closer to flick the rubble away from one of the pages, trying not to smudge it into the fragile paper. I wish I had some kind of brush or cloth.

My light shines near my fingers and my mind catches several of the words before I've cleared them.

Like you this way.

A tingle of warning jets through my belly and I hold my breath, trying not to show any kind of reaction as I clear more of the dirt away, my eyes straining to read the faded, curlicued cursive.

Before I could stop him, he touched my cheek and whispered, "You're beautiful, you know that? I like you this way." Never has a man spoken to me thusly!

My breathing is ragged and tight, but my eyes are already darting ahead.

Especially not Mr. Quinn Avery, whom every girl in town is pining for, though he be only a newcomer. I should have struck his face, walked away, shamed him. But I only stood, as though spelled there. Mayhap I was. Spelled by those green eyes.

I refuse to look back at Quinn—it can't possibly actually be his name, not after this. Pretending I saw nothing, I gingerly flip the pages, looking for the title page.

I know what I'm going to find, but I need one more scrap of proof. My fingers are shaking as I turn to that front page and read the name etched there.

Rebecca Fielding.

Becca.

I whirl around to face Quinn before he can do whatever sinister thing he has planned, my phone held up like a weapon. But my beam of light shows an empty space where Quinn was standing. I haven't decided if he's a run-of-the-mill stalker/murderer, or maybe in league with Sunglasses Guy and whoever else is chasing me, but I am *not* waiting for him to come back.

Sweeping up the journal, I run for the entrance, bursting out without bothering to close the door. I have to get to Benson!

I stop.

My footprints are completely gone.

A good couple of inches of unbroken snow has covered everything in the brief time I was in the dugout and now I have nothing to follow. I'm disoriented, but I have a fuzzy sense of which direction we came in. As long as I keep running that way, I should—at worst—pop out on the main road.

I'll be able to find Benson from there. Hopefully, before I freeze to death. And before the people hunting us find *me*.

I don't even know which people that means anymore.

My ears strain for the sound of footsteps behind me as I tear through the forest, not bothering to keep quiet. My leg throbs and my lungs ache from the frosty air, and it's all I can do to keep running at all. The snowflakes sting my already-freezing face and blur the forest all around me until I feel like I'm running in circles.

Maybe I am.

Gratitude fills me when I see lights peeking between the tall tree trunks, and in a shorter amount of time than I thought possible, I'm back on the road.

But I'm not safe.

I'm on the wrong side of Camden; that's why I got to the road so quickly. In order to reach Benson, I'm going to have to go all the way through the middle of the city.

There's no other option. I have to keep running.

It's past two in the morning now and the streets are full of ghostly silence and a few drunk people, probably wending their way back to chintzy bed-and-breakfasts. I stand out, I'm sure. But I suspect no one will stop me unless they see a tall guy in Revolutionary War era clothing chasing me.

And then *he'll* be caught.

And he won't be able to bother me again.

I hate that tears are streaking down my face, making icy lines along my cheekbones. I was so certain—every instinct within me screamed that I could trust Quinn. It's bad enough when you can't trust your family or your therapist. Now I can't even trust myself.

Maybe I never could.

My body is so exhausted I can barely see when I finally get to the other side of the town. The sidewalk ends and turns into a crumbly shoulder thick with wet mounds of new snow and my feet skid out from under me. I can't think of a word bad enough to express the agony that shoots up my hip when I land hard on my side, so I clamp my teeth down against a weak whimper instead. I take one second—maybe only half a second—to sweep my eyes back, peering into the flake-speckled darkness behind me.

A hint of movement.

Quinn?

I don't know, but I'm on my feet and running again before my mind can process whatever my eyes did or didn't see.

Finally I reach the road where we parked the car. Every muscle in my body hurts, and my hands are so numb they can hardly grip the keys as I dig them out of my pocket. I throw the door open and crash into the driver's seat, my finger instantly pushing the lock button. I'm still fumbling the keys into the ignition when Benson's voice reaches my ears.

"What's wrong?" he demands, not sounding particularly sleepy. "What happened?"

"Quinn found me; we're leaving."

"Quinn? But you"—he hesitates, then adds in a small voice—"you came here because of Quinn; you . . . you like him."

"Not anymore," I say, but the pain in my chest calls me a liar.

My lungs burn and my leg muscles complain as I press on the gas pedal, forcing myself to stay within the speed limit, grateful to be alive.

I should never have come to Camden. I'm so stupid. Quinn's never been trustworthy—never given me the time of day. Why did I think this time would be different?

My entire body is filled with the deepest, most mournful sorrow I've ever experienced. Somehow worse even than the moment I realized my parents were dead. The world swirls around me and I want to scream, to curse the universe for taking him from me, just as I was getting a taste.

I want to cry, but I'm past the point.

He's gone.

I'm alone.

And a part of my heart I never knew shatters.

CHAPTER TWENTY-FOUR

I focus on the news on the television the next morning. Anything to keep from looking at Benson. There are more victims of the mystery virus—these ones in a small town in Texas. It makes me think of Jay. Mark. Whatever the hell his name actually is. I wonder briefly if he really was working on the virus or if that was a lie too.

"We can find no connection between the victims or their towns. No common threads whatsoever," the reporter says, staring into the camera like this is the most important story in history.

Who knows, maybe it is.

I flinch as the chime on the front door dings, and I try to turn and look without being too obvious. Just some guy in Wranglers. His eyes drift by me before his face lights up and he waves at a woman waiting in a booth.

I let myself breathe again.

"Okay. I'm done," Benson says, smacking his hand down on the table.

I jump at the noise, nearly spilling my tea.

"Tave," Benson says, softer now. Probably because everyone in the dinky little restaurant is looking at us. Waitresses included. The whole restaurant is way too intimate for my taste—it's like one of those diners you see in old movies, the tables so close together that you can just turn your head and join in someone else's conversation.

Which I have no doubt happens frequently.

I'm not sure what town we're in. Last night I just drove until I felt safe. Not *safe*, but safe enough to sleep.

For a little while. As much as one can in wet jeans.

Benson didn't ask questions, but I had the sinking feeling he hadn't actually slept much while I was gone.

And judging by the shifting of our bodies once I found a new place to park, neither of us slept much in the wee hours of the morning, either.

When the sun came up, I could see I had brought us to another oldish town like Camden—a throwback to the fifties with the addition of smart phones. I think they do it on purpose, actually—bright storefronts, rocking chairs in front of the shops. I even saw a guy sweeping his sidewalk.

The people here look set in their ways, and I bet most of them don't even have to order their breakfast anymore. *My regular, Flo*, I can hear them saying in my head. And she just nods and brings it out because the cook already had it made.

"Please, talk to me." Benson reaches for my hand.

I flinch away before my weary mind comes back to the present.

"I haven't pushed; I've tried to give you space. I haven't asked any of the *million* questions I have about everything we learned yesterday. But *you* brought us out to Camden, and don't try to tell me that was some random decision," he says, cutting off a protest I didn't even have the energy to make. "I know it had something to do with Quinn. So I waited; I trusted that you had a reason not to tell me. Then you snuck off in the middle of the night under the pretense of a bathroom break and came back *two hours later*—yes, I noticed and worried about you every second since by the time I realized you were not, in fact, peeing, I couldn't follow you—covered in snow and half frozen and said you found Quinn and you don't like him anymore—which, just so you know, I'm totally in support of—and proceeded to drive like a crazy person for two hours and then conk out in the front seat in some waffle place parking lot in the middle of nowhere without saying a word. Talk, Maple Bar."

I have to smile a little at his pastry nickname.

"There we go," he whispers, touching my bottom lip. "Come on. You'll feel better if you tell me." I feel his fingertip rub under my eye, and it's the first time I notice there are tears rolling down my cheeks.

Benson hesitates for a moment, then scoots off the bench and comes over to my side of the booth and wraps both arms around me, squeezing me tight against him.

"Go ahead, cry it out. My shirt needs to be washed anyway."

I giggle and hiccup, and that just makes me laugh and cry all at the same time. For a few minutes we sit, my face buried against Benson's shoulder, his arms tight around me. "You must think I'm so stupid."

"Nah," he says, trying to tuck a strand of hair behind my ear, but it's still too short to stay. "People do irrational things for the people they love all the time." He pauses, then adds in a whisper, "Really stupid things." I look up when he stops speaking, but after a few seconds he squishes me a little harder.

I give him a sort-of smile, but I don't really feel it. When I woke up this morning, curled unnaturally into the front seat with my knees braced against the steering wheel, every muscle in my body ached. On top of that, now I have a long scab across my face from a tree branch. My legs are sore from running and my arms from simply being terrified.

But it balances out the numbness that has enveloped me on the inside.

"You were right," I whisper against the soft fabric of his jacket. "About Quinn, I mean. He's—he's dangerous and obsessed and . . . and . . . you were right."

His hands are suddenly tight on my arms. "Did he hurt you?" he asks, eyes flashing fire. "Did he lay a single finger on you? I'll kill the bastard!"

"No, no," I say before he can get any louder. "I'm fine. I promise. I just . . ."

"Do we need to call the cops?"

I feel tears build as Quinn's betrayal sweeps through me again, but I push them back—I will *not* shed another tear over him. "No. Technically he didn't do anything. And I have nothing to tell them even if he did. His name's not even Quinn. Everything he ever told me is a lie."

"Tavia, seriously, did he hurt you?"

"He never touched me. He just led me to this old . . . cellar, I guess. It was kind of hidden."

"A hidden cellar?" Benson asks, not exactly disbelieving, but there's a hint of that.

I open my backpack and, after a quick look around, pull out the ancient journal.

An impressed whistle escapes Benson's mouth as he reaches for the book. "You're good," he says, smiling in earnest now, and I feel a faint glow at his compliment. I crave his approval, though I'm not sure quite why. Maybe I just need *someone* to believe I'm not out of my mind.

Just psychic.

And magic.

And something called an Earthbound.

I'm *so* in over my head.

"This is seriously impressive." Benson flips through the pages, and something clanks onto the table.

"Holy crap," I say, picking up the gold coin. "I didn't mean to take this."

"Is that . . . ?" Benson's eyes shoot up to mine.

"I think so."

He holds it up, turning it and watching the light glint off it. "Is it really awful if we keep this?" he asks, his voice tense.

"I am *not* taking it back," I say. "I'm never going there again."

"Ten tanks of gas," Benson says, pocketing the coin and turning his attention back to the journal. "So this was just sitting in there?"

"Whoa! Benson, look!" I close the journal, and on the front cover is a triangle, each side at least six inches long. "You can see *that*, right?" I ask, a little paranoid.

"Yeah," Benson says quietly. "The triangle; I can see this one."

I trace the small indentation with my finger, going around all three sides. A strange flicker crosses my vision and I see another hand following my fingers.

But I blink, and it's gone.

Holding back a sigh at yet another disappearing image, I flip to the front of the journal. "Right before we went in, he called me Becca."

"Rebecca Fielding," Benson says softly, his eyes on the curly script. "1804."

I skim the book in silence, Benson giving me peace. The darkness inside my chest spreads as I find more and more familiar words. "It's all in here," I say, paging carefully through the book, each new entry making the waffles I just ate feel heavier and heavier in my stomach. "Everything he ever said to me. Look, here she talks about how he had *things to show her*. Here he asks her to trust him. How he messed everything up and frightened her. And this part"—I point at the book—"this is the part I read last night. It's word for word what he said to me. He's obsessed with this dead Rebecca and trying to reenact his sick fantasies with modern-day girls. With . . . with *me*. But there could be others. He could be a freaking serial killer!"

A hard look is pasted on Benson's face as he leans over the book. "This is so weird," he says.

I flip back toward the beginning and a name catches my eye. "Benson!" I can feel all the blood draining from my face as I read the passage.

"What?" he asks, leaning over the page and looking where I'm point-ing, his vague expression indicating that he doesn't see what I'm so upset about.

"It says she first saw him when she was walking past his house, and he was minding his little sister."

Benson is trying really hard, but his face is completely blank.

"There was a little girl with Quinn when *I* first saw him! In Ports-mouth, a few days ago. Do . . . do you think he kidnapped her?" My heart is beating wildly as I wonder just how major of a psychopath I've run into.

"There's no way," Benson says. "I don't know how he got that girl to play the part, but we'd have heard something on the news if a little girl was missing."

It makes sense, and I try to latch onto Benson's confidence to calm myself. "But the house was gone too," I think aloud. "When I went back, it wasn't there anymore. It *wasn't real*. Maybe the little girl wasn't real either."

"Maybe this Quinn guy isn't real," Benson says, and there's a low simmer of hostility in his tone.

"No," I say dismissively, still focused on the words in the journal. "He talks to me. He got that door open in the dugout. *He* is definitely real."

"The journal's real too," Benson says. "Not just physically real," he adds, rapping a knuckle softly against the cover. "It appears to be authentic. Do you think Quinn just stumbled onto it somewhere?"

"I don't know," I admit in a small voice. "Honestly, I haven't had the time or energy to think of anything except that I was a complete moron."

"No," Benson says, rubbing a hand on my arm. "People like this are always über-charismatic and nice and all that. I mean, come on, every time a serial killer gets caught, what do the neighbors say? *Oh, he was such a nice guy.*"

"You're not making me feel better," I mutter, laying my head down on the table.

"Point is, it's not your fault he's a creeper; it's his."

Mentally, I know it's true, but I don't feel that way.

"So . . . it looks like maybe Quinn has nothing to do with . . . the . . . the Earthbound thing?" he asks hesitantly.

I stare at him, uncomprehending for a moment. "Oh, right," I say, feeling even more defeated. "The fact that I can create matter out of thin air just got bumped down to second on the list of drama in my life. Fabulous." I clasp my hands in front of me. "But no. I think he's like me, Benson. I think he can do what I can do. At the very least he knows about it."

"You talked to him about it?"

"Sort of. Do you think he's working with Sunglasses Guy?"

"Dragging you out somewhere alone in the middle of a snowy night and abandoning you? Whether he's working for that guy or not, I think we can assume he is some seriously bad news, Tave."

I let my head fall onto my arms. "No kidding," I mutter. I feel like such a complete moron.

Benson rocks back and forth a few times. "Maybe we should look up Rebecca and the original Quinn. On microfiche." Benson continues with an eyebrow raised, "Though considering the era, we're likely to find more on Quinn than Rebecca."

"Why?"

"Because he was a man," Benson says dryly.

"True."

He leans his head close over the table and grins. "Surely along with the chipper attitudes and polyester pants, we could find a library around here somewhere."

I nod stoically. "Okay, let's do it."

He scoots out from the booth and holds out a hand for me. I wince as I stand, and Benson's hands go to my waist. "Are you sure you're okay?" he asks. "You look like you're hurting."

"I'll heal," I tell him. And I hope it's true. My bruises will go away, but I can't imagine ever losing this amazing but terrible compulsion I feel toward Quinn. I take one more look up at the television, where the reporter is still going on and on about the virus. She looks at the camera, her face so serious it borders on grave.

And then flickers.

I gasp aloud and Benson looks back at me.

Along with half the restaurant.

"Did you see that? She flickered."

About ten heads turn to the TV.

"Were you watching?" I ask an older woman sitting close to me. "Did you see her flicker?"

"Well, sometimes the service isn't perfect. But Flo gives us the television for free, so I don't think you should be complaining."

"Not the television, the woman. The reporter." My head is screaming at me to keep my mouth shut—to avoid looking crazier than I am and, at the very least, to not make a scene. But now that I've started talking, I can't seem to stop. "The woman, not the scene behind her, just the woman. She was gone for just a second. You didn't see it?"

I look around me. Forget half, now *everyone* in the restaurant is staring.

"Tave, we gotta go." Benson's voice finally breaks through, and I duck my head and turn in the direction he's leading me. He keeps one hand at my elbow and escorts me around to the car. "What was that?" he asks when we're finally out of earshot.

"The reporter, she flickered. Just like the lady who gave me the Band-Aid and the guy at the candy store. No one sees it except me."

Benson purses his lips and studies me for a long moment. "We need to get out of here. We have to assume that if Quinn knows we were in Camden last night, other people do too. We have to keep moving."

I nod, not sure if Benson doesn't believe me or if he's just as bewildered as I am. "Can you drive for a bit?" I ask.

"Drive the Beemer again? I'm afraid you're going to have to twist my arm," he says, grinning.

I roll my eyes as we both get in. I guess I shouldn't be surprise that even in the face of death and magic and mystery, boys still like their fancy cars.

CHAPTER TWENTY-FIVE

"Hey, Baklava, we're here," Benson says, poking my ribs.

I must have fallen asleep. "Did you seriously just call me Baklava?" I grumble, throwing my arm over my eyes as I blink against the midday sunlight.

"Don't sweat the small stuff—I found a library."

I grumble something that was probably better unheard.

"Your phone rang a bunch of times while we were driving," Benson says, ignoring my mutterings. "I couldn't get it out of your pocket to turn it off."

And I was apparently so zonked I didn't even hear it. I take my phone out and check the screen.

Six missed calls.

"Jay," I mutter as I shove it back into my pocket. "The man doesn't give up."

Once inside, we make our way to the microfiche lab and I realize I feel better already. Benson is someone who's proved I can trust him, and a library—even a new one—feels like a safe haven. While I'm here, with him, I can deal.

As Benson predicted, when we look up the names in the database, there's one reference to a Rebecca Fielding, and seven to Quinn Avery.

"*Captain* Quinn Avery," Benson says. "Looks like he owned some kind of boat." He writes down some references, then starts pulling tiny films out of file cabinets with a practiced efficiency. "Here," he says, handing me the first film. "You start while I pull the others."

Library nerds are the best.

"There's a whole story on him," I say, skimming an article. "You were right—he was the captain of a shipping boat." I keep reading as Benson opens and closes file cabinet drawers. "Weird," I murmur, then louder, so Benson can hear me, I add, "So this article says that just as he was really starting to make a name for himself in the shipping biz, he disappeared."

"Disappeared?" Benson asks. He places a small stack of films on the desk beside me and pulls up another chair.

I point at the screen as I keep reading. "Yeah. He lived at the edge of Camden—that totally explains why Psycho Quinn told me to go there—and one night there was a huge disturbance, gunshots and tons of noise. Neighbors went to his house, and all four walls were, like, totally riddled with bullets, everything inside ransacked and destroyed, but the house was empty." I lean forward and keep skimming. "They never found any bodies, but neither he nor a local banker's daughter was ever heard from again." I turn to Benson. "Do you think that was Rebecca?"

"It seems likely," Benson says, his eyes fixed on the screen.

"This would have been a *major* scandal, right?"

"Murder and an illicit love affair in the early 1800s? Oh yeah."

"Can it be a coincidence?"

"What?"

"That the original Captain Avery seduced women and may have

either murdered them or been murdered for his deeds?" I ask, fear fluttering in my chest again.

"Coincidence? I doubt it. But the question is, did today's Quinn choose this identity because of its sordid past or did he just find someone in history to match his preferred crimes?"

Crimes. I hate using that word to describe Quinn.

What is wrong with me? Even after last night, I'm still trying to find a way to justify his actions.

"And why me?" I ask quietly. "I don't see how any of this relates to me." I read another paragraph, then turn fully to Benson. "Do you think he tracks down people who can do what I do? Do you think there *are* more people like me?"

"It seems possible," Benson says hesitantly.

I wonder if he found any. If they're still alive.

I swallow hard and scroll down farther. Suddenly the world swirls around me and I can't stifle the loud gasp that escapes my throat.

It's *him.*

It's a sketch, not a photo—possibly done after his disappearance. But it's definitely him. I can't tear my gaze away from those eyes. Soft green eyes that the artist has captured well, even in monochrome. I reach out and touch his sharp cheekbones, then am shocked when I have to hold my breath to stifle a sob. My emotions are a hurricane inside me fighting to get out.

"That's *him,* Benson!"

"Quinn? Like, the guy you saw last night?"

I can't speak; I only nod. Before I have time to process the thought, I hit the print button.

"That is seriously weird," Benson says. "You're sure?"

"That's *exactly* what he looks like," I say, and my voice is unsteady.

"This guy must be way hard core," Benson says, leaning in close to the picture.

Zac Brown Band starts playing, and it takes about five seconds before I realize it's my phone's ring tone. Instinctively I hit the talk button and put the phone to my ear, my gaze still fixed on the microfiche screen. "'lo?"

"Tavia, thank goodness. Please don't hang up."

I freeze as Reese's voice sounds in my ear, pouring jagged ice down my spine.

"I just got back and Jay told me. Please let us talk to you. You're in so much danger. Where are you? Just tell us—"

I hit the end button with a shaky finger and feel all the blood draining from my face. *I answered my phone? What the hell was I thinking?* That's the kind of mistake that could get me killed. Me *and* Benson. "I have to get rid of this," I say, and I'm not sure if I'm talking to Benson or myself. It's been easy to push Reese and Jay into the back of my mind since leaving Portsmouth—my head has been full of Quinn.

But my phone is a tether to them and I can't keep it anymore.

I walk over to the printer and gather up the small handful of papers and clutch them to my chest. "I gotta go," I mumble, not sure who I'm talking to. What I'm doing.

The phone.

Get rid of the phone.

Completely distracted, I turn to walk out and almost yelp when I feel Benson's hand on my arm. My instinct is to yank it away, but rational thought wriggles into my consciousness and I remember who he is.

He's Benson. He's helping me.

He's the only one who can.

"Tavia?" His hand is still on my arm.

I slow my breathing and make myself focus, feeling a semblance of calm start to fill me again. "Yeah?"

"Wait for me," he says quietly. "Let me grab my stuff."

Everything I'm feeling about Quinn and Reese and Jay and Elizabeth right now is too big. It fills my mind and heart until I'm too full to feel anything for Benson. And I can't be around him when I feel this way.

Flee! my mind is shouting at me, and my breath is shallow and short. The desperation to get rid of my phone—to cut off all contact with Reese—is like a compulsion it almost hurts to resist.

As soon as he turns, I start walking again—making my way to the doors.

"Miss, miss?" It's not Quinn's voice, but the memory of the words he said last night covers me, smothers me with despair. I duck my head and walk faster.

"Tave!" Benson's voice is too loud for a library, but still I don't stop. I know I'm running away, but it's too much. I can't stay in there, not one second longer.

"You need to pay for your copies," the librarian calls after me, scolding.

As I pull on the doors, I chance a look back at Benson, standing by the reference desk with desperation in his eyes and pulling out his wallet in a panicked hurry.

It's now or never.

The wind hits my face as I exit the library and stride out onto the street. I don't know anything about this town, so I just pick a direction and start power-walking with my head down, my phone clutched in my hand.

I wish I could close my fingers and crush it to pieces.

Once I'm out of sight of the library I pause to catch my breath and lean against the red-brick wall of a nondescript office building. I glance down at the printouts, now wrinkly from being crushed against my chest. When I hold them out to get a better look, a big raindrop plops down, smearing some of the text. I gasp my dismay and jog a few more steps to the shelter of an overhang before crouching down against the wall. At least it's not snowing. Yet.

My thoughts whirl as I stare at the sketch. It looks *exactly* like Quinn. I mean, it's not a photograph, so there could be subtle differences, but they would have to be damn subtle. Their faces are the same, right down to the bone structure. I've drawn the shadows beneath that prominent brow, the rise of those cheekbones, the square straightness of that jaw. You can't fake that kind of thing with a costume and a dye job.

I'm not sure you could reconstruct it even with surgery.

Who the hell *is* Quinn Avery?

As if hearing his name in my thoughts, Quinn walks around the corner of a building, kitty corner from where I'm crouched. My head turns to him, and I realize I don't need to see his tall, lanky form to know when he appears; I *feel* him. He's walking my way and my eyes find his face. He looks right at me and the purpose in his eyes terrifies me.

Paralyzes me. My limbs are stone. He's still coming, his steps long and leisurely. I finally jerk into action when he's less than twenty feet from me. The clatter of my phone hitting the sidewalk and shattering means nothing as I spin around, running in an instant.

I don't know where I'm heading, only that it's away from *him*.

But then the screams start.

My eyes widen and time seems to slow as I look back to see a dark blue car slam into Quinn's body and pin him against a wall for an instant. An endless, slogging instant. Then a sharp crack reaches my ears, fills my world, the wall giving way and burying Quinn in a mound of broken bricks.

The last thing I see before my world begins to spin is a familiar face. The face that means they've found us again.

CHAPTER TWENTY-SIX

I wake in a comfortable darkness, floating slowly out of a haze to the sight of an orange sun piercing through a canopy of nearly bare-branched trees. It takes me a few seconds to remember where I am.

Reese's car. Quinn. Benson. Quinn!

Through the lingering haze of sleep, I try to remember what happened. What happened after—

After the car hit Quinn.

After the car *killed* Quinn.

There's no way anyone could have survived that.

The scene flashes through my mind even as I try to push it away: the mangled car covered in shattered bricks, its hood swallowed by a gaping hole in the brick wall.

Don't make me see it. Him. The blood.

I squeeze my eyes shut and try to push the memory away. Try to forget the last time I was surrounded by blood and death. But closing my eyes only makes it worse. I have to get out of the car. I shove the door open, desperate for a breath of fresh air, fighting not to puke on the upholstery.

Thankfully, when I push the door open and swing my legs out, my head doesn't pound like when I first woke up from the coma after the plane crash.

I really was just sleeping this time.

I manage to stand, but it takes more effort than I feel it should. My body is completely wrung out, like I've been climbing a mountain for the last three days. It feels like those first few weeks after the plane crash, when even simple movements were tasks of herculean scope.

I don't like thinking about those days.

I wrap my arms around my waist and look around. Benson. Where is he? Is he here? Surely I didn't drive myself.

It takes a few more seconds, but then I remember. Benson pulling me to my feet, dragging me away before the cops could arrive.

And something else I saw . . . someone. Someone I knew.

Then there was the hysteria. Completely out of control, like someone was pulling my puppet strings. Tears, desperate words, telling Benson about Quinn. The hard line of Benson's mouth. Him, pushing me into the car, draping his coat over me.

Then nothing.

I shiver at the awful memory. I'm still tired, but at least I feel like myself. I never want to be anyone but me ever again.

A sound pulls me out of my thoughts. I can hear Benson, but not see him. We're pulled off on the side of the road somewhere I don't recognize, and I finally find Benson behind a tree talking on his phone.

Arguing.

I step closer, trying to catch words, but he keeps cutting off, like someone's talking over him.

". . . not what we agreed to. But—" I watch his hand fist against his hip. "I understand," he says a few seconds later, then hangs up without saying goodbye.

"Who was that?" My voice sounds creaky.

Benson whirls around with a gasp and sighs when he sees me. "Make some noise, will you?" he says with a half grin.

"Sorry." It sounds lame, but what else is there to say? "Are you all right?"

"Yeah, roommate stuff," he says, pointing at the phone.

I nod. I don't know what he means and my brain is still too fuzzy to care.

"How do you feel?" he asks.

I laugh. "Like I'm never going to sleep tonight."

Benson shrugs helplessly. "Sorry, I couldn't bear to wake you up." He pauses and then puts his fingers just under my chin. "I worry. You're so tired."

"Hey!" I counter. "Under-eye circles are the new black." But my joke falls totally flat.

"I don't mean physically." He studies me for another long moment, like he wants to say something else, but I don't drop my challenging gaze, and after a few seconds he lets his hand fall.

The look on his face is so strange—there are more emotions there than I can interpret, and I find myself wishing I'd brought my charcoals so I could capture him on paper—maybe figure him out that way. I lift my hand to his face and he leans into it, trapping it between his face and shoulder. I step forward for more, but he clears his throat and holds up his phone and I stop. "I found a small online report of what happened today," he says.

"Oh yeah?" I say, instantly curious.

"It didn't say much, just that an unmanned car was parked on a hill without the e-brake set." He looks up from the screen on his phone and says, "They're saying no one got hurt."

"No one got hurt? But—" I close my mouth to cut the words off. "Are you sure?" I have to ask. I *know* what I saw. The images are branded into my brain.

"That's what the report says. They commented that the office staff had just left for lunch, so the building was empty."

"And there's nothing about . . . about . . ."

"Nothing about Quinn," Benson finishes for me.

I stand for a long time in the crisscrossed shadows of the trees. I have no idea what's happening to my life. It feels like it's slowly splintering. Not breaking apart yet, but full of spidery cracks barely clinging to each other.

Things were starting to get better.

And then this.

It's like all the emotional healing I went through after the plane crash never happened.

"I saw him," I say.

"I believe you."

"Not Quinn—I mean obviously Quinn too, but—" I take a steadying breath as the shadow memory finally solidifies. "I saw the Sunglasses Guy. From Portsmouth. Just out of the corner of my eye a second after the accident, but I *know* it was him," I say quickly before Benson can cut me off.

He doesn't try. It's like he already knew. But then, he was there. He probably saw the guy too and didn't want me to know.

I look up at Benson, force myself to meet his eyes. "Is *everyone* in on it? You asked me yesterday how deep I thought this went and I didn't know. Is this a cover-up, Benson?"

Benson is silent. He folds his arms across his chest, then changes his mind and shoves them into his pockets instead. Though my mind is screaming for him to just speak, I stand silently, watching him. There's a possibility my eye is twitching.

"What if Quinn's a ghost?" Benson says softly.

A bark of laughter bursts from me before I can stop it. "Seriously? No. There's no such thing as ghosts."

"There's no such thing as people who can pull ChapStick and pencils and stress balls out of thin air either. Think about it, Tave, it would explain everything: the old-fashioned clothes, the thing with Rebecca Fielding, having that car run into him and no one notices."

"There's no such thing as ghosts," I repeat, but my voice is so quiet it's almost a whisper. My mind is racing. I saw him die. But did I actually see the blood or was that my mind filling it in? I shake that thought away and try to analyze what I *know*. Quinn *is* always in old-fashioned clothes; he comes and goes so quickly it's like he disappears; he *never* lets me get a word in edgewise—it's almost like he can't hear me. And that weird place he led me to last night, it seriously looked like no one had stepped into it for . . .

For . . .

Two hundred years. My mind forces me to complete the thought.

"He never touched me," I say, looking at Benson with wide eyes.

Benson says nothing but he's studying me with a grim expression that says he knows it makes sense.

"All those times—even when we talked—he never touched me." My chin jerks up. "Am I a psychic now?"

"Like a medium? Maybe."

"Benson, the fact is that I see things that *other people don't see*. All the time. I can't deny that anymore."

Benson nods, but says nothing.

"Do you think this is because of my surgery?"

"Your brain surgery?"

"Yeah. When I was in the hospital, I found this wacko website that suggested that trauma to the brain could give you paranormal abilities. I thought it was stupid at the time, but now?" I spread my hands out helplessly.

Benson pushes his glasses higher on his nose. "It doesn't sound very likely to me. But what do I know? Nothing, apparently."

Something doesn't fit. "Except . . ." I say, the idea gelling even as I speak. "It couldn't have been *totally* triggered by my brain injury. Reese and Elizabeth got me on that plane. They were *expecting* something like this to happen. You can't just predict that anyone who has brain trauma is suddenly going to turn into . . . I don't know, an X-Man or something."

"I wish I knew what they know," Benson says with a sigh.

"Me too." I sink down onto a moss-covered stump.

Two weeks ago I was a regular old sole-survivor-of-a-plane-wreck orphan being hidden from the media. Today? I don't even know what I am.

"Elizabeth called me an Earthbound," I say after a while. "What do you think that means?"

Benson stares at me blankly. "I don't know," he says.

"It all comes back to Quinn Avery," I finally say. "The old one, I mean. Everything. I think . . ." I don't even want to say it. "I think I need to go see that place he took me to again."

"You said you'd never go back there . . ." Benson answers, a spark in his eye betraying his interest.

"I know, but I think maybe that's what we're going to have to do to figure all of this out."

Benson nods thoughtfully. "If Quinn had any answers, it makes sense that that's where they'd be."

"I don't want to go alone. Will you come?"

"Of course," Benson says, and there's a ripple of excitement in his voice.

The place scares the bejesus out of me, but I guess it's kind of a grown-up field trip to him.

"Sun's going to set in about an hour, but I can pick up a flashlight in Camden," he says, then flushes. "I stopped in some town we passed through while you were sleeping and sold the gold coin. I hope you don't mind; we were out of gas money."

I wave his worries away. "That's what it's for."

He nods and drapes his arm lightly around me as we head back to the car. I have no clue how an over-two-hundred-years-dead guy—I cringe at the thought—is going to help us, but everything revolves around him. There *must* be a connection.

Besides, the irrational part of me is desperate to find out more about Quinn. It doesn't matter that he's dead—that he might have been a ghost all along—he's still the one with the answers.

I steer the car away from the shaded clearing and Benson helps me get oriented on the right highway. Once I set the cruise control, he squeezes my hand before releasing it and opening Rebecca's journal, leafing through the beautifully scripted pages. "Have you had a chance to read any more of this?" he asks.

"Since this morning? When would I have done that?" I drawl. "Before or after I eluded my assassin?"

Benson is flipping pages—slowly, but not slowly enough to really be reading much.

"Look at this," he says, tilting the journal toward me.

"Benson, I'm driving. Read it to me."

"I can't. It's code."

"Code? Really?" And I chance a look over, but the tiny, perfect cursive is too small to make out.

"Not actual code, I think. More like another language, but I don't recognize it. It's kind of Latin-ish, but not exactly. Maybe an old form of a different Romantic language?"

"Great," I say, my heart sinking a little. "A different language *and* in 1800s speech."

"It goes like that for the rest of the entries, it looks like," he says, flipping until he reaches blank pages. "The weird language and a whole bunch of drawings."

"What happens right before the change?" I ask, forcing myself to concentrate on the road.

Benson goes back and turns pages more slowly. "It's all about Quinn. How in love she is. How he has things to show her, just like he told you."

I cringe at the memory, especially now that Benson and I are ... what exactly are we, if Quinn is out of the picture?

Well, physically.

Sadly, he's still very much haunting us.

"Let's see, she's supposed to meet him. It's a secret. She thinks he's going to propose." He turns to the next page. "Then that strange language. I wonder..."

"What?" I ask when he pulls out his phone but doesn't finish his sentence.

"I'm putting it into Google translate to see if anything comes up."

"God bless Google," I murmur sardonically.

"That's weird," he says after a few minutes.

"What?"

"Well, it *is* Latin. Sort of. It's *close* to Latin. Google isn't translating everything because most of the words are spelled wrong."

"Do you think there's any way we can translate the whole thing?"

"Maybe. I can figure out some of the roots of the words that are misspelled, but"—he looks up at me—"it's going to take a really long time to even get the gist of it."

"What have we got if not time?" I reply quietly.

But it's a blatant lie.

Ever since the car almost hit me, it's like I've been hearing a clock ticking down in my head.

And I'm not sure what's going to happen when it reaches zero.

CHAPTER TWENTY-SEVEN

T he door's still ajar. Just how I left it.

"See?" Benson says when I point that out. "He's totally a ghost. Can't touch anything."

"Whatever," I say, not wanting to encourage him. Benson's insufferable when he knows he's right.

And he usually is.

But I love that about him.

Love? I try not to dwell on that.

"Do you think anyone else has been here?" I ask, my voice a hushed whisper—as though we were encroaching on sacred ground.

"No footprints," Benson notes. "And it stopped snowing in the middle of the night last night. So unless they snuck in right after you left, I suspect we're safe."

"We're not staying long," I say, pulling my coat a little closer.

"No arguments here," Benson says dryly.

I start to slip through the open doorway, but Benson stops me and examines the locking mechanism instead. "This is seriously brilliant," he says when I explain how it works. "It's like a combination lock. This

Quinn guy is—was—smart."

I blush. *Why does it feel like he's complimenting me?*

Reaching into a messenger bag hanging from his shoulder, Benson pulls out the huge Mag flashlight we acquired half an hour ago. *So* much better than my lame cell phone light.

The cell phone that's eighty miles away, in pieces on a sidewalk. Probably smashed by a brick as well. That tiny, simple thought makes me feel less afraid, if only a bit.

The dank smell hits me as soon as we enter the small burrow. With it come memories of last night in startling clarity–Quinn's face close to mine, not looking ghostly in the least. "Hey, aren't ghosts supposed to be see-through?" I ask as Benson shines the flashlight around.

"I don't think anyone knows that for sure."

"He looked so real," I say, and I'm a little embarrassed by the longing in my voice.

"Come over here," Benson says with a wave, beckoning me to the table where I found the journal.

"Paintings," I breathe as he turns over a few curling bits of paper. "I didn't really explore when I came down here last night." The paintings are small, casual watercolors of Quinn as I've never seen him before; smiling up at the artist, his hair loose and tousled, looking into a fire in a cozy hearth in contemplation. My breath catches as Benson turns over the last one.

Quinn with a woman.

It portrays the two of them from the back, walking hand in hand. I can't see her face, just a tall, slim form and brown hair bound into a braid. A roiling possessiveness that makes no sense whatsoever rolls over me, filling me with an odd hostility that makes me sick to my stomach.

"Rebecca?" Benson suggests from over my shoulder.

I swallow hard and answer in a weak voice, "Probably." I've never understood what it means to truly hate someone, but as I stare at that painting, my fingers gripping the corners so hard they're turning white, I think this must be what it feels like.

"Holy crap!" Benson holds up a dirty coin and blows some dust from it. "There's a bunch of them."

"Take 'em," I say. "I think Quinn owes me that much for blowing my life all to pieces."

While Benson's trying to decide how much this cavern is worth, I start poking around. "Think we can use your flashlight to smash into these crates?" I ask.

"Why don't you just make a crowbar?" Benson suggests.

I suck in a breath. I don't want to. It feels superstitious, but every time I use my powers, something bad happens. But what else am I supposed to do? Ask Benson to tear the lid off with his bare hands?

My fingers shake as I hold up my hand and picture the tool in my head. An instant later I'm holding a rather short crowbar. I avert my eyes as Benson takes it from me. After that it's a matter of seconds before he's pried the lid off.

We both drop to our knees to peer into the box.

"Sweet," Benson says, lifting a heavy pouch that jingles with the clink of metal. A quick look inside and he whistles. "Damn, this Quinn guy was seriously loaded."

"Give me that," I scold, snatching it away. "We're not grave-robbing."

"This is not a grave," Benson says. "And that pouch has got to be worth five figures. At least." He grins. "Think about how much gas and trail mix that is."

I glare at him and put it on the ground beside me.

Though I do love trail mix . . .

"Ooh, check it," I say, pulling out a book with a familiar triangle pressed into the leather cover. "It's another journal." I flip it open, expecting Rebecca's flowery script, but a bold, masculine hand greets me instead. "I think this was Quinn's."

There's no name on the front cover, but the second page has a list of names and dates, with Quinn's name at the top. There are no repeating surnames and there doesn't seem to be a pattern—though they do go backward until 1568. Then there are three more names without dates.

I turn the page and hold the book out at arm's length as I'm greeted with words three times the size of the precise list on the previous page.

If you are not friend to me, then the gods have mercy on your damned soul if you read on.

My eyes are wide as I reread the words. "Benson?"

"There's a painting and a pocket watch in here too. Weird."

"Benson?"

"Hey, this painting has a house on it. What do you want to bet it's the—"

"Benson!"

He looks up and I turn the book to him. "Am I a friend?" *Friend to a ghost?*

Benson raises an eyebrow. "Do you think it really matters? He's dead."

"He's already haunted me for a week!" I retort shrilly, though *haunting* isn't really the right word for it.

Still, Benson freezes. "You've got a point." He purses his lips. "He did show you the combination. I think that's a pretty good sign that he doesn't mind if you read this."

I nod, but adrenaline makes my fingers tremble as I turn the page and the writing returns to normal.

I am Quinn Avery. I am Earthbound. I am a Creator. If you are reading these words, I pray thou be a trusted friend or mine own reborn. Within this box find ye the tools needed to restore me. But when ye have, seek and find Rebecca. Nothing in this wide world is of greater import. Find her. Give her the necklace.

"Rebecca." I whisper her name quietly, feeling it burn on my tongue. He wants me to find her? Her ghost, I guess. Why? So they can live ghost-ily ever after? I force my fingers to relax when I realize I'm gripping the journal so hard I'm beginning to bow the covers.

"So—" Benson hesitates. "So you were right. He's also an Earth-bound. Was. You know."

I ignore the unspoken declaration that that means *I'm* an Earthbound too. I don't know what that means and I'm not sure I'm ready to find out.

"I wonder if his stuff also disappears," I muse quietly.

"Well, next time you see Quinn's ghost, you should ask him," Benson says, peering back into the crate.

"He doesn't answer questions," I say, flipping through the journal only to find that it's blank after about the first ten pages.

"You said you had conversations with him."

"I *thought* they were conversations, but everything he ever said to me I can find in Rebecca's diary. It's like . . ." I let the journal rest in my lap. "Like he's not a ghost so much as an *echo* of the past. I think that's why he called me Becca, even though I told him my name was Tavia." I remember how angry it made me. Now I feel strangely apathetic.

Briefly I wonder what that means about me, but I have too many other questions to answer first. Bigger questions. *Much* bigger.

I turn my attention back to the journal. "Hey, look!"

Benson turns to peer over the pages with me as I point to two carefully drawn symbols.

"It's the one from the files in Reese's office," I say, pointing to a drawing of the feather and the flame with the word *Curatoria* written beneath it. "That's the word Elizabeth used. I guess it's a name, not a word."

"Makes sense," Benson says quietly.

"I wonder. I don't have my phone anymore, but a couple days ago I took a picture of a really worn-down symbol on a building in Portsmouth. It was so faded I could only see something round over something with wavy lines. But it definitely *could* have been this symbol."

I move my finger to the opposite page. "But not this one. It's totally the wrong shape." This one is an ankh, but instead of the circle at the top connecting, one side curves out and makes the shape of a shepherd's crook instead. "Reduciata," I say. "Jay and Elizabeth both said that one." I try to read, but Benson keeps moving the light back to the box he broke into.

"Look at this," he says, tilting a small framed painting up for me to see. It's clearly done by the same artist as the others on the table, but this one is much smaller and it's the only one we've found in a frame. It's of a yellow house nestled in a grove of trees that are about halfway through the autumn change. "I bet it's the house he was killed in."

"He wasn't killed there." The words are out of my mouth before I have a chance to consider them.

I gape at Benson—how did I know that?—and reach for the painting. As soon as my fingers touch the brittle edges of the oil paint, I'm bombarded by an avalanche of distorted images and blended sensations.

"It was a trick," I manage to say as the barrage of sensation breaks my focus. My fingers wrap around the frame, gripping it tighter as words pour from my mouth and I can almost *feel* Quinn again, somewhere in the distortion and noise, but I'm nearly deafened by a scratching buzz, blinded by billowing fog. "They were never really in danger—not from the guns—but they had to . . . had to . . . I can't! Help me, Benson!" I'm holding the painting out to him, but I can't make my fingers let go as the sensation of fire licks up my arms and rattling static fills my ears.

Benson yanks the painting away from me and tosses it on the ground behind him before wrapping his hands around my upper arms. I almost collapse against him but manage to wring the last vestiges of strength from my weary muscles in time to catch myself.

"What happened?"

"I—I don't know. I touched the painting and it was . . . like I knew what happened to Quinn. Or, what didn't happen, I guess." Black dots swim in front of my eyes and I'm afraid I'm about to faint. I feel like I've just run a marathon on an empty stomach.

"I can't stay here any longer," I say, my hands covering my eyes.

"No problem. We can come back another day."

I nod mutely—not wanting to come back *ever*—and Benson reaches for the painting and tosses it back into the crate, pushing it into the darkness. He gathers up several of the other objects and packs them into a leather bag he brought along. I lean against the crumbly dirt wall and avert my eyes so I don't have to see the painting again. Even the thought of it makes me a little queasy, like I'm riding a bad roller coaster.

It's not supposed to be this way. The thought comes unbidden to my mind.

The journal starts to slide off my lap and I slap both hands down on top of it.

"It's just me," Benson says.

"I want to take this."

"Whatever you say. As long as it's not going to mess you up like the picture."

"It won't," I insist. I have no reason to assume that, but somehow, I know it's true. "I need it."

The words come out of my mouth, but they don't sound like mine.

CHAPTER TWENTY-EIGHT

"I don't think I can drive," I say when we finally catch sight of Reese's car half an hour later through the swirling gusts of sharp, icy winds. The shiny dots are back in front of my eyes as I try halfheartedly to help clean a thin layer of snow off the windshield. "Can you gemefood?" My words are slurring and I have to concentrate on standing upright as I dig the keys out of my pocket. I'm too tired to even worry very hard about the people following us, although, after the car incident, I ought to be doubly on edge.

Especially because I'm completely useless right now. But given our freezing journey through the woods and how he had to half carry me and his messenger bag filled with stuff from the dugout, I can't imagine Benson's feeling too spry either.

After helping me get in and buckle my seat belt, Benson asks, "Do you need to throw up? You look sick."

I shake my head and the motion makes me nauseous. "Need food. Starving."

"I think you should magic yourself something."

"Won't help," I argue, leaning my forehead against the window and closing my eyes. "Disappear in five minutes. Even the stuff I already ate."

"Yeah, but if you keep making more for the ten minutes that it'll take me to get you some *real* food, you'll keep replenishing the food that disappears. It's got to at least help a little," Benson says, his eyes pleading with me not to fight him on this.

It takes a few seconds for the words to register and I realize it's a rather brilliant idea. I fight it, though. The thought of actually ingesting something I made with my freaky magic makes me nauseous. *More* nauseous.

I can last; there's gotta be some fast food here. French fries. I can stay conscious long enough for some good, salty fries. The picture in my head is so vivid I have to resist the urge to lick my lips.

It's only when I feel the heat starting to seep through my jeans that I look down and see a carton of perfect french fries sitting in my lap. My hands grab for them even as my mind screams that they aren't real, that I shouldn't touch them. But Benson's right—I have to eat something *now*. I almost burn my tongue pushing them into my mouth and try to remember to chew. In less than two minutes the carton is gone.

"Make more," Benson says, and he sounds very serious now as he bumps onto the paved road and heads back toward Camden.

I don't fight it this time, and soon I'm making my way through another carton of fries. They warm me up and replenish my blood sugar faster than I would have thought possible. When the second carton is gone, I take a few deep breaths before making another one. The first carton will be disintegrating soon and I realize I have no choice anymore: I have to keep eating to prevent my blood sugar from crashing again. Probably harder this time.

I make another batch of french fries and conjure up a big cup of hot chocolate to go with them. Steadily, but not at the frantic pace I started out at, I munch and sip as I start to feel normal again.

"Hamburgers or tacos?" Benson asks dubiously as he looks between two non-branded fast-food joints that look questionable at best. At least they're open.

"Oh, hamburgers, please. Some kind of double with fries—real ones—and a Coke. Not the diet kind." I stuff another handful of fries into my mouth as it starts to water at the thought of a hamburger.

There's no drive-through and Benson turns to look at me sternly with his hand on the door handle. "Keep eating. I'll be back as soon as I can."

"Hurry," I say with a smile. I'm conning my body and I don't know how long I can keep it up before it rebels.

A handful of fries stops midway to my mouth when I realize that the last few days have been just like when I woke up from the coma. I ate and slept almost all day long. They told me it was because my brain needed immense amounts of resources to heal. It makes me wonder just what the hell my brain is doing now, what that picture did that my body needs this much help recovering from.

Reese's words about burning me out come back to me and I'm sick to my stomach again. What kind of horrible metamorphosis am I undergoing? I try to push the thoughts aside and conjure up a second hot chocolate. Nauseated or not, I have to keep eating or I'm going to be in big trouble.

Twelve minutes pass by the time Benson slips back into the car, and I've gone through five cartons of fries and both cups of hot chocolate. The smell of the burgers fills the air, and I push the magic fries off my lap and onto the floor in my hurry to reach for the two to-go bags.

"Watch it, Tave!" Benson gasps as fries scatter everywhere. "This is a Beemer!"

Such a guy. "Gone in five minutes," I remind him. "Grease stains and all."

"Well, these ones are real," Benson says grudgingly. "So be careful."

I take a second to spread some napkins on my lap before unwrapping my humongous hamburger and taking a big bite. We munch silently for a long time as I slowly feel my system start to stabilize.

"That was a really good idea," I say when I get a moment to take a breath. "I'd have blacked out before we got here for sure."

"And I don't even want to think about how I'd try to explain *that* to some stranger who saw us on the side of the road," Benson says grimly.

"No kidding," I murmur. We eat a while longer. "Thank you."

"It's just food," he replies with a grin.

"No, seriously." I turn to face him fully. "Thank you for *everything*. Not freaking out, believing me even when I sound crazy; everything, Benson."

"You're welcome, I guess," he says, and I can't help but notice there's a smear of mustard just above his lip.

I smile and reach a finger out to wipe it off. "You missed a spot," I whisper when his eyes darken—no, deepen—pinning me to my seat in a flutter of nerves and delight. He reaches for my hand and lifts my fingers to his lips, kissing each one briefly.

"Thank *you*," he whispers, with an intensity I don't understand but revel in. I hide my sappy grin behind my sandwich and we both finish our meal in silence.

When my food is gone and I'm so full I'm just on this side of being uncomfortable, I wipe the oil off my hands and reach for Quinn's journal while Benson finishes.

"Listen to this," I say, pointing to a short passage. *"Of the brotherhoods trust ye the Curatoria but tenuously, and the Reduciata not at all. Give none of them your secrets. Above all, tell the Reduciata nothing of Rebecca. If you know her whereabouts, deceive them."* I think about Elizabeth blurting out that name—Reduciata. "Who do you think the Reduciata are?"

"No clue," he says around a big bite.

"Must be someone bad," I say, flipping another page. "Reese and Elizabeth were worried Quinn was a . . . Reduciate? That must be what they call their members." I point at that paragraph. "I have a feeling he wasn't."

"Sounds like this Rebecca chick was in some serious trouble," Benson says, peering over my shoulder.

"Quinn too. It's got such old-fashioned wording—I'm going to have to read it carefully—but he talks about storing the gold *to brace against disaster*, and here, *running to ground like a hare in the hunt*." I pause as a sinking feeling hits my heart. "Sounds like us, doesn't it?"

"Sadly."

"He says not to trust the Curatoria, but from what I can tell, it's the Reduciata they're always running from." I pause, mulling the name over in my head. *"Reduciata;* it sounds kinda like *Illuminati.* Maybe they're both secret societies trying to . . . I don't know, run the government?"

"Wasn't much of a government back then," Benson says. "Or at least not much of a United States. Not yet."

"True. But I don't think they were just based in the United States. Look." I tilt the book toward him. "You can see a drawing of a pyramid here, and the ankh symbol is from ancient Egypt." I read that section, trying to make sense of Quinn's old-fashioned prose. "It looks like the Reduciata and the Curatoria were behind all the pharaohs of ancient Egypt—fighting to be the one in true control. It says the pyramids were built to hoard their belongings, kinda like Rebecca and Quinn's dugout."

"That sounds a little far-fetched. People took their myths pretty seriously back then, though."

"Well, that *is* what they did with the pyramids, right? Filled them full of the pharaohs' belongings? They would even bury servants alive in there."

"Yeah, but . . . the pyramids, really?"

My fingers hesitate at the bottom of the page. "The pyramids. Benson, the pyramids are triangles. Triangles that face all four directions."

"I'm . . . not following," Benson says, sounding almost wary.

"The Curatoria and the Reduciata have symbols; doesn't it seem like the Earthbound would too? It's got to be the triangle. That's why Reese said the triangle changed everything. Think about it. If you were an ancient Egyptian and you saw someone do the things I can do, what would you do?"

"Stone him?" Benson suggests.

I smack his shoulder. "Or make him your *leader*. In fact," I add on, grinning as the idea occurs to me, "you might decide your pharaohs are *gods*. Even though they really aren't," I tack on quickly. "I think it makes total sense."

This time Benson nods. "I can see that. Does he say anything else in there?"

"It's hard to make it out," I say, not bothering to hide my disappointment. "I've only figured out that one bit about the two groups." I chuckle morosely. "I'm just making the rest of this stuff up."

"And you're sure Quinn didn't die in that cabin?" Benson asks as he crumples up our trash.

"No. They were supposed to," I say, wrenching my attention away from the journal—what little there is of it. "But . . . they escaped." An ache starts as I try to think about that, but it's not so overwhelming now that I've eaten.

"How do you know?"

"It's like remembering a movie you watched a long time ago. You remember the basics, but not all the details. And the more I try to remember, the harder it is."

"Maybe Quinn is trying to speak through you and that painting was, like, some kind of supernatural gateway."

I raise my eyebrow at him. "He picked some random, totally broken teenage girl to communicate through?"

"Not random," Benson insists. "Another Earthbound. Like him. Maybe that's the only way it works."

I consider that and it makes a horrible sense. I admit, I don't want to be an Earthbound—whatever that really means. I don't want to be special. But if Quinn chose me, there must be *something* I can do for him. "I think we need to go to the house, Quinn's house, the one from the newspaper article."

"Problem. We don't know where—"

"I do," I whisper, realization dawning, "I know where it is."

Benson peers at the clock on the dash, his skepticism unconcealed. "It's too late to go now, and honestly, I don't think you're in any condition to do *anything*."

I nod wearily. "Tomorrow, maybe?"

His brow furrows in concentration. "If you want."

A contented drowsiness is starting to overtake me. "I do. I have to— to figure this out."

"I know," Benson says with a loud sigh, and it strikes me as an odd answer, but he's probably exhausted too.

"We should find a place to sleep; I'm going to pass out soon."

A smile crosses his face now. "Your wish is my command." He checks the rearview, then pulls out. "Go to sleep," he says as he scans the sparse traffic. "It'll take about twenty minutes."

"Where are we going?"

"Just sleep. It's a surprise."

I feel like I've scarcely closed my eyes before Benson is nudging me.

"We're here."

I don't understand why he's waking me up just to let me know it's time to sleep until my fatigue-heavy eyes catch the light.

I've never been so happy to see a simple Holiday Inn. "Are we staying here?" I ask, practically pushing my nose up against the window.

"No," Benson says. "I just drove you here to tempt you with a real shower. We can leave now."

This time, his shoulder gets a punch, but my brain has a death grip on the words *real shower*.

I grab my backpack—feeling a little guilty that I'm the only one who has a clean change of clothes—and scan the items in the trunk, trying to decide what's most important. "The journals," I finally decide. "I need to bring them in. I have to read them." My brain is still fuzzy, and that's as far as I get before Benson scoops them up.

"Let's just get inside. I don't want anyone to see you."

"It'll be fine," I say, as though the words would make it so. "Where are we?"

"Freeport. It's about sixty miles from Camden, but it's a town we

221

haven't been to yet. I'm trying to keep us safe," he finishes in a mumble.

"You're doing great," I say, glad he's being careful. Whoever's following us is smart and persistent, and as much as I generally admire both those qualities, I like them much less when they're working to make me . . . dead. As we cross the parking lot, I step a little closer to Benson, letting my shoulder brush his. "You're my Superman." I reach up and tap his glasses. "Specs and all."

"I'm no hero," he says softly.

Feeling bold, I reach down and slip my hand into his instead, entwining our fingers. "You're *my* hero."

He squeezes my hand and unlocks the door, and I try not to feel fluttery about the fact that I'm going into a hotel room. Alone. With Benson.

"Why don't you go ahead and shower," Benson says, hovering in the doorway, probably having just come to the same realization I did. "I need to go sell some more of this gold."

"Now?" I ask, the panic of him leaving way worse than the similar panic of him staying.

"I'd rather go at night when the car is less likely to be recognized," he says, looking down at the carpet. "I saw a pawnshop on the way into town—had one of those 'we buy gold' signs. If I get it done tonight, tomorrow we can just take off."

His shyness is oddly emboldening, and I step forward and rest my hands on his hips. "I wish we could just take off now."

"Me too," he says, barely loud enough to hear. He hesitates and then draws his head a little closer to mine. "Are you sure you'll be okay on your own for an hour or so?" he whispers.

What does *okay* mean, really? It's not the same definition I had yesterday, or last week, or last month. For the moment, *okay* means I'm alive. "Sure," I say, but I know I can't sound very convincing.

Benson tugs me closer. Our foreheads touch, and for a while I think that's all he's going to do. Then he traces one finger down my jawbone and lifts my chin. The kiss is barely more than a brush of his lips, but it's like liquid comfort pouring into my belly and spreading through my limbs.

"Take a shower. And it's okay if you go to sleep—I don't know how long I'll be."

I nod, knowing I'll never be able to sleep until he's back and I'm sure he's safe. "Be careful."

"Don't open the door for anyone," he warns, even though he knows I don't need it.

"Only you," I promise, holding eye contact until the door closes between us. "Only you," I repeat, setting the whispered words free.

CHAPTER TWENTY-NINE

Five minutes later I step into a scalding shower and sigh in sheer pleasure. After lathering twice I knead my sore neck, then look down to take stock of my sad, battered body. The pink scars on my right side from the plane crash—small lines where two broken ribs pierced through my skin, a staple-marked scar on my thigh where they put the worst of my broken bones back together with a metal plate, even my comparatively tiny trach and feeding tube scars—are so familiar now that it's hard to remember what I looked like without them.

I shake my head, thinking of Elizabeth's declaration that I'm an Earthbound. This body, riddled with scars and aches, should be proof enough that she's wrong. Mistaken. A supernatural being couldn't be so broken. If not for my *gift*, I wouldn't believe her at all.

And now I have new marks.

An enormous bruise is purpling on my left hip from where I fell running from Quinn last night. The edges are just starting to turn yellow and the middle resembles an eggplant. My knees and hands are both scraped from the pavement earlier today and still sting a little from the vigorous scrubbing I gave them a few minutes ago.

Visually seeking out a vague throbbing on my upper arm, I see the shadow of forming bruises where Benson's fingers dug in when he dragged me away from the car crash.

When he rescued me.

The coming bruise makes me chuckle and shake my head. I won't tell him. He'd feel awful. Benson would never hurt me. Not intentionally.

Sometimes I think he's the only one.

My mom.

My dad.

But they're gone.

A small surge of guilt shoots through me as I realize I've hardly thought of my parents the last few days. Slowly, so slowly I didn't realize it until just this moment, Benson has slipped into their place. The person I can trust with everything. Not just life-altering secrets like my powers and the people trying to kill me, but silly ones. The time in fourth grade when I laughed so hard I wet my pants, the baby bird that fell out of its nest that I tried to save . . . and how I cried when it inevitably died. The kind you only share with true intimates.

Family.

I straighten in surprise as the word races about in my brain and then settles.

But why *shouldn't* Benson have become my family?

I think of Elizabeth's warnings against him yet again and a prickle of anger makes my face heat. No one, *no one*, has proved as loyal as Benson. I would take him over the whole lot of them.

I stand under the hot spray until my whole body is pink, then take my time getting dressed, first blow-drying my short hair with the loud hotel blow dryer, then pulling on a simple baby tee and yoga capris and finally slathering some hotel lotion over my scratched arms and hands. It all feels like such a luxury.

I'm too keyed up to sleep. I try watching TV, but all the stations are talking about another breakout of the mysterious virus—this time in a small town just north of the Canadian border.

A one hundred percent fatality rate. It makes my stomach churn.

Jay's words echo through my head: *My work, we've found connections between the Reduciates and the virus, and if you walk away, I'm not sure I—*

What was he going to say next? For the first time, I almost wish I'd stayed. I wish I'd listened. Could something this devastating, this random, be the work of an organization that had nothing better to do than hunt down an eighteen-year-old girl? It seemed impossible.

There's a doctor on the news now, outlining the symptoms of the virus, the possible vectors of infection. I close my eyes, not wanting to hear.

I'm so sick of bad news.

I click off the television and turn to look at the two ancient journals. I haven't had a chance to even skim through Rebecca's journal since this morning, so I flip to the end so I can check out this mystery language.

The handwriting is the same, but Benson's right: it's impossible to read.

I turn to Quinn's much shorter diary instead.

Quinn's journal doesn't go into depth, but the brief descriptions are enough. If Quinn is to be believed, these two groups—*brotherhoods*, he calls them—have had their fingers in everything from the French Revolution to the Knights Templar to the councils of Nicaea. History changing.

History *making*.

And I should have realized how ubiquitous the triangle has been as a symbol throughout history. The Templars, the Masons, the Egyptians; hell, it's on our dollar bills. The Earthbound—and through them, these brotherhoods—are etched across the history of civilization.

If I was scared before, I'm *terrified* now.

No wonder they seem to always be a step ahead of us. They've had *thousands* of years of practice.

When I hear the door unlock, my heart leaps and races. Benson pokes his head in tentatively—probably to check if I'm sleeping—before slipping in.

I glance at the clock and am shocked to see that it's been two hours since he left. I scarcely noticed the time passing.

He comes in and shuts the door behind him without a word. He stands with his back to me for a long time, and when he finally turns, I lift both of my hands to my mouth with a gasp. His eye is purpling in what's sure to be a major shiner tomorrow, and a scrape on his upper cheekbone has a smear of blood across it. His hair is mussed and the knuckles on his right hand are bleeding through a napkin.

"Holy crap, Benson, what happened to you?" I rush to him, but he puts out a warning hand and I pull up short.

"Please don't," he says, and his voice is brittle, almost to the breaking point. "I think my ribs are bruised."

"What the hell happened?"

"Get your stuff, we have to go."

"What do you mean go?"

"Not far, but we aren't safe here. There's another hotel across the street."

"But—"

"Please Tavia, there's no *time!*"

The desperation in his voice shocks me into action. I circle the room, grabbing everything I can see and throwing it into my backpack. I hold my loaded bag against my chest and huddle beneath my coat as Benson opens the door again. Chilly air rushes in and swirls around my bare calves and sockless feet shoved into tennis shoes, but when Benson turns to ask if I'm ready to run, I nod.

We sprint through the snow, struggling not to slip on the iced pavement as we cross from one hotel parking lot into another. Benson leads the way around to the far side of a long wing of rooms and then reaches into his back pocket. "Stand over there, in front of me," he says, pointing.

I do, confused, but understand when I see Benson working on the old dead bolt with his tiny lock picks.

"You didn't *book* us a room?" I whisper.

"Do you *want* to be dead by morning?" he retorts, in a completely uncharacteristic display of impatience.

That's when I understand how scared he is. "No," I answer softly. "Thank you."

The door opens moments later and Benson gestures me inside. He drops my backpack as he flips on the light, revealing what could have been a mirror image of the room we were just in. Different colors, one less lamp, utterly interchangeable.

The silence feels thick between us.

"What happened to you?" I finally ask, hating the suspicion that he ran into *my* trouble. My mind flashes back to Sunglasses Guy, who apparently managed to track us up to the library. And we really haven't been that careful this evening. Not careful enough.

"Can we not talk about it?" Benson asks, and he sounds so weary that I almost relent, but I can't just *not* know.

"The quick and dirty basics," I say.

"I went to a pawnshop like I told you and turned in the gold for cash, and I was so focused on how much I got us that I was sloppy. Didn't watch out. It was dark and I . . . I was easy to sneak up on."

"Oh no," I say, knowing what's coming.

Benson turns away and starts emptying his pockets onto the bedside table, including a thick fold of twenties. Or are those hundreds? He continues wearily. "So a guy jumps out and puts a gun to my head and demands to know where you are."

"Where *I* am?" I was right; my stomach feels sick. "What did you do?"

Without turning he lifts his wrapped fist. "I punched him in the teeth." He chuckles mirthlessly. "He didn't like that very much," he says, gesturing to his blackening eye.

I swallow hard, wondering if he broke any bones in his hand or just the skin. "How'd you get away?"

"I got in a couple good hits, gun fell in the snow, and I managed to get in the car. He didn't shoot. Probably didn't want to kill me before he found out where you are."

"Benson." My fingers skim up his back, over his damp coat.

"Just don't," he says. "Please."

"Okay," I whisper, not understanding.

"You're clean," he mumbles in halfhearted explanation. "And I totally reek. You don't want to touch me."

"I—" But what am I supposed to say? The truth is that I want to touch him so badly I can hardly keep myself still. But that won't help anything.

"I should shower," he says, and I turn, trying to give him the privacy he's so blatantly asking for, but after a few seconds I hear muffled cursing.

I turn and see that he's managed to slide his peacoat off but is struggling to unbutton his shirt with his injured hand.

"Let me help." I rush up and Benson jumps away like a skittish rabbit. He looks almost as weary as I do—as though he's aged five years in the last week.

I pause and study him for a moment with my artist's eyes. I wonder if I look that way too, if that's what had Reese so concerned. Does it show in my face the way it does in Benson's? If so, I *can't* hide it.

"Benson," I whisper, soft but firm. He settles down, but his eyes still have that wild look. I move slowly, unfastening all the buttons down the front first, revealing his white T-shirt beneath. Then I unroll the sleeve on his left arm; the right one's already ripped up to his elbow.

"I can take it from here," he says, but I fix him with a firm glare and he remains docile as I carefully peel the wet fabric away and lift the tail of his undershirt to look.

"Oh, Benson," I whisper. His entire torso is covered with purpling bruises that look about as bad as the one on my hip. "Turn," I say, but he grabs the bottom of his shirt and plants his feet firmly without a word.

I give up. It doesn't matter. If his back is anything like his chest, I'm not sure I *want* to see it. "Are you sure none of your ribs are broken?" I say, shocked at the beating he took.

Because he wouldn't betray me.

"I'm not sure of anything," he says in a low, raspy voice.

Slowly, I reach for his chin and turn his face from one side to the other, examining. He closes his eyes, and I bite my lip at the split skin on his cheekbone and a scratch I didn't see at first that goes up into his hairline, probably from the bent earpiece of his glasses. "Ben," I murmur, and from beneath his closed lids a single tear slips out, tracing down his cheek. Stepping on my toes, I lift myself without leaning on him and kiss it away, the salt bitter on my lips, and I seethe inside at the person who would do this to my Benson.

I crouch and realize just how much this has broken Benson's spirit when he sits on the bed without even being told and lets me untie his shoes. He protests briefly when I start to pull off his socks, but he doesn't put up much of a fight.

His breath sucks in as I reach for his pants. "Just the button," I say from where I'm bent close to his shoulder, "then you can shower."

He nods, and after I carefully unfasten his pants, I take what looks like an unbruised elbow and help him up. He stifles a groan and shuffles into the bathroom.

I stare at the closed door for a long time. Guilt boils inside me, filling me with acrid shame. Benson wouldn't be here, wouldn't be hurting, if it weren't for me. There's no way to argue my way out of it; this is my fault.

I lie helplessly in the bed listening through the thin walls as Benson gets in, then out of the shower. The hotel blow-dryer turns on and runs and runs, and I wonder if he's actually doing something with it or just trying to cover up the sound of his soft noises of pain. Almost half an hour passes before Benson opens the door, freshly showered and looking a little better.

Not quite so defeated.

"You're still awake?" he asks, averting his gaze, hiding behind the door so only his head and shoulder are visible. His water-darkened hair is wet and freshly combed, but not styled, making him look younger than usual.

"Waiting for you," I say from the bed, wondering where I found the courage. I twist my fingers together, not sure if I'm more drunk on fear or anticipation.

A red flush fills Benson's face as he turns off the bathroom light and steps out from behind the door. Now I understand and have to hide a little smile. Unlike me, he doesn't have any clean clothes—he's clad in his undershirt and a pair of boxers, probably fresh-dried courtesy of the blow-dryer.

"I'm sorry there's only one bed," he mumbles, still not meeting my eyes. "I didn't have time to check out the place. I just . . I just . . . I'm going to sleep on the couch."

"You don't have to," I blurt. "I mean, you know, there's plenty of room."

"I—I don't think it's a good idea."

I nod, trying to disguise my disappointment. I pull up the heavy but warm blankets that feel cloud soft after trying to sleep, cold and wet, in the car. But my eyes might as well be glued open.

Benson grabs the extra blanket out of the closet and shakes it out, then spreads it over the couch that's more like a love seat. With his height I know his feet will hang over the edge, and I can't decide if the mental image is more hilarious or devastating. As he leans over, his white T-shirt stretches across his shoulders and underneath I can see the shadow of something black. I force back a little smile when I realize it's a tattoo. It's what he didn't want me to see when I was trying to take his shirt off. I wonder what kind of ink a guy like Benson would get.

I wonder if it's something he regrets.

When he's done making his "bed," Benson looks down at the sparse couch. I wish I could *make* him something better. Despite my reluctance to use my powers, I wouldn't hesitate for him. Not for a second.

But what good is a disappearing bed? I feel so helpless.

I realize Benson's staring at my bed, over to where a second fluffy pillow sits beside the one I'm lying on.

I see his hesitation, but this tiny piece of comfort gets the better of him and he walks forward and gestures at the pillow. "May I?"

"Of course."

I feel so *proper*.

His long arm reaches out for the pillow and I grab his wrist. "Stay?" I ask.

Just one word.

He gives me a tight smile. "No, really, we'll both sleep better if . . ." His voice trails off and he gestures at the sofa, backing toward it even as words fail him. He turns the light off and I hear him settle on the couch with a rustle of the blanket.

I try to sleep, but the bed seems too big and I feel oddly unsafe. "Benson?" I whisper after twenty minutes of trying to calm my racing brain.

He shoots straight up at the sound. "Are you okay?" he asks, panicked.

Guilt shoots through me; he had probably just gotten to sleep. "I'm cold."

"I'll turn up the heat," he says, without a trace of reluctance in his voice, his blanket already tossed aside.

"Not like that," I say, and my heart pounds in my ears.

"What?"

"Not like that," I repeat. "Ben, please just hold me." My voice is strong at first but barely audible as I finish.

"Tave, I . . . I shouldn't. You don't—" Something oddly sob-like cuts his voice off and then before I know what's happening, the blankets are flung back from the empty side of the bed and Benson's arms are pulling me almost savagely to him—he groans as his arms crush me against his ribs.

"Careful!" I warn. "I'm hurting you."

"I don't care," he gasps, his lips brushing against my neck, his fingers buried in my soft, clean hair. "I want you so badly I don't even care." He brings me hard against him, his fingers digging into my back in a pain that feels like pleasure, and I understand him better now.

And then his lips are on mine, part savage, part flower-petal soft, and I grasp at his shirt, pulling him to me. My legs tangle with his, our hips meeting, melding, as his fingers skim the skin between my pants and T-shirt.

Every nerve in my body is on fire, singing angelic refrains that echo in my head, blocking out all words, all doubts, all fears. I kiss him with abandon, not caring that I hardly know what I'm doing. It doesn't matter; with Benson everything is right. I don't stop until we're both gasping for air. His hands sweep my short hair off my forehead before pulling my face against the warmth of the skin just above the neck of his shirt, tucking my head beneath his chin.

There are no more words as we lie there together, our hearts beating fast at first but slowing to thump almost in tandem. I release my breath in a long sigh, and my whole body relaxes for the first time in what feels like weeks. I want to stay awake, to savor the feeling of lying in Benson's arms without the frantic desperation that has accompanied most of our interactions that even hint at romance. But my consciousness floats away all too soon, and when I open my eyes again, it's morning.

CHAPTER THIRTY

He's beautiful in the morning sunlight.

Beautiful seems like a funny word to use for a guy, but it's fitting. The line of light shining in from the window makes the tips of his eyelashes glow, and despite the purple bruise beneath his eye, he looks boyish without his glasses.

He wakes up slowly and smiles when he realizes I'm watching him. "I was a little afraid it was a dream," he says, his voice gravelly.

We must have both been totally exhausted, because it's almost eleven by the time we wake up. I'd like to linger—even spend the day shut up together with one shower and one bed—but the fact that we've managed to evade my tails for a full twelve hours makes both of us anxious to get back on the road and *stay* one step ahead of them.

Especially since we're going back to Camden today.

I shoulder my backpack while Benson grabs the journals, but as we leave the room, Benson veers right instead of left, heading *away* from the hotel we actually checked into last night. Where Reese's car is still parked.

"Where are you going?" I ask.

"To get us a car," he says, that same grim look on his face he was wearing after he got jumped. Like something bad just happened and something worse is coming.

I don't understand why he seems so reluctant until he looks both ways and leans down next to a dark green Honda, fiddling with the lock. "Are you *stealing* this car?" I ask, horrified.

He pauses, then looks up at me. "I would do a lot of illegal things to keep you safe, Tave," he says with an intensity that makes my toes warm. "Just be glad this one doesn't actually hurt anyone."

I try to pretend I'm not aiding and abetting a crime—*another* crime— as I slip into the passenger seat. Benson hesitates, then turns the car and drives around the building toward the Holiday Inn. "I just want to see."

It's impossible to miss.

Four cop cars and a fire truck are parked around our former hotel room, their lights flashing. My eyes immediately go to the black smoke wisping off the charred hunk of metal that used to be the BMW. A fire fighter is dousing it with a weak stream of water, and it takes me a second to realize the car is upside down.

I tear my gaze away and turn in my seat to look at the hotel room we almost slept in. The door is lying on the sidewalk in several pieces, and shattered glass from the large front window blankets the ground. The curtains hang torn on the other side of the empty window frame, and I can just make out the mattress leaned against the wall and the TV stand tipped over.

"Don't look anymore," Benson says, and I turn my eyes forward.

"Let's get the hell out of here," I say, not the least bit ashamed of the quaver in my voice. I reach for his hand, loosening my grip when I remember it's his injured one. He gives me a pained smile in response.

"So where are we going?" he asks as we approach the highway.

"The house was just outside of Camden," I say after a hard swallow. "Head that way."

I know what Quinn is now—he's not like the people hunting me: the Reduciata or Sunglasses Guy or Reese and Jay, whoever they are—he's like me. He's an Earthbound.

He's also a ghost who can't hurt me. But he can do *something*. Since I first saw him, he's had some kind of control over me, over my emotions. I wouldn't say that he can make me *do things*, exactly, but it's mortifying to think about the way I sneaked away from Benson and followed him into the woods.

In the dark.

Anything could have happened. And what's worse, I *knew* it. And I went anyway.

But that hotel room. That car. I don't think I understood until now just how vicious the people after us could be. The night I went off with Quinn, it could have been Benson burned to a crisp.

He could have died because I left him.

As that thought sinks in, holding his hand isn't enough. I loop my arm around his, hugging it against my chest with my head resting lightly on his shoulder while he drives, needing to feel the warmth of his skin, the sound of his breathing, the faint beating of his heart. All signs that he's still alive.

That he's still mine.

And I promise in my mind that I will never let these people take him away.

I just wish I had a better idea of who *these people* are. Or, at the very least, who specifically pulled the job at the hotel. Sadly, I have several options. Reese and Jay—but I don't believe they'd do something like this.

Violence like this seems more like a Sunglasses Guy thing. But who does he work for? The Reduciata? This whole thing would be a hell of a lot easier if I knew *who* I was actually running from.

We're about five miles from Camden when a pit forms in my stomach. Revisiting a town we've already been to twice seems more than a little dangerous, even though we're not going to the exact same place. In a town as tiny as Camden, going to Quinn's house versus his hideaway isn't much of a difference. Whoever's tracking us has to know we stopped here yesterday before proceeding on to the Holiday Inn. It's likely they know about the first time we stopped here too. I have visions of them lying in wait, guns in hand, and it doesn't seem very fantastical.

"You ready?" Benson asks as the sign welcoming us to Camden comes into sight.

I don't know if I'm more afraid of what might be waiting for us . . . or that nothing will be. No house, no answers, not even any clues. If I don't find some answers here, I'm not sure we'll have the resources to survive until tomorrow. "Ready as I'll ever be."

In a few minutes we're turning down a street just outside Camden, and I feel my chest finally start to relax as the buildings grow sparse. Fewer places for an assassin to hide. I'd like just *one* day to go by without someone trying to kill me. It doesn't seem like too much to ask.

We're on crumbly county roads now and there's forest on both sides. "There should be a turn coming up soon," I say, leaning forward and searching for it.

Benson points to a faint dirt road that speaks of decades of neglect, and the car bumps off the pavement. He grins. "Glad you're not a serial killer," he says, leaning to nudge his shoulder against mine. "Because this would be an awesome place to ditch a body."

Thank you for that visual, I think, knowing the comment was supposed to lighten the mood. Somehow, it only made everything feel more serious. More dangerous. "At least we haven't seen anyone following us," I manage in response. I can *feel* the house approaching us instead of the other way around. "It's coming up," I say, peering into the trees. I catch sight of a barely there path that isn't nearly wide enough for even a compact car and point it out.

"Time to hoof it?" Benson asks, and I nod, though no words come out. My throat is frozen.

In a complete turnaround from last night, the sun is out in full force today, melting all the snow it dumped on us two nights ago. I'd like to take it as a good omen, but really, it's yet another sign of how screwed up the world is.

The path is muddy and slick with wet grass, and baby leaves drip water droplets onto our heads when we disturb them. But we don't have far to go; the path ends at what I know used to be a white-picket fence. There's nothing left of it, though.

It, or the house.

Disappointment surges through me. It was foolish to think Quinn's house would still be here, looking just like the painting. I pick my way across years of fallen leaves, reminding myself that two centuries is a long time. My eyes follow the path to the house that's invisible except in the memory that feels as much mine as Quinn's.

I step closer to where the house used to be.

It's almost nothing now—a broken outline of what *might* have once been a foundation, covered in green moss. There's a pile of old stones that hints at a fireplace on the north side, but it could just as easily be a heap of rocks some kids made twenty years ago. My toes find the edge of a stone barrier that's more or less straight and I follow it carefully, hoping that it'll give me some insight into the structure that existed here so long ago. It's only when it turns a third corner that I'm sure this was, in fact, the foundation.

"Wow," Benson whispers when I reach him again, coming to the same conclusion. "This is really it."

It is.

I can *feel* it.

It's the familiarity I expected to feel in Camden. And now I understand—it's not the city, it's *here*. This place. *This* is where Quinn meant for me to come.

As though hearing his name in my thoughts, Quinn's presence resonates within me, filling my soul with a silent music like the vibrations of an enormous bell. My backpack slides from my shoulders as I stand before what would have been the front of the house. It wasn't large—not that homes in that era ever were. But big enough for one.

Two, my mind whispers, and I nearly hiss aloud in jealousy as I push the thought away. *Why am I jealous?* I don't want Quinn! He's not even real!

And Benson is here. Benson, who took a beating for me. Who kept me warm last night.

I force my eyes back to the hint of ruins and imagine what the house looked like from the brief glance I got of the painting at Quinn's secret hideaway. Yellow, with smooth wooden slates. Two windows on either side of the door.

And curtains. The thought comes unbidden. *Red gingham curtains.*

The picture that flashes in my head is so vivid that I step back and look up.

At a house.

A real house.

Not exactly real, I remind myself, even as I gasp at the vision that has appeared in front of me. It's like Quinn—it looks real, but it can't be.

I'm standing on what would have been the front porch. It spans the entire length of the house and thin white pillars support the roof. Glistening wind chimes sway in a gentle breeze.

Wind chimes.

Just like the ones on the porch at Reese and Jay's.

I hung them across the front veranda myself. Found them a couple months ago at a flea market downtown. Reese laughed and told me I could hang a dozen if I wanted to.

So I did.

Quinn's house has wind chimes too.

Now I'm seeing connections where there really aren't any, I berate myself. *Tons* of people collect wind chimes.

Of course, I'm seeing a *lot* of things lately, so perhaps that's not the best argument.

But when I look to the front door, I can't hold back a gasp.

A triangle glows gold above the door so brightly it's hard to look at. Boldly proclaimed for anyone to see, it might as well be spelled out: this is an Earthbound home.

The door beckons me, tempts me, and though a rational part of my mind knows it's not real, I can't resist. I walk forward and reach out my hand.

It melts right through the doorknob. Of course I can't touch it. But . . .

I set my jaw and walk forward. A tingling sensation crackles over my skin as I walk through the opaque door and find myself inside the house. With my mouth agape, I look around the room, catching sight of the cheery, wood-burning stove in the corner and the soft gray stone mantelpiece over the fireplace.

I allow my eyes to drift to the other corner and startle when I see a woman standing there. Her back is to me and I sense she's humming, though I don't hear anything. It seems like all my senses have been muffled except sight.

She's pulling a quilt over a delicately carved four-poster bed. Once it's in place, she tosses a pillow into the air, fluffing it in her hands before plopping it down at the head of the bed.

I can't see her face, but I recognize the thick brown braid from the painting. *Rebecca.* They must have lived here together.

Again that misplaced, irrational envy washes over me and I gasp. As if hearing me, Rebecca turns.

I stagger backward when I see her face.

She's me.

Or someone who looks just like me.

That doesn't make any sense. Not unless my crazy brain is projecting myself into the scene . . . ?

Her eyes stare into space—her thoughts clearly wandering—and her hands reach up to touch something at her throat.

I see a necklace, and a jolt of possessiveness burns through me. I want to reach out and snatch the shining silver from her fingers. I push my knuckles against my teeth and force myself to remain where I am.

Still silent, Rebecca turns toward the door and her soft brown eyes light up.

I tremble, forcing myself not to turn to the front of the house to see who has walked in.

I know who it is.

Quinn.

A hat flies by me, landing on the bed, and my arm explodes into tingles as I feel him pass, brushing through me. Then he's in my sight line and my legs shake, then crumple beneath me as every feeling I've tried to deny for the last few days floods through, fills me, overflows—too much for my skin to hold inside.

His coat comes next and my fists clench against the floorboards as it slips down his long, lanky arms and joins the discarded hat on the bed.

Quinn reaches for Rebecca and she steps forward, their bodies melding together with a rightness I can't deny. A cry of dismay builds up in my throat and I grit my teeth shut against it.

I hear Benson behind me, but only vaguely, like an echo from another world. Someone I used to know.

I should turn—I should listen, but my eyes are fixed on the excruciating, sweet pain of seeing Quinn hold someone else. His hand cups her cheek, his thumb traces her jawline. I reach my hand up to my own face, as though I can will those hands to be on me instead of her.

My heart races, then immediately slows, and every breath is an effort as I wonder if agony or ecstasy will kill me first—I'm certain one of them is going to. I can't bear this much longer.

Just as I realize agony is going to win, I feel as though my soul is ripping from my body and then I'm looking down on myself.

But only for a moment.

I'm settling.

Settling into a familiar place.

I'm home.

Where I belong.

A cool metal is heavy against my throat and my eyelashes rise to meet a white-shirted chest in front of my eyes. Insistent fingers are tilting my chin up to meet warm lips, while an arm pulls me close.

Of course. My mind sees it before I do and my heart rushes to catch up.

He's holding this woman.

He's caressing Rebecca.

He's kissing *me*.

CHAPTER THIRTY-ONE

Quinn's lips are indescribably soft on mine, and I'm half afraid I'll die from the burst of ecstasy that surges through me. Inside I'm quaking, but Rebecca's hands, *my* hands, are steady as they find the ends of his cravat and pull gently. A raw wanting floods through me as the length of cloth loosens and the knot comes apart under capable fingers.

I look up at his face.

And everything comes together in a flash of insight. My fingers, my eyes, my mouth.

My Quinn.

Rebecca's thoughts flow through my brain. *My* thoughts. Not now; they *were* my thoughts. I try to fight them, to block the invasion of my brain, but it feels too right, too familiar, and finally I relax and allow myself to just *be* Rebecca.

Again.

I'm helpless to resist when my hands—Rebecca's—pull Quinn's face down again, his gritty stubble velvet under my fingertips. His head snaps up and I try to force him back to me, but my hands won't obey. I'm not in control—this is something that already happened, two hundred years ago. I can't change it; I can only play my role, think the same thoughts she thought.

Once I understand that, our consciousnesses blend, and instead of feeling like I'm watching a movie, I'm there, in the scene. *I run to the window beside him and gasp in fear as his arm tightens around me. A semicircle of at least fifty men on horseback surrounds us, their faces masked, torches burning. Each man has a rifle on his shoulder; many have two. I don't know if they're witch hunters or Reduciates; we've faced down both.*

The problem is if it's the Reduciata, they actually know how to kill us.

I cling to Quinn, watching through the windows as the riders spread out and close the circle around the entire house.

There will be no running.

Tears sting in my eyes and I have to take deep, gulping breaths to push them back. Not because I'm afraid—we're far from defenseless—but because this means we'll have to leave. We've lived here together secretly for more than a year. It has been a haven.

A heaven.

It's always a fight for Earthbounds to be together, but here we'd won that fight. We found each other and unlocked a love most humans can only comprehend in blissful moments of sweet dreams.

And it's been our reality.

These men—these beasts—are taking it all away.

Quinn's hands are in my hair and his lips murmur, "Be strong." His nose brushes my earlobe. "I need thirty seconds." My fingers clench fistfuls of his shirt, drawing on his strength to feed my own. One more breath and I look up to meet his eyes.

It must be now.

I tear myself away and fly to the door, bursting out into the frigid night. The icy wind slaps my cheeks and I pull frozen air into my lungs, only to cough on the winter-kissed chill.

With my arms wrapped around my aching chest, I raise my head to the snorting horses surrounding me.

And the black gun barrels.

Dozens of them, pointed at me, their horses shoulder to shoulder in an arc so tight I cannot escape.

My eyes rise past the guns to the faces of the mounted men. They're well covered, but even a mask can't hide their eyes. These eyes—all of them—burn with hatred.

With murder.

Not a spark of mercy.

Twenty-eight, twenty-nine, thirty. Please, gods, let him be ready.

I spin back to the house, my braid flaring out in the darkness, the end stiff with cold. Without letting myself hesitate, I turn my back to them, praying they will give me the three seconds it will take to close the door.

I hear amused chuckles, and though anger slices my belly, I know their heartlessness is what will ultimately save my life.

I slam the door shut and the slam is drowned out by the explosion of guns from everywhere. My mouth opens in a piercing scream, then a steely hand wraps around my wrist and yanks me downward. A soft cloth covers my mouth to stifle the sound, and Quinn's leaf-green eyes meet mine, calming me in an instant even as the roar of gunshots continues over my head.

Suddenly, his eyes roll skyward and we're encased in total blackness.

"No," I whisper, and it echoes in my mind instead of coming out of Rebecca's mouth.

I can't see him. He's gone!

"No!" I cry louder, but it only makes my head hurt as my skull fills with the echoes of a scream that can't escape my mouth.

My soul rips away again and I'm back in Tavia's—*my*—broken body, surrounded by the ruins of my—Rebecca's—home. Something's restraining me and I thrash against it, trying to get free.

Trying to get back to him.

Quinn!

"Stop. Tavia, it's me."

"No, it's not—it's not you," I sob. "You're gone! Come back." The keening sound is loud in my ears again instead of trapped in my skull, and somehow I figure out I'm in the present again.

I'm me. I'm not Rebecca anymore.

I've never hated being me so badly.

My chest shakes and I realize—so agonizingly slowly—that it's Benson's arms holding me in place.

"Tave, look at me," Benson says, and I feel fingers on my chin, pulling my face up. Blue eyes boring into mine.

Blue.

Not green.

Blue.

Benson.

Tavia.

My mind can't handle it and I feel like I'm ripping in two as Tavia and Rebecca struggle for control.

"Tavia, talk to me!"

He's afraid.

Why is he afraid? *I'm* the one who's dying.

The crunch of dead leaves under my back as I collapse onto the ground finally jolts me back to reality and I suck in a deep breath as my head whirls.

Was I holding my breath?

I breathe again and soothe my aching lungs. I must have quit breathing entirely. "I'm okay," I whisper. I'm trying to convince myself as much as Benson.

"Are you sure?" His face is close to mine and his eyes look terrified.

All my bones are jelly, but I manage to nod.

"What happened?"

"We escaped." The words are out of my mouth before I realize I know what happened. "We escaped!" I struggle to stand and push Benson away as I run to the very middle of the crumbled foundation and begin digging. Rocks and sticks tear at my fingernails, but I feel no pain. "Help me," I beg Benson, desperation clawing at my chest.

"Help you what?" he asks, beside me.

"Dig."

He pauses, and at first I think he won't, but in a few seconds he brings over two thick sticks. He hands me one and holds onto the second.

It takes twenty minutes and nearly a foot before we hit something solid. "This is it," I say, letting out a sigh of relief.

I'm not crazy.

And just this *one* time, maybe I'm not wrong.

Time slips by as we dig out a square of iron. We're both filthy by the time we try to open it, and it takes the two of us pulling on the cast-iron handle with all our might before it begins to lift up and away from the ground.

I squeak in dismay as several large bugs crawl out, but soon I'm on my knees, peering in.

"Are there skeletons?" Benson asks, squinting at the edge of the dark hollow.

"No, we *escaped*," I say again. The panic is gone and I feel strangely confident as I hop down into the cavern, which can't be more than four feet by four feet. "I distracted them while Quinn got this place open. I came back, we hid, he made a shield first of wood to blend in with the floor and then cast iron, to protect us from the bullets. We took the tunnel. I created new dirt to fill in the path behind us. No human could have followed. That's how we got to the dugout!"

Benson is staring at me in horror and I'm half horrified at myself. What did I just say? Created new dirt? But in my mind's eye I see it—I *feel* it! Crawling down a tunnel, finally leaving the awful sound of gunshots behind. Thinking of dirt, picturing it, imagining it, just like everything else I've ever created.

And then it's there—as clear as if it were happening right at this moment—blocking the tunnel, dulling all sound, leaving Quinn and me in silence and darkness.

Darkness.

The memory of being Rebecca is slipping away, leaving me empty, and I push at her, wanting my body to myself.

The necklace, her voice says in my mind just before relinquishing her hold.

"The necklace," I echo aloud, almost without will. "I have to get the necklace. It . . . it has the answers." My words make no sense, but they ring through my body with truth. I reach out my hand and Benson helps me crawl over the shallow edge of the grimy hole, where I pause, kneeling on the ground, trying to understand myself.

Who am I?

It used to be an easy question.

"Tave, please, you're not making any sense. What the hell just happened?"

The sound of my name—my name *now*—jerks me back to the present and I look up at Benson.

"Benson." His frightened eyes meet mine. I've hardly registered his presence, but now I see his face again, streaked with mud. And suddenly, I remember. I remember him. Remember that he's the most important person in my entire world. I fling my arms around his neck, cling to him as he kneels in front of me. If I just hold onto him, the emotional hurricane won't be able to blow me away.

"Tavia, you have to—"

I cut him off, covering his mouth with mine. Savagely I grasp at his jacket, pulling him closer. I throw a leg over his knees, sitting on his lap, my thighs hugging his torso, my face above his now, begging him to remind me of who I am.

That I am Tavia.

That I love Benson.

The thought makes me flinch back. I look down at his blue eyes—worried, confused, mirrors of my own—and I realize I want to see those eyes every day for the rest of my life. Screw Elizabeth, screw her warnings; this is my choice. *He* is my choice.

"Benson." The words are a whisper before I kiss him again. *I love him.* The truth of that realization fills me, revitalizing me, giving me a strength I didn't have ten seconds ago.

He tries to pull away, to say something, but I don't let him. My mouth presses against his, just hard enough to hurt, but I don't back off and neither does he. *It's not enough.* Hands push into jackets, groping at skin. His. Mine. I feel him under my legs, against my hips, and a primal greed creeps over my body.

More.

He groans, and dimly I remember how battered he is, but I can't care right now. I need the solidness of his weight pressed against me, the feel of his racing heart pulsing in his neck as my fingers caress his warm skin.

I need to feel *grounded.*

Benson's mouth leaves mine and tiny gasps escape me as his lips trail down my neck, feasting, loving, needing me as much as I need him. We're frantic, as though we have only brief, borrowed time.

It seems likely.

No.

"Don't leave me," I manage to say before claiming his mouth again.

"Never," he growls. Our bodies are so close we feel like one as I wrap my arms around him, pulling him as tight against me as I can—filled with an irrational fear that he'll disappear if I don't.

I can almost hear Rebecca wailing in my head, but I shove all thoughts of her aside. All thoughts of Quinn.

I will not let Rebecca take Benson from me. I know what she had with Quinn. What *I* had with Quinn. The depth of that devotion, the joy of being a lover, of having that one person who knows everything.

She had it with Quinn.

Now I want it with Benson.

CHAPTER THIRTY-TWO

Sobs are wracking my body before I realize I've started crying. And almost as soon as I do, I'm laughing, laughing at the power Rebecca's trying to exert over me as soon as I want someone who isn't Quinn.

"Get out of my head!" I scream to the sky, and she retreats, but her presence is still there, slowly melding, and I know it's only a matter of time before it is not her and me, but *us*.

"Tave," Benson says, his hands still on my face. I take a calming breath and ground myself by studying him—his wire-rimmed glasses, slightly askew, the streak of mud across his forehead, his lips. They're red from my rough affections and all I want to do is kiss them again.

I try to speak, but my teeth are chattering from both cold and nerves and I can't get anything understandable out.

"Come here," Benson says, opening his jacket to me. I tuck myself close against his chest and he wraps me up as best he can, holding me tight as the chattering turns into full-body shudders, then slowly subsides.

"Can you talk about it now?" Benson whispers.

I don't lift my head; I'm not sure I can make this confession while looking at him. "I saw the whole thing. The night they were supposed to die."

"You mean like you were seeing through Quinn?"

I shake my head violently. "No, I had that part totally wrong. This was never about Quinn; it was about me! Quinn's not trying to possess me—he's just trying to get me to remember who I am."

"And who are you?"

"I'm Rebecca Fielding." Saying it aloud threatens my grip on reality. Less than a week ago, I thought *loving a stranger* was crazy. Where does that leave me now? "I *was*. Two hundred years ago, I was her, and I was here. With Quinn. We're . . ."

We're Earthbound. That word in Rebecca's head. The word Elizabeth spoke. The one I read in Quinn's journal.

But there's another word, too. One that terrifies me to my bones.

Gods. I am a goddess. But I don't say the words out loud. I hardly dare to think them, but their truth resonates through me. Even though I'm still not entirely sure what they mean.

For months I've accepted my limitations, accepted the parts of me that will never heal. Accepted that I am less than I once was.

But now I'm not.

I'm *more*. So much more.

I am forever. I am eternal. I am powerful beyond imagination. It's why I can make things. Rebecca could. Quinn could. And now I can. The cast-iron covering Benson and I dug up, like the cast-iron manacles I trapped Elizabeth in. I understand why, in that moment, it seemed so familiar.

And that's only a fraction of what I can do.

Rebecca and Quinn were better than I am now. My creations disappear—two hundred years later, theirs are still here.

I have the potential to do the same thing.

But I have to *do something*. And not just *anything*—the most important something in the world.

It will unlock my abilities . . . . if only I can remember what it is.

My body starts to shake again. That kind of power makes everything more dangerous, more dire. Maybe I can harness it, but if I can't, it could destroy us all.

"I don't understand," Benson says, and his voice is unsteady. "Like, a past life?"

"Yes. And not just one. A hundred. A thousand. At first I saw Rebecca, the same way I've always seen Quinn. But then, it's like my—my soul, I guess, came out of me and I was *inside* Rebecca, looking out of her eyes and feeling everything that she felt on the night they tried to kill her."

Benson is silent, but his brow wrinkles in obvious thought.

"And it was . . . familiar. I knew I'd been in that body before." *It was like coming home*, I think. But I don't say it.

"So, do you . . . remember things now?"

"Sort of. Flashes. It's not much," I admit. "But she . . . I was so afraid. They're after her, Benson."

"Who?"

"The Reduciata." Just saying the word makes a storm of fear roil in my chest.

He swallows hard.

"And that's why they're after me. Because she *is* me. I can't let them catch me. They'll—they'll—" I don't know how to end that sentence. But the terror that twists my insides in knots is enough to let me know that I would rather die than be in Reduciata custody.

Again.

Again?

"You can't even imagine what they'll do," I finally say, my voice soft. I shake off the awful memories.

Not even memories—shadows, hints of memories.

"We can't go to the Curatoria either. I have to do this on my own." Panic quivers inside me and I spin back to Benson. "Not *alone*," I emphasize when I see the despairing expression on his face. "Please help me?"

He reaches for my shoulder, then changes his mind and lets his hands drop. "What do you need me to do?"

"I need—"

The necklace. Rebecca's voice, I think. It sounds so much like my own.

"The necklace," I obediently parrot. "The one Quinn wrote about in his journal—then I'll remember." I don't want to give Rebecca more access to my head—to my heart—but somehow I know that getting the necklace will give me more power, not less. I *have* to have that power.

"Do you think it's in the dugout place?" he asks.

"It's got to be."

"Let's go back to the car." He helps me to my feet, but my fingers and toes are numb and I stagger.

"Easy," Benson says as he curls his arm around me and leads me away from the ruins of the house I lived in, lifetimes ago. I lean my head against his shoulder and wish we could forget about all this for a few hours and just go back to the hotel. Any hotel. The farther away the better.

But I can't. I have to remember and then get the hell out of here before they catch up with me. I can protect myself, protect Benson, but only if I remember.

Remember.

A few drops of melted snow from the trees drip onto my face as a gust of wind finds the towering boughs above us. The sudden cold pricks on my skin and I'm myself again. Completely now. Even though I know—know as surely as I know the sky is blue and grass green—that I was Rebecca Fielding in another life.

"I'll drive," Benson says. "We shouldn't stay in one place very long while people are following you—especially around that house. What used to be the house. If they know about Quinn, they might know about this place already."

"Just a sec," I say, reaching past him into the passenger seat. "It might be in the stuff you grabbed." I open Benson's messenger bag and sort through the contents.

A ring, a small pouch still mostly full of gold, and a lumpy bundle wrapped in a handkerchief.

That's it.

An energy only I can sense pulses through it and I know what's inside even as my fingers reach for it, pulling at the sparse stitches that hold the yellowed handkerchief closed.

The necklace.

It's here.

It's mine.

My hands are shaking too hard to undo the strings. "Benson? Can you please?"

He takes the delicate fabric and holds it in his hand for a few seconds before untying the thin strings to reveals a heavy pendant that glints silver and red.

It's the one from my vision.

He looks down at the necklace with a tight expression. "So this will bring everything back?"

"I think so."

He tries to speak, but his voice cracks and he stays silent for another few seconds. "And then what?" he finally asks, not looking up to meet my eyes.

I step forward and he draws the necklace closer, as though to keep it from me, but I'm not reaching for it. I run my hands up and down his arms the way he so often has with me.

Slowly.

Calmly.

Somehow I have to help Benson deal with all this. Help him see I still need him—need the guy who has seen me through absolute hell the last week. He didn't ask for this, wouldn't have had anything to do with this if I hadn't walked into his life. Come to the library for help.

Help. If only he knew then what he was getting into.

My hands freeze, and the words are out of my mouth before I can stop them. "Benson, if you could go back in time to the day we met, and you knew everything that was going to happen, would you opt out?"

He looks down at me, and his eyes are hollow.

And he thinks.

Really *thinks*.

A prickle of annoyance threatens at his hesitance, but I stamp it down. It's an important question and not one to be taken lightly.

"No," he finally whispers.

"Me either. And this," I say, pointing at his fist, still clenched around the necklace, the thin chain spilling out like sand, "isn't going to change things. I don't care what Rebecca thinks she wants, Benson. *I* want you. All this is going to do is give us answers."

"You don't understand," he whispers. "You won't feel the same."

"Benson Ryder, put that necklace down!" I snap.

He drops the necklace on the trunk of the car with a thud, wary and confused. As soon as it's out of his hand, I push my arms inside his jacket, just under his shirt. He shudders when my fingers touch his bare skin.

"Benson?" My heart beats wildly.

He just looks at me, and I could drown in the pain in his eyes.

"I love you. *You*." I kiss his bottom lip, more of a gentle brush of skin than a kiss. Tingles spread through my body and I suppress a smile.

I said it.

I meant it.

I stand on tiptoe and kiss the scrapes on his face, then his nose, his cheeks. I let my hands slide up his neck and pull him down to me, kissing him gently, coaxing him with my mouth. "She can't change how I feel," I murmur against his lips.

"You don't know that," he whispers, and his voice is filled with an agony I'm desperate to heal.

I entwine our fingers and hold them against my heart. "I *do*. You are the best thing that ever happened to me, and I think you've more than proved the lengths you'll go to for me." I kiss his knuckles, one at a time, avoiding the reddened, broken skin on his right hand. "Now it's my turn to prove it to *you*."

I look up at him, and his entire face is tight with an emotion I can't quite read. He draws in a ragged gasp and pulls his hand away. He turns halfway and picks up the necklace. "Shall I?" he whispers with near reverence.

"P-please," I stutter.

He lifts the necklace, and rubies sparkle in a beam of sunlight. The chain is long, and Benson holds it up and gestures for me to turn around. Then the pendant hangs in front of my face, still suspended from Benson's fingers. He hesitates, and I feel his breath close to my ear—in and out in a loud hiss.

"No matter what happens next," he whispers, "I love you too."

He drops the necklace over my head.

CHAPTER THIRTY-THREE

The instant the metal touches my skin, I'm in a whirlwind of light and color that flashes before my eyes, brilliant, excruciating, blinding in its radiance. My fingertips dig into Benson's arm as I try to find something to grasp onto to keep from being carried away.

But the storm rages only in my mind, and soon I have to close my eyes to the world and try to force the turmoil inside me to calm, to hush to a reasonable volume. As the pain builds, I grasp for respite. *Rebecca has done this before; she knows how to manage it.* Desperate, I surrender my mind to her and somehow she *takes* the invading burst of memories from me.

They solidify, somehow, though it's still like watching a movie in fast-forward. Scenes in a montage that flash before my eyes for only the briefest of instants before they're gone—long before I can make sense of them. But soon they grow bright again, wild; Rebecca can't handle them either.

"Benson, I can't stop it!"

The pressure is still rising inside my head and I clutch at my temples, willing it to slow, to just give me a moment of rest. An instant to catch my breath. I can feel Rebecca trying to do the same thing, but nothing is working and the pressure is building, pushing out against my skull until I'm afraid my cranial bones are going to literally burst.

She's no good to us if her brain is destroyed. The words skitter through my mind and now I understand what they were worried about.

Someone's screaming and I think it's me.

Hands are on me, arms wrapped around me, and even though my eyes are open again, I see only blackness. Images race, and just as I'm ready to give up, I see a flash of gold in the smeared scenes.

"Quinn, help me," I whisper through clenched teeth that rattle as I speak.

And then his eyes are there, still and green amid a sickly sea of memories. I focus on those eyes and the crazed turbulence ebbs the tiniest bit.

But it's enough.

I grasp for control and it's like swimming through tar toward the dimmest of lights. But it's there. Quinn's eyes sustain my equilibrium and Rebecca's mind and mine meld—we are one, we are *us*—and I know what to do. Together, our thoughts reach out like a net to bridle the energy that's been poured into me and somehow, I hold it. It fills every inch of me until I swear my skin must be stretched to bursting, but this time I can contain it.

My breath slows and when I blink again, a fuzzy green greets me. It takes a while longer before I can see the sun-imbued leaves clearly, but eventually my focus returns. My head is on Benson's lap and I'm lying on the sparse grass just behind the Honda. I try to move and everything hurts. After a few seconds I give up and just turn my eyes to Benson.

The forest is a glade of silence until Benson breaks it with a deafening whisper. "Are you okay?"

I nod. I ache like I've been struck by lightning, but I'm okay. I'm more than okay.

I'm *full*.

But I don't have words to express that; not ones that he would understand. I wouldn't have understood before either. It's beyond normal human comprehension.

I must be beyond human comprehension.

I am something else. My head aches and I close my eyes—the sunlight overwhelms my senses. But I know what I am now.

"Does it still hurt?"

I don't try to deny it. "Not as bad as before." And even speaking makes me want to whimper. "It's like an entire library just got poured into my brain and there's no room," I choke out.

"Is that why you screamed?"

I look up at him and for the first time since touching the necklace I see him clearly, with my Tavia eyes. He's pale and a sheen of sweat dots his brow. *What have I done?* "I'm so sorry, Benson." Though I don't know exactly what I'm sorry for. Scaring him? Putting him in this position at all?

Everything?

"You screamed and screamed," he whispers, and his voice quavers and he won't meet my eyes. "I thought you were going to break inside and die. I really did."

"So did I," I say, reaching for his hand.

He moves his arm, runs his fingers through his hair, a flash of hardness shining in his eyes.

But I don't have the capacity to analyze it.

I lie with my head on his lap, my knees curled against my chest, for minutes that feel like hours as the pain recedes, slowly, so slowly, like the tide going out. Staring at the green leaves, the crumbly brown earth, straggly grass blades, distracts me enough to let my mind carefully make room for everything I've learned.

Everything I am.

"I'm exactly what they said," I whisper, loosing my confession into reality.

"They?" Benson asks, his shaky words the barest hush on the wind.

"Elizabeth. Jay. They weren't lying. I'm an Earthbound—I'm a goddess." The word passes my lips for the first time and it's not quite as frightening as I feared. But almost.

"Like . . . God, capital *G*?"

"No. Something else. Something different." Ideas are whizzing through my head, making it hard to think in words. "I'm a creating goddess. But . . . cursed. I did . . . I did something wrong. A long time ago."

Benson stays silent, but I have to talk. I discover my knowledge as it falls from my lips, and somehow it relieves the pressure in my head.

"I make things, from nothing. I'm a Creator, like Quinn. We're Creators together. Lifetimes and lifetimes together. I can make anything. Anything," I say with wonder.

"A goddess," Benson says, and his voice is so quiet I'm not sure I would have heard him if my ear weren't pressed against his belly.

I feel a little giggle build up in my throat. "Like a tree," I say through a hysterical laugh. "Or a mountain. Or a building. Just *poof!* Anything."

"Like a pyramid," Benson says, following my manic thoughts.

I nod. "I was an Earthmaker. There were lots of us. We created the landscape of the whole world. It was—it was ours. Gifted to us by . . . I don't know. Someone bigger. Someone stronger. But we got greedy."

Wringing out specific memories is like trying to squeeze a brick of steel with my bare hands, and my body begins to tremble from the effort. "We created humans. To—to be our servants. We overstepped. We were cursed."

"Cursed by who?"

I shake my head. "I don't know."

"You remember this?"

"No. But I remember Rebecca remembering it." *Quinn told her.* "We failed our stewardship." The words are part of a proclamation—a sentence—burned into my memories. "Our immortality was taken away. Kind of. We became mortal, but with our souls tied—bound—to the earth. We live again and again, among the beings we created. Searching, always searching."

"Searching for what?"

"Our *diligo*," I say, trying out the unfamiliar word on my tongue.

"What does that mean?"

"Lover," I say, not meeting his eyes. "Bound to earth, bound together," I whisper. *"Reus ut terra, reus una."*

Quinn.

But . . .

No.

"The Reduciata try to kill the Earthbounds before they can reunite with their lovers."

"That's why they're trying to kill you?" Benson murmurs.

But I shake my head. "It's more than that with me. I . . . I know something. A secret. A secret that could destroy everything."

"What secret?" Benson asks, breathing in short gasps now.

But I just shake my head. "I don't remember. Something, something

I didn't even tell Quinn because it was too dangerous. That's what the men who came to our house were trying to get rid of. That knowledge. Something . . . something about the Reduciata and the Curatoria. Arg!" I growl. "It hurts to even think about it." I force a deep breath into my lungs and bury my face in Benson's shirt.

"Those names have Latin roots," Benson says, and I look up at him, confused. "What?" he asks sheepishly. "I looked them up on my phone after I saw them in Quinn's journal. *Curator* means 'to keep and preserve.' *Reduco* means 'to—"

"'Reduce,'" I interrupt with bitterness. "'To kill.'"

"No," Benson says softly. "It means 'to lead.'"

I'm silent, trying to affix meaning to this new information, but my brain is too tired.

"I guess that's why their symbol is that ankh thing. The ankh for eternity and shepherd's crook for leading."

"What about the other?"

"Other?"

It hurts so much to think. "The feather and flame."

Benson chews on his lip and looks up at the sky for a few seconds. "Maybe a *phoenix?* You know, they die and are born again, like Earthbound."

"And stronger every time," I say, unsure whose words they are. "If the Curatoria does their job, the Earthbound get stronger."

I don't even know what that means, but the effort pulls me into silence again.

"Can you sit up?" Benson asks after a while.

"Maybe."

He helps me up and lets me lean against him. My muscles ache and I'm hungry again. I stiffen as I realize every time I do anything that has to do with being an Earthbound, I get hungry. "I'm hungry. All the time," I say in a flat voice.

"What?" Benson asks.

"Ever since the crash, I'm hungry all the time. But especially since I started using my powers." I look up at Benson. "And Reese and Jay, they're always trying to get me to eat more. Even Elizabeth told me I had to get over my guilt and eat. They all knew—my Earthbound body needs to eat more."

"I guess it makes sense," Benson says slowly. "You make something out of nothing and I suspect your brain works on overdrive. That kind of thing needs fuel."

"But it was only after the crash. I've always been an Earthbound; you don't *become* an Earthbound. Everything started happening after the crash. What was it about the crash that made this part of me . . . wake up?"

Benson sighs. "I have no clue, Tave. I'm discovering just how little I really know about anything," he mutters.

Is he mad? Or just confused and frustrated, like me?

I can't think anymore.

"We should go," I say. "I need food and we have to get away."

"I think you need a few more minutes," Benson says, steadying me as I wobble to my feet.

"We may not have a few minutes. Someone's got to know about this place." My words are slurring and I take a deep breath and concentrate harder. "Don't underestimate the brotherhoods. It'll kill you."

Rebecca's memories flit through my head like fireflies, shining and dimming almost at random. Meeting Quinn, our life, our escape, the dugout, writing the journal.

The journal.

"I need the journal," I say. "Rebecca's." I'm moving toward the car door and Benson is scrambling to help me stay upright. "I need to make sure . . ." I snatch it up and rifle through the pages until I reach the strange language, and a smile curls across my face. A grin. A chuckle. Then I throw my head back and laugh, the sound filling the trees. "I can read it! Oh, Benson, she was brilliant! This is Latin—not exactly Latin, like you said. A common Latin. It's—" I think, trying to get the specifics from a memory bank that's like a closet I can't open more than a crack. "It's from Rome—ancient Rome." My head pounds from the effort of retrieving that tiny fact.

I look up, surprised, when Benson snorts. "Vulgar Latin?" he asks. "You can read Vulgar Latin?"

"It's not vulgar," I counter.

"No, that's what the common Latin is called—I read about it last semester. It's from like 800 A.D. when the Romans were trying to create a universal language throughout the empire. It's basically the parent language of *all* the Romance languages. And you can read it." He grins. "That's awesome."

I sober as I look down at the journal. "This is where my answers are. She left it in the dugout for me. It's our own personal pyramid, just like Quinn's journal said. A place where we stashed all our stuff so we could remember someday. We created it just for something like this. So we could rely on each other, not on either of the brotherhoods. After that night, we left. We never came back."

"But you escaped. You didn't die. What happened?"

"I died eventually," I say, and something snaps within me and the memory trickles back and I want to gag and clench my fists against it, pushing it away. *Please don't ask, please don't ask.* If he asks, it'll re-ignite the sensations and I'll have to feel it all over again and I'm not sure I have the stamina for that.

"How did you die?"

I look up at him as the all-too-familiar, body-numbing chill crashes over me. "I—" I brace myself against him as the cold that exists only in my mind paralyzes me. "I drowned. In a lake."

The nightmare of my last moments as Rebecca replays in my head until my whole body is quaking with cold. I can't sense any details— don't know why, where, when. All I know for sure is that *they* did it—the Reduciata. That fact burns in my mind like a searing fire, melting a tiny layer of ice. "They've been hunting me. For over two hundred years. Me, specifically. They've killed me so many times. I . . . I think they're the ones who made my plane crash."

Benson's hands tighten on me.

My body courses with crazy energy now. "Of course, Benson, it makes total sense."

"Total," Benson says dryly.

"I've been reborn. Not just now, a hundred times. A thousand times." I lean against him with a groan as the scope of that thought makes my brain ache. Then my eyes pop open. "And they're chasing me through lifetimes, trying to keep their secret—whatever it is—quiet! The Curatoria located me—lured me to them with the promise of a fancy art school, to protect me until they could awaken me, just like Eliza-beth said. But the Reduciata found out—brought the plane down. All to silence their secret." My eyes widen and the implication sinks in. "They'll kill anyone to get me. *Anyone* who stands in their way."

Anyone like him.

CHAPTER THIRTY-FOUR

"You need to find him, don't you?" Benson says after a while, his face a tableau of anguish.

"Who?"

His hands are chilly to the touch. "Quinn. Whoever he is now."

"Quinn?" I'm not sure how we even got to this subject. It feels foreign. Wrong. I don't need Quinn, I need Benson.

Don't I?

When did even the barest doubt enter into my mind?

And how can I get rid of it?

"If you've been reborn, then he has too, right?"

"Yes, of course," I say, as though it's the most obvious thing in the world. And right then, it is. "The Earthbound are never dead—their souls simply move from one body to the next."

His hands are tight around my fingers and I can hear his heart beating.

Not beating. Racing.

Pounding.

"You have to find him, then. It's . . . it's the only way you'll be safe."

I stare up at him part in horror and part in wonder. I won't leave Benson—but my mind is screaming that I *will* be safer with Quinn. How does Benson know that?

"And—and I won't stand in your way," he continues in a whisper. "I knew things would change when you remembered. And even though I—"

"No," I interrupt. "No, Benson. That's not what I want." I force these feelings, this doubt away. I am my own master. I may be a goddess and the brotherhoods may think I have a path I'm not allowed to stray from, but they're wrong. I can *choose*, and I will.

"These people are chasing you because of a secret you knew two hundred years ago—do you think they're just going to give up now?" Benson shakes his head, as if frustrated with himself. "You two need to be together. And I—" His voice breaks off and his hands tighten even more and the next words he says seem to take physical effort to force out. "I'll help you."

My head feels too heavy on my neck, but I force my face up so I can meet his eyes. "No, Benson, no. I don't want him. I want *you*."

"But—but you're Rebecca now."

I lift my hands to frame his face. "I am *not* Rebecca. I *was*, absolutely. But I'm not now. I'm Tavia and I love *you*, Benson."

He's silent for a long time before he whispers, "It's not as easy as that."

"It can be."

"People are trying to kill you, Tave. That's more important."

My thumb touches his cheekbone, just under the cut. "*Nothing* is more important than this."

His voice sounds frantic, and icy fear clenches at my heart. "But at the house, after your vision, you said—"

"*I* didn't say anything," I counter, a little pissed that he believes I would turn on him so easily. "*Rebecca* said a lot of things before I got control back. It's what *she* wants, Benson. But she's not in charge this time around. *I* am."

Benson's eyes are wide and then he closes his mouth and clenches his teeth, the muscles standing out on his cheeks. "I just . . . I assumed, I mean you've had lifetimes with him, right?"

"I guess, but—"

"Everything you've done the last three days has been about you trying to get to Quinn, to figure out Quinn, to complete this mystery task Quinn had for you. Not Rebecca—*you*." His hands are tight on my arms, not holding me back, more like holding himself back from me. I loosen his hands, and his expression turns chastened until I step forward and lay my head on his shoulder, wrapping my arms around him as lightly as possible.

"I thought I might be in love with him; I did. I thought that desperate feeling of obsession was love. And maybe it's a *kind* of love. But it isn't the kind I like." I pull back and look at him. "Rebecca will always be there inside me. And there are—others—who may come out in time. But I won't let them choose my life." I lean my head back so I can see Benson's face, so I can look him in the eye. "I don't want him, Benson. I want you. I don't love him." I take a deep breath. "I love *you*."

The moment stretches and everything is still. Benson's eyes stare into me, searching for truth. Maybe searching for lies.

But there are none. The feelings I have for Quinn will always be there—I understand that now, and I can't purge an entire part of me, especially one as big as my past lives—but if there's one thing I've learned from my long recovery, it's to live every day like it's my last.

And if today is my last day, I want to spend it with Benson.

He looks shocked, so I reach for the back of his neck and bring his lips down to mine. Benson comes to life, his arms twisting around me, holding me close. Pained groans sound against my mouth, but he doesn't release me; his kiss is hard, as though branding me his in a way words alone cannot.

His fingers stroke close to my scar and then across it. I freeze, waiting for him to . . . I'm not even sure. Pull away? Push against it? At the very least, ask questions. But his cheek rubs across my forehead and his hands continue their gentle exploration as though he didn't notice. He slides his fingers to each side of my face, warming my clammy skin.

"Tave," he whispers, his lips feather light.

"What?" I whisper back, my fingers finding a sensitive curve of his neck and making him shiver.

He bends his head so his mouth is right by my ear. "Run away with me."

"What do you mean?"

"Let's go underground," he says, gripping my hand in tight fists. One of the cuts on his right knuckle cracks open and oozes a tiny droplet of blood. "These people chasing you—Reduciata, Curatoria, whoever—if you stay here, they're going to find you. And when they do, they are going to *kill you.*" He looks down and shifts back and forth a few times. "I was going to suggest you take the money and leave on your own to find whoever Quinn is now, but if—if you really want me—"

"I do, Benson," I interrupt, not willing to let him have the slightest moment's doubt about that.

"Then—then I'll come too. But we have to be fast and thorough. These people, they've found us again and again and I can't let them hurt you. Not now. We have to go seriously underground, Tave. It's going to be hard core. Leave my phone, ditch the car, change our identities, *everything*." The fear in his eyes terrifies the glee out of me.

"What about your family?" I ask. "This isn't like when you left Portsmouth with me. If we run tonight, I don't know if there's any coming back. Ever."

"There's not," he says, determined.

"You've already made your decision."

"I decided yesterday—with or without you, I'm going to run. I'm hip deep in all this stuff already. If we both went to ground in different directions, we'd probably be safer." He sighs and bunches his fists on his hips. "But to tell the truth, I'm willing to risk just about anything to be with you."

"I have no family anymore, Benson. But I can't pretend it's the same for you. You might never be able to see your mom and brother again."

He looks down, his emotions burning in his eyes. "I can't—I can't live my life for them anymore. Some bonds are stronger than blood; *you're* my family now."

The same words that filled my own thoughts just yesterday. It's the final confirmation I need.

Me and Benson.

Benson and me.

We'll take on the world and win.

Benson squeezes my hand. "We should go. Now."

I nod, feeling sudden confidence in our plan. "How should we leave?" I ask. "I mean, since we have to ditch the car?" The *stolen* car. Maybe the cops will find it and give it back to whoever it belongs to.

"Greyhound?" Benson suggests. "It's not luxurious or anything, but it'll get us far enough away to consider our options. We can park a few blocks from the nearest station and leave the Honda behind. You pick the city," he says, stepping forward, his face close to mine. "Anywhere you want to go."

"As long as we're together, it doesn't matter."

He kisses my forehead, then pulls his phone out of his pocket, looking even more like the Superman I've always thought of him as. "I'll look up a bus station and then ditch this in a Dumpster."

"You got that from a movie."

He laughs. "Maybe, but the good guys always win in the movies, right?"

I start to turn to get into the car, but Benson holds onto my hands. "When we get on the bus," he says hesitantly, "we need to talk. Really . . . talk."

"Absolutely," I say, but my heart speeds a little at the look on his face.

"I think we should talk now."

We both spin at the intruding voice only to see what still appears to be an empty clearing. Then, in a circle around us, we hear the unmistakable click of guns being cocked. I cling to Benson, my eyes scanning the trees. Just as I'm sure no one is going to appear before they shoot us, Jay steps out from behind a tree.

CHAPTER THIRTY-FIVE

"Let's all stay calm," Jay says in a soft, even tone that makes me want to reach out and smack him. My mind spins with defensive plans.

More cast iron, insta-shotguns, bulletproof glass . . . assuming I could make something that high tech, which I'm suddenly not convinced is within my capabilities.

But Benson is here.

I won't risk him.

Can't risk him.

This is the problem with love.

"Peace offering," Jay says, drawing my attention back. He's holding up what I vaguely recognize as several of the organic, all-natural protein bars that Reese keeps around the house.

A weird nostalgia hits me. That will never be my life again.

"No one's here to kill you, Tave," Jay says, as though reading my mind. "All of this—" His hand takes in the unseen guns surrounding us, hidden from sight by the broad-leafed trees. "Just a precaution. After what you did to Elizabeth and me, I think it's understandable."

He edges forward like he's approaching a skittish colt. Despite what he just said, he doesn't seem afraid of *me*; he looks like he's worried I'm afraid of *him*.

Which I am. Terrified. But I don't want him to know.

The sun is shining down into the middle of the clearing with a vengeance that defies the bitter cold of the last few days, but despite that, my veins are ice water.

"I know you need to eat," Jay says, still holding out the bars. "I'm not sure what you've been doing, but I've seen enough Earthbounds on the run to recognize that look; you're about five minutes away from fainting."

Even though every nerve in my body is poised to bolt, I force myself to meet his eyes and then take two slow steps forward and snatch the protein bars, immediately retreating back to Benson as soon as the food is in my hand. I rip open the wrapper and take a bite, keeping my eyes on Jay the whole time.

To tell the truth, he looks awful. Those circles under his eyes—they speak of more than sleep deprivation. And his skin has a weird quality to it—like it grew a size too big and is now hanging off him. Melting, almost. "Are you all right, Jay?" I ask through a half-chewed protein bar.

Jay doesn't answer, just makes a small motion, and Reese and Elizabeth step out from the brush and join him with that same tentative slowness. I've already torn open the next protein bar and taken a big bite, but at the sight of those two my mouth turns dry.

Even though I know they were telling the truth.

Even though it was probably a mistake to leave them in the first place.

But they're still the ones controlling the guns pointed at me—at the guy I love. It's hard not to think of them as the enemy when they're pointing weapons at us.

"We just want to talk," Reese says, before I can speak.

"Why are you doing this?" I ask when the second bar is gone—which takes a remarkably short time, and I'm already opening the third. "I thought you were Curatoria. Aren't you supposed to help Earthbound?"

Are they?

Supposed to. Or so they say.

Rebecca considered them *more* trustworthy than the Reduciata, but what kind of standard is that?

"We are," Reese says. "And we're trying our damnedest to keep you alive, but you're not making it very easy."

The shock of the whole situation is wearing off and I'm not afraid anymore.

I'm pissed.

"If you had trusted me with *any* amount of information, maybe I wouldn't have been so high strung. Do you have any idea what the last week has been like for me?" I snap.

"If you had trusted *us* with any information about what you were experiencing, maybe we could have helped," she replies without emotion.

I close my mouth. I'm not going to play this blame-trading game. "You're not my aunt and uncle, are you?" I ask, not bothering to hide the accusation in my voice.

The question hangs in the air, one they obviously don't want to answer. "No," Reese finally says. "My name is Samantha. Sammi."

I almost laugh at the nickname. It matches her pert blond hair and doll-like stature but is completely at odds with her formal, businesslike personality. "And you?" I say, whipping my head around to Jay, who I realize is leaning against the tree now—like standing takes too much effort.

"Mark. Just Mark," he adds awkwardly.

"Why pretend?" I ask, shooting my words at him.

"To get you into protective custody without shocking you with everything all at once. It was hard enough for you to deal with your parents dying—not to mention the physical trauma—without pushing a bunch of supernatural stuff on you as well. We were trying to be gentle, while still keeping you safe and hidden."

"Did you kill my real aunt and uncle before you stole their identities?"

"That is *not* how we work, Tavia," Sammi snaps, plainly offended. "They're alive and well and think you died in the crash. And trust me, falsifying TSA documents is no picnic."

"Tavia," Elizabeth says, speaking up for the first time, "if there's anything I have *ever* said that you believed, please believe this: Sammi and Mark and I have dedicated every waking moment for more than the last *year* to keeping you safe."

"Not to mention eighteen years ago," Reese—Sammi—adds in a mutter.

Elizabeth shoots her a look and continues. "We almost lost you in the plane crash, and that failure has plagued us every single day. There are no three people in the world who you're safer with than us. I promise you that."

Safer than with Benson? I think wryly. *Not a chance.* But I say nothing, just reach back for Benson's hands. He's staying quiet, letting me speak, rant, accuse. But he hasn't moved an inch, his warm chest a solid support against my back. As steadfast as any of these ancient trees. He makes me feel strong. Bold. Better.

"Please," Elizabeth says, "let us take you somewhere safe—we'll talk about anything you want then, but we're tempting fate by staying out here in the open."

"We're pretty off-road," I reply sarcastically, gesturing at the thick foliage around us.

"Anything but bulletproof walls is *out in the open* as far as I'm concerned," Sammi snaps. "Please, let us take you to a safe house."

"I'm not going anywhere with you," I retort. "I don't want anything to do with the Curatoria or the Reduciata."

"To be honest, I don't think you'll last long on your own. I've never seen the Reduciata hunt someone this seriously. Taking down an entire plane?" Mark says, confirming my suspicions. "That's brutal even for them. We managed to get to the car crash in Bath about an hour after it happened, and to tell the truth, we thought they'd gotten you at that hotel in Freeport."

I clench my jaw. They were *never* far behind. But still farther behind than the Reduciata, who have been getting progressively closer and closer. I want to take Benson and run—I want it so badly—but would it be a death sentence for us both?

"They want *you*," Mark continues. "Specifically, and very badly. After the plane wreck we had to take you and hide you because when you were the sole survivor, the Reduciata immediately knew they'd failed to assassinate you. Only an Earthbound could have survived that crash."

My fingers clutch Benson's icy skin. "What is it about this crash that started everything? I don't understand. I didn't know anything then."

"An Earthbound's self-preservation instinct is incredibly strong," Sammi says simply, as though we were discussing the migratory patterns of butterflies. "Awareness that borders on precognition, impulse self-defense in disciplines the Earthbound has never learned in conscious memory, that sort of thing. Sudden re-awakenings of powers in life-threatening scenarios is the least of what I've seen in my time. The simple need to stay alive brought your ability forth. We're not sure exactly *what* you did, but somehow your instincts kicked in and you created something to save yourself."

My throat is constricting now as the obvious question slams into me like a boulder. "I did it? I kept myself alive?" I whisper, and I can see in Elizabeth's eyes that she knows what's coming next. I blink, but that only makes the tears spill onto my cheeks—searing spots on my skin. "Then why couldn't I save them too?"

"I don't think your unconscious instincts could do anything beyond self-preservation," Mark says, empathy—real or not—heavy in his tone. "You can't feel guilty about that, Tavia."

But I do.

If I—even without consciously understanding my powers—could rescue myself, then I could have rescued them.

And I *didn't*.

Benson wraps his arm around my waist and I cling to him, forcing myself to fill my lungs several times even though it feels like knives are stabbing my chest.

The truth should be simple. And this is not simple. This is a fairy tale. And not the Prince-Charming-kissed-the-princess kind of fairy tale; the kind where the wolf eats the grandmother, the mermaid turns into sea foam, and the dancer gets her feet cut off.

"How did you guys even know who I was?" I choke out.

"Oh, Tave, so much research," Sammi says, and she looks tired at the thought. "*Generations* of research. My family have been Curatoriates for more than ten generations; membership in both brotherhoods is often a family affair."

"Like the mob," Benson says dryly, speaking for the first time.

Sammi shoots him an annoyed look but continues as though he hadn't spoken. "Since I was sixteen and trained under my father, I've spent my life searching for the Earthbound. We have a lot of methods, none of them simple or foolproof. Honestly, if you didn't look the same from lifetime to lifetime, I think we'd be hopelessly lost."

I remember the vision of Rebecca. Longer hair, but otherwise identical.

"I—I have a bit of a connection with you, actually," Sammi says.

"What kind of connection?" I ask, and I can't keep the suspicion out of my voice.

She reaches into the large bag at her hip and I step back and throw my arms out in front of Benson, but Sammi's hand emerges clutching a file folder with the symbol of the feather and the flame. She walks toward me, raising the folder like a white flag.

It feels strange, exchanging folders of documents in the forest, with brown leaves crunching under our feet, but what about this whole experience hasn't been strange? I take the folder warily and try to keep my eyes on Sammi even as I open the cover.

It's odd to see my face stare out from a picture I don't remember being in. It has that sepia tinge that old photos take on, and I see myself in a wide-necked sweater and high-waisted jeans, lying on my stomach, reading a book. "When is this?" I ask, studying all the little facial details I've become so intimately acquainted with over the years.

It's strange how foreign they look now.

"Eighteen years ago," Sammi says, and I remember her cryptic statement a few minutes ago.

I wrinkle my brow. "I died young."

"You did."

My finger reaches out to touch another face in the picture—the sharp chin of teenage Samantha. Shorter hair, a little thinner, but definitely her. "That's you."

"Yes, that's me as a teenager, and that's you as Sonya. And despite everything," she adds with a laugh, "you are *so* much easier to live with this time around."

"'*Belligerent*,'" I recite from the next page in the file, but there's no humor in my voice. I'm not ready to think of *any* of this as amusing.

"That basically sums it up. You didn't trust us, even after we were able to give you your memories back. And you wouldn't tell us *anything*."

I reach the bottom of the file, and everything inside me clenches up in denial. "It says here that I killed myself. If you Curatoria people are so helpful and trustworthy, why did I do that?"

Sammi is quiet for long time, twisting her wedding ring around and around. When she speaks, her voice is low and serious. "The bond between partners is so strong, it often becomes an Earthbound's motivation for living. Right before we found you, we found your partner. His name was Darius then. But we weren't the only ones who found him. Unfortunately, he left too much of a trail and the Reduciata located him . . . and . . ." She spreads her hands out in front of her. "You have to understand, Tavia. For an Earthbound, death isn't the same as for the rest of us. It's not the end; it's more like a reset button. It wasn't that you stopped wanting to live but that you wanted to be on the same timeline as Darius. Quinn. Whatever you want to call him. You didn't want to be twenty-three years older than him when you found his new incarnation. You wanted to be at the same stage so the two of you might have a chance of a long life together."

"So I *killed myself*?" I ask. The cold logic of the act doesn't make it any less gruesome.

"It was hard on me too," Sammi admitted. "Even though I understood what it meant. Since then I've dedicated much of my service as a Curatoriate to finding you and Darius and getting you together again. To right that wrong. It's been my life's work. So when I recognized your painting style last year from a few pieces we have by Rebecca, I was finally able to complete the first step in my mission."

"Well, you can stop now. I don't want to be with him." I take Benson's hand again, twine my fingers through his, and smile. "I want to be with Benson. We don't need you and we certainly don't need this guy—Darius, Quinn, whoever. We only need each other."

Benson smiles back, but he looks nervous—edgy. His hand grips mine like he's afraid I'll bolt at any moment.

"Don't you even want to see him?" Sammi asks.

"See who?"

"Your partner, Quinn Avery. Who he is today?" She holds out another file.

I try not to be affected. I have a boy who loves me; I certainly don't need another one. But Sammi continues to hold it out, and finally I give up my show of nonchalance and grab it and read the label.

"'Logan Sikes,'" I read.

I hold the file, count to three, open it.

And there he is.

An eight-by-ten of a guy—a teenager, just like me. Somewhere in the back of my head a new voice I vaguely recognize as Sonya cheers. *It worked!* And even as I push her away, I realize she's right. We're the same age. We could be together—have an entire lifetime.

Except.

I don't want him.

Not *me.*

They do. They want him so badly I'm not sure my brain can handle the split decision without tearing apart.

Stalling, I reach my fingertips out to touch Quinn's familiar face, made modern in this Logan guy. His hair is shorter, tousled and hanging almost to his green eyes instead of tied with a ribbon. Jeans and a T-shirt look so odd on him, and yet he seems very at home, glancing just over his shoulder.

I can deny my heart, cling to Benson, ignore Elizabeth's warning, shut out Rebecca and Sonya's voices.

But I can't escape those eyes.

I know those eyes. I've loved those eyes. Looked into them while they loved me. Hundreds of times. Thousands. My breath feels sharp as I stare into his eyes and am hypnotized.

Desperately, I push my gaze to the date at the bottom of the picture. "This was taken yesterday?" I gasp, and Sammi nods, mistaking my dismay for delight.

"As he was walking to school. I saw him myself. In the flesh, not this vision of Quinn Avery that you've been seeing the last week. He's real. It's the reason I had to go to Phoenix so abruptly. That's *where he is.*"

Phoenix. I almost went there. Meeting up with *ghost* Quinn nearly ripped apart my heart and soul; what would seeing the real Logan have done to me?

Sammi leans forward. "I'm sorry I didn't tell you before that I thought I'd found him—I see now that I should have—but . . . Tavia, it almost destroyed me when you killed yourself while under my care. I was there when my father told you Darius was dead. You—you can't even imagine the devastation I saw in your eyes. Maybe you can," she said wryly. "Surely you remember that part."

I hesitate. "I don't, actually. I don't remember a lot of things. Mostly just my life as Rebecca, but even that's vague. I . . . I *sense*," I decide on, not really sure how to better describe it, "that this isn't the way it's *supposed* to happen. That this whole remembering thing should be easier." I let the unasked question hang in the air.

"You don't remember anything about Sonya? At all?" Sammi asks.

"Just a . . . familiarity," I admit. "A trickle of a voice in my head."

"Do you remember—" But she cuts off. "Now's not the time; we can discuss Sonya later. Liz did a ton of research after the plane crash, and she theorized that the damage your brain suffered would make things more difficult. The same way it was so hard for you to start drawing again."

"It's why we were worrying about damaging you further," Elizabeth tacks on.

"Will it always hurt?" I ask in a weak voice, my whole body on edge at even the thought of the pain the necklace had invoked.

Sammi's chin shoots up. "It—"

"The brains of Earthbounds don't function quite the same as ours— not even the same as those of us who have Earthbound as kin," Elizabeth interrupts. "It's the reason you see things the rest of us can't." She pauses. "Like the glowing triangles."

My eyes widen and I try to ask about that, but Elizabeth cuts me off.

"As far as we can tell, the synaptic pathways both connect and fire differently. What we aren't certain of is how the damage to your brain will affect that. But no, it *shouldn't* hurt." She hesitates, understanding how bad it must have been even though I didn't say so. "I don't know if it will continue to be a painful process or not, but now that you've had your initial memory pull from one of your creations, the *worst* should be over. From here on out it will hopefully just be a matter of sifting through the memories from the change you've already invoked."

"I had hoped to find a way to bring Logan back with me and pull his memories while you were together." Sammi's voice is soft and even, but I've lived with her long enough to hear the current of frustration. "But your running away kind of put a wrench in that."

"If you're waiting for me to apologize, it's going to be a long night," I say, leaning closer to Benson with my arms folded over the files, holding them against me.

I'm not giving them back.

"I'm not waiting for anything. We know where Logan is; we'll take you to him tonight." She looks up and meets my eyes. "By force, if necessary."

"What do you mean by force?" I snap. "I think you're being a little melodramatic."

Sammi looks at Mark and they have a silent conversation with their eyes. I rest one hand on my hip to wait for them to finish deciding if they are going to continue lying to me. But Mark gives a tiny nod and Sammi turns back to me with genuinely haunted eyes.

"Mark has the virus."

CHAPTER THIRTY-SIX

"The virus? The one from the news?" I ask, and reach for Benson's hand. I grip his fingers so tightly I know I must be hurting him, but he doesn't complain.

"I estimate he's got twelve to eighteen hours," Sammi chokes out.

I look over at Mark, understanding his limp skin, deep under-eye circles—even the signs of fatigue I was seeing before I ran away; he's dying.

And then, as I'm about to look away, he flickers. I draw in a loud breath.

I get it now. I see it when others don't because I'm an Earthbound. The reporter on TV—probably dead or dying. The woman who gave me the Band-Aid, almost certainly gone. What about the man by the candy shop? If flickering is the virus, what is disappearing entirely? I shake the thought away; there's no time. "What does that have to do with me?" I ask shakily.

"Something changed when you survived that plane wreck, Tave. At that point, they wanted to kill you—wanted it desperately. Now? They want to *take* you."

"Could have fooled me," I grumble, thinking of Sunglasses Guy shooting at me, the car that almost hit me, the charred BMW at the hotel.

"Trust me," Sammi says, "if the Reduciata really wanted you dead, that
car in Bath *wouldn't have missed*. They're not amateurs: it wasn't a failed
assassination attempt, it was a message—a warning. I only wish I know who
it was for. They *want* you to remember, and then they'll try to take you.
And our sources say it's because you know something about the virus."

"But I don't!" I protest.

"Tavia, Mark's only chance of survival is getting you back with
Quinn—Logan—connecting you two, and getting you to resurge. Hopefully in that process you'll remember what the Reduciata need you for."

"But I can't . . . I don't—"

"Tavia, I'm offering you a chance to be with Logan. At *eighteen*," she
adds, and I hear a frantic edge in her voice. "To have a whole lifetime
together. It's what you've always wanted; why are you fighting me?" she
asks, her patience starting to loosen at the seams—completely unaware
that not fifteen minutes ago I pledged my life to Benson instead.

I'm keeping that promise.

Somehow.

Sammi takes a deep breath and runs her fingers through her short
hair, getting a better grip on her control. "I have a private jet waiting for
us; you can sleep on the way and we'll get some better food into you."

"No." My voice seems to boom around the clearing, and I swear I
hear people shuffle around in the trees behind me.

Sammi freezes. "What do you mean, no? You *have* to do this. And
we're running out of time! Not just for Mark, but for everyone. Sixty-four
people died of the virus today, and that number is only going to go up."
She flings her hand out, pointing at nothing, at the world, at everyone

else. "I don't know exactly what the Reduciata want with you, but it must have something to do with the virus; otherwise they would just kill you. You don't understand—they have plans, something is brewing, and in the last few years their methods have *changed*. They're getting ready to—"

"I don't care!" I scream, finally stopping the words falling from her mouth. "Whatever they're planning is just a moment amid *thousands* of years of history of blood and schemes and I want *out!*" I turn to Mark. "I am truly sorry, Mark, but I. Can't. Help. You. I know nothing about this virus." I turn back to Sammi and Elizabeth. "I don't want anything to do with the Curatoria or the Reduciata and if you're as interested in aiding me as you say, then you'll respect that." My legs are quaking, but I force myself to stay calm—to appear in control.

"Think about it, Tavia," Sammi says, carefully avoiding looking at Benson as she changes her tactic. "This is your chance to be a true goddess and *save the human race*. After your curse, don't you think this is the ultimate redemption? And on top of that, it's your opportunity to have a *whole lifetime* with your partner. You're going to give it up to spend a couple of years with a guy you just met?"

"No offense," Mark says in a wry mutter.

"Mincing words isn't going to help anyone," Sammi retorts without looking away from me. "Do you think you can fight the thousands of years of longing and love that you're going to remember more of every day? And why would you want to when you can be with him *and* do something to stop the Reduciata?"

"You can't make me fall in love with someone just because it's 'supposed to' happen," I argue, and my stomach feels hollow as I try to push away the guilt. But I can't be the heroine they think I am! I don't know anything about this virus!

"No," Sammi says softly. "I can't." Then she points at my head. "But *they* can. The hundreds of women inside you, the hundreds of women who love him. And they'll grow stronger and louder until you resent the day you didn't run into Logan's arms when you had the chance. That's simply the reality of it. Do you think you're the first Earthbound who had a life before their memories awakened? The people I've seen, the journals I've read—you can't fight this, Tave. And by the time you realize that, you'll be dead, the majority of the human race will be gone, and it will be too late. Think very carefully about that."

I stare at her, defiant, and she stares right back, her eyes razors of anger and fear.

She's not lying—at least, she's saying what she believes to be the truth.

But truth, like beauty, is in the eye of the beholder.

"Tavia." Benson's voice is small and weak, but it vibrates to the center of my chest. "Maybe she's right."

"No, Benson, she's not!" I turn to him and he catches my face in his hands, cradling my cheeks, his face inches from mine.

"I will stay as long as you want me to," he says in a whisper meant only for me. "But this virus, it's going to devastate the world. And if you're the key to stopping it—you need to take that chance. If she's right, someday you'll regret making this choice. I know what that feels like and . . . I don't know if I could handle it."

"I don't think she *is* right," I argue. "I know nothing! And I don't think Rebecca knows anything either."

"Is it worth the risk?"

"Yes," I insist, and I don't bother whispering—don't care if they hear. "Benson, every person I have ever loved in my life has been ripped away from me either by death or deception," I say, flinging my hand out at the people I had come to love as Reese and Jay. "The chance to choose my own heart's desire and be with the person I want is *worth it*." This is my truth; *he* is my truth.

Sammi blinks, for once unruffled. "Tavia, I didn't want to bring this out too, but you *have* to reunite with your partner," she says flatly. "Or you're both going to die. Forever."

"What are you talking about?" I demand. I step forward, my chin raised. "I'm an Earthbound. My soul is immortal and tied to this earth for all time." *Rebecca's voice again.* I don't push her away; she knows what she's talking about.

"That's what we've believed for thousands of years," Sammi replies. "But thanks to a Reduciata Earthbound who came to us a few decades ago, we've discovered that's not entirely true. We've tried to keep it quiet, but you need to hear the truth."

I feel shaky and have to lean against Benson's chest to stay upright. Though I can't remember all my lives—any of my lives, really—I can sense a bedrock of truth that goes back thousands, maybe millions of years, that there's *always* another day, another life, another chance to do better, be better. Even the hint of a threat against that shakes me to my very core. "My existence is dependent on my choice of boyfriend?" I snap, my voice dripping with disbelief.

Sammi looks at me strangely as Elizabeth steps forward. "You don't remember why you have to find him, do you?"

I'm afraid to answer. To look stupid and dependent on them.

"This isn't about romance, Tave. This about life and death—your curse."

"The one for creating humans?" I ask shakily.

Elizabeth nods. "You know how the things you create disappear in about five minutes? Once you reconnect with Quinn, they'll stay permanently."

"Which is actually the *less* important part," Sammi adds. "The powers of the Earthbound are like . . ." She pauses. "What's the best way to explain this? They're like a battery. And each lifetime you find each other is like charging that battery. Your powers become not only permanent, but stronger. And each lifetime you don't connect, they weaken." She glances at Mark and I don't like the fear in her eyes. Not fear *for* me, fear *of* me. She's afraid to tell me this. Afraid what I'll do. "And like batteries, they eventually go dead."

"No," I say, dismissing her words. "We've existed since the beginning of time. We don't just *go dead*."

"You do if enough lifetimes pass."

I say nothing.

It's *impossible*.

"For centuries we've believed that the Reduciata are motivated by greed—mainly a desire for power. And while that *is* true, it's worse than we thought. Both the brotherhoods keep meticulous records. The Reduciata discovered it first, but once we found out, it was easy to confirm. Earthbounds have some kind of finite source of power, and it takes a great deal of that power to reincarnate. If they don't find their partner for long enough—replenish that source—eventually, they run out of the energy necessary for their soul to . . . migrate."

I hold out my hands as if I can stop her from speaking. As though it won't be true if she simply doesn't say it.

"So eventually, when you die, you're gone. Just like the rest of us," she adds in a whisper. When I say nothing, she continues, probably as much to fill the awkward silence as anything. "That's what the Reduciata are trying to do. They believe that if they can permanently kill enough sets of Earthbounds that their power will revert to the remaining gods. They're trying to return themselves to the level of strength the Earthmakers—the Earthbounds before the fall—were originally endowed with. And they've done a fairly good job already."

"How many?" I whisper.

"How many what?"

"How many lifetimes?"

Sammi hesitates. "Seven."

The math is instantaneous. Two hundred years since I was with Quinn. "This is my seventh lifetime, isn't it?"

Sammi nods.

"And Logan's?" In my mind he has already reverted to his new self, his new name.

"As far as we can tell, his too," Sammi confirms.

The message is brutally clear: if I run away with Benson, Logan and I both end as soon as we die.

And maybe the world perishes with us.

Five minutes ago, I thought I would give anything up for love—but now, will I have to give up love to save the world?

I let my head drop and Sammi interprets it as concession. "You won't regret this," she says, a flutter of excitement in her voice.

Before I can contradict her, she sifts around in her briefcase for a few moments, then steps toward me with something held between her palms. "When I first met you," she begins, "when you were Sonya, you were so afraid of us. Afraid of being discovered by the Reduciata, especially. And then when you found out Darius had been killed, you ... you never wanted to remember that life. At all. You wouldn't give us anything to do a memory pull with, never told us more than was absolutely necessary. But one day I came in and you had been lying on the floor reading and, without thinking, you braided the edge of the carpet. It wasn't much, but technically, you made it."

"Do you mean I made it with my powers?" I ask, not understanding.

She shakes her head. "I've been telling you for months that being an artist is integral to who you are. You don't have to do anything supernatural to create something that will help you remember—or else what would Destroyers be left with? You just have to *make* it. Generally in the form of art, painting, sculpting, or"—she gestures at my necklace—"jewelry. Simple as it is, I'm pretty sure this bit of carpet counts. I tied both ends and cut it off. It shouldn't have mattered that much; a memory pull with a creation from any of the lifetimes should restore them all. But I kept it just in case. And now?" She raises her eyelashes, showing intense blue eyes. "I don't know if you do want to remember that life or not. Whatever happened to make you so paranoid, you didn't tell us. Maybe it's better left buried. But I think that's a choice *you* should make for yourself."

I'm afraid to reach out my hand, but I don't have to. Sammi is already shaking her head.

"Don't touch it," she says. "Don't even look at it. Not until *you* decide if you want to. Those memories *might* be somewhere in your head—but if Elizabeth is right, you may need *this* to get Sonya's memories back. I'm going to tuck it in here." She slides a Ziploc bag into a small pocket of my backpack and holds it out to me. "Now it's up to you." Then, before I can even process her confession, she's walking away.

"I'll call the pilot and have him start preparations. Grab anything you want to take with you from this car that you *borrowed*," she calls over her shoulder. "We're leaving it here. Maybe it will find its way home."

I turn to Benson and lean my forehead against his shoulder, drawing strength from him as his arms wind around me, pulling me close. I feel like my whole body is devoid of energy after everything I've learned and heard today.

Hell, the last several days.

He's my anchor to reality. No, more than that—my own sanity.

"I don't know what to do," I admit, my lips close to his ear.

"Let's start with collecting our stuff," he whispers. "That way, if you want to run, you're ready. But"—he pauses—"if you *do* still want to, maybe it's best if we go with them tonight and run tomorrow. At least we'd be thousands of miles away."

"Forgive me if I don't share your confidence in a plane getting us anywhere safely," I say darkly.

He squeezes my hand in understanding before reaching into the center console and grabbing his phone. He holds it, looking down at it for a moment, and then his expression grows hard and he throws it as hard as he can into the trees.

I eavesdrop on Sammi as I fill my backpack to bursting with all the things from the dugout and the journals from the front seat. I look up when Mark curses. He's staring at his ringing phone but not answering it. "It's Daniel again. I have to answer eventually. What am I supposed to tell him?"

"Anything but the truth," Sammi says wryly.

"Who's Daniel?" I ask, recognizing the name from the conversation I overheard in their bedroom.

Another conversation that included hiding the truth from this Daniel person.

"Bigwig in the Curatoria," Elizabeth answers for Sammi.

My heart pounds in warning. "Then why don't you trust him?"

The three adults look back and forth at each other and don't speak.

"Oh please," I say in such a bitter tone that all three heads jerk up. "We got into this mess because you wouldn't talk to me. Have you learned nothing?"

Sammi nods and beckons me closer. "We've been seeing some signs of . . . corruption, so to speak . . . among the higher authorities of the Curatoria. Regarding your case, specifically."

I think about Sunglasses Guy, not to mention everything else that's happened since. I was certain they were Reduciata assassins, and Sammi indicated that they were too. Are we both wrong? I grit my teeth, wishing I could remember whatever it is that the Reduciata thinks I know.

"So, just to be safe, we're trying to keep our plans as out of their hands as possible. Even the six guns I brought," she says, pointing to the trees, "are old friends of my dad's who know not to report to their superiors. We could be wrong about everything," Sammi hurries to add. "But we want to keep you safe."

I swallow, Quinn's words echoing in my head. *Trust ye the Curatoria but tenuously.* Tenuously indeed. Apparently that's how much they trust themselves.

"Let's get out of here," Sammi says, making a gesture to her hidden bodyguards and leading the way.

"No."

The word is soft, almost inaudible, but Sammi hears.

"Tavia—"

"No." I say it louder now. I hold out the files. "Thank you for these, but I won't be your pawn."

"It's not about that."

"It doesn't matter. I have to make this decision on my own. And that means not going with you tonight. That doesn't mean I won't help with the virus," I add before she can speak. "But the fact is, I don't trust Curatoria."

"Tavia," Sammi begins. "Don't make me force you. I don't—"

"Let me walk away, and I promise you'll hear from me again. And soon. Show of good faith," I say, challenge in my eyes. "But if you try to . . ." A movement over her shoulder catches my eyes and I nearly gasp when I realize it's Quinn.

Vision Quinn, not real Quinn.

He's in the same coat and hat he was wearing when I first saw him and he looks out of place standing close to the Honda.

He's not looking at *me*; he's glaring up the pathway we drove down hours ago.

I feel like I'm fixed in cement. Benson pulls away and says something, but I'm deaf to his words as I stand there gaping.

Quinn takes half a step forward, thrusting his chin toward the path with that same studious gaze. Then, with no warning, his head whips around and that glare is directed at me for a fraction of a second before he begins to fade from sight.

And I understand.

We stayed too long.

"They're here," I whisper, my head spinning to look in the same direction Quinn had been glaring.

All motion stops—everyone is silent.

"They're here!" I shout, some forgotten instinct taking over. I hear only a sharp crack, a blinding light, before I'm enveloped in an explosion of searing heat and blistering flames.

CHAPTER THIRTY-SEVEN

Something inside me wrenches away control of my mind and I fall to one knee. My hands swoop out to the side and swing over my head, pages of files scattering to the ground around me.

The space around me vibrates with a sound that pierces my eardrums and yet is strangely muffled. Hot air fills my lungs and I stifle the urge to cough.

Then it's quiet.

No, not quiet; fire crackles and roars. But the explosion is over.

I touch my arms.

I'm not burned.

Dancing orange flames lick up the trees, devouring the crackly leaves. I look up, but there's only blackness. I'm standing in shadow.

"Ow! Damn it!" Benson swears beside me after scrambling to his feet only to clang his head on something above us and sink to the ground again.

We're in a rounded shelter of something black. I lift my hands to it, my fingertips skimming the surface, almost hot enough to burn me. "Cast iron," I whisper, recognizing the material. Just like the shield that protected Quinn and Rebecca from the bullets two hundred years ago.

Well, at least I know who to thank.

"Tavia, Benson," Elizabeth snaps. I turn to her with wide eyes as I realize what happened.

"I made this!" The words burst out in a shriek. "Holy shit, Elizabeth, I did it! I—" *I saved more than just me this time.*

"We have to get out of here," Benson says, his hand squeezing mine so tightly it hurts. "I can't—why—*this is all my fault.*" He releases me and runs both his hands through his hair, ragged gasps loud in the tiny space.

"Ben, it's all right," I say, trying to grasp for his hands, but they flutter just out of reach.

His eyes meet mine and it's like he just realized I'm here. He throws his arms around me and his fingers grasp against my back. "I'm sorry," he whispers against my neck. "I didn't mean to. I was trying to get away."

"Benson, what are you—"

Benson rises to his knees and pulls at his jacket, yanking it down his arms. He grips my leg to get my attention. "Scissors, Tave."

"What?"

"Make me some scissors. Please," he adds.

There's no time for my ethical quandaries. Not when there are three lives to save. I can do this! *Scissors.* I close my eyes and force my mind to focus. A weight fills my hand and I give a pair of sewing scissors to Benson.

They're identical to the ones that used to reside in my mother's sewing basket. Hauntingly familiar. It's like the locket I accidentally created. Somewhere at the periphery of my consciousness a firefly memory glows. *I make what I know.*

Benson grabs them and begins cutting his jacket. I still don't understand what he's doing, but I trust him with my life. With Elizabeth's life.

"Water," he says before coughing. But I'm ready this time.

Liquid spills from my upturned palms and he soaks the pieces of cloth and hands one to each of us.

"Shouldn't I just use water to put out the fire?" I ask, confused, remembering the huge surge of water I managed to make when Benson's roommate was such an asshole.

But Benson shakes his head. "If we can get away, the fire might hide us. You put it out, we're sitting ducks."

I nod and we all press the wet fabric to our mouths as we crouch together, the temperature in the air rising fast.

"That way," Elizabeth shouts over the sound of the flames devouring the trees as she points. "Our cars are just up the road—maybe we can get to one. Whatever you do, don't stop running."

Benson nods with a calmness I can't imagine he actually feels.

"What about Sammi and—" I try to ask, but Elizabeth cuts me off.

"Don't think about them," she orders. "We have to go. This shield isn't permanent; it's going to dissolve any second."

Sammi and Mark. Reese and Jay. They weren't close enough to save.

I failed again.

My feet skid a few inches when I step on something.

The files!

In the barest seconds that are left, I gather the pages I can see. Several are singed, and I'm sick wondering how many are gone forever. I don't have time to put them in my backpack so I clamp them against my chest with one arm and grab Benson's hand with the other.

Elizabeth looks at us and nods. "Go!"

We duck out from beneath the shield and I gasp as a nearly tangible wall of heat slaps my face, paralyzing me into stillness for just a moment before cool spots dot my forehead, making the heat bearable.

It's raining.

More than raining; it's suddenly pouring. But it has no effect on the roaring flames.

Benson's hand tightens on mine and he drags me along.

My heart freezes when I see them.

Their bodies are half charred and I wouldn't even recognize Mark if I couldn't tell it was Sammi cradled protectively in his blackened arms. He threw his body over hers, but a frail human shield wasn't enough. The explosion must have seared up her left side, killing her instantly but leaving her right side eerily preserved. Her eyelids are mercifully closed but blistering red even as I tear my eyes away and feel the urge to retch rise in my throat.

Elizabeth leads the way, skirting the flames while Benson and I follow her.

She's almost at the edge of the clearing when something catches her foot and she stumbles toward the burning car. She screams as she falls against the blistering hot metal, and the sound is almost swallowed up by the raging fire.

And then, instantly, the flames are gone.

Gone.

The destruction remains, but the orange fire has disappeared. Almost as if magicked out of existence.

Out of existence.

Of course. I remember now. Equals and opposites. There are Creators like me.

And there are Destroyers. The term Sammi used. I didn't question it at the time because I knew intrinsically that it was right.

There's another Earthbound here.

Benson pulls me away, yanking me toward the edge of the clearing. "We have to go *now!*"

Even as we turn, I hear another sound—this one so completely dissonant that I think I would have heard it over a hurricane.

A chuckle.

A long shadow approaches, but the twilight air is too murky to make out a face until she raises her head.

"Marie?" I whisper, completely baffled. Her hair is pulled sharply back from her face instead of falling in its usual soft waves, and her sleek pantsuit and large silver pendant are worlds away from the dresses and cardigans from the library. She's tall and stands straight, with a regal air that speaks of both power and pride. Even with rivulets of rain coursing down her face, she *looks* like a goddess.

Benson's arm tightens, pulling me against him so hard I can barely breathe. "Run," he orders, then pushes me away.

I force my legs to move, bursting with sudden speed, but before I've gone three feet a thick forearm snakes out and catches me across the throat, and suddenly hands are grasping at my waist, my legs, pulling me away from Benson. The icy barrel of a gun presses against my temple and I still as I hear the words, "One more move and you're dead. Forever."

I force myself to be still, but my eyes search for Benson, who's fighting against his captors. "Stop! No! Leave her alone. I told you—" His words cut off with a sharp crack and I can't stifle a cry as Benson's head snaps to one side with the force of a blow to his temple.

I glance around at the dozen or so faces. I don't see Sunglasses Guy, but without his distinguishing shades—not to mention the shadows of the tree branches crisscrossing all of the faces—he could be any of them.

"Ben, it's okay," I chance saying, though I don't move a muscle. "I'm all right."

"Aw, isn't that cute," Marie says in a tone so unlike her quiet librarian voice that I freeze. "He got the Earthbound to crush on him. That was over and above even for a Reduciate, Benson."

"It's not like that," Benson says, still struggling toward me. Blood trickling down his cheek, mingling with the pouring rain, making red streaks like macabre tears. "Let me go!"

"All in good time," Marie replies—the embodiment of calm—eyeing me as the world seems to spin, everything turning upside down. "You know, when that hotel room was empty this morning, I was pretty sure you had run away on us, but I see you took your little *lesson* to heart," she says, brushing the purple bruise under Benson's eye. He flinches away from her touch.

Time flows around me in slow motion as I turn my head. "Benson?" Did I even say it out loud?

His face is a mask of desperation. "Tavia. I didn't mean to. I thought—you have no idea."

"You did this?" I whisper. I can't believe it. I *won't* believe it. "No!" I yell the word at Marie. "You're lying!"

"Am I?" the woman says, so quietly I barely catch her words. "Show her his mark."

The man holding Benson spins him roughly around and Benson groans as the man tightens an arm around his bruised ribs, yanking his T-shirt up until I can see the skin of his left shoulder.

The shadow of the tattoo I saw through his white shirt last night.

It's part ankh.

Part shepherd's crook.

No.

It's true.

The whole time.

My stomach clenches and I want to double over and clutch it and it's all I can do to stay upright. A crash of lightning chooses this moment to split open the sky and I gasp at the sudden light.

Everyone is motionless. *One, two, three, four.* Then a deafening rumble of thunder envelops the space around us, filling everyone's ears. Only when the silence returns does the chaos begin to move again.

The man behind Benson lets him go, but a foot to his back knocks the boy I was sure I loved to his knees. He looks up at me, his injuries suddenly making more sense. *A message*, Sammi had said a few minutes earlier. *I only wish I know who it was for.* She'd know now. If she was alive.

"I didn't want to," Benson says, pleading in his eyes. "I had no choice! Last night—I tried to get away."

I sift through memories of the last few days—the candy bars and french fries he knew I needed to eat, the way he accepted my powers so easily, running away with me, even the stupid wallet-size lock picks. The reality of how much he lied—how far he'd gone to deceive me—snaps into place with a clarity that makes my stomach writhe.

"The entire time, you were—" It's all I can get out before the urge to retch overtakes me and I gag, my hand clasped over my mouth, the drum of the rain filling my ears. My head, blocking out my thoughts.

"Tave, please," Benson pleads, but Marie interrupts with an almost casual wave of her hand.

"Take him to the truck."

Another man grabs Benson's arms and starts dragging him away.

"Tavia! Don't listen. Don't tell them—ah!" Benson gasps for air as the man elbows him in his already-bruised ribs. I can't tear my eyes away. My heart aches for the cruel way he's being treated even as everything inside me feels like ashes, crumbling to nothingness. Turning me into nothingness.

I can't move.

I can't breathe.

Benson, who has been there through everything. Who told me he loved me.

And I believed him.

But my mind races, finding more proof I refused see before—knowing what the Latin names for the brotherhoods meant, his knowledge that I had to get to Logan, his insistence that we needed to talk on the bus, his cryptic apologies, even his quick thought to use my powers to get us out of the fire when I forgot I had them.

Because he's been a Reduciate all along.

He's known about Earthbounds all along.

My heart pounds a too-slow rhythm that feels like a funeral dirge and part of me wishes it was mine.

"The truth hurts, doesn't it, Tavia?" Marie says, and for the first time, she pronounces my name correctly. I wonder if she got a sick pleasure out of annoying me with that for so many months. "But that's what the Reduciata are all about. The truth. The cold, hard truth that nobody else wants to face."

Her voice is poison in my ears.

She looks over where a truck door closes on Benson, muffling his protests.

"You should have a little sympathy for him, I suppose," she says, almost sounding kind. "It took a lot of effort to get him to go along with it. The guy we had follow you, the car that almost ended you, all reminders to Benson of what would happen if he failed."

"Doesn't matter," I say, trying to wrench my arms away from the two people holding me. "He accepted the job."

"Yes, he did," Marie says, a very small smile sliding over her face.

"The Reduciata kill Earthbounds," I say through gritted teeth. "Why are you helping them?"

She laughs now, and it's a laugh I've heard before. A laugh that sounds like a warbling bird. A laugh I remember from back when she was Marie, the sweet, hovering librarian. Now it vibrates down into my bones, rattling my sinews. Another crack of lightning, but this time the thunder follows more closely. "I don't *help* the Reduciata, Tavia Michaels; I *lead* them. And there are *many* Earthbounds among our members. Elite Earthbound, who want to restore us to the lives we were meant to lead. You could join us. Willingly, I mean. I think it's obvious that we want you—need what's in that pretty, damaged little head of yours. You could accept your role and be one of the privileged. It would certainly be easier on you. There's no true reason for this enmity to go on."

A groan escapes my clenched teeth and Marie laughs again.

"I didn't think so, but never let it be said that I didn't give you the chance."

My mind races and I try to think of what I can create to get out of this mess.

As though reading my thoughts, the woman clucks her tongue. "I wouldn't try anything if I were you. I'm far more powerful than a pitiful demigoddess a step away from permanent death."

"Then why don't you just kill me?" I snarl between clenched teeth.

"Because it turns out you're not who we thought you were. Or, more appropriately, you're *more* than just who we thought you were. When we saw what you did to that plane—" She sighs and shakes her head. "And to think we almost lost you." She steps forward, and even though I try to jerk away, I have nowhere to go and have to grit my teeth as she runs one fingernail down the side of my face. "Don't you remember? A bitter-cold night in England, on the hard, unforgiving ground, under a park bench? A night when no one should have been about. Where this game of chase all began?" She chuckles again, and I'm shocked by how badly I want to wrap my hands around her throat. "Benson told us you weren't really remembering things, but I wasn't convinced he was telling the truth. Maybe he was. Still, surely you remember *me*."

Her expression softens and she looks directly into my eyes. My chest constricts and a pain builds up in the back of my head and even though I try to fight it back, for the second time that day, my soul is ripped away.

CHAPTER THIRTY-EIGHT

I'm lying on something hard and lumpy and my clothing is slightly damp, making the freezing wind all the more biting. My nose is so cold it feels like needles are jabbing into it and I'm afraid to open my eyes.

But I have to.

Because whenever this happened, I did, and all I can do is lie here and replay the memory exactly as I once lived it. I give in and let the vision overtake me.

Voices draw near, and soon my view of the snow-covered park is blocked by a voluminous black skirt with silver brocade. Leather boots and the bottom of a greatcoat join her and I stifle a tiny sigh of relief as the thick fabrics block some of the punishing wind. I try to go back to sleep—to take advantage of the slight warmth before they stand and leave, but the words they're saying keep waking me up.

"It will destroy nearly all of them. And half the Earthbounds. We can start over. It will be the Reduciata's finest moment. Our finest moment."

"It's not ready yet. You cannot release it without the antidote."

"How many more lifetimes? Three? Ten? I grow impatient and the Curatoria . . . they grow bothersome."

"Don't you think I know that better than you?"

Earthbound . . . Reduciata . . . Curatoria.

I don't know what the words mean, but my mind latches onto them and clings, forcing my eyes open, my thoughts spinning.

And spinning.

And then something else.

A sensation unlike anything I've ever felt before. Pictures flash before my eyes, and it feels as though someone has opened up my head and poured in hot broth. It fills me with warmth, with knowledge, with voices.

Voices that warn me into silence.

I try to remain quiet, but as lovely as the warmth is, it's also a hurricane of . . . something I have no words for. Like suddenly I am a hundred people all at once.

I gasp and feel beads of sweat forming on my brow, despite having been so desperately cold only moments before.

Moments?

Yes, it has only been moments.

Suddenly a hand is wrapping around my arm and the man yanks me out from beneath the bench. His face is inches from mine and he shakes me with teeth-rattling force. I am still too full of those strange feelings to hear a word he says, but I manage to whisper, over and over, "I heard nothing, sir. I heard nothing!"

He stops shaking and it's all I can do to keep my head up at all. I stare at that face, craggy, with a short beard and a scar along the side of his cheek. I can't be sure if he's a gentleman or a rough sort.

But his eyes are a light, ale-colored brown and I stare at him for long, silent seconds.

I know this face.

I'm certain I've never met him before, but I know this face.

"She's just a little human child," a woman's voice says from out of view. I spin my eyes over to her. She's going to save me!

But what greets me is the small barrel of a flintlock pistol, nearly touching the skin on my forehead, held in a delicate, gloved hand.

"No one will miss her," the woman finishes. My eyes widen and I look into her face. She looks kind, regal, almost beautiful.

But she shows no remorse or hesitation as she draws back the hammer of the gun, and my last moment is flooded with the earsplitting report of a shot as my head snaps backward, alight with pain.

And then my soul rips away again.

I gasp for breath, my lungs begging for air. I touch my forehead and find whole skin there. Perspiration mingles with splattering rain, but I am unharmed.

I'm alive.

It was only a memory.

I look up at Marie; there is no gun this time, but I see that same look, devoid of emotion.

"It's such a shame," she says evenly. "You and I, we were friends once, before you sided with the Curatoria. So many aeons ago and yet I still remember the ages we spent making a river, a canyon, whose great walls and beautiful landscape would be legendary, just because we *could*. You creating high mountains, me carving out those deep ravines. Give-and-take, balanced exactly the way the Earthmakers were intended to be. The two of us making something beautiful while our lovers quarreled and fought. I still have a tiny twinge of regret every time someone speaks of the Grand Canyon."

I'm still trying to make sense of her words when a stinging slap flings my head to the side.

"That's for leaving me behind," she says softly.

Anger roils inside me, filling me with a rage that blots out any pain from the slap. My life, my parents, my love; she is responsible for everything I no longer have.

"You have taken *everything* from me," I shriek, a flash of lightning accentuating my words.

"Yes, I suppose we have," she says, utterly calm.

But even as I'm sure the rage is going to overwhelm me, something shifts inside and a black calm settles in my mind.

No more. Voices I don't recognize echo in my head as a razor fury makes a pit in my stomach, white-hot anger at wrongs I can't remember—and yet the pain, the agonizing loss, *that* I recall with perfect clarity. *Not one. More. Damn. Thing.*

I push my hands out in front of me, pour out my rage, and instantly I'm standing before a mountain: a dusty red behemoth of crags and sharp boulders that towers hundreds of feet above my head, the sheer face of a cliff an arm's length away. The forest that was is nothing more than a destroyed memory, swept away by stone.

For an instant.

It blinks out of existence. Not the normal five-minute way—it's *forced* out of existence, leaving Marie standing there, looking almost bored, surrounded by splintered trees as far as I can see in the murky dusk.

Marie the Destroyer.

But I'm not done. That was only a test.

Lava, steel, bullets. They come from every direction as the women in my head pick weapons from memories out past my reach. And I let them. I surrender my mind, allowing the Tavias of old to let loose every drop of anger and pain I've built up for millennia.

One voice, one memory fights to the surface.

The night I was in the water, when I was Rebecca—the face I saw above me, just past the icy surface.

It was her.

How many times has this face been my last sight?

My concentration wavers. She's killed me before—she's going to do it again.

No.

I won't drown; I won't die. Not this time.

Power surges within me, filling my body to bursting and creating a noise in my head so loud I'm sure I'll be deaf if I survive this.

If.

I don't even care.

More rage, more white-hot heat, more molten anguish pours from me. I can't see anything as the fullness begins to ebb, leaving me completely bereft of energy. I teeter, not certain I can stand any longer. Rain falls in soft rivulets down my face, but it feels almost warm.

"Tavia, come on!"

Elizabeth's voice, her hands, dragging me. I can't see and stumble as I try to follow her, running blindly, steered only by Elizabeth's hand clenched around my arm. The sound of a car door, a shove that sends me down onto a seat.

I blink and stars swim in front of my eyes. My head lolls to the side as Elizabeth drops into the seat beside me. Thank gods the car wasn't crushed by my mountain. I've just made a hell of a lot of trouble as it is.

And I'm not even sure just what I did.

I look out at what's left of the forest, and an enormous pile of rubble, silhouetted by the glow of molten rock, stares back. Every kind of matter I can imagine is in a smoldering heap where Marie was standing, barely visible through the trees.

It won't last long; she's too good. It's already blinking away, bit by bit, as though I never made it at all. As nonexistent as the mountain that once was. People are running toward us. I recognize one as the guy who dragged Benson off. They've almost reached the car.

The engine roars and Elizabeth peels out backward, smacking a tree, the crunch of the bumper a macabre harmony with the squealing tires.

Dark shapes whirl around us and I feel the dull thud of flesh on metal at the back of Elizabeth's car. I try not to think too hard about that as my throat convulses. But Elizabeth is already throwing the car into drive, lurching forward, gaining speed.

I don't look back; I don't want to see anything else. I already have the sight of Sammi and Mark's decimated bodies to haunt my dreams.

And Benson's betrayal.

I can't even think of him without a vile sickness clutching at my stomach.

Desperate to distract myself, I click my seat belt just before Elizabeth almost dumps me into her lap turning a sharp corner.

"There's no time to get to the plane—assuming the Reduciata haven't taken control of it already," Elizabeth shouts, forcing me to pay attention. "I'm going to drop you off at an alley two blocks south of the Greyhound station," she continues, her eyes glued to the road. "Take this."

My fingers wrap around the cell phone she proffers even as she spins the car around another bend. As soon as I've taken the phone, her burned hands are back on the wheel, and as we pass under a streetlight, the steering wheel glints wet.

Blood.

I remember her falling against the charred car—the scream she let out. This drive must be killing her hands.

"Get on a bus—the next bus," Elizabeth orders, her eyes still fixed on the road. "It doesn't matter where it's going. Just *get on it* no matter what it takes. Understand?"

"Yeah," I say weakly, bracing my arms against the door for another squealing corner.

Another flash of light; her hands are red and seeping.

"Elizabeth, your hands—"

"Will heal," she says through gritted teeth. "I'll call *you* when it's safe. I don't know when that will be. Don't *you* call anyone. Especially Benson. You have to accept it; you can *never* have any contact with him ever again."

Benson. I nod, hating the truth of it. It's worse than him being dead. It might be worse than *me* being dead. Elizabeth hits a curb, throwing my head against the window. Distantly I feel pain, but it doesn't seem to matter anymore.

"Open my purse," Elizabeth instructs. I look around at my feet and find the black bag that's tumbling around. "Take my wallet."

"But I have—"

"Take it, Tave!" she orders.

I unzip the leather bag and fumble around for the wallet, transferring it into my backpack.

"There's some food—it's not much, but you'll need it."

I sift around and find part of a candy bar and a large package of trail mix. Gratefully, I slide the trail mix into my backpack and stuff the entire piece of candy bar into my mouth to fight off the blackness that's trying to close in around the edges of my sight.

Seconds of silence pass as my mind tries to take in what just happened.

As soon as I choke down the candy, I blurt, "I beat her." *They* beat her. *This time.*

"Yes, you did." Her words hold a softness and I hear *thank you* in them.

But it feels empty. I didn't save Sammi and Mark.

I saved Benson instead.

And he betrayed me.

Elizabeth spares me a glance as she continues to drive erratically. "You did good."

Not good enough. Marie's still out there. She's probably not even hurt. I got away, but I didn't actually stop her.

"Quinn was there. I saw him," I say, trying to push away my despair at *still* being on the run from this woman.

Elizabeth is silent, one lip pulled between her teeth.

"He warned me. How can he do that? He's not real. I mean, every time I've seen him, he's been an illusion, right? He's not . . . . real." My mind hasn't stopped whirring since I saw him tonight—I don't know how to justify it, what he did. "His soul isn't here; it's with Logan. It *is* Logan."

Elizabeth spins around another corner with her eyes glued to the rearview. I'm completely lost. "The mind is an incredibly powerful thing, Tave. But it's also very fragile. Your memory unlocking must have started when you saved yourself in the plane crash, but your brain was too damaged to survive such a drastic change. So when the memories couldn't be held back any longer, your mind seems to have done something to protect itself. Created something to personify it; a comfortable person you could accept. Someone safe. A defense mechanism, if you will, to ease you into your full awakening without burning out your synapses." She sweeps me the barest of glances. "You wouldn't be the first."

"So he didn't save me?" I ask quietly, not wishing he had exactly, but wanting *someone* to have been on my side.

Elizabeth turns and for just a second our eyes meet. "No," she says, and she sounds very certain. "You saved *yourself.*"

"Elizabeth?" I hesitate. "Sammi was right, wasn't she? The Reduciata actually want me so badly they sent their *leader* after me. For a secret I'm too damaged to even remember?"

She doesn't look at me, but I see her swallow. "They want you *bad,* Tave. Something's going wrong. I think they released the virus too soon. It's affecting everything too strongly. The death time that's too short to go unnoticed, the crazy weather that people are starting to realize can't be natural," she says, gesturing at the downpour that looks like it's trying to turn into either hail or snow. "It's all wrapped up in their screwup. They miscalculated, and now everything is spiraling out of their control and it's only going to get worse." She looks over at me. "They wanted you to die in the plane crash, but something about what you did . . . now they think *you* can fix their mistake before it destroys all of us—including them. That's all we know."

An oily fear coats my stomach. "They've got to be wrong. Elizabeth, I can't help. I can't *do* anything. I don't remember whatever it is they think I do."

Her eyes narrow. "If there's one thing I've learned in my years as a Curatoriate, it's that the Reduciata are almost *never* wrong. Tavia, *do not die.* Somehow, you are humankind's last hope. You need to figure out why, and then you need to stop them."

I sink back against the seat and say nothing. I've never felt so small, so inadequate. If I'm humankind's last hope, then humankind is doomed.

Elizabeth glances at the rearview again as we drive through a nearly dark section of town with half the streetlights burned out. Seedy-looking and more than a little scary. "I don't know if I've lost them, but they're at least far enough back that I can't see them anymore. When I pull over, you jump out and hide. Wait for about thirty seconds so I can get away from you. Then run in that direction," she says, pointing toward a shadowy alley sided by two lines of decrepit wood-slat fencing. "You'll reach the bus station in less than two blocks. You can't miss it—it'll be all lit up."

"Elizabeth?" I say desperately.

"What?"

I want to tell her that I'm not ready, that I don't really understand how I saved myself on the plane or in the fire, and especially not from Marie. And I'm not convinced I can do it again.

Not alone.

Not without Benson.

No, don't think about him.

"Thank you," I finally whisper instead.

"Thank me if we live through this," she says, so quietly that I don't know if she intended for me to hear her. "Ready?"

I pull my backpack over my shoulder and unfasten my seat belt. My fingers are poised over the door handle as I choke out, "Ready."

It's the biggest lie I've ever told.

The car screeches to a halt, and the second we stop moving, Elizabeth's hands are pushing at my back and I'm wrenching the door open and almost tumbling out, staggering down to one knee as my shoe slides on the oily cement beneath my feet. The car's already moving again. I'm bathed in dark shadows, but I force my knee straight and dive behind a Dumpster anyway, not daring to peer out to watch the taillights disappear. The icy rain soaks my face as I begin counting.

One.

Two.

Three.

Four.

At eighteen the earth beneath me trembles, the light of flames reaching my eyes before the slower sound waves echo in my ears.

An explosion.

It's to the east.

The direction Elizabeth drove.

And it's exactly the distance a speeding car would cover in eighteen seconds.

CHAPTER THIRTY-NINE

No one could have survived an explosion like that.

Agony presses against my chest, pushing the air from my lungs, and for a few seconds I lose count. Lose my will to fight, to run, to live. But I force myself to finish counting to thirty, my teeth chattering in terror the whole time. Then I dart out from behind the Dumpster and tear through the alley without looking back, trying to keep to the shadows even as my leg threatens to buckle beneath me.

I have no idea where the bus station is and I hope it's as easy to find as Elizabeth said.

Elizabeth.

Don't think about her—don't think about her. Don't think about any of them. Think about surviving.

I nearly burst into tears of relief when I see the telltale bright lights ahead. My lungs are aching, but I'm almost there.

Then I hear it.

The clattering of footsteps behind me.

Something whistles past my ear and I shriek when the cinder blocks beside me shatter, spraying me with tiny beads of rock.

They found me.

The lights of the bus station are so close, but I'm not sure I can reach them in time.

And even if I do, what then? I don't have minutes to stand in line— seconds to buy a ticket—much less hours to sit around and wait for the next bus.

I'll be dead by then, my body riddled with bullets.

And then the world will slowly die because I was too blind to realize what Benson really was.

It's too much—I can't think that big.

A boyish face with golden hair flashes into my mind, almost certainly courtesy of Rebecca.

Logan. I can focus on Logan.

He doesn't know.

I have to go to him.

I grit my teeth and hoist my backpack higher. If I die tonight, I'll never find Logan. Never again. It will be over for both of us. In a flash of understanding, I realize I don't want to cease to exist without meeting him—even if it's for the last time.

With his green eyes vivid in my mind, I reach for one more surge of energy and force myself to ignore the screaming pain in my leg as I run, stretching my strides, feet slapping the pavement, lungs burning for air.

Once I reach the lights, the people, surely the Reduciates chasing me will have to back off to avoid being discovered. Or at least take a more subtle approach. But then, human life is obviously not high on their priority list. They'd probably just kill all the witnesses. More deaths to be laid at my feet.

Just run!

I hear the gentle rumble of a bus before I see it. It's the only bus that isn't silent and parked behind a fence.

It's ready to go.

I *have* to get on that bus.

But I'm a full fifty feet away when the last person in line boards. The driver smiles and then looks around the sparsely populated bus station. "Pittsburgh?" he yells. "Anyone else for Pittsburgh?"

Pittsburgh. Good enough.

I don't have a ticket.

Yet.

Twenty more feet.

Ten seconds.

I squeeze my eyes shut for an instant and try to remember the last time I took a Greyhound bus. It was when I was sixteen and went to visit a friend who had moved out of state.

The ticket. What did it look like?

My mind swirls and I try to recall the details, the feel of the cardboard in my hand, the green of the logo, the meaningless words.

The bar code.

What if they have to scan a bar code? My heart beats so wildly it feels like the flutter of a hummingbird's wings.

I can't do this.

I'm going to die.

I can almost feel the bullets ripping through the skin on my back already.

The driver makes eye contact with me and smiles. I stagger to a walk and refuse to let myself look around. As I cover the last few steps, sweat pours down my neck and yet I shiver.

I stop in front of him.

He holds out his hand.

I lift my arm, but it's only when my hand reaches waist height that I feel the sharp corner of a cardboard square prick my skin.

The uniformed man scarcely looks at the white and green miracle before waving me onto the bus with a pleasant, "Just in time."

I cling to the handrail with wet hands, my palms sliding down it as I try to pull myself up—to make a leg that no longer has the strength to stand lift me another step. The adrenaline is gone and my entire body feels like spaghetti.

The driver seems to sense my desperation and I feel a large, warm hand at my elbow, helping me climb those last two steps.

"Noticed you were limping as you came up," the bus driver whispers. "You just rest now."

God bless you, sir.

But I don't say the words out loud. If I open my mouth, I'm going to lose it entirely. I nod instead and try to show my appreciation with my eyes.

As I set down my backpack, I accidentally drop my ticket. My fingers fumble desperately for the piece of cardboard that saved my life. It has a corner folded down and I straighten it with near reverence.

Truth be told, I didn't do a very good job. Garbled letters march along the bottom, and I think the only word I really got right is *Pittsburgh*. There *is* a bar code, but as I squint in the darkness, I realize all the bars are the same length and width. It would never have worked if they'd actually scanned it.

But the logo is there, looking very much as I remembered. My breathing speeds up again as I realize just how crappy my ticket is—how lucky I am the driver didn't look closer.

But he didn't.

And so I am alive.

The doors are unfolding now—closing—and the driver is pulling his seat belt across his wide belly. I look out the window and see two men in black pants and polos jog into the parking lot.

Go, go, go! I silently urge, and the bus driver settles in and begins to ease the gearshift out of park. I keep my eyes on the two men, knowing they can't see me through the tinted windows. They glance at the bus, but it was literally thirty seconds between my running into the parking lot and the bus leaving.

I shouldn't be on this bus.

Still, they've got to suspect.

A pounding on the door startles me and I lean forward and see the two men gesturing for the driver to open the door.

"I gotta go!" he bawls.

They flash him some kind of shiny badges that I have no doubt are fakes and the driver sighs and stops the bus.

Oh please, no! I'm trapped now. A rat in a cage. After all of that— everything Reese and Jay and Elizabeth did for me—the Reduciata are still going to get me. I feel like sobbing, screaming to the sky the unfairness of it all.

Life's not always fair. I must have heard my mother say that a hundred times.

My mother.

A crazy idea bursts into my head and I panic, knowing I have only seconds.

I hear the door open and I force my eyes shut and think of my mother. Only my mother. Her light brown hair, long plump arms, contagious smile. I gather all my mental energy and try to remember every detail about her. Her smile, her short fingers, her long brown hair, so much like mine used to be.

"Excuse me, ma'am. Ma'am?"

I look up at the breathless man who was shooting at me not two minutes ago. He peers into my eyes and I struggle to hold a neutral face. His jaw tightens and he moves on, shaking his head.

"... not here ... waste of time ... canvas area ..." They don't even try to muffle their voices as they leave the bus without a word to the driver.

The driver grumbles about their rudeness, but finally the door closes and I breathe again as the bus eases away from the station—rumbles onto the highway.

I need a mirror.

I rummage through my backpack until I find a compact in my make-up bag. I open it, and as the bus crosses under an orange streetlight, it floods light over me. And in the mirror is my mother's face.

A soft gasp escapes my lips and I reach out to touch the mirror.

No, I have to touch *my* face.

It's me.

It's her.

I touch her lips, her cheeks, her eyelashes, look into her green eyes. Then I smile.

And it's *her* smile.

A funny sensation distracts me as it tickles my palm and I look down to see the cardboard ticket starting to dissolve. It reminds me of the feeling of sand washing out from under my feet when an ocean wave recedes.

In a few seconds, it's gone.

My eyes leap back to the mirror. The ticket's already gone; I have only a minute—maybe two—to gaze at the familiar face. Technically, I could do it again, but somehow I know that after tonight, it'll feel false and this is the only true chance I'm going to get to see my mother.

I stare, willing the seconds to last, but time isn't like that and soon the long nose is melting into my short one, the muddy-green eyes turning brown, the hair shortening.

And I am myself again.

And my mom is still dead.

My fingers tighten on the mirror that now shows me nothing but myself.

Everyone I loved is dead. Or worse.

Except Quinn, Rebecca's voice reminds me, but I push her away. I can't let myself hope right now. I'm too full of anguish and there's no room for anything else.

I curl my knees up to my chest and rest my cheek against them. A glance from under my eyelashes allows me to take in the passengers on the half-filled bus around me.

A mother is rocking a toddler back and forth on her lap. His face is curled against her shoulder, but I still hear his soft sobs. I don't want to stare, but I can tell by the shaking of her chest that the mother is crying too. A few seats back, a man lays his head against the window and is silent, but I can just make out tears running down his cheeks. A teenager sits across the aisle from me, a hood pulled over her face, headphone wires trailing to an iPod in her hands. *Clenched* in her hands. I wonder if she's sleeping until a loud sniff comes from her shadowed face.

And so, because I'm not alone, I let my tears come too. On this late-night Greyhound, rolling down the road under an inky-black sky, no one will even notice.

▲

"I came as soon as I heard."

"I wish you hadn't." I'm standing in my office—my real one, my secret one—staring out the windowpane into blackness.

"Are you sure you're all right?"

"Fine enough." My throat is tight and I give voice to the unfamiliar feeling shooting spikes through my gut. "I failed," I whisper.

"No."

"Yes," I hiss. "She was . . . she was so strong. She shouldn't be so strong!" My voice is rising, and I despise that I'm so out of control, but I can't seem to rein it in. "She should be weak—hardly able to function. It should have been child's play to bring her in once Benson helped her awaken her memories." I clamp my teeth shut. I won't let him see me cry. "I don't understand what happened."

He's silent for so long I finally turn and look, expecting to see an expression of disapproval. Instead he's wary. "What if . . . what if she didn't just change? What if she also . . . reset for lack of a better term?"

"To her original strength?" The thought makes fear close around my neck, cutting off my air. "Surely the gods wouldn't be so cruel."

"But it is possible."

"I think we've established that nothing is impossible at this stage," I say, turning away from him again.

"At least we know where she's going."

"To him," I say bitterly. "Could it get any worse?" I face him—face the man I've known and loved for longer than even my memories stretch. "It's your turn to be the hunter."

He nods but says nothing. He already knew. It's why he came here tonight. To take her off my hands.

He can have her.

We stare at each other for a very long time—sometimes I think words are scarcely necessary between us anymore.

Then, without a word or even a goodbye, he turns and leaves—nimbly working the hidden catch on the secret door. I look at the door that only looks like a wall now and I distantly hear the minutes ticking away on my grandfather clock.

"Do better than I did," I whisper.

CHAPTER FORTY

"Phoenix!"

The call wakes me and I rub my arm across my face. Last time I woke up, I was drooling.

I unfold myself from my seat, half afraid my skeleton is going to be permanently fused into the shape of a bus seat. Eight buses, over three thousand miles, and four nights sleeping on the ground. Technically I could have slept in the stations, protected from the elements. Or even in a hotel—I have money and, well, a small fortune in gold coins, not to mention the ability to make more if I really had to. But all those choices were bound to get me caught and, most likely, killed. So spiderwebbed bushes and wet, cold grass have been my hosts for the last few nights.

It's been murder on my spine—not to mention my leg—and every muscle in my body is aching as I shamble toward the bus door. The last step proves to be a little too much and I stumble out into the sunshine and throw a hand over my eyes, like a bear cub emerging from hibernation.

And into a subtle feeling so unfamiliar it takes me a few seconds to recognize it.

Warmth. Beams of sunlight spreading soft heat through my body,

warming my skin, heating the air that I breathe. I give myself a few moments to stand there, soaking in the revitalizing rays. I'm not sure I've
been completely warm since the night I left Portsmouth. We've driven
through snow, hail, even had to delay a drive due to a fluke tornado in
Montana. People all around me were theorizing about global warming
and solar flares, but I kept my mouth shut. I don't yet understand the
connection between the extreme weather and the virus—but Elizabeth
said it was there, and I know now to believe her.

It takes a few minutes to orient myself, to get used to walking on a surface that doesn't move and sway. Being still doesn't feel normal anymore.

Jeez, I smell. The hasty washings I've managed to get in bathrooms
on my way across the country haven't been nearly enough. *But better than
being a Reduciata prisoner*, I remind myself.

I hardly feel like myself anymore. No, that's not quite right. I hardly
feel like *Tavia* anymore. The last five days I've let the voices that came
out when I was fighting Marie become part of me. I've filled half a note-
book with what I can remember of them. Shihon the warrior queen from
before time had meaning, Embeth the faceless scullery maid with dreams
she couldn't understand, Kahonda, an Indian huntress who died young
on a search for something she couldn't put into words.

And Sonya. And Rebecca.

They are me now, and I am them.

And we all need one thing. To find *him*.

Because now that I've had a chance to read the secret part of
Rebecca's journal—twice—we all know just what we're running from. I
don't know what kind of future I do or don't have with Logan, but I have
to find him and protect him from these people. It's more than a little terrifying to realize how many disasters I've read about in history that can

be attributed to Earthbounds—usually affiliated with the Reduciata, but not always. The Mongol invasion of China, the great Indian famine, the Deluge of Poland and Lithuania, and even—if the Curatoria are to be believed: the Black Plague—a practice run of the virus now devastating the world. It ravaged Europe seven hundred years ago, but apparently that wasn't enough for the Reduciata. This virus is supposed to be ten times worse. Ten times as deadly.

That this is *success* in the Reduciata's eyes sickens me.

It makes me wonder what they've been involved in since Rebecca's account. The Great Depression? World wars? Even natural disasters like the huge tsunamis of the last decade could potentially be laid at their feet.

I push those thoughts away again. I have to focus on step one—finding Logan. Step two is too big to think about now.

Too impossible.

I look at the scrap of paper I copied Logan's address onto, even though I have it memorized.

A cab. I need a cab.

I need to get to him—to make sure he's still alive.

And if he is, then it'll all be worth it.

No. Not *worth it*. But somehow justified. I need this Logan to be the right one. To be Quinn. Because I can't save anyone without my partner, of that much I'm certain. And I need their deaths to *mean* something. Sammi, Mark, Elizabeth.

Benson, my mind says, but I shove that thought back. He's not dead.

But I kind of wish he was.

Still, too many people have died for me, for us. And not just in this life.

I look around. I don't know how to find a cab. I stand in the parking lot looking lost for several minutes before I realize the three neon-green cars on the far end of the parking lot are taxis. Neon green?

Whatever.

I walk over to one and hold out the torn piece of paper. "Can you take me here?" I ask.

The guy reaches for the paper, but I draw it back possessively. It's proof of where I'm going—my own little paper trail. I've learned the value of paranoia.

He nods his understanding—he probably drives a lot of crazy people—and leans forward to study the address. "Easy," he says, a heavy accent in his voice. "'Bout ten miles."

I nod with a jerky motion as adrenaline surges through me. Ten miles. I could walk if I had to. My body tenses at the thought and I'm grateful I won't need to.

"Bags?" the driver asks, gesturing to the bus.

I shake my head. I have nothing but my backpack, and I grip its straps even tighter when the driver offers to take it. The journals are in there—my journal and Quinn's—the few pages of the files I managed to save, the gold, the money, the necklace. No one's taking my connections to my past away from me—not for a second.

He opens the back door and I slide into the cool vehicle. He starts the car and more chilly air flows from vents on the ceiling, hitting my face like a slap that sends goose bumps across my skin. As he pulls out of the lot, the cold air chills the nervous sweat on my body, and I shiver.

The driver notices and turns down the AC—which I appreciate—but it doesn't matter. It's nerves.

Every minute, every *moment* that ticks by brings me closer to him. I've embraced the feelings I once fought against. Let the attraction—

Rebecca's love—come through. I don't care anymore than it's not my choice. Who can fight fate, really?

I was stupid to try. I wish I had listened to Elizabeth. About everything. Maybe she and Sammi and Mark would still be alive if I had.

But even without Elizabeth's words, I should have known.

Humans and goddesses. That never ends well; I've read the stories. I belong with my own kind.

I belong with Logan. He needs me.

Maybe . . . maybe this is what I want.

I wish I didn't have to work so hard to convince myself of that. It's Benson and Quinn all over again—except that the lingering feelings I wish I didn't have are for Benson this time.

Focus, focus on how much they all love Quinn.

Leaning forward as far my seat belt will allow, I study the meter. The driver glances at me from the corner of his eye. He sees how fixated I am on the ticking red numbers and probably thinks I'm worried about the fare; now he's afraid I can't pay.

He couldn't be more wrong. I'm willing the red numbers to scroll up *higher*, faster. Wish the driver would speed a little more.

I hear a turn signal click and sit up straight, staring out the front windshield. The driver pulls off the main road and into a quiet neighborhood. Not fancy, but nice.

Unfortunately, it's also the kind of neighborhood where a taxi will be noticed.

"Hey." I lean forward. "Can you drop me off like a block from the address?"

"Of course," he says, then adds in a grumble, "You're the boss."

He pulls over about ten seconds later in front of a two-story stucco and brick house, and as he circles the cab to come open my door, I'm frozen in terror. Terror? No, it's not precisely that. It's fear and nerves and giddiness all mixed together and it glues my feet to the floor. Then the door is open and warm sunlight pours in, thawing my skin and somehow melting my paralysis. I move slowly, but at least I move.

The cabbie is looking at me with real worry in his eyes now. "That's twenty-nine eighty," he says, obviously assuming I can't pay. I don't blame him—I *look* like I can't pay. But I peel two twenties from a small wad of bills in my pocket and hold it out to the driver, my eyes already traveling up the street toward my ultimate destination. He says something, but I don't hear. I make a noncommittal sound and step away from the car.

The driver almost runs back to his seat—probably afraid I'll ask for change—but I don't have the energy to pay attention to him. I'm barely managing to breathe. I can feel my chest starting to convulse and have to make myself take a breath and hold it for three seconds to keep from hyperventilating.

Again.

Again.

My heart is still racing—my pulse deafening in my ears—but at least I'm not light-headed. My feet move, carrying me up the street.

I don't have a plan. Four days of thinking about Logan and I still don't have a plan.

It's Saturday. He should be around. It's still early afternoon—too early for dates and parties.

What if he has a girlfriend? My mouth dries up. I hadn't even considered that.

A smile hovers at the corners of my mouth. *Just one more hurdle.*

If there's anything the last week has taught me, it's that I can jump hurdles.

I'm here.

What now?

Ring the doorbell? That seems a little awkward. Hang around like a stalker? Probably not the best idea, but I have nowhere else to go.

I'm hesitating there in front of his house—probably looking like a moron—and as though he can sense me, the front door opens, then slams shut and a tall guy comes out of the house. My breath is ragged as my eyes drink him in, but his head is down and he's peering at a cell phone. All I can see is his golden hair.

Quinn's hair.

It's *got* to be him.

My throat is too dry to make a sound even when I realize he doesn't see me and is about to plow me over.

He's almost on top of me before he lifts his head and jumps to the side. "Whoa!" a low, quiet voice says. "I'm so sorry. Texting—I'm a total jerk. You okay?"

His eyes meet mine and my lingering doubts flee.

It's Quinn. My Quinn, with shorter hair, more muscle on his arms and shoulders, and a quick smile.

And in that moment I realize I can't wait to discover this person, who he is now—what the last two hundred years have turned him into. Warmth steals through my body, and the reality that I've found him fills me up and overflows. My lips smile, and I can't make them stop.

"Do . . . do you live here?" I ask, finally finding my voice.

"Here?" Logan says, jerking his thumb toward the blue house. "Yeah."

"I—I—" I stumble for words, but then the plan snaps together. I shove my hand into the side pocket of my backpack. "I found this out on the sidewalk," I say, forcing my fingers to open. "It's looks like it might be valuable. Is it . . . your mom's maybe?" I finish lamely.

My palm is sweaty and I know Rebecca's charm will be slightly damp, but I'm not embarrassed. As soon as he touches the locket, none of that will matter.

He holds out his hand and I turn mine over, purposely brushing his skin with mine, almost gasping at the thrilling rush that courses through me. It's better than all the dreams I had of him, the vivid memories the necklace gave me.

Because this time, it's real.

Real in a way that Benson never was.

I kick that thought away and let go of the necklace.

It falls from my palm into his, pooling like a liquid.

He's studying it.

He keeps staring at it.

I want to scream at him to look up at me, but perhaps this incarnation of him is shy.

That's okay; I can wait.

For a second.

His shoulders shrug. "I can go ask her if you want," he says casually, "but I've never seen her wear anything like this."

My mouth drops. He's toying with me. He must be. This isn't the way it's supposed to happen.

"Do you want me to come with you to ask my neighbors?" His green eyes turn up to me.

They're blank.

My heart dies. I'm not sure my legs will support me.

It didn't work. Not my touch, not the necklace. He's still just Logan; he's not my Quinn.

Not yet, Rebecca reminds me. And from somewhere deep inside—a reserve I didn't know I had—I find new strength. New resolve.

Back when Quinn met me as Rebecca, *I* was the one who didn't know *him*. Maybe it's only fair that the tables are turned now.

The important thing is that I found him. He'll remember, eventually. I have the old journals to help me—Logan's sparse file that I've practically memorized. The answers are there somewhere, and I'll find them.

Until I do, I'll stay with Logan. I'm not simply his partner; I'm his protector too. The Reduciata are looking for me. For us. Eventually they'll find us.

Again.

Hell, Benson's probably already told them we're in Phoenix.

And if I don't wake Logan up before they kill me—or him—and do whatever it is that's supposed to recharge us, then we're done.

He needs me.

And the world needs *us*.

I hold out my hand for the necklace and shrug casually. "I don't think that's necessary. But if someone tells you they've lost it, will you let me know?" I dig into my backpack, trying to shield its contents from Logan's eyes. I cringe as I rip a corner off the file Sammi gave me, but it's the only paper I've got. The tip of my pen touches the page before I remember that Elizabeth's phone is in a landfill in Pennsylvania. After she died, I didn't chance it; I got rid of everything.

"Shoot, I totally spaced it," I mutter, feeling my cheeks heat up. "I lost my phone and I'm not sure when I'll be getting a new one. Can I get *your* number?" I ask as I peer up at him from beneath my lashes.

"Uh, yeah, sure," Logan says, and rattles off ten digits.

"How 'bout a name?" I ask, playing dumb.

"I'm Logan," he says, shoving his phone into a pocket and holding out a hand to me.

I shake his hand, feel our warm skin meet, and euphoria tingles through me. He's a little different—modern, I guess—but most parts of him are the same. The eyes, that lopsided tilt in his smile. I don't know if I've ever managed to find him this young.

A lifetime. That's what we have.

A twinge shoots through me at the memory of Benson saying those same words, but I push it away.

I don't have time for regrets.

"Tavia," I say, and cling to his hand just half a second longer than necessary. "Thanks for this," I add, holding up the scrap of paper. "I'll call you."

"Sure," Logan says.

I stride down the street, peeking once more over my shoulder at him. I don't know where I'm going, don't even have a place to stay tonight, but it doesn't matter. We're both here now, and somehow, it will work out.

It's fate.

"Wait," Logan calls out only a moment after I manage to tear my eyes from him.

I stop and he takes a few steps forward, looking almost sheepish. "Do I . . . I know this is going to sound weird, but do I know you?"

I grin, confidence bursting in my chest. "No," I say playfully, "not yet." I hitch my backpack higher and turn away, holding our eye contact as I look over my shoulder. "But you will."

ACKNOWLEDGMENTS

Wow. This book has ended up being one of the scariest things I've ever done and I would probably be a crying, quivering mass curled up on the floor if it weren't for the people who seriously forced this book into awesomeness.

To Jodi Reamer, my agent, thank you for giving me courage when I didn't have any. Ben Schrank, my publisher, for taking a chance on me even when it looked like things weren't going to work. Gillian Levinson, my editor, for having the guts to ask the one thing you should never ask a romance writer! That, more than anything else, is what made this book shine.

To my amazing cover designer, Emily Osborne. Seriously, I. Owe. You. One.

To Scott and Ashley, for letting me steal so many aspects of Scott's injuries and for letting me share in this journey with you. Writing it is so much easier than living it, but watching the two of you work through this together has brought a realism and life to this book that could never have existed any other way. Just remember, Tavia had a brain injury before Scott did! I promise!

Kenny, for letting me leap. It may have been even scarier for you than for me, but you let me do it anyway. Thank you for believing in what I knew I had to do.

To Audrey, Brennan, Gideon, and Gwendolyn, who are more important to me than my books. Thank you for dealing with all the eccentricities of your "Writer Mom."

And lastly, thank you again, Kenny. Because you deserve two mentions. Nah, you deserve ten. But two will have to do.

Tavia's heart
has found its match,
but for how long
will it beat?

**Find out in book 2
of the Earthbound series
Coming Summer 2014!**